MW01483890

.

THE HAPPINESS COLLECTOR

ALSO BY CRYSTAL KING

In the Garden of Monsters

CRYSTAL KING

THE
HAPPINESS
COLLECTOR

///MIRA

/II MIRA™

ISBN-13: 978-0-7783-8727-5

The Happiness Collector

Recycling programs
for this product may
not exist in your area

MIRA
22 Adelaide St. West, 41st Floor
Toronto, Ontario M5H 4E3, Canada
MIRABooks.com

HarperCollins Publishers
Macken House, 39/40 Mayor Street Upper,
Dublin 1, D01 C9W8, Ireland
www.HarperCollins.com

Printed in U.S.A.

For Joe, who knows I'm the opposite of funless.

Happiness is a ball after which we run wherever it rolls, and we push it with our feet when it stops.
—JOHANN WOLFGANG VON GOETHE

The art of being happy lies in the power of extracting happiness from common things.
—HENRY WARD BEECHER

PROLOGUE

Rome, Italy

1986

A MAN IN A bejeweled black cat mask sidled up to Effie. "You look so happy," he said in English.

"Always," Effie replied, used to such compliments. Her own white lace half mask revealed her smile, her best feature, standing out against the deep copper of her skin. Behind the man, the ballroom glittered with the bold fashion of the era—puffy sleeves, cinched waists, and double-breasted suits in daring colors—a perfect backdrop for the annual masquerade ball hosted by a prestigious Roman arts association. She loved masquerades and had attended at least one every year since her first in Venice, lifetimes ago.

The man was slightly taller than her, pale, but with hair the same obsidian color. His eyes—a crystalline blue—mirrored her own rare shade. *How curious*, she mused.

"I'm Effie," she told him.

"Damon," he said, holding out a hand.

He had a firm warm shake. "Damon. That's an old name."

"Perhaps I'm an old soul." He chuckled. "Care to dance?"

"I thought you'd never ask."

Effie let him take her arm and lead her to the center of the crowd, where they joined the other masked dancers gyrating to a Blondie song. The deejay played the popular Italian bands Litfiba and Diaframma, but the hits in English made the crowd most ecstatic: The B-52s, Erasure, and Duran Duran. He was a terrible dancer, worse than most everyone else on the floor, but Effie didn't mind. He seemed happy, and that made her happy. She loved the vibe of a club, and there was something magical when everyone was masked, bodies twisting and flowing together with the rhythm.

No one seemed to care about Damon's awkwardness—not a soul gawked or laughed at his strange movements—although Effie was sure some of that was due to his proximity to her. People couldn't help themselves when she stepped into their periphery. They let their guard down, smiled and laughed more; they loved each other and felt pure, unbridled joy in whatever they were doing. She couldn't see Damon's face, but she was sure there was a smile under the cat mask.

After New Order's "Bizarre Love Triangle," Damon took Effie by the hand and led her back to the bar. "I bet you could dance all night. You make me think I could too. But I definitely need a break." He motioned to the bartender. "Prosecco, *per favore*."

Effie grinned. Prosecco didn't affect her at all, but she delighted in the way each bubble hit her tongue. And she loved Damon's gallantry. She tried to imagine him pounding down a beer and couldn't.

"To a wonderful night full of surprises," he said as they clinked glasses.

"It's not easy to surprise me." And truly, it wasn't. She had witnessed every imaginable courting ritual, their nuances replayed through the ages in endless variations. Yet she found herself amused rather than startled by these familiar displays. She could already see the evening's end in Damon's hopeful eyes. But instead of the conclusion he envisioned, she would lean close, her breath a gentle murmur of bliss in his ear, steering him into a car—alone. He would wake in his own bed, cradling a delightful but entirely fabricated memory of their night, unharmed and blissfully ignorant.

"That sounds like a challenge," he said.

"No challenge." She laughed. "Just truth."

"I'll take the challenge anyway." Damon fumbled in his suit jacket for an awkward moment and pulled out a jewelry box.

"You aren't asking me to marry you already!" It had happened before.

"No, I'd like you to model a necklace for me."

She raised an eyebrow at Damon. "Model a necklace?"

Damon nodded, his cat mask glinting in the strobe lights. "I'm a jeweler, you see, and having a beautiful woman model my pieces helps them sell even better in the store. You'd be doing me a great favor, Miss Effie. Turn around. Let me put it on you, and I'll take some photos. The surprise will come when you see yourself adorned in my creation. The bartender has been holding on to my camera for me." He motioned to the bartender, who pulled a Polaroid camera off the shelf behind him and handed it to Damon.

"Well, well, how could I say no to that?" She gave him a brilliant smile and turned around, pleased at this turn of events— she was truly surprised, and delighted. She lifted her long hair to expose her neck.

Damon draped the thin necklace across her skin, the metal feeling strangely warm when it touched her. He clasped it, then turned her around. Standing back, he began snapping photos with the camera, setting the Polaroid photos on the table in front of her to develop.

Effie smiled for the camera, but something felt wrong—the necklace. It was growing hot against her collarbone. She reached up to touch it, and her smile died.

Damon picked up the first photo and began waving it in the air to help it develop faster. Finally, he held it toward her. She beamed within the fuzzy image, and there, as Effie had feared, she saw a thin gold necklace with two small adders biting a gold ring. Their heads each adorned with a large emerald, their eyes rubies.

For the first time in many an eon, all mirth died within her. The lights in the club darkened, and the music shifted to a dolorous Bauhaus song: "Stigmata Martyr." There was a crash behind the bar as a server dropped a tray of wineglasses. The world seemed to shrink so it only encompassed Effie and the man. The people beyond them were suddenly irrelevant. Panic took hold of Effie, and she reached for the necklace's clasp.

"Don't bother," the man said. "You know it won't work. You're familiar with Harmonia's necklace."

Effie dropped her hands. "Who are you? You're not a god." She would have known if a god had approached. But how could someone other than a god have this necklace?

Then she felt it. Her brother's presence. He stepped out of the shadows, wearing the same cat mask as the man who had her model the necklace.

Her brother gave her a broad smile. "It's good to see you again, sister. You remember Pandora, don't you? Like her, my messenger is wrought from gears and dreams."

Effie's voice sharpened with her curse. Where had he found an automaton?

"Now, now," her brother chided, "such language doesn't suit you. The necklace? Merely a precaution. Consider it insurance. Sending my messenger with it was the only way to ensure you'd accept my invitation."

He was right. She would never have accepted a gift from a god she didn't trust, especially her brother. The necklace was burning hot. It wouldn't mar her skin . . . would it? This was no invitation—it was a kidnapping. "Who wants to meet with me?"

He held out an arm. "I'll take you there. Come."

"Do I have a choice?" She seethed. She wasn't sure she had ever had cause to *seethe* before. It made her stomach roil uncomfortably.

"Of course, sister of mine. You always have a choice. But, as you know, choices have consequences."

Effie knew the consequences of wearing Harmonia's necklace. It had turned the goddess Harmonia and her husband, Cadmus, into serpents. Later, when it had passed to Queen Jocasta of Thebes, she wound up marrying her son Oedipus. And less known to most, after wearing the piece, Anne Boleyn and Marie Antoinette both lost their heads. She had to get the cursed thing off—and fast.

She gritted her teeth and let her brother lead her out of the club, the masked automaton trailing in their wake.

I

December 2018

Aida stared at the email from her publisher hovering on her laptop screen like a digital albatross, the cursor blinking expectantly for a response she didn't have.

Dear Ms. Reale,

It is with deep regret that we inform you that due to a financial setback, Ovidian is ceasing operations immediately. Unfortunately, this means we will not be able to move forward with the publication of your book. We understand how much work you have put into this project, and we deeply apologize for any inconvenience this may cause.

Aida wanted to throw the laptop across the room. Why did they choose to send this email on Christmas Eve, of all days?

The news was particularly devastating. After numerous rejections from academic publishers, three months ago she had finally secured a contract with Ovidian, a small but respected publisher known for its niche focus on history and art. Her book about food featured in Italian tapestries was supposed to be her breakthrough, a scholarly work that would boost her reputation. Instead, the sudden closure of her publisher meant her manuscript, which had taken years of research and writing, was now in limbo.

As if that wasn't enough, she had just completed her final semester of teaching. At the end of the spring semester, the university announced her department would be downsizing due to budget cuts, reducing faculty and course offerings. With the semester over and no new job lined up, Aida was officially unemployed. She had spent the summer and fall applying for positions, but the competition in history departments was fierce, and the loss of her book contract was another blow to her prospects. Now, the reality that she might not have a job in the new year loomed large.

The comforting scent of cinnamon wafted from the kitchen, where Graham was attending to the holiday details she couldn't muster the energy for. "Where are the goblets?" he called out.

"Top shelf in the pantry," she said, eyes still glued to the screen. "Red box. Can't miss them."

A few minutes later, the soft shuffle of feet announced her fiancé's presence in the doorway of the living room. He had five years on Aida's thirty-four but looked much younger. With his wavy brown hair and blue eyes that had a boyish charm, he could have just stepped out of a holiday rom-com. He held a glass of mulled wine. "What's wrong, love? You look like the world just ended."

"Ovidian is shutting down. They won't be publishing my book. I don't know what I'm going to do. This was supposed to help in my job search, but now . . . And with the wedding coming up, how can we afford it?"

Graham's expression softened, and he immediately crossed the room to sit beside her, handing her the wine. "Oh, Aida. I'm so sorry. I know how much this meant to you." He wrapped an arm around her, pulling her close. "But listen to me, we'll get through this. The job market is tough, I know, but you're brilliant, and there will be another opportunity out there. As for the wedding, I've told you a hundred times that we'll make it work. We won't let this ruin everything. We've come too far, and I'm not going anywhere. We'll think outside the box."

Aida leaned into him, the warmth of his embrace easing the tightness in her chest. His words were like a balm, soothing the jagged edges of her anxiety. "Thank you," she whispered. "I don't know what I'd do without you."

"You won't have to find out," Graham replied softly, running his fingers over her necklace with a little silver star pendant, an engagement gift he had given her that she wore daily. "We're in this together, for better or worse, remember?"

She wanted to cry, but the tears wouldn't come. "It just feels like everything I've worked for is slipping away."

As if on cue, the doorbell rang—a discordant jingle that seemed oddly out of place in the quiet moment. Aida reluctantly got up to answer it, expecting Graham's parents to have arrived early. But instead, she found a luxurious black envelope with golden embossing placed meticulously on the welcome mat. No courier in sight, no sign of who had left it. No stamp or address, just Aida's name printed in gold block letters. When she picked it up, it was quite cold—whoever had delivered it had not kept it in a purse or a coat pocket. There was only a neat line of footprints in a dusting of snow. They came from one direction, up to the town house, then back down the walk and off in the other direction.

Returning to the living room, her curiosity piqued, Aida broke the wax seal and opened the envelope with a sense of anticipation she hadn't felt in a while. The invitation inside was printed on luxurious paper, embossed with gold lettering that caught the glow of the Christmas lights.

Lady Ozie requires your attendance in the Seaport on December 30th at 11:00 a.m. to discuss a matter of importance to your future. A car will be sent to collect you.

Aida stared at the paper. The elegance of the invitation and the sheer audacity of receiving it on Christmas Eve made it feel like something out of a fairy tale.

Graham peeked over her shoulder. "What's that?"

"A joke, I think."

"A joke? Who would do that?"

"It must be a scam. There's no return address, phone number, or email." She handed it to Graham.

He looked it over, an eyebrow raised. "Is Lady Ozie related to Ozzy Osbourne?"

Aida chuckled at the ridiculousness of the idea. But more sobering, why would this "Lady" think anyone would agree to hop into a strange car without any other information? Imagining her face on episodes of shows like *Unsolved Mysteries* or *48 Hours*, she shuddered. Aida plucked the invitation out of Graham's hand and picked up her laptop.

"I think it's Oh-Zee, not Ah-Zee. Let me put this away and I'll help with dinner."

She had just set her laptop—and the invite—on the desk in the alcove off the bedroom when her phone buzzed in her pocket. Digging it out, she saw the text was from Felix, a tour guide in Rome who had quickly become a friend after she met him several years ago when she was researching her book and needed information about specific Renaissance period locations in the city. When he learned she was no ordinary tourist and not only spoke the language but had a strong understanding of Italian history and culture, he had quickly taken to her and happily guided her through the city, sharing his expertise and connecting her to scholars she might not otherwise have had easy access to.

Buon Natale, amica mia! I think someone may reach out to you soon about a job. Rich client of mine, a Lady Ozie.

Aida stared at the envelope in front of her. The gold lettering shone in the gleam of the holiday lights in the window.

A job? Is this a joke? she texted back. Although she desperately needed a job, this seemed too strange to be true.

Felix took a moment to respond and then it wasn't by text. When Aida's phone flashed with his video call, she took it immediately.

"*Cara!* It is much better to see your lovely face. You cut your hair!" Felix smiled through the small rectangle of her phone. His russet locks were tousled and fell over one eye.

"I did!" Aida held her hand up to show off her new shag cut. "I almost went pink but thought it might make me look too young."

"Ha! You don't need the pink. The blond looks good on you," Felix remarked, before briefly pausing to address someone in the room. After the sound of a door closing, he resumed. "My handsome Christmas present," he joked. "But he doesn't need to hear this."

Aida grinned, glad to know he wasn't alone on the holiday.

"So, this Lady Ozie," she began. "I received an invitation from her today and I was just about to throw it away. I thought it was some kind of prank."

Felix's expression grew serious. "No, no, Aida, it's not a joke. It's a real job offer. So, this is the thing. I'm not sure if I've met Ozie—if I have, I never knew it. One day, I received a letter praising the expertise of my tours and asking if I would give specialized private excursions to anyone who came to me and was referred by her. But I'm not to talk about them to anyone. I've been sworn to secrecy about the whole thing. It's all quite clandestine."

Aida raised an eyebrow. "You're talking to me though."

Felix chuckled. "Indeed, but only because I've referred you to Lady Ozie. Despite the rather unnecessary shroud of secrecy, she compensates me at quadruple my standard rate."

"Wow, that sounds like a nice arrangement. Do you do a lot of tours for her?"

He shrugged. "For the rates she pays, one might expect A-list clientele, but it's only been a historian from South Africa—a Mr. Johannes Khumalo. The tours I gave him were specialized, primarily more obscure locations. I had to prepare pretty well beforehand, making sure I could get access and that I had all the information he might need."

"What types of locations?"

"There have been so many, I can't remember them all. Most recently, Princess Isabelle's apartment in Palazzo Colonna—a room of extraordinary beauty—and the optical illusion frescoes of Trinità dei Monti convent. Before Lady Ozie's team canceled, I was preparing to show him the secret rooms of Saint Philip Neri in the Santa Maria in Valicella church. Neri is considered to be a saint of happiness. The spirit of God was said to visit him with a flame that made his heart grow double in size, and he was filled with warmth and thereafter preached joy to his congregation. But not many people have heard of him."

"A saint of happiness?" Aida could use a bit more happiness in her life.

"That's right. According to him, 'A joyful heart is more easily made perfect than a downcast one.' He believed we should aspire to be joyful and happy."

"Well, don't most people aspire to that?" Aida asked. "Unfortunately, the world is pretty good at ripping happiness and joy right out of our hot little hands."

"That doesn't mean we shouldn't keep aspiring to it, no matter how bleak things become. Besides, you don't really believe that. You are the most optimistic person I know," he said.

Aida didn't have the heart to tell her friend that her optimism wasn't exactly brimming over these days. Her money was trickling away, straining under the cost of her upcoming wedding to Graham at the end of May. He was a teacher and certainly didn't make bank, and now that she was out of a job, her uncertain future didn't exactly elicit joy.

Felix prattled on. "But back to the historian. The tours I have arranged for him are to strange and beautiful places that most tourists wouldn't ever know about."

One of the things that Aida had always loved about Felix was how animated her friend grew when he waxed historical. "So, what does this have to do with me?"

"I had a call very early this morning from Lady Ozie's assistant. Apparently, the historian is no longer working for her. She was asking if I could recommend an expert on Italy who may need work. Of course, I thought of you. It's a three-month gig to start, then if the person works out, they will offer a five-year employment contract. I know it might be a stretch for you two . . . moving overseas, but figured it might be worth looking into it."

Aida's heart ballooned at the kindness of the gesture.

"She called you on Christmas Eve?"

Felix nodded. "Well, one of her employees did. Everything about Lady Ozie is bizarre, but you know what a guide's salary is like. She pays so well that I'd take calls from her at three a.m. if I had to."

"Your Christmas present wouldn't take kindly to that, I expect," she teased.

He laughed. "Probably not."

"Why didn't you offer to take the job?"

"She's looking for a historian with credentials, and I don't have that kind of experience. Besides, I love the work I do and if she keeps paying me extra on the side, I'm happy."

The prospect of meeting Lady Ozie and conducting hands-on research in Italy was intriguing. Living in Italy was certainly tempting. But it didn't make much sense to give it any real consideration. Graham didn't speak Italian, and what job opportunities could a high school physics teacher find there?

"What kind of name is Lady Ozie?" she mused. There was a story in this strange scenario and her curious side was keen to know more.

"It's anyone's guess. My amateur internet sleuthing has turned up nothing. I like to imagine she's an eccentric duchess running a secret society of librarians," Felix offered.

Aida snorted. "You've been reading too many novels."

"Or binge-watching Netflix," he countered. "What are your plans for Christmas? Where's Graham?"

"He's cooking dinner. I should go help him," Aida said. Just then, the door behind Felix cracked open and a hushed conversation ensued.

"Bedtime," Felix said, winking at Aida. "Hang in there, *cara*. And let me know if you meet with Lady Ozie!" He blew her a few air kisses and then ended the call.

"WHO WAS THAT?" Graham asked when she finally joined him in the kitchen. Aida pretended she didn't notice his irritation as Graham pulled the goose out of the oven and set the steaming pan on a nearby cutting board.

"Felix in Rome. He says hi," she said. "You know that letter I just got?" She explained the situation to her fiancé.

Graham took off the oven mitts and looked at her. "It sounds really cool, but a job in Italy? I'm confused. Why would Felix suggest that? He knows we're getting married in a few months, and that I teach."

Aida shrugged. "I think because the trial period could give me a quick infusion of cash, even if I decide not to take it long-term. It does sound interesting."

"Interesting? More interesting than me?"

She swatted him on the shoulder and gave him a conciliatory smile. "Don't be silly."

Her fiancé laughed and enveloped her in a hug. But as she stared over his shoulder at the steaming goose, she had to admit that a little piece of her wanted to do it. She pushed the thought away and hugged him tight.

The doorbell rang again, but this time it was Graham's parents, Brennan and Miriam, with an armful of colorfully wrapped presents and a plastic-wrapped tray of cookies. Miriam was the first to step inside, her perfume filling the room with a familiar floral scent. She was a petite woman, her hair gone gray but carefully coiffed, her ensemble stylish in a conservative way.

"Merry Christmas, darling," Miriam said, her lips landing on both of Aida's cheeks in quick succession. "You look a bit thin. Good thing I brought cookies."

Aida suppressed the urge to roll her eyes, instead offering a tight smile. "I'm fine, Miriam."

Brennan was next, a tall lanky man whose stern demeanor was etched into every line on his face. Unlike Miriam, he wasn't one for effusive displays of affection, but he managed a slight smile and a nod in Aida's direction. "Aida," he greeted.

"Graham, darling," Miriam cooed, turning to her son with a warm smile. "Thank you for hosting us."

Aida felt a familiar twinge in her chest, the one that reminded her how much his parents didn't like her, and regularly made subtle digs to make sure she knew it. They'd never approved of her—too academic, not enough connections, not enough money. It was strange and inexplicable, considering Graham himself had a job as a high school physics teacher and they weren't exactly made of money either. But for some reason, to them, Aida wasn't a good enough match, and they never missed an opportunity to make that clear.

"Our home is your home," Graham replied, already angling toward the kitchen with the cookies.

"So, what's for dinner?" Brennan asked, taking off his coat and scrutinizing the living room as if inspecting it for defects.

"We've got a goose, some sweet potatoes, green beans, and a chocolate mousse pie for dessert," Aida listed off.

"A goose? My, aren't we fancy?" Miriam remarked.

"It was an old family tradition in my house," Aida said. "Graham was excited about the challenge. But you know him. Everything he cooks is delicious."

As she spoke, Aida couldn't help but think of her own parents, who had passed away in recent years. They had been much older than Graham's parents and couldn't have been more different. Where Miriam and Brennan were always judgmental, her parents had been joyful, welcoming, and free of pretense. Aida missed them most during moments like this, when she had to put up with Graham's family's constant scrutiny.

Miriam walked over to the Christmas tree, carefully arranging the stack of colorfully wrapped gifts at its base. As she straightened, her gaze lingered on the tree and the room's decorations, a few with her and Brennan's names on the present tags.

"Well, everything looks very . . . quaint," she said, the word hanging in the air like a thinly veiled critique.

Aida bit her lip, a flicker of irritation rising. Miriam's comments, as always, came laced with judgment, like she had something to prove. Choosing not to respond, Aida gently guided her in-laws toward the dining table, eager to escape the prickling atmosphere near the tree.

UNFORTUNATELY, THE DINNER table was a battlefield, with Aida's attempts at humor falling flat amid awkward silences and strained politeness, while Graham's jokes drew genuine laughter from Brennan and Miriam. Brennan dominated the conversation, boasting about his role as a municipal court clerk. Miriam, who had also been a teacher—of high school English—offered up stories of her former students who had recently published articles or secured high-paying jobs, each tale an arrow in Aida's already-thinning armor.

"So, Aida, what's new with your book?" Brennan asked, as if remembering to include her in the conversation.

"Yes, do tell. When will it be out? It will give you the needed credibility," Miriam chimed in.

Aida hesitated, feeling cornered. The room seemed to shrink as all eyes turned her way, and she reluctantly responded. "It's not good news. My publisher folded, so I'm back at square one."

Brennan frowned, cutting into his goose. "Why can't you find another publisher?"

"It's not that easy," Aida said, her voice tinged with frustration. She didn't want to get into the details; they'd never understood the nuances of her university career nor cared to.

Brennan seemed like he was going to say something else but thought better of it and took a long draft of wine instead.

Miriam, however, wasn't ready to let it go. "What are you going to do?" she asked, her tone dangerously close to condescending. "Maybe you should focus less on the book and more on hitting the pavement to find—"

"The book was supposed to help make that easier," Aida cut in, her voice sharper than she intended. "I am *hitting the pavement*. But my timing is way off. They've already filled faculty positions for spring at most places. Even if I found something tomorrow, I wouldn't be starting until summer at the earliest, and more likely, the fall. I thought I might find an adjunct position, but I haven't had much luck. I may try to find something temporary to tide me over while I keep looking."

"It's a good idea," Graham said, putting his arm protectively around the back of Aida's chair. "But mostly so you keep your mind occupied. Job hunting is such a downer. Maybe Felix had the right idea suggesting something to you."

"Felix? The tour guide friend of yours in Rome?" Miriam asked.

"Yes, that's him," Aida confirmed.

Miriam reached for the bread basket, her expression carefully blank. "I'm sure a tour guide is full of useful career advice."

At the slight to her friend, Aida clenched her fists beneath the table. She forced herself to relax. "He knows someone who might be able to offer me some temporary work. A bit like a research fellowship."

Brennan straightened and laid his napkin on the table. "I suppose Graham is right. It is a good idea. You shouldn't expect Graham to support you both on a teacher's salary." He gave a conspiratorial nod toward her fiancé.

The sting of Brennan's words was sharper than she'd like to admit. Before she could give the heated response on the tip of her tongue, Graham's voice cut in, firm but calm. "Actually, we're doing just fine. Aida's been working really hard, and I'm confident her book will find a new publisher. It was accepted once, so it has a strong chance." He gave Aida's hand a reassuring squeeze under the table.

Miriam smiled approvingly at Graham, the warmth in her expression reserved entirely for her son. "Well, aren't you lucky to have someone so responsible looking out for you?"

Aida seethed.

Miriam waved her fork at Aida. "Maybe you should hold off on the wedding."

Simultaneously, Aida and Graham both responded with an emphatic, "No!"

Aida's heart surged with love. She had mentioned this same idea to Graham when she lost her job, but he understood that her fear wasn't about the money, but about him not wanting to marry her because she couldn't pull her own weight. Then, as now, he was adamant that they would find some way to make the wedding work. She wasn't sure she believed him, but she loved him for having such unwavering faith when she did not.

"We would lose too much money on all our deposits if we canceled now," Aida tried to explain.

"We're keeping the wedding," Graham said, his tone clear that the decision was final.

Brennan gave a snort and raised his glass with an air of forced cheer. "Well then, to the future."

Aida clinked her glass with the others, but the last vestiges of her holiday spirit dissolved as she drained the wine.

THE FOLLOWING DAY, Aida showed her friends Yumi and Erin the mysterious envelope. Yumi was Aida's bestie, a petite Japanese woman with striking features and dark expressive eyes that always seemed to be analyzing everything around her. Erin was her oldest friend, with fair skin and rich auburn hair that fell in soft waves around her face.

Aida and Erin had been inseparable as children. Their summers were spent racing bikes through the neighborhood, building forts in the woods, and whispering secrets late into the night during sleepovers. Erin had always been the one Aida could rely on—the friend who knew every little detail about her life, the one she could turn to without hesitation. Even after Erin moved away ten years ago, they'd managed to stay in touch, though mostly through social media. Their connection had become something of a shadow of what it once was—likes on posts, the occasional comment, but nothing compared to the tight-knit bond they'd shared growing up.

After Erin left, Aida met Yumi at a friend's party. At first, Aida had been intimidated by Yumi's sharp, analytical mind. But as the night went on, they bonded over a shared sense of humor and a mutual love for reality television and indie music. Despite their different paths, the two women clicked. Over time, Yumi became the person Aida turned to for advice, the one who grounded her when life felt overwhelming. Yumi's pragmatic, no-nonsense approach to the world balanced out Aida's more creative tendencies, and their friendship had only deepened over the years.

And now, Erin was back in Boston. When she called three weeks ago to let Aida know she had moved back, Aida's heart had leaped. The joy of reconnecting with her childhood best friend had been immediate. She was grateful to have Erin back and excited to introduce her to Yumi, who had quickly taken to her.

The three were sipping drinks at a bar a few blocks from Aida's house on a tab that Yumi had declared she was picking up. Yumi had a high-profile role at one of the big cybersecurity companies in Cambridge, a job she had snagged after showing off her amateur hacking skills.

"This interview sounds a little dangerous—and exciting." Erin twiddled the straw of her mai tai. "What does Graham think?"

Aida sighed, conflicted. "We talked about it last night. Apparently, there is a trial period before they offer the contract, which pays well. He isn't thrilled about my being away from him, but he thinks it could be good for connections and help me find a fresh perspective."

Yumi's eyes widened. "Wait, are you seriously thinking of going?"

"Maybe," Aida admitted. "It might be the only way right now to have the wedding. Without some form of cash infusion, I think we'll have to call it off and have a small civil ceremony." She picked up the envelope and waved it around. "Plus, all of *this* is so weird. I want to know what the story is."

Erin was more enthusiastic. "I think it would be worth checking out. It sounds like it might be a cool job."

"Hmm." Yumi considered this for a moment. "If it's only for three months, maybe Erin's right—it will be worth it. God knows you need the money. It'll be an adventure. But if you really want to do this, you shouldn't go to the meeting alone. You are taking Graham, right?"

"It's a job interview! Wouldn't that be weird?"

Yumi rolled her eyes. "They sent you a freaky hand-delivered note on Christmas Eve that said a mysterious car would pick you up. No phone number, no website, no nothing. If it weren't for Felix, you'd think it was a scam and a half. Wouldn't you say that's weirder? They could hardly blame you for wanting to be safe in this Hashtag-Me-Too world. Which means you need to take him with you."

Aida flipped on her phone, scanning the calendar. She shook her head. "I can't. Dang it. He's helping one of his buddies move that day."

Yumi patted Aida's arm. "You know what, I'll go with you."

"I'm sure she'll be fine going alone. It can't be bad if Felix suggested it," Erin said.

Yumi shook her head. "That's not the point. I don't care if Felix trusts them—I don't trust mysterious notes with no contact info."

Aida bit her lip, torn. "But you don't have to—"

"I *do*," Yumi interrupted, her tone firm. "I'm not letting you walk into whatever this is by yourself. This is the kind of sketchy situation that sets off alarm bells. I'm going with you, end of discussion."

"Thanks, Yumi. It's probably nothing, but . . . I'll feel better with you there."

Yumi grinned. "Besides, if it turns out to be totally normal, we can grab lunch afterward and laugh about how paranoid we were."

Aida nodded, the knot in her chest loosening. Whatever this strange opportunity was, at least she wouldn't face it alone.

2

December 2018

IN THE DAYS leading up to December 30, Yumi spearheaded efforts to uncover the mysterious Lady Ozie's identity. Despite combing through social media profiles, public records, and business filings, they came up empty-handed. Even narrowing the search to Boston didn't help; all their attempts led them down a rabbit hole of Ozzy Osbourne fan pages.

Yumi arrived ten minutes early on the day Lady Ozie's car was supposed to pick them up. The Boston winter was living up to its reputation—crisp and piercingly cold.

Yumi sported a long black coat, over-the-knee boots, a huge pink scarf, and a matching pair of big fuzzy earmuffs. Aida had always admired her friend's ability to appear both elegant and adorable at the same time. She waved her phone at Aida. "I connected my sister to my GPS app so she'll know where we are. If I haven't called her by midafternoon, she'll send out the troops to look for us."

"I did the same for Graham and Erin."

A sudden knock on the door interrupted their conversation. A man in his mid-forties in an immaculate chauffeur's suit and hat appeared as if he'd walked straight out of a classic film. Aida had been chauffeured before, but never by someone so impeccably dressed. Behind him, a gleaming black Rolls-Royce Phantom sat double-parked. Aida's heart lifted. Perhaps Felix was right, and this job would pay well, after all.

"Miss Aida Reale?" He arched an eyebrow, his gaze shifting between Aida and Yumi.

"I'm Aida," she confirmed, slinging her purse over her shoulder and wrapping a scarf around her neck. "My colleague Yumi will be joining me."

The chauffeur shook his head. "Lady Ozie's invitation is for you alone."

Aida drew a breath and stood taller, a trick she had learned to steel herself against the condescending scholars she often encountered during her research. "Please forgive me if I refuse to get into a car with an unknown person to go to an undisclosed location alone."

The chauffeur paused, considering her, gave a curt nod, then headed down the path toward the car, where he stood near the rear door to let them in. He swung it open, revealing the car's luxurious interior, which screamed opulence—from the blue leather seats and blue-furred floor mats to the ceiling speckled with tiny twinkling stars.

It had just begun to snow, the pretty, fluffy kind that was unlikely to stick. The air felt charged with possibility. Aida climbed into the waiting Rolls-Royce, buoyed by a mix of hope and anticipation.

Once she and Yumi were inside and seated, the chauffeur returned to the driver's seat and activated a console on the back of each seat in front of them.

"If you desire, choose the massage you would like, then press the button."

Yumi looked at Aida, eyes wide.

"Has anyone ever declined a massage?" Aida asked as she fiddled with the settings.

His eyes smiled in the rearview mirror. "No, Miss Reale, not yet."

"Where are you taking us, anyway?" Yumi asked.

"The Boston Harbor Hotel on Rowes Wharf."

Aida's fingers were already flying across her phone's screen, texting Graham.

Within twenty minutes, they were pulling up to the hotel, its grandeur marked by a massive flag that billowed from the center of the wide arches defining the seaside structure. Beyond the arches lay the hotel's dock, a haven for luxury yachts adorned with helicopters and swimming pools. Nearby, a covered floating ballroom boasted a checkered floor that seemed to dance on the water's surface. Aida recalled the days of her early childhood spent there, long before her parents became ill. She'd been too young for cocktails but delighted in sipping ginger ale as if it were a grown-up drink, her eyes wide with wonder as she watched the swing dancers whirl and dip. Those were magical times, filled with laughter and the gentle sway of the floating dock, a stark contrast to the more complicated years that would follow.

A white-gloved bellhop swung open the car door and paused as if he were unsure he had opened the right door. "This is Aida Reale and friend," the driver told him. Masking his puzzlement, the bellhop warmly greeted them before escorting the two women into the hotel's lobby, where a woman stood by a window overlooking the seaport. Her ink-black hair was pulled into a severe ponytail, offering a striking contrast to her ivory skin and impeccably white pantsuit.

"Aida Reale and friend," announced the bellhop before promptly disappearing.

The woman eyed Yumi with a furrowed brow. "You are Yumi Tanaka."

"How did you know that?" Yumi bristled and crossed her arms.

The woman did not respond. "The invitation was only for you," she said, addressing Aida.

"Please forgive me, Miss . . ." Aida paused for the woman's name. After an uncomfortable moment when it became clear the woman was not going to indulge her, Aida repeated the rationale she'd given the driver earlier, insisting on the presence of a companion for her own safety.

The woman's dark eyes narrowed, and Aida thought she caught the flicker of a smile at the edge of her lips. "Fine." The woman flicked her hand at the two of them to follow, then led them to a private elevator, where she inserted a key card and selected the penthouse.

A thrum of unease coursed through Aida as she stepped into the elevator, her mind racing with questions. How—and *why*—did this woman know who Yumi was? What else did she know about them? The elevator doors slid shut with a soft hiss, sealing them in a silent ascent. Aida wanted to speak, to demand answers, but the woman's icy demeanor stifled any attempts at conversation. The illuminated numbers above the door ticked higher with each floor they passed, ratcheting up Aida's tension.

As the elevator neared the penthouse, the woman finally broke the silence. "Miss Tanaka, you will be escorted to our theater room, where you'll be made comfortable. Both of you are required to sign a nondisclosure agreement."

"I need to sign an NDA even if I'm not part of the conversation?" Yumi asked. "You know so much about me. I hardly find it fair."

The woman only raised an eyebrow at her. "Lady Ozie requires the utmost privacy for her affairs," she explained. "I'm sure you've worked with clients that require the same."

The door opened, not into a hallway as Aida had expected, but a stone-inlaid foyer. The woman led them through the vestibule into a palatial space with a high-vaulted ceiling and a massive glass chandelier blooming downward from its center. Several upholstered gray and white couches were carefully arranged beneath it. While opulent, the room's muted color palette of grays and whites lent it a chilly air. Beyond was a wall of floor-to-ceiling windows that led to a vast terrace with a panoramic view of the Boston Harbor.

"Dear god," Yumi said as she took in the view.

Ignoring the chef carrying a tray of pastries and a red-haired woman engrossed in her tablet, their host guided Aida and Yumi to a long table near a plush sofa. She opened a drawer, presenting each with a pen and sheet of paper. "The NDAs."

Aida quickly skimmed the document. It was standard fare, similar to contracts she'd signed at corporations she had worked at before her academic pursuits. The language was clear: No discussion of what took place within these walls, no photos or recordings of any kind, and no mention of the meeting to anyone, not even in passing. It was a simple but effective way to ensure whatever happened here stayed here. A glance at Yumi showed her friend had already picked up the pen and was signing her name. Aida scribbled her signature at the bottom, sealing her silence just as Yumi handed the document back to the waiting assistant.

"Our next step," the woman said, lifting the lid of a sleek black leather box on the table. "Please place your phones here. Photos, recordings, and messages are not permitted beyond this point."

Aida watched as her friend gave a resigned shrug, as if to say, "Well, we're in it now," and relinquished her phone to the box. She followed suit, wondering what kind of meeting necessitated such secrecy.

"Now, Miss Tanaka, come with me."

Yumi trailed after the woman, leaving Aida to stand awkwardly at the table. She marveled at the view and the opulent suite, but her insides were churning. She wasn't one to usually be nervous in interviews, but this was an extraordinary location for an interview for a strange position. Fortunately, she wasn't alone long—the woman returned, passing Aida with a gesture to follow.

"You'll be meeting Fran now," she said, leading her toward the dining area.

The red-haired woman, engrossed in her tablet a moment before, stood to greet them. Aida's eyes were drawn to an elaborate gold belt at her waist, with an interlocking ancient motif. A meander, or a Greek key, Aida recalled. She wanted to remark on it, but the woman addressed her before she could say anything.

"Miss Reale, it is a pleasure to meet you." She took Aida's hands in hers. They were warm, as was the smile upon her face. "I'm Fran." She pronounced it like *frown*, which made Aida question the way the woman who had escorted her had said it earlier. Had she misheard, or was there something more to this unusual pronunciation?

"Thank you, Disa. Please, Aida, sit." Fran indicated the seat next to her.

Fran was even paler than Disa. There was such a similarity in their features that for a fleeting moment Aida wondered if they could be sisters.

It was odd that despite Aida having signed the NDA, Fran failed to give their last names, but then again, everything about the scenario was odd. Disa pulled out the chair for Aida, and she sat, feeling awkward at the head of the long table. A white runner edged in the same gold meander ran down its length, and a bowl full of shiny red apples rested a few feet away, the only bit of color in the room. A single golden apple sat on top.

"Are either of you Lady Ozie?" Aida finally asked, curiosity winning over caution. "The invitation was from her, so I assumed . . ."

"No. We are here to represent her interests," Fran explained, her smile undiminished.

"Ahh," Aida replied, feigning understanding while internally puzzling over the situation. Why extend an invitation under the guise of a personal meeting if Lady Ozie had no intention of attending?

Disa seated herself on the other side of Aida. "Lady Ozie is a very eccentric individual. You will likely not meet her."

Alarm bells went off in Aida's mind.

"Now then. Let's discuss why you're here," Fran said, her tone considerably warmer than her colleague's.

Aida reached for her purse, intending to pull out a notepad and pen.

"No need for that," Fran interjected, placing a gentle hand on Aida's shoulder.

"So, no notes either?" Aida was growing increasingly perplexed about the nature of this meeting.

Fran shook her head. "I'm afraid not."

Aida hooked her purse on the back of the chair and folded her hands in her lap. She smiled, an attempt to ease the rising anxiety in her chest. She remembered the stories from a friend of hers who lived in the North End about the way the mafia worked in the city, primarily through secrecy and threats; this felt strangely similar. She contemplated these two women and pushed the idea out of her head. There was no threat. Felix had given them her name.

"We've read your published papers," Disa continued. "We're quite impressed by your knowledge of Italian history and the depth of historical detail in your work."

A warm glow of pride spread through Aida. The irony wasn't lost on her that strangers were validating her craft while so many publishers had been reluctant to publish her book.

Fran patted her arm again, the gesture of a consoling friend. "We also understand you may be somewhat blocked in continuing your success."

Aida stiffened, but she kept her face neutral. "How could you possibly know that? You seem to know a lot about me and my life."

"We do our own research," Disa said. She was all business, sharp edges, whereas her counterpart was all kindness, soft and reassuring. "We must be able to trust those we bring into our employ."

"And what sort of employ would that be?" Aida asked. It came out more defensive than she intended, but she didn't like the idea that these people might know of her money situation. No one, save Erin, Yumi, and Graham, knew of her financial concerns.

Fran leaned forward slightly, her voice warm and inviting.

"We need someone to craft a narrative around specific periods and items in Italian history."

"What do you mean? For what purpose?" Aida pressed, her curiosity piqued yet mixed with a growing unease.

"Because Lady Ozie requests it," Disa said. She did not expound upon her statement, letting the name hang in the air, as if that explained everything.

Fran shot Disa a withering look before turning back to Aida with her dazzling smile. "I'll elaborate on the position, then we can address any questions you may have."

Nodding, Aida began seriously contemplating grabbing Yumi and making a quick exit. Even if this was just for research, something felt off about all of it.

"This position is based in Rome. Your travel, relocation, and accommodations have already been secured for you."

Aida opened up her mouth to protest. She hadn't agreed to this job. But Fran didn't pause. "You'll work from a palazzo in the center of Rome, which will serve as your home base. Everything is taken care of: meals, laundry, housekeeping, and so on." Fran waved an elegant hand as if brushing away any concerns Aida might have. "You'll have transportation at your disposal for professional and personal use. Exceptional guides will assist you at every location where you work."

Aida couldn't believe her ears. All expenses paid living in Rome? This was surely too good to be true. Yes, definitely too good to be true. For a fleeting moment, she thought Yumi must be playing an elaborate joke on her, but she discarded the idea; her friend would never be so cruel as to tease her about her financial situation.

Fran continued. "We believe you would find the work as a scholar for MODA very fulfilling. You'll be expected to thoroughly catalog certain locations, events, and objects throughout the Italian peninsula. This research will be submitted partially through the MODA database and partially in person, every three to four months."

"MODA?" Aida echoed, trying to grasp the full scope.

"Lady Ozie's organization," Disa interjected sharply, her tone carrying a chill that seemed at odds with Fran's warm presentation.

Aida hesitated, caught by Disa's attitude. She gave a nod toward Disa's outfit. "*Moda* means fashion . . . Is there a connection?"

"No," Disa clipped out, her brisk dismissal adding an icy layer to the conversation.

Aida was unsettled—not just by the presumptuousness of the arrangements but also by Disa's response. It was clear that working together could be less than harmonious.

"There's something I don't understand," Aida finally said. "If this is just a research job, why do you need to know everything about my personal life, my family and friends? That seems . . . excessive for a historian role."

Fran's smile remained serene, almost maternal. "It's a fair question, Aida. Our projects often require a deep understanding of our team members, not just their professional skills but also their personal motivations and values. This helps us create a cohesive and trusting environment. We want to ensure that those we bring on board are not only experts in their field but also a good fit for the unique demands of our work. And I assure you, any personal information we gather is handled with the utmost discretion."

Something about Fran's response still felt off, too rehearsed. "And this job . . . it's all aboveboard, right? I wouldn't be doing anything illegal?" Aida asked.

Disa laughed, a rich peal of noise that rang through the vaulted room. "Only if you want to."

"Don't mind her," Fran said, waving a dismissive hand in her colleague's direction. "Nothing illegal, I assure you. It's just that our work sometimes involves accessing private collections or restricted locations, and we must be discreet. Hence the thorough vetting process."

Aida exhaled, still grappling with the nebulous outline of the job. "Could you describe what a typical day or week might look like?"

Fran shook her head. "There's no *typical* in this line of work, but I can give you a sense of the projects." She began to outline one such project that Felix had mentioned Aida's predecessor had focused on: documenting the private apartment of Isabelle Colonna in Rome's illustrious Palazzo Colonna. The historian's assignment had been exhaustive, involving the cataloging of the art, objects, furnishings, and alterations made over the years. There was also a great deal of modern information relating to the room, such as an estimate of how many visitors had seen the room over the years it had been open to the public, what restorations had been made, and the number of tours that had been given. A videographer and photographer accompanied the historian on occasion. There were also several interviews with individuals who viewed the rooms, asking them about their impressions of the beautiful space. "Projects can last from a few weeks to a few months, but once you complete the three-month trial period and become a full employee, you'll give quarterly reports in Lady Ozie's offices in London."

During Fran's extended exposition, Disa had grown visibly bored. She got up to look out the window at the cold bay beyond, returning to her seat just as Fran concluded her explanation.

Aida pondered the idiosyncratic nature of it all. "Is there a common thread among these projects? Some guiding principle?"

Disa chuckled and began to say something, but Fran cut her off. "Not really. Lady Ozie is just particularly curious about some of the more obscure, unusual, and beautiful places, items, and events in Italy. Her objective is to compile a comprehensive historical database on these, albeit an unconventional one."

"What happened to the previous historian?" If the job was as great as they said it was, Aida couldn't understand why someone would voluntarily leave such a role.

Fran shook her head and pursed her lips. "Unfortunately, Mr. Khumalo died of a heart attack. He had worked for MODA for the last four years, and we were sad to lose him."

Disa tsked. "Smoking will do that to you." She lifted two fingers to her lips and mimicked the movement of a cigarette.

"Now, Disa, be kind to the dead."

Her colleague rolled her eyes. "I'm going to check on Miss Tanaka." She stood and headed toward the doors on the opposite side of the vast suite.

"Remember our conversation," Fran called after her. Disa didn't look back.

"Forgive her," Fran told Aida. "She loves to sow a bit of discord. Now then, where were we . . ." She drummed her fingers on the table.

Aida's thoughts briefly flitted to Graham, her soon-to-be husband. "And what about my partner?"

"Of course, he will be able to join you once the trial period is up. He'll be subject to our NDAs around the nature of the work you do. We will also employ our services to help him find suitable employment."

"That's generous," Aida said cautiously, tucking away her real intention—accept the role for three months as a trial and then gracefully exit.

"Lady Ozie has the means to be generous."

"I have to say, this is an unusual interview. You haven't asked me any questions," Aida noted.

"This isn't an interview. We're offering you the position," Fran clarified with a confident smile. "We've conducted an extensive background check and are convinced you're the ideal candidate for this role. Your work speaks for itself. We expect you to prove us right during the next three months. Also, on the publishing front, we have some connections that might interest you." A subtle offer hung in the air. "And we hope this new role will inspire more books."

Aida wasn't sure what Fran meant by *connections*. It sounded both intriguing and fishy at the same time.

"Well," Aida said, gathering courage. She had never liked the monetary negotiation part of the job process, but it was better to get to the point. "You haven't mentioned the salary."

Fran flashed her a brilliant smile. "Yes, the money. It always comes down to that, although I suspect with all living costs included, the additional amenities, plus love for the type of work you are doing, the salary might seem secondary."

Aida thought of the astronomical amount of credit card and wedding debt weighing on her, but instead of objecting, she offered Fran a patient smile.

"We are prepared to offer you four hundred thousand US dollars per annum."

Aida's jaw dropped before she could catch herself. "I'm not sure I heard you right," she finally said, her heart racing.

"You heard right, Miss Reale. Lady Ozie values the work and compensates accordingly."

"I . . . uh, I'm not sure what to say. This sounds too good to be true."

"It is good, and I also assure you, it's true. You will begin work right away. We'll also provide you with a twenty-five-thousand-dollar signing bonus to help you wrap up any affairs in Boston before you are sent to Rome."

But $25,000 . . . *Dear god*, she thought to herself. That would stave off worries she had about paying for the wedding. And the salary, on top of all living expenses paid? She could research and write solely for the joy of it, her financial concerns silenced in one stroke.

But a tremor of hesitation shook her resolve. The money was more than enough for both her and Graham. Technically, he could leave his teaching job; they could start a new life in Rome together. Yet the thought lingered uncomfortably in her mind—did she really want that? Would he want that? Graham loved teaching physics with a passion, and aside from words like *spaghetti* and *espresso*, he didn't know a lick of Italian.

She imagined him in Rome, restless without the structure of his classroom and the intellectual challenge that came with it. Graham was a man who thrived on puzzles and equations, the kind of person who needed a purpose to channel his energy. Without the ability to teach, what would he do with himself all day? Sure, he could learn the language, but that would take time—time during which he might feel like an outsider, disconnected from the very things that gave his life meaning.

Pushing those swirling thoughts aside, Aida tried to refocus on Fran's words.

Fran seemed to pick up on her unease. "While we don't expect you to decide right now, if you're interested in the role, we'll need the signed contract submitted by this next Wednesday. The position starts with a three-month trial period to ensure a mutual fit. If all goes well, you'll then sign a five-year extension."

Next Wednesday. That was only a few days away. Aida stared at the bowl with its golden apple just a few feet away. The apple, with its brilliant shine, almost appeared as though it were truly coated with the precious metal.

"Miss Reale, are you all right?" Fran's voice cut through her thoughts.

"I am. I'm just a little stunned. I need time to consider this."

"As expected. You'll find several items from MODA when you next check your email. First, a reminder of the NDA you signed, which emphasizes that this conversation and anything related to Lady Ozie and the organization must remain confidential. We expect that your fiancé will be part of your life in Rome, and as such, he will also be required to sign a separate NDA, allowing you to discuss certain aspects of your work with him within strict limits. For anyone else, you can tell them that you've taken a position involving research on Italian antiquities. It's truthful and should satisfy any curiosity without breaching confidentiality." Fran paused, ensuring Aida was following. "Additionally, you'll find a link to a site with pictures and details of the palazzo in Rome where you'll be living, along with the contract to sign electronically."

"*If* I take this position," Aida said firmly.

"Of course. But I'm confident you will," Fran replied with a small knowing smile.

The offer was undeniably alluring, but Aida felt a pang of conflict.

"I need to consider how this would fit into my life, especially since my fiancé is a high school teacher and can't easily relocate."

Fran looked at her thoughtfully, as if weighing her words. "We're aware of your situation with Mr. Pechman. Don't worry, Miss Reale, we've had employees in similar circumstances before. There are plenty of opportunities for someone of your fiancé's abilities, and I am sure we'll have no problem helping him find placement."

Aida's stomach twisted. She wanted to demand answers about how they knew so much about her life, but managed to keep her expression neutral, schooling herself not to react. She needed to stay calm, to not let Fran see her surprise. She simply nodded, forcing herself to remain composed.

Fran extended her hand, and although Aida knew she hadn't made her final decision, the gesture felt weighty, almost as if accepting it would bind her to the path ahead. She hesitated for just a moment before clasping Fran's hand. The warmth of the handshake sent a ripple of unease through her, the job still seeming too good to be true.

"I'll respond by Wednesday."

"Excellent. I look forward to hearing from you," Fran said.

Yumi appeared with Disa, as if on cue. Her friend's eyes were unreadable.

Disa accompanied them on the elevator but did not step out when they reached the bottom. "Remember, ladies, you signed an NDA. You won't speak of anything you discussed today, right?"

"Right," Aida and Yumi responded. No one would even believe them if they told the story, anyway.

"Good."

Then Disa was gone, and a bellhop escorted them back toward the waiting Rolls-Royce.

A nudge and a shake of the head to Yumi as they walked to the Rolls had signaled not to speak of Aida's offer in front of the driver. Instead, they chatted about the Netflix show that Yumi had watched while she was in the theater room. But as soon as the luxurious car had driven off and Aida closed the town-house door behind them, Yumi began to pepper her with questions.

"I need a drink to explain all this," she said as she removed her coat and placed it on the hook near the door. "Come on." After texting Graham that she was safe and would tell him everything when he got home, Aida led Yumi into the kitchen, where she mixed up a gin and tonic for each of them. She trusted Yumi, and since Yumi had signed an NDA too, she reasoned it was safe enough to divulge the details. After all, they were in this together.

"Is the salary worth it?" Yumi asked as Aida dropped a lime slice into each glass and handed one to her friend. When Aida told her the number, Yumi picked up the drink and took a huge swallow. "Damn."

"Let me check my email. I was so stunned I didn't think to look in the car on the way back." Aida went into the next room to grab her laptop. She climbed onto the kitchen barstool next to her friend and logged in.

"She said she would send me pictures of the place where I would live in Rome." Aida opened up the email with the subject *MODA palazzo*.

"Dear god," Yumi said as Aida flipped through the digital carousel of photos. "This is ridiculous."

Aida had always understood *palazzo* to mean a palace in Italian, but she knew it also referred to apartment buildings, many of which were converted palaces. For her stay in Rome, she had pictured a modest apartment, perhaps quaint and charming in its own right. However, the photos she was now looking at painted a completely different picture.

She flipped through the images with growing astonishment: a massive master bedroom, multiple living areas adorned with Renaissance frescoes, ceilings that could have been masterpieces from centuries ago. The terraces opened to views she had only dreamed of, and the central garden was lush and inviting. Further images revealed a library, a gym, a massage room, a sauna, and a well-equipped kitchen. This was not just any palazzo apartment—it was a living space fit for royalty.

"This just can't be real," Yumi said. "It has to be a scam. Hand me your laptop. Let me put my fingers to work." After Aida showed her the documents she had been sent and mentioned Mr. Khumalo's heart attack that had ended his career, Yumi got to work. She quickly copied and pasted everything into a new document and uploaded it into a shared drive that they used to trade photos and GIFs. With a nod, she jumped off the stool and headed toward the door. "I'll text you when I find anything."

Aida didn't need Yumi to hack up the information to tell her that the whole scenario was likely a sham. But what didn't make sense was Felix's endorsement of Lady Ozie and her strange company. He trusted the woman, and if he said he had done work for her, he must have. He would never have referred her to a company that would steer her wrong.

The money was a good lure, that was certain. She could pay for the wedding and a nice chunk of her credit cards.

As she scrolled back through the images of the palazzo again, excitement mixed with a touch of apprehension. This could be a fresh start, an adventure. It was only for three months, but a small part of her couldn't help but wonder—what if the job was as incredible as it seemed? What if she found herself wanting to stay longer?

AIDA HAD JUST finished tidying up the kitchen late in the afternoon when she heard the front door open. Graham stepped in, shaking off the cold and unwrapping his scarf. He looked tired but content, like he always did after a long day of teaching.

"Hey, you," Aida called out, her voice carrying from the kitchen.

Graham smiled as he walked in, leaning down to kiss her on the forehead. "Hey, yourself. How was your day?"

"It was . . . interesting. They offered me the job."

Graham straightened, his eyebrows shooting up in surprise. "Wait, already? That was fast!"

"Yeah, and it's . . . well, it's kind of unbelievable," Aida said, trying to gauge his reaction. "They want me to leave next week."

Graham's eyes widened. "Whoa. Next week? That's not just fast—that's weird. Why the rush?"

"I guess they're really eager to get started."

Graham ran a hand through his hair, processing the news. "Wow, that's . . . a lot sooner than I expected. Do you think it's worth it?"

"They're offering a hundred K for three months, plus a twenty-five-thousand-dollar signing bonus."

Graham froze, the skepticism momentarily overridden. "You're kidding." He blinked, then ran a hand through his hair. "A hundred and twenty-five thousand dollars for three months of work? Aida, that's . . . holy crap . . . that's . . . ."

"I know," Aida agreed, feeling a rush of relief at his enthusiasm. "It's a game changer."

"I mean, it's incredible, but is it legit? I just don't want you getting involved in something sketchy."

"Yumi's already on it," Aida assured him. "She's digging into the company, making sure everything checks out. Felix vouched for them too, and you know how careful he is. He wouldn't have sent me their way if he thought something was off."

Graham visibly relaxed. "That's good. I trust Yumi, and if she gives it the green light, then I'm all in. Oh man, Aida, this could make all the difference for us." He paused, thinking.

"That's a lot of money for them to just let you walk away after three months. What if they pressure you to stay?"

Aida shook her head. "I'm not staying, no matter what. It's a trial period to see if they like me or not, and that has to go both ways. Plus, with Yumi on the case, we'll know before I leave if there's anything weird."

"All right, but, Aida . . . just be careful. That kind of cash isn't handed over for nothing."

Aida wrapped her arms around him. "We need this, Graham. It's only three months. I'll take the money, we'll pay off everything, and then I'm back home."

Graham sighed, still uneasy, but Aida felt a little of the tension leave his shoulders. "Okay, but promise me you'll stick to your plan. Get the money, then walk away."

"I promise," Aida said.

He hugged her tight and kissed her on the nose. "I love you, Aida. I hate the idea of you being so far away."

"I know. But it will make coming back and getting married all the sweeter, right? Absence makes the heart grow fonder?"

Graham lifted his hand, his thumb brushing lightly across her cheek. "I don't think I can get any fonder of you than I already am." He leaned in, his lips meeting hers, slow and deep, the kiss pulling them closer, as if he could imprint the moment into memory. When they broke apart, he smiled, eyes warm. "Wait . . . maybe I can."

With a playful grin, he swept her up into his arms, laughter bubbling between them as he carried her toward the bedroom.

3

January 2019

NEW YEAR'S EVE came and went with no more fanfare than a clink of champagne as they watched Ryan Seacrest at the ball drop in Times Square. The day after, Yumi came by for lunch. Graham was at the grocery store, and Aida was searching the web, trying to find the best place for Graham to rent a tuxedo for the wedding.

"I think the MODA org is legit," Yumi said when Aida opened the door.

Aida's heart sped up, thinking about the ridiculous salary and all-expenses-paid palazzo. "It is?"

"I think so. Although there isn't much information about the company and even less about the mysterious Lady Ozie. The problem is that in the States, MODA isn't a corporation but an LLC. And it seems that everything tied up with this LLC is in a trust, so the owner is anonymous. But I was able to track down a few things."

She set her bag on one of the empty kitchen barstools, pulled out her tablet, and flipped it on. She touched a few points on the screen and then began reading. "The MODA company's headquarters are registered in Switzerland, which shouldn't be surprising given the amount of money they seem to have. From what I could tell, they don't have an office there, but I verified the legitimacy of their London location, where MODA has been a tenant for the last ten years. The name on the lease is Ozie Momus."

"Momus? Like that Scottish art musician you made me watch on YouTube?"

Yumi nodded. "The name is spelled the same, but I'm pretty sure there's no connection."

"Did you find anything out about this Ozie Momus?"

"No. There isn't anyone with a name like that. I looked everywhere. All the search engines, Facebook, LinkedIn, and I dug deep into the dark web, but Ozie Momus doesn't seem to be a person's name—real *or* imaginary."

"How could they have their name on the lease if they aren't real? Wouldn't there need to be credit checks and the like?"

"I'm not sure how British property laws work, but I guess that's true. They don't sell anything from the space, so perhaps it functions like a residence? Also, if this person has the money they seem to have, then perhaps there could be a convenient arrangement of looking the other way. I don't know."

"What about the South African guy who worked for them?"

"Ahh, Johannes Khumalo. Now that's where we start to get somewhere. He was a native of South Africa. He graduated with top honors from Sapienza University of Rome before returning to teach at the University of Pretoria. He wasn't there long, only three years before MODA snapped him up. I asked one of my hacker friends to dig into the South African Revenue Service . . ."

Aida gasped. "Wait, you had someone hack into that?"

Yumi laughed at her discomfort. "Don't worry, I wasn't the one who did it! And he owed me a favor."

"I don't want to know why he owed you a favor, do I?"

"Probably not," Yumi said with a wink. "But, you know, it's not exactly the kind of favor you'd ask your neighbor to do. The hacker community is a close-knit network, and while not everything we do is strictly lawful, it's not all malicious either.

There's a lot of gray area. Some of us work in cybersecurity, help-ing companies protect themselves. Others, well . . . they tread a bit closer to the line. And yes, most of us are anonymous to each other. We use pseudonyms, encrypted channels, all that jazz. It's safer that way."

Aida's eyes widened. "So, you're saying this whole thing is . . . illegal?"

Yumi shrugged, a little more serious now. "Technically, yeah. It's a gray area we operate in. But honestly, I didn't think much about it at first. Most of us are just people trying to do what we're good at. Sometimes that means bending the rules . . . or breaking them."

"And you're okay with that?"

"It's not about being okay with it—it's about knowing the risks. Most of the time, we're just solving problems, but some-times those problems cross legal lines. I've built up trust in this community over the years. That's how I got this favor."

Aida shook her head in disbelief. "So, you've got a whole network of people who do this, and none of you really know each other?"

"Pretty much," Yumi said. "It's a different world, Aida. One where you're judged by your skills, not your identity." She turned back to her laptop. "Anyway, my friend was able to find records of him working for MODA with the same salary they are offering you. Or at least it's close. Six million rand in South Africa is around four hundred thousand in our dollars. He worked for them for four years, just like they told you. It's really sad though . . ."

"What do you mean, sad?"

"I found his obituary. He was almost our age—thirty-three. So young to have a heart attack."

"Ugh. The poor guy."

Yumi turned off her tablet. "But it means the job is legit. They told you how he died, and that checks out. They paid him what they said they would pay you, and of course Felix verified him working there as well."

"Oh, to work with Felix would be so fun."

"I hate the idea of you not being here, and I know Graham will miss the hell out of you, but I think you should take it," Yumi said.

"I was thinking I would," Aida admitted as she poured her friend a glass of wine. "You really think it's a good idea?"

"Hell, when will you ever get a chance like this again? This will set you and Graham up for a new life together."

Aida raised her glass. "To my best friend, my personal therapist, and the person I trust most in the world."

Yumi raised up hers. "To my best friend, my therapy client, and the person I trust most in the world."

They clinked glasses with a grin and drank.

"One more," Aida said impulsively, raising the glass again. "To happiness."

Yumi agreed wholeheartedly. "To happiness. We deserve it."

THAT AFTERNOON, AIDA gave Erin the sanctioned spiel from MODA—that she would be researching Italian antiquities, though she didn't know many details yet. She had faith in Erin, but after not truly knowing her for the last ten years, Aida thought it best to stick to the NDA she had signed. Yumi was her most trusted friend—even above Graham in some ways—and had come with her to the hotel, so she got a pass.

"I think I'm going to take the job. What do you think?"

"Oh my god, Aida! Rome? That's incredible! Yes, you have to take it. You're going to have the time of your life. Italian antiquities? That's literally the dream!" The excitement radiated off her. "You're going to be living in a palazzo, drinking wine, and uncovering secrets of the past. This is fan-fucking-tastic!"

Aida smiled, her own excitement swelling in response to Erin's enthusiasm. "I know, right? It's definitely a chance of a lifetime."

Erin leaned forward, grabbing Aida's hands. "I'm so happy for you. This is exactly what you need—a chance to begin again."

"I feel bad that you've just moved back and I'm leaving."

Erin smirked and shook her head. "Don't be ridiculous. This is amazing! Plus, you'll get to explore all those places we used to dream about when we were kids. I mean, the Colosseum! The Pantheon! The food! You're so lucky. You better send me pictures every day. Seriously. I want to live vicariously through you."

That night, Aida sat at her desk, staring out the window at the lightly falling snow. Graham had gone to the wine store for what he called "supplies," and the house was silent save for the occasional salt truck going by to keep the roads clear. Staring at the open pdf on her screen, ready for her electronic signature, her heart twisted with indecision. She had read through the contract at least ten times, careful to make sure she wasn't committing herself to MODA for more than the initial three months.

Her phone dinged, and she picked it up to see a text from Erin with a GIF of someone standing in front of the Colosseum, taking a picture of the ancient arches against the golden light of the setting sun. Erin's message read, This will be you soon!

Aida grinned, then turned back to the contract.

"You're right. That will be me soon," she said aloud as she typed her name into the signature field, then without any more hesitation, she hit Send.

THE WEEK FLEW by in a flurry of packing and preparations. Before Aida knew it, the morning of her departure had arrived. She stepped out of the apartment, the crisp January air nipping at her cheeks. A taxi idled by the curb, its exhaust forming misty clouds in the stillness of the early hour.

Graham emerged behind her with her carry-on. "Are you sure you didn't pack bricks in this thing?" he joked, setting it down next to her other suitcases.

Aida was about to retort when she heard Yumi's cheerful

voice. "There's our jet-setter!" Yumi bounded up the sidewalk, her breath visible in the cold air, Erin at her side.

Aida felt a wave of warmth despite the chill. It had been Erin's idea for them all to see her off, and having her three favorite people here, supporting her, made her heart swell.

"Perfect timing," Graham said, nodding toward the taxi cab.

"Well, this is it," Aida said. Her stomach was doing backflips—the familiar anxiety she sometimes had before she traveled. "I'll be back before you even notice I'm gone."

Graham hugged her tight. "Trust me, I'll notice." He kissed her temple, the warmth of his lips lingering in the cold. "Don't forget to call me when you land."

"I won't," Aida promised. She glanced over at Yumi, who was practically bouncing on her heels.

She grinned and clapped her hands together. "Oh man, you're going to have the best time! Don't forget to send me pictures of that palazzo. I want a full virtual tour, all right?"

Aida laughed. "You know I will. You'll be getting pictures of everything."

"Are you sure you're okay leaving all the wedding planning to Graham?" Erin asked, glancing at him with a playful skepticism.

Graham raised an eyebrow. "Hey, I can handle this," he said with mock offense.

"Seriously, let me help. It would give me something to do," she said.

Aida waved her hand in a sign of approval. "Hey, if you want to give Graham a hand, I'm sure neither of us would say no. But I'll have plenty of input from Italy."

"Well, I'll help streamline things. Having a woman's touch for things like the invitations and the cake will be good."

Graham chuckled. "Erin, don't say that unless you mean it. You have no idea what I'm about to unleash on you."

"I'm ready," Erin shot back with a grin.

The taxi driver honked lightly, signaling they were out of

time for farewells. Yumi pushed off the steps and walked over to hug Aida. "Go kick some ass over there, okay?"

"I will," Aida said, hugging her back tightly.

Graham helped her with the suitcase, lifting it into the back of the taxi before turning to face her one last time. "Stay safe," he said, his voice quieter now, more serious. "I love you."

"I love you too," Aida replied, feeling the moment's weight settle in her chest. They kissed one more time, and then she forced herself to step back, opening the door to the taxi.

She waved one last time to her friends, trying to absorb the sight of them before she climbed in. And then she was off, wondering what sort of wild adventure she was rushing toward.

January 2019

A PRIVATE CAR WHISKED Aida to the city center, letting her out in front of a massive palace on the historic Via Giulia. The five-story building was etched right out of a Renaissance painting.

The butler, a middle-aged man named Dante, who was dressed in a very smart suit, led Aida around her new home.

"I think I'm in a dream," she told Dante in Italian.

"Then we are both having the same dream." Dante beamed. He seemed to take great joy in her utter delight over the historic palazzo. "This gallery has frescoes by Pietro da Cortona." Dante guided her into a vast ballroom with ancient statues in niches around the room. Above them, busts backlit with a golden glow, interspersed with beautiful paintings of the myths, looked out over the space. A long table with a massive candelabra stood in the center of the room, flanked by at least thirty chairs. A credenza at the end of the table displayed a precious china dinner service. "This room is perfect for entertaining. But I imagine you may want to take your meals in one of the smaller salons or terraces, or perhaps the garden."

Aida found the *sala dei mappamondi*, the map room, even more wondrous than the gallery. Frescoes depicting scenes from the stories of biblical hero David adorned every inch of the walls. In the center of the room rested two massive globes, one depicting

the heavens and the other the earth. Aida longed to turn the
globes but wasn't sure if she should touch them.

"If you are careful," Dante said with a smile when she asked.
Aida turned the heavenly globe, and a rush of joy filled her. Her
father loved big globes, and one of her fondest memories was of
a trip she took with him to New York when she was young. He
showed her the metal Verrazzano Globe in the Morgan Library.
She had been eight and it was the first time she had really understood that America was a young country—the map showed
how little Europeans had known of the New World in 1524.
As a young adult, she always sent her father pictures of the big
globes she saw when she traveled through Europe. Never in all
the times she had stood in a map room had she imagined she
might live in a house with one.

Out of habit, she pulled out her phone with the intention
of taking a photo, but Dante placed a warning hand on her
arm. "I won't police you, but I am obliged to remind you of
your NDA. No photos are allowed here. You can take photos
of places you visit externally but not in areas where MODA is
stationed. You'll learn more about these restrictions when you
meet Trista, your aide."

The name was familiar from emails with Fran, who had mentioned she would be assigned an aide to manage her travel, keep
track of her calendar, and guide her on projects. Aida pocketed
her phone, feeling frustrated, but she had agreed to the rules
when she'd signed up for this gig.

"How many bedrooms does the palazzo have?" she asked
Dante after he had led her to the breathtaking space where she
would sleep every night. Aida's bedroom, which Dante called
the *stanza di Ulisse*, was an embrace of classical elegance. The
ceiling boasted a tableau of Ulysses's adventures, his cunning visage captured in frescoes edged with golden cornices that glinted
under the soft chandelier light. Rich yet worn by time, damask
patterns adorned the walls, echoing stories of a grand past. The
polished checkerboard floor, cool to the touch, led to windows

that framed the city's silhouette. Amid this historical canvas, the furnishings spoke of unabashed luxury—a four-poster bed with carved wooden posts and a canopy of sheer fabric, a pair of velvet armchairs facing an ornate fireplace, and a mahogany writing desk by the window, inviting Aida to pen her thoughts while overlooking the lush Renaissance-style courtyard.

"Fifteen. Half are occupied by staff."

Dante led her around the rest of her palatial home, introducing her to the staff—three maids, a groundskeeper, the chauffeur, the chef, and the sous-chef. Aida blurred the names during the tour, except for the chef and his assistant, who immediately made an impression on her.

The palazzo's chef was not much taller than Aida's five foot five, a thin bald man with rounded glasses and a salty goatee. His chef's coat was pure white, and he wore a black-and-white scarf knotted around his neck. "And you must be Signorina Aida Reale," he said in English, approaching her when she entered the kitchen. The aroma of cooking tomatoes and basil wafted toward her.

"Sì, I am," she said as he took her hands.

"I'm Chef Ilario! I'll make you anything your heart desires. Please, signorina, tell me you like to eat."

Aida laughed. "I do! Perhaps too much."

"No! Not too much in this place. Your mouth and your belly will be filled with joy. Is that not right, Pippa?" He turned back toward the interior of the kitchen, where a young woman was chopping onions on a wooden board. She looked up, briefly nodded, and returned to her task.

"You will learn, signorina, that Pippa is very serious, but I promise her seriousness will benefit you with every meal."

Someone behind Aida nervously cleared their throat. Chef Ilario let go of Aida's hands, and she turned to see who had interrupted them. It was a young woman in her mid-twenties with large features—big blue eyes and full lips. Freckles dotted her nose and cheeks, and her mousy brown hair was pulled back into a severe bun at the nape of her neck. Her eyes were sad-looking, as though she might burst into tears any minute. She held a tablet in her hands.

"*Mi dispiace*," the woman apologized. "I need to update Miss Reale on her first assignment." Her accent marked her as British.

"This is Trista Acheron," Dante said.

Trista nodded at Aida, but did not extend a hand in greeting.

"Signorina Reale, please call me if you need anything," Dante said, providing her with a phone number to reach him at for any reason—a modern-day bellpull, as he put it. Then he departed.

"Come with me," Trista said, not looking back to see if Aida was following.

"How long have you worked for MODA?" Aida asked as they walked.

"Long enough. Maybe seven, eight years?" she muttered, barely audible.

Trista wasn't as young as Aida had thought. "Do you enjoy it?" she asked.

The aide glanced at her, as though contemplating how serious Aida might be. "Of course. What sort of question is that?"

Aida drew in a small breath, shocked at the vehemence in the woman's voice. She looked timid, but clearly was not.

"A sincere one," she said to Trista.

Trista remained silent but gestured to an open door, leading into a library. Towering shelves lined with books flanked the room, and plush velvet couches in Baroque design invited leisurely reading. The grandeur of the double doors drew the eye, revealing a balcony that offered views of the manicured garden below. At the room's center stood a desk, its antique facade belying a trove of modern conveniences—a retractable keyboard tray, monitors that rose from secret compartments, and a discreet panel with buttons to summon Dante, the kitchen, or security. To illustrate, Trista pressed a button, placing an order for tea with Chef Ilario.

"My office is adjacent to this room," Trista noted, pointing at an inconspicuous door. "There's no button for me, but I'll hear you if you call and I am there."

Trista handed Aida a sleek new MODA-issued laptop, phone, and a Post-it note bearing a neatly printed password. "You can use MODA devices for personal communication, but remember, all access to Wi-Fi in this building is monitored. As stipulated in your contract, all digital, visual, and audio materials you generate—on any device—while on this property and during MODA business are owned and can be accessed by MODA at any time."

Aida groaned inwardly. She must have glossed over the part about *every* device. "I brought my laptop and phone. Are you saying I can't use them for personal purposes?"

Trista's eyes narrowed, her expression unwavering. "You may, but you won't have Wi-Fi access for your personal devices on MODA properties. We have a vested interest in maintaining the confidentiality of our operations. It's not about curiosity; it's about control and security. But if your personal projects are purely historical research, unrelated to MODA's interests, you shouldn't have anything to worry about."

Aida recalled a brief clause in the contract about data generated on-site, but she'd dismissed it as typical legal jargon—a formality. In her past jobs, personal use of company equipment or time had been quietly tolerated, a perk of the office culture. This somehow felt different, more serious. She would never have imagined her personal devices would be subject to this sort of monitoring.

"As for your work here," Trista continued, "most of it will be digitally rendered. However, if you prefer paper, you are welcome to use the MODA-provided portfolio for your notes." She patted a portfolio on the table before them. "All notes must be stored within this portfolio and submitted with your quarterly report in London. There's no exception to this."

Aida nodded, trying to mask her unease. "Understood," she said, her tone neutral.

Trista's expression softened slightly. "And regarding your fiancé, Graham," she added, almost as an afterthought, "he has already signed the necessary NDA. This means you can discuss certain aspects of your life here with him, but remember, the confidentiality rules apply—no specific details about your work or anything related to MODA's proprietary information. This is the same for your friend Yumi."

Aida managed a faint smile, relieved at least by the thought that she wouldn't have to keep everything entirely to herself.

Trista gestured for Aida to follow her to the velvet couches, where she sat and activated her tablet. "Now then," she said, "your first assignment is at the Casa di Goethe."

Aida was pleased with this revelation. She had always intended to visit the museum dedicated to the celebrated German author.

"I'll be guiding you through the process. Before you spend time in the museum, you should research and read up on Goethe, particularly his time in Italy." She paused and looked at Aida, her big blue eyes wide. "Have you read his *Italian Journey*?"

"Yes, but it was a long while ago."

"You'll have a week to research what you can about Goethe and his life. Read *Italian Journey* again. Brush up a little on the rest of his works but don't dive deep. You're mostly looking to understand everything you can about his time in Italy. Every last detail, anything you can uncover. You will work fast, but you will be thorough."

"What am I searching for?"

Trista gave Aida a look that suggested she might be daft. "I literally just told you," she said with all seriousness.

Aida raised an eyebrow. "You told me what I would be doing but not what I would be looking for. Am I trying to understand a particular correlation between different sets of information? Am I trying to uncover some sort of new fact about his time here? Or perhaps an untruth in what we think we know about him? What you described is fairly unnecessary—his life has been well cataloged. That's why a museum is dedicated to him, after all."

Trista stared at her, expression empty, and finally, Aida broke eye contact, uncomfortable with the gaze.

"I see," Trista said after a long pause. "Lady Ozie is interested in Goethe's emotional impact upon the world and the qualities that made him compelling. In particular, how he sparked joy in others as a result of the time he spent here and the way in which he wrote about it."

If Trista had shown an iota of emotion, Aida might have made a Marie Kondo joke about sparking joy, but she sensed that the woman wouldn't understand the humor. She still wasn't sure what Lady Ozie really wanted. To understand joy? It sounded so strange coming from Trista, who looked like she had never experienced joy in her life.

Chef Ilario interrupted them with a cheerful "Tea is served." He crossed the room with a massive tray.

"Excellent, thank you, Chef."

"These look delightful," Aida told him.

"You both look as though a little delight is needed. *Siete troppo serie.*"

Too serious indeed, Aida thought. She was tempted to ask him to stay and have tea with them, but Trista dismissed him with a wave of the hand. Chef Ilario winked at Aida and departed.

Aida could hardly believe the elegant afternoon tea setup before her. A sterling silver teapot gleamed among fine bone china cups. An array of scones, their surfaces dusted with a golden crumb, were nestled beside pots of clotted cream and strawberry preserves. Neatly cut cucumber and salmon sandwiches lay in precise rows with fillings peeking out from their crustless borders. Petits fours, iced and tempting, added a splash of color. It was a tableau of comfort and civility that Aida found herself warming to, the kind of ritual that could easily become a cherished part of her afternoons.

Trista, however, was not one to linger over teatime delights. She was all business, briskly outlining the plan. "You will have a week to settle in here and get accustomed to living in Rome. Take the time to do your research on Goethe and reread *Italian Journey*. Next week you'll be given full access to the museum and its staff."

"And why not employ the museum's Goethe experts for this task?" Aida questioned.

A smirk flashed across Trista's face. "Because then you'd be out of a job."

"Fair enough. But it's an honest question. What could I uncover that these individuals wouldn't already know?"

Trista powered down her tablet. "Let me be clearer. In all your projects for MODA, you'll focus on cataloging happiness, a perspective other historians have overlooked. You'll understand as you immerse yourself in the work."

"Cataloging happiness?" Aida was bewildered yet intrigued.

"Yes. Lady Ozie is keenly interested in how certain people, objects, and places have brought the world happiness, levity, glee, euphoria, joy."

"Will I ever meet her?"

"She's never visited. Don't expect that to change."

"But you've worked here nearly eight years and she's never come? Isn't that odd?"

Trista shrugged. "I don't ask questions. I'm well compensated; that's what counts."

Aida found this unsettling. "Aren't you the least bit curious?"

"Curiosity killed the cat, did it not?"

That sounded like a warning.

Trista took a sip of her tea and then stood. "Feel free to explore and familiarize yourself with the palazzo. I'll set up meetings with you if needed, but of course, I'm always at your disposal. Once you log on to your laptop, you'll find information from me in your email, and you'll see that your calendar is already populated with various meetings in the next few weeks. I'm here to help you manage all that. If you need anything done, simply ask, and I'll take care of it. Your job is to focus on the research."

Trista departed through the door to her office and Aida was left alone in the vast library. She polished off a couple more of Chef Ilario's delicious treats, then took a cup of tea to the window to stare at the garden while pondering her new assistant's strangeness. Finally, she turned to her desk, sitting in the elegant and ergonomic chair. She wondered how much it cost, then realized that if she questioned that about everything she encountered in this house, she wouldn't have room for any other thoughts.

It occurred to Aida she hadn't let Yumi know she had arrived. She'd called Graham as soon as she landed, but she should let her best friend know she was in one piece. Plus, Yumi would undoubtedly have something witty to say about the place's weirdness. Aida pulled her phone out of her pocket to dash off a quick message, but cursed when she saw there was no signal.

She set her phone aside, turned to the MODA laptop and phone, and followed the steps to connect to the Wi-Fi and set up fingerprint and facial recognition. Aida looked at her own phone again. She could understand not connecting to the Wi-Fi, but it was strange not to even have a cell signal. She attempted to reset it by turning it off and on, but that proved to be useless. Trista hadn't been kidding about being unable to use her own devices. There must be some sort of jammer in the palazzo that prevented her from connecting. Clearly, MODA had no intention of letting her communicate with her own technology.

Irritated, she used the MODA phone to text Yumi.

Hey Bestie. Sending from my new work phone. Made it to Rome in one piece. The palazzo is breathtaking and the job sounds amazing, if strange. I hope you aren't having any more 404 issues. I'll check in with you later to find out.

Aida hit Send. When she and Yumi were in college, they established 404 as a code to signal that their conversations weren't private. It began as a joke to cover up talking about people that she and Yumi didn't like, relating the http error code to the idea that the conversation had crashed because someone might overhear. She trusted Yumi would understand that her communications were being monitored, given all the emphasis that had been placed on secrecy and NDAs. Aida would find a way to call her from her personal phone tomorrow if she could.

Yumi must have been looking at her phone because the response was nearly instant.

Gotcha. I can manage the 404, just glad you are there and ok.

Aida spent a little time familiarizing herself with the MODA setup on her new laptop and phone, but it wasn't long before fatigue overtook her, despite the infusion of caffeine from the tea. Somehow, she managed to find her way back to her room. Dante had set out her luggage on racks next to the walk-in closet, but she passed them by and collapsed on the plush velvet couch that looked out toward the courtyard.

She fell asleep, caught between disbelief that this palace was her new home and the unsettled feeling that all her communication would be monitored. She didn't have anything to hide.

But MODA clearly did.

5

January–February 2019

THE WORK BEGAN right away, starting with Aida taking stock of Goethe's *Italian Journey.* "As you go through the book, please record a reading of the passages that refer to joy, happiness, and pleasure," Trista explained. "Note if anything makes you particularly joyful. If you delight in his phrasing or his description. This will be an important part of your work in general."

It was a strange instruction, but it matched the idea of cataloging what makes people happy about an object or place. But now, as Aida thumbed through the volume, she realized she would be reading about a third of the book aloud. She loved a good book, and Goethe's memoir was full of gorgeous scenes. It was no wonder—Italy wasn't called *il bel paese*, the beautiful country, for nothing. Aida pressed the record button and began reading aloud:

"'As evening draws near, and in the still air a few clouds rest on the mountains . . . I feel at home in the world, neither a stranger nor an exile. I enjoy everything as if I had been born and bred here and had just returned from a whaling expedition to Greenland . . . The bell-like tinkling noise the crickets make is delightful—penetrating but not harsh . . . Every evening is as calm as the day has been . . . I have the pleasure of feeling this happiness which by rights we ought to be able to enjoy as a rule of our nature . . .'"

Aida hit Stop and set the microphone aside. It was strange to record her notes verbally, her voice echoing through the library she now called her office. Yet, having spent so much time in Italy during her three-plus decades, she felt a kinship with Goethe. His joy at the simple beauty of an Italian evening was something she knew well. It was the kind of happiness that crept up on you—the quiet joy of being perfectly at home in the world. It was a happiness that readers could relate to, those fleeting moments when the world seemed just right, even if only for a moment.

Dante appeared in the doorway. "Your friend Felix Goodman is here to see you."

"Wonderful! Please send him in." Aida was grateful for the interruption. As much as she enjoyed getting to know Goethe, it wasn't how she preferred to do her research.

Felix took a moment to pause at the doorway to the library, his breath sucking in with the wonder of the scene. "Oh, my giddy aunt," he exclaimed in a faux British voice, sending Aida into a fit of giggles.

"I feel the same way every time I enter this room."

"And I really can't take a photo?" he said, his face hopeful.

"I can't even do that."

His eyes widened. But instead of saying something else, he kissed her on both cheeks and hugged her.

"It's *so* good to see you again," she told him.

"You too. Let me whisk you off to a little wine bar I know nearby that has the most *eccellente* charcuterie."

Aida led her friend out of the palazzo, her mind buzzing with everything she wanted to tell him, but after Trista's stern warning, she wasn't sure she should.

ROME WAS WARMER than Boston, so winter wasn't nearly as frigid. Aida was delighted that she only needed a jacket, not the heavy winter coat she'd been sporting for the last two months.

The sun made the buildings glow with the golden, almost otherworldly light for which the city was well-known. Walking through the streets of the Eternal City, the breeze barely kissing her cheeks, filled Aida with unbridled joy and contentment.

"What a perfect day." Aida slid into a seat at a slightly weather-worn table under the awning of the wine bar's patio. They ordered a bottle of Cesanese wine and a selection of local cheeses and salumi, including a wild boar pâté with a smear of chocolate.

"So, tell me," Felix said, "how are you liking the new job?"

Aida reflected on Dante and Trista's insistence on confidentiality and decided to power down her MODA-issued phone. She had long thought her own iPhone was listening to all her conversations to serve up ads. What could the MODA phone do?

"It feels like a dream. But there's this undercurrent of surveillance that's . . . unsettling."

"Yeah, a Big Brother element to it all." He gave a nod toward her purse on the chair next to her where she had put her phone.

"You had to sign an NDA too, so you know how weird they are." Aida didn't feel like she should say the name MODA aloud in public, although logic told her the locals would think she was talking about some new fashion.

"Very weird. When I worked with Johannes, he would record most of my tour and have it transcribed afterward. I definitely cut down on my lively banter knowing every word I said might be read again at a later date."

"It was probably to help him manage the research. I've been told to do the same. He would have picked through the text afterward to get at the essence of what he was looking for. You probably don't have anything to worry about."

"Still. I never really understood the reason for all the secrecy. The NDAs, the restriction on photos, you know. It's just history. I'm glad I'm just a guide they use occasionally, and not fully employed like you are. I would never submit to all their rules and regulations in my personal life. They certainly don't need to hear all my racy phone calls!" He laughed. "So, what *are* you researching?"

"Goethe and his time in Italy."

"Ahh, you'll be going to the museum then."

Aida took a sip of her wine. "*Sì.* Next week."

"But he's already been well studied. That *is* why there's a museum dedicated to him here."

"It's the angle I'm taking that's unique."

"Oh, do spill the tea." Felix leaned in, ready for details.

"I'm not supposed to talk about it," Aida said, torn between adhering to the rules of her contract and confiding in her dear friend.

"I signed the same NDA, remember? Plus, you turned off your phone."

Aida looked at the other diners around her. No one was paying them any attention. "I'm studying happiness . . . what made Goethe happy, how he made others happy, and everything related to that in his life and works."

Felix wrinkled his brow. "Happiness?" he said, a little too loudly. Aida gave him a stern look and he lowered his voice. "That's it?"

Aida nodded. "Strange, huh? I don't know why I can't talk about it."

Her friend chuckled. "Well, does it make *you* happy?"

Aida raised her glass. "So far, it's like a fairy tale. I'm learning endlessly, living in splendor, dining like royalty, and I have Rome's treasures at my doorstep. The work, the place, the luxury—it's more than I could have ever imagined. So yes, you could say I'm quite happy. Immeasurably so. But I really miss Graham. It's hard to be away from him."

As she sipped the wine, her gaze drifted past the table, lost in thought. She was in Rome on a day that seemed to have sprung from a painting, accompanied by a dear friend. Soon, she would be married to the love of her life. But for the next three months, she was living in a palazzo, her whims catered to at the press of a button, and her job was so financially rewarding that it seemed ludicrous to think she would soon resign.

"I have you to thank for it. And I already have a new idea for a research project," Aida said, her eyes alight with excitement.

Felix grinned. "Now that is music to my ears. Okay, tell me about it."

Aida took a sip of wine and a deep breath. "I've been so inspired by Goethe's *Italian Journey*. I want to explore the overlooked connections between early botanical studies and cultural life in Italy during the eighteenth century. Goethe was fascinated by the natural world and often wrote about the flora he encountered and even wrote a book about botany. I'm thinking of investigating how the study of native plants influenced the art and literature of the period. There's an intriguing intersection between science and the arts that hasn't been fully explored."

Felix leaned in. "That does sound like a fresh angle. How scientific discovery and cultural expression influenced each other . . ."

"Exactly," Aida replied. "For instance, I could examine how certain Italian artists incorporated botanical elements into their works, possibly inspired by the botanical explorations of their time, or how literary depictions of nature reflected contemporary scientific understanding. There's a wealth of untapped primary sources, like letters and personal diaries, that could offer new insights. Goethe is a great start because he corresponded with so many people."

"Damn! You've already thought it through that much? In barely a week?"

"Your fault for getting me to come here. I needed something new to pursue. Thanks for inspiring me."

He put a hand to his heart, beaming. "That makes me immeasurably happy."

She lifted her glass to toast. "To happiness."

Felix grinned. "To happiness!"

AIDA SPENT THAT afternoon in the depths of Goethe's writings, her voice giving life to his reflections as she recorded passages for her research. The room was quiet, save for the soft rustle of pages and her measured tones.

Just as the light started to fade and Aida's throat became a bit hoarse, Trista appeared in the doorway to the library. Aida shut the recording off.

"How is the research going?" Trista asked as she sat down and smoothed out her skirt.

"Good. Although there is a lot to record. Italy made Goethe quite ecstatic."

She gave the slightest nod. "Yes, I suppose that is so."

Aida waited for Trista to tell her why she was there.

The woman pulled herself upward out of her slouch. "Well, Miss Reale . . ."

"Please, call me Aida."

Trista's expression was a blank mask. "I've arranged for your first visit to the Casa di Goethe. They will receive you next Monday for the entire week. The whole staff will be at your disposal, and the museum will be closed, so you have no interruptions."

Aida's jaw dropped. "They're closing the museum for me?"

"Yes, this is standard for many projects you will have in smaller locations."

"Don't they need that revenue?" The words were out of her mouth before she realized that Lady Ozie was paying the museum for any lost revenue.

"Miss Reale, you will become accustomed to all doors being opened without any worry about money."

Aida wasn't sure she would ever be accustomed to that, just like she didn't think she'd ever feel comfortable with Trista refusing to use her first name.

"I have a lot of paperwork to sort through, so I'll leave you to finish up your work." She stood and drew in a deep breath. After a long pause, she said, "I trust your time with Mr. Goodman went well today. I must remind you that although he has signed an NDA for his work with us, that does not mean he is privy to the true nature of the projects you are working on. Please be thoughtful of that when you are visiting with friends. And make sure to leave your phone on."

She turned on a heel and hurried out of the room and into her office, leaving Aida stunned at what was clearly a stark warning.

WHEN AIDA WASN'T recording Goethe or correlating information between his various works, she explored the palazzo, the entirety of which was open save the quarters where the staff lived. Walking through the rooms filled Aida with wonder, and every pass through one, she delighted in finding something new, whether it was a detail on one of the palazzo's many frescoes, a previously unnoticed tile pattern, or an antique of exquisite quality. She was exploring the grand ballroom when her phone buzzed. It was Graham. Settling onto a velvet-covered bench, the plush fabric brushing against her palms, Aida answered.

She smiled when she saw his bed-head hair. "I see you just got up. Oh, I miss waking up with you."

He gave her a sleepy grin. "But it won't be long until I'm there."

The day after she'd arrived, she'd called him on her personal phone during a walk outside the palazzo. She'd explained that they shouldn't discuss her plans to leave after the trial period over the MODA phone, suggesting instead that they pretend he might move to Rome after the trial and the wedding just to keep everything smooth with MODA's expectations.

"You are really going to love it here. I've been walking every morning, wandering the streets and getting lost. There's something amazing around every corner! Right now, I'm at the palazzo, in a majestic ballroom. Imagine ornate frescoes and crystal chandeliers. I can almost hear the echoes of centuries-old waltzes."

Graham chuckled. "Only you could be so poetic about a room. But honestly, how's the job? And the people?"

"The job is . . . unique, more than I expected. And the people . . . they're different, but that's just part of adjusting to a new place. But, oh, Graham, you will love Rome. There's so much history, and I keep imagining what it would be like exploring it together," she said, maintaining their agreed-upon pretense.

"I'll be happy anywhere you are," he said.

Aida brightened. "How is the wedding planning going? Have you figured out the limo yet?"

"Yep, we'll travel in style in a 1959 Silver Cloud Rolls-Royce. Oh, speaking of the wedding," Graham said enthusiastically. "I ran into Erin yesterday at the grocery store. She's offered to help us figure out the favors and gift bags. We're going to meet up this weekend and put something together to show you."

A mix of gratitude and relief filled Aida. "Oh, that's so sweet of her! I'm so glad she's back in town. I know wedding planning isn't exactly your favorite thing."

"It's not too terrible. The outcome is what matters . . . that walk down the aisle."

Just as Aida was about to respond, she heard the faint clearing of a throat and turned to see Trista at the door. The woman's expression was unreadable.

"Oh, I have to go," Aida said quickly, a surge of discomfort tightening her voice. "We'll talk soon."

"What? Wait—" Graham's voice crackled with confusion and a hint of disappointment.

"I'm sorry, really, I need to take care of something for work. I love you." Aida hurriedly ended the call, pressing the disconnect button. She set the phone down, her thoughts swirling uneasily. She didn't like cutting Graham off, but something about the way Trista had been standing there, overhearing their conversation, left her with a gnawing feeling of unease and foreboding.

Turning her attention to her assistant, she tried to steady her voice. "Is there something you needed?"

"I've left some new information on your desk to prepare you for tomorrow's visit to the museum." She gave Aida a curt nod and then departed.

Aida stared at the empty doorway, confused and irritated that her aide thought something so trivial was worth interrupting her call with Graham. She considered calling him back, but the thought of MODA listening in was so unsettling that she decided against it.

THAT NIGHT, AIDA lay awake, unable to sleep. Finally, a little before midnight, she threw on a robe. Hearing voices, she wandered to the kitchen, where she found Ilario and Pippa sitting at the little table in the corner, sharing a glass of wine. They both stood quickly when they saw her.

"Signorina, tell us how we may help you."

"Please, please, sit. I don't need anything. I just couldn't sleep and thought I'd take a little walk. I heard someone else was still up."

"Ahh, then you must sit and let me . . . what do those Brits say . . . make you a nightcap." Ilario left her with Pippa and headed toward the interior of the kitchen.

"I hope I didn't interrupt your conversation."

Pippa shook her head. "Nahh. It's al' right." Her cockney accent was thick.

"Where are you from?" Aida asked, curious.

"Essex originally, but me fam moved 'ere when I left school, and I thought I'd come too. This—" she waved her arm expansively "—place is way better than any borin' university back in England."

Aida had to chuckle. "I suppose it is."

Chef Ilario returned with a dark bottle of something and three glasses.

"My nonna's *nocino*," he said proudly. "My grandparents were from Modena and owned a walnut orchard. It's tradition that every year on the night of San Giovanni, you harvest the walnuts all night by hand, by the light of the moon, or by the light of torches if there is no moon. I loved being able to stay up to help pick the walnuts." He poured the thick brown liquor into the glasses and passed them around. "One of my last few bottles."

"I'm honored," Aida said, taking a whiff of the aromatic mixture. "But I thought only virgins could harvest the walnuts," she teased, remembering her history of the drink.

Ilario waved a hand in dismissal. "Virgins are hard to come by."

"You know this ain't Italian," Pippa said before she took a sip. She closed her eyes to savor it. "This comes from me people. The druids were gettin' blotto on this stuff long afore you Romans come in and pinched it."

"But, we Italians, we perfected it."

Aida drank in the mahogany-colored liquid. "Mmm. Cloves, cinnamon, vanilla, and . . ."

"Juniper and coffee too," Ilario said. "I know what goes into this bottle but have never figured the recipe out. I think there is something else, something special that she never told anyone about. We will never know, since she is long gone."

The drink warmed Aida's insides. "It means our enjoyment is that much stronger, because it is special."

"*Esattamente*," Ilario said. "You understand."

"How long have you worked for Lady Ozie?" Aida asked.

"Not even six months yet for me," Pippa said. "I was workin' as a chef in a li'l restaurant in the Campo de' Fiori. Mo found me and made me an offer I couldn't say no to. Even if I gotta work under this *rompicoglioni*." She raised an eyebrow at Ilario.

"I am not a pain in your ass," Ilario said in Italian, lightly smacking his sous-chef on the arm. "You are the pain in mine."

Aida loved their banter and comfort in teasing each other so roundly in front of her.

"Mo found me in much the same way. I was working in Bologna as a sous-chef at a Michelin restaurant." Ilario smirked at Pippa, who stuck her tongue out at him. "That was two years ago. It is nice to be paid so well to not work so hard and still do what I love."

"Who is Mo?" Aida asked.

"You'll meet him soon enough . . ." Ilario began before Pippa interrupted him.

"He's a bit smarmy, that Mo. Too bleedin' cheeky for me. Somethin' ain't right about 'im."

"But he found you the job," Aida pointed out, puzzled.

"Don't mean I trust 'im."

"Mo works for Lady Ozie," Ilario explained. "You'll understand what Pippa means when you meet him. He can be . . . a little . . . how do you say, sarcastic. You'll get used to him."

Pippa shook her head and gave Aida a contrary look.

"Trista never mentioned this person," Aida said.

Pippa snorted. "That girl keeps to 'erself. Don't know what rock they dug 'er up from under. She never shows emotion. Even when that poor sod Johannes died. Thought I might see 'er face crack, but nah."

Johannes—the man who had held her position before Aida arrived. "I heard he died of a heart attack?" The *nocino* was already making her sleepy, but she wasn't about to lose out on the gossip.

"That's what they told us," Ilario said. "It was quite a shock. That man was . . . how do you say, *era sano come un pesce?*"

It took Aida a moment to translate the idiom, healthy as a fish. "We say healthy as a horse."

Ilario rolled his eyes, causing Pippa and Aida to giggle. "He was like this healthy horse of yours. Always going jogging. Ate mostly vegetarian and only rarely let me make him something with meat."

"And just a month before 'e died, he was rabbitin' on to us about the clean bill of 'ealth his doctor give 'im," Pippa added. "All 'is blood work was good, 'is blood pressure was bleedin' perfect, barely a bit of body fat on 'im."

"I thought he smoked," Aida said, recalling Disa's words at that first meeting in Boston when she had asked about her predecessor.

Pippa snorted. "Absolutely not. Johannes could 'ardly manage to sit on a rest'rant *terrazzo* with someone smokin' near 'im."

"If someone like him can die from an attack on the heart, what hope do we have?" Ilario said. He lifted his glass. "We have this."

"Liquid 'ope," Pippa agreed, raising her glass to his.

Aida clinked her glass against theirs and downed the rest of her *nocino*, unsettled by the conversation about Johannes. Why had Disa lied to her? She excused herself afterward, thanking them for the drink and the company.

On the way back to her room, Aida passed by her library office, and next to it she saw that the light was on under Trista's door. She paused outside to see if she could hear her assistant and was met with only silence. But as she continued on, Aida heard Trista's voice, hushed, low, talking as though there were another in the room with her. She could only catch snatches of the conversation and couldn't make out who the other speakers might be.

"Easier than him . . . don't worry . . ."

A man's voice. "So slow . . . tired of . . ."

Another voice, a woman's but not Trista's. "Patience . . . centuries. Patience."

There was a whoosh of air, like the release of someone standing up from a vinyl cushion, then silence. The light went out.

Aida rushed away before Trista could open the door and find her standing there. But who on earth would she have been talking to at 1:00 a.m.?

6

January–February 2019

A IDA ALMOST WALKED by the museum, its facade blending unassumingly with the commercial hustle of the busy Via del Corso.

"Here," Trista said.

Amid the vibrant displays of the ground-floor shops shouting LUXURY OUTLET! -70%! Extra discount! *Saldi!* was a more subdued doorway. A small red flag marked Casa di Goethe fluttered above it.

Trista sniffed dismissively at the cheap store and pulled open the door indicated by the flag. They found themselves in a nondescript office-like hallway that led to an old-fashioned elevator cage. The contrast between the commercial vibrancy outside and the silence inside struck Aida as she stepped into the building.

The museum occupied the very apartment where Goethe had lived from 1786 through 1788, sharing it for three months with the painter Johann Heinrich Wilhelm Tischbein, who was rumored to have been more than just his host. Prominently displayed in one of the main galleries was a replica of Tischbein's iconic painting of Goethe, poised contemplatively amid the Italian landscape. Although small, the museum was densely packed with artworks, including pieces by Warhol and drawings by Toulouse-Lautrec and Dalí, which they passed on their way to what would be their office for the week—a modern library bathed in light, its walls lined with ancient books encased in glass.

After settling in, Trista outlined their plan for the week. "They've assigned a curator to walk you through the museum this afternoon and tomorrow, providing a highly personalized tour of each item. Before then, you should wander through the rooms on your own and record your impressions. MODA is not as interested in what is in the room, but rather how you think and feel moving through the museum and as you view each item. If you are drawn to a certain piece, indicate why. Above all, describe how you feel looking at the various items. If any artwork brings you joy, that's especially important and you should take more time in your description."

Aida had known that recording her own happiness was part of the process, but now the whole idea of sharing her emotions about the history and the art seemed strange. Would the very action suck the joy out of the experience?

"How should I capture this information?"

"Ideally you should voice record your impressions." Trista reached into her bag and handed Aida a small handheld digital recorder. "If you find that too awkward, you can write your thoughts down, but that could prove to be very time-consuming. I recommend you try recording this time and if it doesn't work, you can switch methods on the next project."

"Will anyone be with me when I do these recordings?"

Trista shook her head and a limp brown lock of hair fell into her eye. She batted it away. "No. I'll remain here and the museum staff have been instructed to leave you be. You shouldn't feel self-conscious."

Aida looked through the glass door out into the museum. It wasn't a big space and she knew sound would travel. She drew herself up and smiled, determined not to let Trista know she was worried.

"Well then, I should get to it."

Aida left the library, making sure the door slid shut behind her. She headed straight for the room housing the striking Andy Warhol painting. The image of Goethe's head, derived from the Tischbein painting but transformed—enlarged and colorized in Warhol's iconic style, albeit with somewhat muted colors— dominated one wall.

Aida had always been drawn to Andy Warhol's vibrant use of color and his bold pop art statements. During college, she'd spent countless hours immersed in exhibitions and reading about his innovative techniques and the sharp cultural critiques embedded in his works. This long-standing interest deepened her connection to the painting before her, making this moment feel like a convergence of her past passions with her current surreal experiences. She pressed Record. "Warhol's painting of Goethe fills one wall here, immediately drawing me in as I enter the room. There's something cheeky about Warhol taking on Goethe, so often depicted in solemn grandeur, and giving him a whimsical pop art twist. Why did Warhol paint Goethe? Most likely because Goethe published *Theory of Colours* in 1810 and presented his scientific views on how humans view and react to color. And Warhol was a man madly in love with color."

She paused the recorder, trying to remember everything Trista had told her to catalog. It was strange talking to the little machine about how the art made her feel, but, she reasoned, she was getting paid an exorbitant amount to do something that was effectively rather simple. She pushed Record once more.

"Tischbein's depiction of Goethe is masterful, and, understandably, it's considered one of the most important German paintings. But Warhol's Goethe takes the serious pose of the author and playfully renders his visage, outlining his hair in blue, taking him to the edge of cartoon but not all the way there. I feel a swell of affection looking at this piece—partly because it's Warhol, whom I adore, and partly because it brings a lightness to an image generally viewed with more seriousness."

Aida rattled on for a little while longer, then decided to view the copy of Tischbein's Goethe reclining—the original was in a museum in Frankfurt. In the painting, Goethe wore a large wide-brimmed gray hat and a creamy white traveler's duster. He reclined on a bench of sorts, with the countryside and its ancient Roman ruins in the background. Aida turned on the recorder, intending to talk about the elevated, enlightened feeling that the painting gave her in contrast to the fun of the Warhol. She had barely begun her sentence when she noticed something in the painting that made her burst out laughing.

"My dear girl, what could possibly be so funny about such a snorrendous painting?"

The voice with the strange unplaceable accent made Aida jump. She whirled around to find a man about her age with ruddy cheeks and blue eyes. His hair was curly black and short-cropped. He was dressed in smart Italian fashion, with a maroon jacket, a white shirt, and a reddish-pink bow tie. Aida was confused. The museum was tiny—how had he slipped in without her knowing?

"You startled me," Aida said, taking a breath to calm her racing heart.

"That was my intention. Are you going to stand there and stare or answer the question? What's funny?" He pointed at the painting.

"Um . . ." Aida was puzzling together the word he used—snorrendous—realizing it was an amalgam of snore and horrendous.

The man waggled a finger at her. "No, um is not an answer."

Aida pointed at the painting. "He has two left feet."

The intruder put his hands on his hips and stared at Goethe's two black left shoes, then burst out laughing. "Well, by the gods, I think you might be right about at least this."

"I'm right about a lot of things," Aida said, indignant.

He guffawed. "That's what everyone thinks. You're no different."

Aida could feel the tips of her ears growing hot. "Who are you?"

"Mo."

This time it was Aida who chuckled. "Ah. I was warned about you."

Mo raised an eyebrow. "Well, perhaps that person was right too. I should come with a warning label. And what did they warn you about?"

"Wouldn't you like to know?" The retort flew to Aida's lips.

"Ha! And an edge to you too. They didn't mention that when they warned me about *you*."

Aida refused to let this man rankle her. "What can I help you with, Mo?"

He leaned a hand against the wall next to the Tischbein. "Nothing."

"Why are you here?" she asked.

"Why not?"

Aida stared at him. He stared back.

"You're mocking me," she said.

He clapped his hands together and pointed a finger at her like a gun. "Bingo! Smart girl. Smart girl."

Annoyed as she was with the *girl* descriptor, she instinctively knew if she called him out, this man would never stop using it.

"I'll take you to Trista. You can bother her. I've got work to get done."

"Funless!" he cried. "You are simply funless."

"I beg to differ," she said as she began to walk toward the library. "It seems you are having great fun at my expense."

"Ha ha! That is the best kind of fun to be had."

Aida rolled her eyes at him and kept walking. She could hear his footsteps behind her. Hopefully Trista would take him off her hands. She wondered what he did for MODA, but he was in such a mood that she didn't think she'd get a straight answer if she asked.

"You, you, I like you just the tiniest bit," he rambled on. "Your hair is all wrong and you have a terrible sense of taste in shoes, but that sarcasm . . . Someone taught you well."

"I've met my share of buffoons."

"Touché."

Trista looked up when Aida led Mo into the room.

"It's you," she said, her voice full of defeat. Aida was surprised to hear the emotion.

"Trista darling, you've missed me."

Trista didn't say anything.

Suddenly Aida wasn't sure if she should leave her assistant alone with Mo. She seemed oddly vulnerable.

"You have, you know it. You are always missing me," he said, giving the woman a light sock on the arm. "I came to see how our newest employee is faring."

"She's settling in very well," Trista said. "But I've told you that already."

Mo shrugged. "I had to see it for myself."

"She's right," Aida spoke up. "I'm doing fine. I'm excited about the work."

Mo held his hands up and wrinkled his nose. "'I'm excited about the work!'" he said, imitating her. "Bullshit! I call bullshit. No one is ever excited about work. Ain't that right, little Trista?"

Aida couldn't believe this exchange was happening. Trista kept her eyes on her computer screen, ignoring him.

Mo slammed his hands down on the table, causing both Trista and Aida to jump. "We know you certainly aren't excited. You're never excited about *anything*."

Aida went to stand by Trista. "You shouldn't treat her like that."

"Perhaps," Mo said. "But if I stopped doing all the things I should stop doing, life would be dull indeed. And, dear girl, I must say, that's no way to talk to your employer."

Aida decided to use Trista's tactic and not respond. Instead, she held his gaze until he finally threw his hands in the air and backed up.

"Fine. Fine. You're lucky I like you. And that you are do-

ing work MODA needs done. I'll let the transgression slide."
He blew a kiss in the air toward them. "Ta-ta, Trista dear. I
look forward to your next report. And you," he said, pointing
at Aida, "don't forget to record your amusement about Goethe's
two left feet."

Mo gave them a little wave, then strolled out of the room.

When she saw him turn the corner toward the elevator, Aida
sat down at the table with Trista. "Are you all right?"

Trista looked at her. The emotionless stare had returned.

"I'm fine, Miss Reale. I appreciate you standing up for me,
but I assure you, it was unnecessary. Mo is mostly harmless." She
seemed to stumble on the word *mostly*.

"Are you sure, Trista? He seemed like he could turn dangerous pretty quickly."

Trista's eyes grew wide. "No, I assure you, he is nothing to
worry about."

Aida was a little skeptical, but hearing the assurance in the
aide's voice calmed her nerves a bit.

"What is Mo's role at MODA? Besides harassing his employees?"

Trista shrugged. "I don't really know. It's not my place to ask.
He checks in on our work from time to time."

Aida thought that odd. Well, she certainly would have no
problem asking the next time she saw him.

"Is he always like that?"

Trista's eyes told her that he was. "He can be very sharp."

"Sharp?" Aida had to laugh. "Bitter and caustic would be
more apt terms."

"That's what I said," Trista responded. "Sharp." She looked
at her watch. "He wasted a fair amount of your time."

Aida caught the hint. But on her way back into the main museum rooms, she paused. "Does Mo have a last name?"

"No. He's just Mo."

"Of course." She let the library door shut behind her. Like

Fran and Disa. It rankled Aida to have such strict formality on so much of what she did and yet she didn't even know the last names of the people she reported to.

MUCH TO HER RELIEF, Mo didn't return during Aida's time at the museum. She spent hours engaging with the curator, delving into every aspect of the artwork, the extensive book collection, and even the curator's personal impressions. They discussed his favorite pieces, the reasons behind his preferences, the art that captivated the museumgoers, and any noteworthy reactions to the exhibits. On her final day, Friday, when the museum opened its doors to the public, Aida planned to observe the guests and interview them about their favorite aspects of the museum.

After the second day, Trista stepped back, leaving Aida to finish the research on her own. That was always the plan, she said, to make sure Aida had everything she needed to be productive. Trista explained that she would occasionally accompany her on location, but there was no real reason for her to spend hours waiting around for Aida to finish her work.

Lost in the sanctuary of the library, Aida was particularly drawn to Goethe's deep appreciation for ancient Greek culture. His journey to Italy was fueled by a desire to grasp Hellenism, and he intriguingly merged his reverence for both ancient Greece and Rome. During his second Roman sojourn in 1788, Goethe set aside many of his Christian beliefs to explore Greek morality and religion. As a historian who had always been captivated by Greek and Roman myths, Aida found this aspect of Goethe's life intensely fascinating. She was especially interested in the myth of Faust that Goethe had made so popular, and why people reveled in the downfall of Mephistopheles.

By Thursday, Aida was confident enough that MODA wasn't monitoring her, so she powered down her MODA equipment on her walk home and tried calling Yumi on her personal device. Aida's conversations with both her fiancé and best friend were constrained to superficial topics due to the restrictions on using the MODA phone at the palazzo. They'd discussed the wedding plans, Yumi's house renovations, regional news, and the general sights Aida had encountered in Italy, avoiding any mention of their jobs. Trista's caution after Aida's meeting with Felix had heightened her wariness, making her doubt whether she was ever truly alone. Yumi's role in software security naturally limited what she could share about her work, mirroring Aida's own reticence. Still, it left a strange void between them, this unsaid part of Aida's life, which she desperately wished she could share with both Yumi and especially Graham.

"I think I'm alone now . . ." Aida said in a singsong voice when Yumi picked up the call.

"For reals?"

Aida laughed. "For reals."

"Okay, I have a solution to our 404 error." Yumi launched into an explanation. "I should have had you do this before you left, but how could we know they would be so authoritarian about your life? You probably can't use it at the palazzo, but you should download Signal on your personal phone. It will encrypt all our conversations—voice, video, or text."

"Really? You sure it's safe?"

"Hell, that whistleblower Snowden uses it. We're good."

"It feels so strange to sneak around just to have a conversation," Aida said.

"But do you love the job?"

Aida had to admit that aside from missing her loved ones, even with the secrecy and the strangeness of MODA, the work was fascinating, and she was enjoying being in Rome.

"Well then, it's worth it. We can play Secret Agent Man on the side. Find me on Signal when you're out and about. You should be able to sneak a text or voice message to me from a bathroom at some point. It will be like a game. Where will Aida text me from next? Ha! Just be careful not to turn your work phone off for too long, and we should still have our regular calls when you're home . . . We don't want them to get suspicious, after all."

They talked for a while and Aida filled her in on Mo's arrival at the museum.

"Wow, sounds like a character out of a novel," Yumi said when Aida had finished. "Just my type." Yumi laughed before shifting the conversation to the wedding. "So, about the bridesmaids . . . Erin's been ghosting me all week. I've tried calling, texting, everything. We need to finalize the dress orders, and she's not responding. It's worrying and, honestly, really frustrating."

Aida frowned. "That's not like Erin. Is she okay?"

"She just won't respond to calls, emails, or texts. I've been trying for days to reach her," Yumi said. "But she's been posting on Instagram like everything is hunky-dory."

"That's strange," Aida agreed. "I'll send her a text. Maybe she'll respond to me."

Yumi sighed, her frustration palpable. "Thanks. It's stressing me out. We're running out of time."

Before Aida could respond, her phone buzzed with an incoming call. She glanced at the screen. It was Graham.

"One second, Yumi. It's Graham."

Yumi chuckled softly. "Go talk to your man. We can finish up later."

"Thanks," Aida said, feeling a little bad for cutting Yumi off but knowing she'd understand. "I'll text you later about Erin."

"Talk soon," Yumi said before Aida switched the call.

She took a breath and answered, seeing Graham's smiling face appear on the screen. "Hey."

"Morning from Boston," Graham replied, his voice warm and familiar. "How's your day going?"

She smiled, already feeling lighter. "Good. Oh, I miss you. How's everything back home?"

"I miss you too. Everything's great, just busy with work. The house feels empty without you though."

"I'm glad you're keeping busy," Aida said. "Hey, Yumi mentioned Erin's been out of touch lately and hasn't responded to messages about the bridesmaid dresses. I know you've been talking with her. Do you know if anything's going on?"

Graham's expression shifted slightly, but he quickly shook his head. "That's odd. Erin's been helping me a lot with the invitation designs. Maybe she's just caught up in something else? I'm sure she'll get back to Yumi soon."

"Could you give her a nudge if you talk to her? Just to let her know Yumi's trying to reach her," Aida asked, reassured by his response.

"Of course. Anything to help keep things on track. Speaking of which, when do we get to do the cake tasting? I'm actually looking forward to that."

Aida laughed. "I'll have Yumi call you to set up a time that works. We found the perfect baker."

"Great. I can't wait. And don't worry about Erin; I'll see what's going on."

"I knew I could count on you," she said, relieved. "I miss you so much."

"I miss you too. Can't wait to have you back," he replied. "Talk soon?"

"Absolutely," Aida said, soaking in the familiar warmth of his words. After blowing him a kiss, she ended the call. Then she downloaded the Signal app and sent Yumi a GIF of Lucille Ball badly pouring champagne. Aida hated GIFs. They drove her mad with their endless looping, but Yumi loved them, and Aida got a good chuckle when her friend texted back a dozen exclamation points of surprise.

Afterward, Aida sent Erin a text, but by the time she reached the MODA palazzo, there was still no response, so she turned off her phone and slipped it into the bottom of her bag. Erin had always been quick to respond, especially when it came to wedding plans.

So why was she ignoring them now?

7

February 2019

Almost two months into Aida's tenure with MODA, she and Trista boarded a train to Florence, occupying a first-class car all to themselves—a MODA standard, as Trista informed her. The revelation that all her journeys would either be in a privately reserved train car or by private jet brought a blend of amazement and guilt, especially considering the environmental ramifications. Yet, for someone like her, who thrived in bustling settings and loved people-watching, this exclusive mode of transport felt oddly isolating. Sure, there was always Trista, but sometimes Aida found solitude preferable to her aide's dreary company. Nevertheless, the allure of champagne, gourmet food, and impeccable service wasn't lost on her. As the Italian landscape blurred past her window, Aida made two silent pledges: never to become numb to such opulence and never to morph into an entitled snob.

Aida had thought they would be going over their itinerary on the way, but Trista settled into a seat at the back of the car and put headphones on, clearly not interested in chitchat. Aida found this strange, but she was also glad for the hour and a half until they arrived and headed to the hotel to dedicate to working on her personal research.

The Presidential Suite at the St. Regis Firenze was far too large, but it looked out upon the Arno and the famous Ponte

Vecchio, where one of Aida's favorite Renaissance artists, Benvenuto Cellini, was memorialized with a bust tucked amid all the gold shops lining the bridge. A suite between her room and Trista's would be used for their headquarters while in the city. Trista busied herself setting up her laptop at the dining room table while Aida took in the view.

A rowing team was practicing on the muddy river, their colorful shirts made brighter by the sun. Aida watched them for a moment, delighting in the way they synchronized each movement of their oars, how their bodies moved in time, and the way the boat cut through the river and left ribbons of water behind. When she turned away, she found Trista watching her.

"What?" Aida asked her assistant.

"You were smiling," Trista observed.

"There's a rowing team out there. It's nice to watch them."

Trista cocked her head. "Why?"

Aida tried to explain, but Trista only looked at her blankly.

"I suppose this is why you are doing the research and I'm not," she said.

Aida wasn't sure what to make of that statement. "Anyone can delight in a small thing. I liked watching the rowers. It made me smile. Surely there are many things that you delight in, Trista."

She frowned. "No, I don't have time for that."

"But you don't need to have time—" Aida began, but Trista cut her off.

"The first place you'll be going today is a car park."

Aida paused a moment to take in what Trista was saying. "Wait, a parking garage?"

"The Garage Nazionale. Founded in 1959. It's on the Via Nazionale, next to the Central Market in San Lorenzo. There are frescoes of cars all over the walls."

Aida watched her pull up Google Maps.

"It's a thirteen-minute walk. Once you're settled, I'll have lunch served and then we can go."

Aida looked out the window. The day was gorgeous. "It's warm today. Why don't we go out for lunch? Have what the locals are having instead of room service?"

Trista straightened in her chair, visibly tensing. "We have work to do. I'd prefer not to waste time over lunch. Of course, you may choose to go out tonight on your own to have what the locals are having."

Aida returned to the window, not wanting Trista to see her frustration. "Very well. Go ahead and send for lunch." She still knew barely anything about her assistant. She was efficient and anticipated problems before Aida ever encountered them, but Trista was all business, all MODA. She refused to share meals unless they were working sessions. She never talked about anything other than work, even if Aida tried to get her to open up her shell.

Aida didn't understand it—they lived and worked under the same roof. Their schedules were largely the same. Not for the first time did Aida find herself missing Yumi and Graham. It reminded Aida of what Mo had called her. *Funless.* While Trista certainly lived up to her name—*triste* meant sad in Italian—the made-up adjective fit her so much better. She was less sad than she was no fun.

THE GARAGE WAS a strange place, and just as Trista had said, there were frescoes of modern and vintage cars lining the walls of the access ramps. To give some oomph to the place, in 1987, the garage commissioned an artist, Carlo Capanni, to paint the two long frescoes. It immediately enlivened the typically sterile, industrial garage environment. Aida spent time recording her observations, and also observing both passersby that peered in and the cars driving past the paintings. Trista left after she had helped the photographer set up, but promptly reappeared at the agreed-upon time to take Aida to the next destination— the Borgo Pinti garden, a little hidden jewel of greenery in the heart of the city, known for having the first jasmine plant in

Italy centuries past, and today for its rare plants, sporting field, and community vegetable garden.

The following days found Aida researching all sorts of other wondrous Florence destinations. There were the centuries-old *buchette del vino*—wine holes—that were essentially places to get takeout for glasses of wine. This aspect of the research was something Aida took great pleasure in, interviewing Florentines and tourists, wineglasses in hand. She visited Casa Guidi, the palazzo where poets Robert Browning and Elizabeth Barrett Browning spent many happy years, and Liberia Antiquaria Gonnelli, an antiquarian bookshop that first opened in 1875. Aida loved the fact that these treasures weren't on every tourist's radar; their obscurity added to their charm.

Trista usually shadowed her during the first hours of an excursion, then left her alone to work. It was during these moments of solitude that she'd reach out to Yumi through texts or video calls, ensuring their bond remained strong despite the miles between them. However, when it came to Graham, their interactions were growing more sporadic and subdued. The excitement of her days in Florence contrasted sharply with the terseness of their conversations. The difference in time zones didn't help, making their calls feel more like obligatory check-ins than heartfelt conversations. Graham was bound by the constraints of his time teaching, whereas Yumi could text or call her anytime.

A week into her Florence adventure, Trista revealed a change in travel plans. While she would be boarding a train back to Rome, Aida's journey would follow the winding roads of Tuscany, making a stop at the fabled Chapel of the Madonna di Vitaleta. A driver would bring her there and back to Rome, and a photographer was set to join her at the chapel, capturing its image for MODA's archives.

Aida spent a few hours the day before researching the chapel before she went, so she was familiar with the history of the little church. Set against the verdant expanse of Val d'Orcia, near the town of San Quirico d'Orcia, the chapel stood resplendent, its silhouette accompanied by six stalwart cypress trees. A UNESCO World Heritage site, the church was one of the most photographed spots in Italy. Aida had glimpsed this scene in countless photos and films, including the dreamy Elysian Fields of *Gladiator*.

The weather that day couldn't have been more perfect. Mid-morning rays bathed the landscape, the air was a cool embrace, and the sky—well, there were precisely what Graham would've cheekily dubbed "*Simpsons* clouds" after the clouds in the cartoon's opening credits. She wondered what he was doing. She snapped a photo of the church and sent it to him.

The photographer and the guide she was to meet had not yet arrived, but Aida wanted a few moments to experience the church alone. She left the driver in the car and walked up the dirt road through the fields to the chapel. It was a Monday and there weren't any other tourists. With no other visitors in sight and the neighboring restaurant's doors firmly shut, solitude enveloped her. It was just her, the soft rustling wheat, and the timeless beauty of the Madonna di Vitaleta.

Gently pushing the chapel door, Aida's gaze wandered into its luminous white expanse. Three tall windows and modern recessed lighting showcased a minimalistic interior: several benches and an altar. At the center was a radiant Madonna statue—a pristine replica of the famed glazed ceramic Madonna crafted by Andrea della Robbia. Legends whispered that the original was, astonishingly, "commissioned" by the Virgin Mary herself during the Renaissance. As the tale went, she materialized before a shepherdess, guiding her to gather the townsfolk and seek a Florentine workshop. There, they would find the destined statue for a church they were to erect right on that very location.

For the next few centuries, the statue remained in the church, and a number of miracles were attributed to it. For some reason that Aida wasn't able to determine, the chapel upkeep was scant, and by the late 1800s, it was falling apart, so the statue was moved to a church in San Quirico d'Orcia.

The chapel was empty, but the lights were on. Aida stepped into the sunlit warmth and looked around. She stood in the center of the aisle, taking in the light and the clean stark lines of the arches.

"It's a bit boring, don't you think?"

Aida whirled, her heart pounding. There had been no one behind her, and no one in the chapel, of that she'd been fairly sure.

It was Mo, in jeans, a black leather jacket, and a white button-down shirt. If his personality weren't so ugly, Aida might have found him handsome.

"Where did you come from?"

He pointed upward. "From the heavens, you stupid cow."

Aida couldn't believe her ears. "Excuse me?"

"The heavens. Don't I look rather heavenly?" He waved a hand up and down his body.

"I was referring to the 'stupid cow.'"

Mo gasped and put his hand over his mouth, mocking her. "Oh, did I offend you? I did, didn't I? Oops!"

Aida turned away and walked down the little aisle of the chapel. She needed a moment to contain her anger. *What an asshole.* Why was it always the jerks that managed to get into the top positions at so many companies?

She stopped before the little altar, at the votive candle rack with a couple of flickering candles. Taking a match, she lit a candle. Though she wasn't religious, she sent a silent prayer to her parents, to look out for her. She didn't like being alone in the chapel with this strange, unpredictable man.

"That doesn't do anything, you know."

Aida steeled herself and turned back to Mo. "Why are you here?"

Mo plopped himself down in one of the chapel's little pews. "Just checking up on you."

"I didn't realize that a basket of insults was the bonus for my work at MODA."

Mo smirked. "Now, now, clearly I've upset you. Not my intention. Well, not today at least."

Aida bit her lip to keep from saying something she might regret later.

He only stared back at her, head cocked as though waiting for her to be the one to speak. His mouth was curved in a little half smile more disarming than Aida cared to admit.

"Why would you come all the way here just to check up on me?"

"I like to see our scholars in their natural environment." He glanced around the chapel.

"I'm not an animal you are viewing on safari."

Mo began to laugh, a rich, melodious laughter that Aida thought she might enjoy if she didn't feel like the butt of his joke.

"Ahh, but, my dear, in some ways you are."

Aida perched on the edge of the pew farthest away from him. "No one has told me what you do for MODA."

He chuckled. "Quality assurance. I poke and nudge and make sure everyone is working."

Why couldn't he give her a straight answer? She tried a different tack. "How long have you been with the company?"

Mo leaned back and put his arms out along the backside of the pew. "From the beginning. I like to think the whole thing was my idea, but my cofounders would likely disagree."

Aida cursed to herself. Of course, he had to be a founder. She likely had no recourse if he continued to harass her. It was no wonder Trista put up with him. "Does the *M-O* in MODA stand for Mo?"

"Yes, and no."

Aida waited for an explanation, but he only looked at her with that same damn smirk on his face. He didn't seem opposed to her questioning, only amused.

"Who is Lady Ozie then? I thought she owned the company."

Mo rolled his eyes. "Oh, Ozie. Is that what they told you? If there is anyone more dramatic than me, it would be her. But yes, in a fashion, she does. But then again, so do I. So do others."

"Others?"

"Yes, others."

Aida had to work to keep the frustration out of her expression. Mo seemed to enjoy making people squirm, but she refused to give him the satisfaction. She decided she would do her job. Her innate sense of curiosity gave her a spectacular ability to keep asking questions, and so she did.

"What is Lady Ozie like?"

Mo gave a shake of his head. "You don't want to meet her. Really, you don't. She's just a bundle of misery, woe, depression, suffering, anxiety, grief, and continual distress. I can barely stand to be around her myself."

Suddenly Aida's strange job made a little more sense to her. "Is that why I'm collecting happiness?"

For a moment, Aida thought she saw him tense up and she realized that somehow she had hit a nerve. But then he relaxed again, and his smirk turned into a brilliant smile.

"Yes, Miss Reale, that's exactly why. So tell me, how is that going for you?"

Aida looked around the beautiful little chapel, the interior aglow from the morning sunlight. A surge of emotion rose within her. "It's going well. I enjoy this work. Being able to see so many beautiful places makes me very happy."

He snorted. "An unfortunate side effect, I assure you."

Aida raised an eyebrow. "I shouldn't be happy in my work?"

"You can be whatever you want. I don't *actually* have control over that."

"And yet, here you are, saying things that, in fact, *do* reduce my happiness." Aida knew her words were bold if this man was actually one of her bosses, but she also had the sense that the only way he would react favorably toward her was if she could take it and dish it back.

"Ahh," Mo said, nodding his head, suddenly contrite. "Yes, I do forget myself. You are right. I should let you do your work. But you are so *fun*. I lose all restraint."

Aida threw up her hands. She really couldn't figure out this man at all. "Last time I saw you, you told me just how *funless* I was."

Mo stood, waggling a finger at her. "See, this is why I like you. I take it back. You aren't entirely funless."

He turned and exited the chapel. "*Arrivederci*, Miss Reale," he called out, not bothering to look back.

What the hell? She went to the door and looked out after him. He was not walking down the road like she expected, but rather he was cutting a path straight through the fields of green spring wheat. Aida wondered where he was going. There were only endless fields in front of him. He was walking north but the road went east. She briefly thought of calling out to him, then decided against it. It was probably what he wanted, and she hardly needed more berating that morning. She ducked back into the chapel and did her best to refocus her mind on her work, but she found herself in a quandary. How could she catalog the happiness of this place now that the encounter with Mo had marred it for her?

Fortunately, the arrival of the photographer set her back on the path of her work. An hour later, having finished their documentation inside the chapel, Aida and the photographer began packing up his equipment. The sheer amount of camera gear and accessories he had lugged in was a testament to his dedication, and Aida felt it only right to help carry some bags out to his car. As she hefted one of the heavy bags up and over her shoulder, the strap caught on her necklace with the little silver star pendant. Before she could react, the necklace was pulled taut, and it snapped off her neck.

"Oh no," Aida cried out, raising a hand to her neck where the pendant had rested just moments before. Only a small part of the original chain remained, still caught on the collar of her blouse, but the force had flung away the rest of the chain and pendant.

The photographer dropped his bag in horror. They both began anxiously scanning the ground near them, but it quickly became apparent the pendant had flown far enough that it was likely hidden within the lush field nearby. Seeing their distress, Aida's driver came over to help search.

After several minutes of combing the area, the driver held up the remaining chain, now disconnected and empty. "Found this," he said, his voice apologetic. But there was still no sign of the pendant itself.

Aida tried to stay calm. The necklace held real sentimental value for her—Graham had given it to her when he asked her to marry him. It had been a spontaneous decision on his part, having picked it up at a sidewalk stall on the way to meet her for dinner. It was a special moment, and the necklace was more important to her than the ring he bought her in the days afterward. The photographer kept profusely apologizing, clearly feeling guilty, though it had been an accidental mishap.

"It wasn't your fault," Aida assured him, though her spirits were crushed by the loss.

She took a deep centering breath. For now, they had to finish packing up and get moving. But as she climbed into the car, Aida couldn't help but cast one last longing glance across the fields, irrationally hoping her pendant might glint in the sunlight and reveal itself.

THE NEXT MORNING when she called Graham, he was in such a terrible mood that she couldn't bring herself to tell him about the mishap with the necklace.

"While you're gallivanting all over Italy, I'm trying to deal with a rat in the basement and a problem with the heat. Again. So, it's freezing over here," Graham said with a strained voice, the underlying resentment palpable. "To top it off, Mrs. Bell from next door has taken to practicing the piano at odd hours of the night. And I feel bad saying anything to her since she got her cancer diagnosis. So, between the cold and the noise, I'm getting barely any sleep."

Aida winced. "I'm sorry, Graham. It sounds really rough."

His sigh was heavy. "Yeah, well, someone's got to deal with the real-world stuff."

"It's not all fun and games here," Aida said, feeling defensive. "So much time has already flown by. I'll be home before you know it."

"Maybe for you it's flown by. Not for me."

Aida wasn't sure what to do with his irritation. Graham was generally good-natured, always managing to look at the brighter side of life.

She attempted to switch the subject. "Hey, I have some good news. Last night I signed the contract for the deejay and started putting the playlist together."

"Great," he said. "Do I even get a say in that?"

Aida drew a deep breath. This side of him was unexpected. "Of course you do! That's why I'm telling you. I just thought I'd get us started."

"All right, okay."

A deep unease rose within Aida. Was being away for so long a bad idea, after all? "Hey, you have spring break coming up. Why don't you come to Italy? We started to talk about that but never figured it out. We can spend a little of the MODA money on a visit."

"I can't. There's a conference on fusion energy and plasma physics that I want to go to."

That he wants to go to more than he wants to come to me, Aida thought, stunned. But aloud she said, "That sounds like a good time."

"Well, it is for me," Graham said. "You're having your adventures, so I will have mine."

"Okay, that's fair," Aida told him, although she thought it was anything but. He sounded like he was trying to spite her. She couldn't quite grasp this emerging side of him. It was a stark departure from the warmth he used to show. Now he just seemed disappointed in her, his words tinged with a cool detachment that was new and unsettling.

"I miss you, Graham. I don't sleep well without you."

"Same here. I need to get back to class. Talk to you soon. I love you." He didn't wait for a response. Her phone signaled the end of the call.

"I love you too," she told the dark phone.

8

April 2019

AFTER HER TIME in Florence, MODA sent Aida to Venice, where she immersed herself in the vibrant energy of the Peggy Guggenheim Collection. She meticulously cataloged the happiness that the museum's modern masterpieces and serene canal-side setting brought to its visitors, noting how the bold colors and avant-garde forms seemed to lift spirits and inspire awe. The Guggenheim, with its eclectic mix of contemporary art housed in an intimate historic palazzo, had long been a sanctuary of creativity and joy, drawing admirers from around the globe to marvel at works by Picasso, Pollock, and Dalí.

From there, Aida shifted her focus to Ca' Zenobio, a palatial residence that offered a different but equally potent form of happiness. Inside its walls, the grand Sala degli Specchi—the Hall of Mirrors—captivated her with its ornate frescoes and mirrored splendor. It was a place where Aida immediately felt transported, her spirits lifted by the sheer beauty and timelessness of her surroundings. She could imagine the many countless dancers who had been spun across the ballroom over the centuries.

With every place Aida visited, her passion for the job only intensified. Venice, with its enchanting canals and rich history, had her dreaming of a life here, wondering how she might persuade Graham to join her in Italy once her contract was up. Yet their conversations had dwindled in recent weeks. Graham pointed to time zone differences and his heavy coursework, but Aida sensed a growing distance.

At last, Erin had called Yumi to apologize for not being involved with the dress selection. She explained that work had been hectic, but she trusted Yumi to make the right decision and would coordinate directly with the dressmaker for her fitting. Aida could sense Yumi's frustration, even though she tried to hide it. But what unsettled Aida more was that, according to Graham, Erin had been really engaged in the wedding planning lately, helping with decisions—especially with the invitations.

It didn't quite add up. Why was Erin so involved with Graham but ignoring Yumi's messages about the dresses? Aida tried to shake off the unease, attributing it to the natural difficulties of a long-distance relationship. Soon, she would be back, and everything would fall into place.

THE WEEK THAT her three-month contract with MODA was up, Aida alighted from a helicopter at the London Heliport, where she had just been whisked from Oxford, bypassing traffic on the M40. A dark blue Bentley limousine was waiting for her. She settled into the creamy leather seat and decided why, yes, she would partake of the Salon Blanc de Blancs champagne the driver offered her.

As the car zipped along the road beside the Thames, Aida sipped her champagne. She wished she could photograph the limo and send a selfie of her drinking the champagne to Yumi. Still, despite the window that separated her and the driver—which, to Aida's amazement, had darkened by the mere touch of a button—she didn't trust that there wasn't some way MODA was watching her. Over the last three months, Trista had given her more than one warning that made it clear Aida's privacy was not what it used to be, and while she wasn't sure that it extended to the limo, she wasn't going to risk another scolding. But, she reasoned, she really had nothing to hide. And to have this level of posh treatment was worth giving up a selfie, wasn't it?

Suddenly, there was a loud crash, and the car slammed on its brakes, sloshing champagne all over Aida's slacks. Despite the dampness, she was glad she always wore a seat belt because the force of the stop might have thrown her face-first into the window between her and the driver.

"My apologies, Miss Reale. But as you can see, we have narrowly missed an accident." He lowered the window, and Aida was shocked to see a car flipped upside down about twenty feet in front of them just before a roundabout, glass sprayed across the asphalt.

"My god, what happened?"

"Probably lost control, collided with another car, and flipped," said the driver, a middle-aged man with graying hair and a calm demeanor that belied the situation's urgency.

The driver offered Aida a pack of tissues to clean her champagne-soaked pants. She dabbed at the stains, feeling a little absurd. It seemed so trivial in the face of a life-threatening accident.

A London police officer, wearing the recognizable black trousers, white shirt, and a black stab vest, with a radio attached to his shoulder, approached the limo, and the driver lowered the window. "Sir, can you stay and provide a witness statement?"

"Certainly, Constable," the driver responded before turning his attention back to Aida. "My apologies again, Miss Reale. This may take a bit. If you don't want to wait, I can call another car for you. But you'll need to walk to the other side of the bridge. I will see your luggage delivered to the hotel as soon as possible."

Aida agreed and exited the car. By then, the ambulance and other emergency vehicles had arrived, blocking most of her view, with the exception of a bloody tennis shoe that had flown far from the wreckage. She gestured to a policeman who quickly came to inspect it.

Halfway across the bridge, Aida paused to look at the Tower

of London a short distance away, its staid presence in sharp contrast to the flowing waters of the Thames. The day was chilly, and the sun was well into its descent toward the horizon. She tightened her scarf around her neck and thought of how lucky she was. The accident had been a startling reminder of how quickly circumstances could change, turning everyday complaints into trivialities. If they had been going just a little bit faster, she could have been smashed up just like that car.

Her phone buzzed in her pocket and when she saw Yumi's name flash on the screen, she happily answered.

"Yumi, you will never believe what just happened," Aida said when her friend's face popped up on the screen.

Yumi was standing outside a restaurant, the sun bright on her face. "Hey, do you have time to talk?"

Aida stopped and leaned against the parapet. "What's wrong? You look like you've seen a ghost."

"Not a ghost. I . . . just . . ." She glanced back toward the glass pane of the restaurant door behind her.

"What's going on? Where are you?"

"I met up with a friend at Barcelona." Aida knew the place. It was a wine bar in the South End known for their Bloody Mary brunches. "And, ugh, I don't know how to tell you this. It's about Graham."

Aida's stomach lurched. Yumi's tone indicated that it wasn't something like a traffic accident. "What do you mean it's about Graham?"

"I hate telling you this over the phone. But given all the wedding stuff, I don't think it should wait." Yumi sighed. "Graham is here at the restaurant too—with someone."

"Who?"

"Erin, but not in a friendship sort of way."

"Oh my fucking god," she breathed. Never in a million years would she have expected either of those two people to cheat on her. She had known Erin since she was two! They had thirty-two years of history together—almost an entire lifetime.

"I'm so sorry, Aida."

"Are you sure it's them?" Aida asked, though she knew Yumi would never make such an accusation without being sure.

"Yeah, I took a video. But . . ."

"Send it, please." Aida knew she would regret it, but she had to see for herself. She ended the call, her fingers trembling as she lowered the phone. Her mind raced back over the last two months, a time spent immersed in cataloging—rather ironically—happiness, all the while a subtle tension brewed between her and Graham. From a distance, she'd felt him grow increasingly resentful of her time in Italy, a sentiment that seemed to shadow their conversations. In response, Aida had redoubled her efforts to show him how much she missed him, sending thoughtful messages and arranging video calls at hours that better suited his schedule. He reciprocated with loving, familiar words, yet carried a tone that didn't quite fall right. It was a dissonance she hadn't wanted to acknowledge.

A minute later, the phone chimed. Aida opened the message to find a video that stole her breath away: Graham and Erin in a booth, unmistakably together, lips locked in an embarrassing public display of affection against the backdrop of the crowded bar. It was like a physical blow, confirming her unspoken fears. Resisting the urge to hurl her phone into the river below, she watched it again, to be sure, she told herself, although she knew the image didn't lie. She wasn't sure whose betrayal was worse—her fiancé's or her childhood friend's. She was so stunned she couldn't even cry.

Her phone buzzed again. Yumi.

"What are you going to do?" she asked as soon as her face appeared on the screen.

"He's still there, right? Well, I'm going to call him." She hadn't known what she planned to do until the words were out of her mouth.

"Are you sure about that?"

"Very," Aida said, anger firming her resolve.

"Oh my. Okay. Then call me back."

Aida nodded and ended the call. Before she lost her nerve, she hit the picture of Graham's face in her recent calls and waited for him to answer.

He didn't.

She hung up and called again. No answer. She tried once more, her patience fraying. This time Graham answered, but not with video, just voice, which was unusual for him. "Hi, Aida, is everything okay? It's a bit loud here. I met Sully for lunch."

"Sully? Really? Don't you mean Erin? No, wait, don't answer that. The wedding is off, Graham."

She hit the button to hang up and heard him call out her name before the screen went dark. Upstream, the Tower of London stood resolute and ancient, its stones a silent witness to her private turmoil. Her fingers tightened around the cold metal of the railing. The unrelenting flow of the Thames below mirrored the chaos in her mind. Each wave seemed to pull at her, threatening to drag her down into its depths. She stepped back, almost knocking into a man walking swiftly across the bridge.

"Easy, luv," he said kindly before continuing on his path.

Aida watched him for a moment before her attention was drawn to a sign a few steps down on the bridge.

SAMARITANS
Talk to us, we'll listen.
Whatever you are going through,
you don't have to face it alone.

There was a number to call, of course, but what Aida found more moving were the things that Londoners had scrawled all over the sign. A heart. *You are loved. One more day. Wait one more day. Your friends would rather hear your problems than go to your funeral. One day at a time, my love.*

Aida was not one to consider suicide, especially over a man, but after seeing the dark swirling river patterns that seemed to map to the despair in her heart, she could understand. She scoffed at the *You are loved*, but there was something in the words *one day at a time, one more day* that not only repeated in the sign, but also inside her, slipping into her mind like a mantra. *One day at a time. One day at a time, my love.*

As she crossed the bridge, a strange empty calm descended upon her, a hollow space within her heart that seemed devoid of emotion. Her gaze returned almost involuntarily to the Tower of London, a monument that had witnessed countless human dramas over its long history. Somehow, the perspective made her feel infinitesimally small yet also oddly comforted.

As she slipped into the waiting Bentley, Aida expected tears, the cathartic sort that would validate her pain. But none came. Instead, there was a yawning emptiness. *I should be falling apart*, she thought. *Why am I not falling apart?*

Ten minutes into the drive, Yumi's face flashed up on her screen. Aida accepted the call.

"He saw me and came over to talk. Erin apparently couldn't bear to face me, and she slinked out like a coward," Yumi said. Her cheeks were flushed, clearly from more than just the weather.

"Oh, Yumi, are you okay?" Aida's concern for her friend momentarily eclipsed her own heartbreak.

"I'm fine. He was just angry. He clearly didn't expect to be caught. He told me that she had seduced him, and it was only a lapse. He wished I had tried to talk to him first."

Aida's hands clenched into fists. The thought of Graham lashing out at Yumi for his own betrayal ignited a fire in her that she didn't know she had left. "And what would that have accomplished?"

"Exactly nothing. I gave him a piece of my mind, which he just stood there and took. He mentioned you had called off the wedding."

"Yeah." A little knot of shame formed in Aida's stomach. "I can't believe this is happening. I really need to get my stuff out of there, and I'm not back for another two weeks. Fuck." She didn't have much furniture—she had moved in with Graham, who had been in the town house for a while. But she would probably need someone with a van to help with what she had. The thought of moving made her sick to her stomach. She had never imagined a life that didn't have Graham in it, or their beautiful house.

Yumi gave her a sympathetic look. "Hey, don't worry. You can stay with me till you are back on your feet. I'll help you figure it out. But I'm not moving boxes, honey. I'm a supervisor."

Aida had to smile a little at that. "The very best supervisor. Oh god, Yumi . . . I just don't understand how he could do this. And with Erin, of all people. She was like a sister to me when we were kids."

Yumi sighed, her expression a mix of sympathy and anger on Aida's behalf. "I know. Everything about this sucks."

Aida stared out the car window, watching the London streets flash by in a blur. "I keep thinking back, trying to see if there were signs I missed about them. Times they were together that seemed off. But I can't think of anything."

"Don't do that to yourself," Yumi said firmly. "This is not your fault. They are the ones who chose to betray you like this. You trusted them, and they abused that trust."

Aida nodded, but the words felt hollow. How could she ever trust anyone again after this?

Needing to feel some semblance of control, she turned the conversation to moving out. Yumi offered to scout out the movers and they decided to split up how they would cancel the wedding plans.

"I'm going to lose all the deposits. My god, what a waste it all was," she said. But it wasn't the wedding she was talking about.

Yumi sighed. "I wish I could reach through this phone and hug you. I know this sucks. But you will get through it. You are strong, Aida. Stronger than you know."

Aida managed a small grateful smile. "Thank you, Yumi. I don't know what I would do without you."

"I've got your back, always," Yumi promised. "Just take it one day at a time."

When Aida hung up a few minutes later, the numbness clung to her like a shroud. The tears still didn't come. Her heart was a dark numb spot that floated empty within the space between her ribs. *One day at a time.* On impulse, she asked the driver to make a diversion from going straight to the hotel. He obliged without question and drove to Baker Street station.

Aida stepped out of the car into the familiar yet altered landscape of Baker Street. The iconic Sherlock Holmes statue stood as proudly as she remembered, but her heart sank at the sight of the nearby museum—closed indefinitely. Its shuttered doors marked a poignant shift from her youth when she had first visited this place, wide-eyed and hand in hand with her parents. Her father had marveled at Holmes's legendary deductive powers, sparking Aida's early fascination with meticulous research that fueled her work and writing. She could still hear his voice, full of warmth and curiosity, explaining the finer points of Holmes's methods to her.

Those moments with her parents had felt so steady, so rooted in love. Back then, the world had been a place where problems were solved together, and her parents' guiding hands made everything possible. Their absence now though left an emptiness that nothing had quite filled.

As she stood on the same street, reeling from her call with Graham, the contrast hit her hard. The warmth and security she had once found in her parents were so distant, and the bitter sting of Graham's betrayal made the void even sharper. She had come to Baker Street seeking comfort, a reminder of a time when love was simple and unconditional. But now, with the museum's closure and the shadow of her crumbling relationship looming large, the memory seemed a distant echo—fading just when she needed it most.

She wandered a bit, heading farther down Marylebone Road, which, she was sure, had another attraction they had enjoyed as a family. The memory was fuzzy, like a word on the tip of her tongue, but she recalled it was a place where she'd been enveloped by a great warmth from her parents.

She paused at the next corner, near two iconic red phone booths. The area felt familiar. In front of her was a circular building with a big green copper dome, like the planetariums she had loved visiting as a kid. This, however, did not appear to be a planetarium. Instead, plate glass windows gave a glimpse inside, of elderly people sitting in recliners watching a big-screen television. A woman with a walker stood at the window staring out at her. Aida, unnerved, continued walking. Sure enough, a couple of windows down, she came to a sign that proclaimed the odd building as an assisted-living facility.

The massive white edifice just beyond the green dome also felt familiar. There were no windows, save above a simple, unassuming entry half a block down, with big old windows on the floor above the front door. A sign above the entrance proclaimed the building as Her Majesty's Young Offender Institution. Aida stared at the front door, trying to understand what she was looking at. She was absolutely sure that neither the old folk's home nor this juvenile detention center was there when she had last visited, perhaps four or five years before when she had been in London for a conference. But what had been there? She stared at the pavement, racking her brain to remember, but for some reason she could only conjure up hazy, half-formed images of Queen Elizabeth, David Bowie, and Darth Vader. Suddenly dizzy, she leaned against a signpost for support. What was wrong with her? Stress, it had to be.

A middle-aged woman in a pink sweatshirt and a teenage boy in a black hoodie emerged from the building. The woman came toward Aida. "Oh, dearie, are you all right?"

"I—I think so. Thank you. Just felt a little lightheaded, but I think it's passed."

"Come on, Mum," the pimply-faced boy said, tugging on his mom's arm. Aida guessed he was embarrassed to be seen near the facility. She wondered what he had done to end up there.

"You look after yourself." The woman let her son lead her away.

"Wait," Aida called after them. The woman turned back. "What used to be in this building? Do you know?"

She looked up at the building. "The YOI? It's been here for as long as I can remember. No idea what it might have been back in the day."

Aida sighed. "Thank you." She watched them retreat, then made her way back to the waiting Bentley. She must have been mistaken about the location.

Still, as she took her seat in the car, she was left with an overwhelming sense of something about the building being wrong, something she couldn't put her finger on. Something that was just beyond the reach of her memory.

The driver honked his horn at someone. Aida's train of thought broke, and she couldn't recall what she'd been ruminating about. But there was an ache in her heart, an ache for what she once had.

9

April 2019

Aᴏᴛᴇʀ ᴄʜᴇᴄᴋɪɴɢ ɪɴ and receiving the key to her room, Aida turned to go toward the elevator and found Disa waiting for her.

"Good evening, Aida."

Aida almost didn't recognize her—Disa's appearance was a sharp contrast to how she'd looked in Boston. She was impeccably but strangely dressed in a wild taffeta mid-length skirt with a navy star pattern, a ribbon emblazoned with Christian Dior on the side. Atop the skirt, she wore a white sleeveless, asymmetrical top with an external white corset. Her white boots were half sandal, and she wore socks with them. Her hair was loose with curls that fell to her shoulders.

Look at her, so self-assured, Aida thought, her mind momentarily sidetracked. *And here I am, an emotional train wreck barely holding it together.* The image of Graham and Erin lip-locked flashed in her mind.

"I didn't expect to see you so soon," Aida managed to say, words strung together by sheer willpower.

Disa cut straight to business. "Are you ready to give your report?"

"I think so," Aida replied, her voice wavering more than she'd like. She wasn't sure what that would entail. She had prepared her presentation like she would an important lecture, making sure she had her narrative and points straight, but she wasn't even sure that was the right approach. Trista hadn't been helpful at all—she apparently had never been to one. She only knew that a number of questions about the research would be asked.

"Well then, let's get to it." Disa turned toward the elevator.

It took a second for her words to register for Aida. Panic surged through her veins. "Wait," she called. "I'm giving the report right now?"

Disa paused. She looked back and raised an eyebrow. "I thought you were ready?"

"I didn't realize that I would be doing it the moment I arrived. I thought it was tomorrow."

"Time is short. You should be rested," Disa said, folding her arms against her body. "You slept on the plane."

Aida took a deep breath, shocked.

"Shut your mouth before a fly lands on your tongue," Disa said. "The flight concierge gave me a report when you landed."

Of course, that makes sense, Aida thought, relaxing a little.

"So, are you ready or not? Your luggage will be delivered to your room, don't worry."

Aida's jaw tightened. *Am I ready? Can I compartmentalize enough to get through this?* But she couldn't afford to show weakness, not now. "Lead on," she said, forcing herself to match Disa's tone. "I'm ready."

She followed Disa to the private elevator, which whisked them up to the penthouse floor. While the view was not half as spectacular as that of the hotel in Boston, the suite was even more luxuriously appointed, with hardwood details, bespoke couches, leather chairs, plush carpets, all manner of trinkets and curiosities on the bookshelves and tables, contemporary wallpaper and artwork, all punctuated by white flowers in vases throughout the room. Disa led her through a small bar area and a little library to the massive living room.

"How big is this suite?" Aida asked, trying to make conversation with her gruff hostess.

"Two hundred and eight square meters."

Aida did the math, over two thousand square feet. "Wow, that's big," she said. The words sounded silly as they left her mouth.

"That's the main suite. There are six bedrooms you can connect, taking over the entire wing." Disa gave Aida a rare smile. "The Manor Wing has its own postal code."

"Oh my."

"Yes, oh my."

Disa left her there. Aida watched her go through the library and enter a sliding door on the other side.

A butler appeared from behind Aida with a tray holding a selection of cocktails and a little bowl of nuts. He set the nuts down on the mahogany coffee table and proceeded to describe her drink choices. Against her better judgment, Aida went for the bourbon. She needed something stiff to calm her nerves.

Muted voices floated from the room where Disa had disappeared. Aida wished she could make out the words, but it was too much like the cacophony of adult voices in the old Charlie Brown cartoons she had watched as a kid. Instead, she reached for her laptop bag and pulled out her notes in an attempt to refocus her attention on the presentation she had prepared. But it was a fruitless attempt. Between her nervousness about the report and the image emblazoned upon her mind of Graham kissing her oldest friend, she could barely focus on the words on the screen.

The bourbon was nearly gone when the door opened and Mo appeared in the doorway. "Ahhh, my funless one. Come along." He waved a hand at her.

Aida cursed under her breath. She hadn't expected him here. His biting humor was the last thing she needed.

The sliding door led to a little dining room with a circular table and eight leather low-backed chairs. Fran sat on the opposite side with Disa two chairs away to her right. The room had a stifling, almost ritualistic aura—a discomforting contrast to the joyful topics they were supposed to discuss.

"Please, sit down."

Aida nervously took a seat across from Fran. Mo began to sit beside her, but Fran shook her head at the man.

"Fine." His voice was petulant, like a child. He sat, leaving an empty chair between them.

The table in front of them was bare, save for a little box about half the size of a cell phone with a sleek black surface and a red button.

"Now then," Disa said, pressing the button. Then Aida understood. The box was a digital voice recorder, although it didn't look like any recorder Aida had ever seen. "Let us begin. We will ask you a series of questions. You will answer them to the best of your knowledge and ability. There is no wrong answer, so you can set aside all the nervousness roiling inside you."

"Am I that obvious?" Aida said with a little laugh. A nervous laugh because, for all of Disa's reassurance, it did nothing to calm her.

"Just get your snark on and you'll be fine." Mo leaned toward her as though he were conspiring.

Aida was not about to *get her snark on* in such a moment. She wished she could take a few deep breaths without it being weird. She needed to calm her pounding heart before she had a panic attack. Staring at the black box on the table, she imagined herself with the same dark shell, able to absorb anything that came her way.

"A reminder, Miss Reale, that you'll not speak of this meeting with anyone else," Fran warned. She had worn her long red hair up high and tight on her head in an intricately braided bun. It made her look much older and somewhat severe.

"Understood."

"Tell us what you felt when you first walked into your new home in Rome."

Aida faltered. Was this part of the report? Or chitchat? Fran's question was rather ambiguous. Why would her living conditions be part of this?

"Go on," Fran said.

"I have to admit being quite stunned. I've only seen such historic places when they've been turned into museums. I never dreamed I might find myself living in such a gorgeous palazzo."

"You are happier here than you would be in Boston," Mo said. It wasn't a question.

Aida thought of Graham and his tongue in Erin's mouth. After a moment's hesitation, she agreed, "I am." She was thankful they didn't ask her to elaborate.

They peppered her with other questions: how she got along with Trista and the rest of the staff, how she liked the food, what it was like being in Rome and regularly speaking the language. Aida answered honestly, although she left out the part about feeling weird about her lack of privacy and her concern about surveillance. At last, the questions shifted to her work.

"Why do you think Goethe turned to the Greeks to build his mythology of Faust?" Mo asked her.

Aida was glad she had spent so much time diving into that side of Goethe. "He believed the ancient Greeks had achieved the perfection of humanity, and this is why they were the masters of literature and art. In his own works, he turned to the ancient myths and depicted humanity in battle against the gods. It was his allegory for the Enlightenment."

Fran sniffed disdainfully.

Worried that perhaps she had given some sort of incorrect answer, Aida continued in a rush. "He thought the Greeks demonstrated their understanding of human nature through the mythology of the classical gods, and he strove to emulate this in his own works, not just in *Faust*, but in poems such as 'Prometheus' and 'Ganymede.'"

"Enough," Disa said, cutting her off. "We already know what Goethe thought about the gods. Let's move on."

The questions bombarded her with dizzying speed, each a pointed query that dug into her meticulously prepared reports. "What did you think the first time you saw the Tischbein painting in the Goethe museum?"

Why are they asking me this? Didn't they read my detailed observations? She offered a rehearsed response. "It was like seeing happiness distilled into pigments and brushstrokes."

The next question shot at her like a bolt. "What made people happy about seeing the Andy Warhol painting of Goethe?"

Her mind raced. She had reported about the blend of modern and classical aesthetics, but was that what they were after? Or did they expect some revelation? "People found joy in Warhol's subversion of the classical—how he breathed new life into a cultural icon," she said, aware that she was also questioning her own understanding of happiness with every answer.

Next, they pivoted to her time in Venice, and after forty minutes of questions, Aida wished she had a cup of coffee. She never slept well the night before flying, and in addition to the emotions weighing upon her, the questioning was mentally exhausting.

After his initial question, Mo had been silent through the barrage from Disa and Fran but finally brought up a new inquiry. "Were you happy in the Chapel of the Madonna di Vitaleta?"

"I was till you arrived," she blurted out, then silently cursed herself. Why did he bring out such a sarcastic side to her?

"And there we have the snark. Now if there is anything that makes *me* happy, that's it."

"My apologies," Aida said, not daring to look at him. "I'm a little tired and shouldn't have been so rude."

"I interrupted your work at the chapel. You were right to shoo me away," Mo said with a laugh.

"I'm about ready to shoo you away now," Fran said to him. Her voice held a dark warning. Aida was beginning to wonder if Fran or Disa liked Mo. They seemed to barely tolerate him.

Mo cackled. "Fine. Fine."

"He has a . . . certain effect on people," Disa said to Aida. "Please, continue."

Finally, after nearly two hours of what Aida eventually came to think of as interrogation, they concluded their questions. As

Trista had indicated, she was asked to turn over the notes she had stored in her portfolio. Disa immediately swept them off the table and into a black metal file box.

Fran set a sheet of paper in front of her. "Now then, we need to discuss the continuation of your contract. We are pleased with your work so far and would like to finalize the five-year extension." She placed a pen on top of the paper.

Aida sucked in a breath. She had spent weeks rehearsing how she would tell MODA she had no intention of renewing the contract.

The weight of the decision pressed against her ribs. She scanned the contract again, but she knew its contents. She'd read it cover to cover when it was first presented to her three months ago, scoffing at the absurd penalties for breaking it. Now, the numbers weren't just ink on a page, but a noose tightening around her future. If she took the job and later walked away, she wouldn't just be quitting. She'd be drowning in debt so deep she'd never claw her way out. MODA would come to collect every cent they had invested in her—salary, housing, training, expenses she hadn't even known were being tallied. With interest and penalties, the total would be staggering, a sum so high it might as well be a life sentence.

A sharp current of panic flickered through her. For an instant, oxygen seemed a scarce commodity, each breath thin and useless against the enormity of what she was about to do. But what did she have to go back to? No home, no job—only an ex-fiancé with disapproving parents she had no desire to face again. Yumi, her one true lifeline to Boston, would support her no matter what, but even that wouldn't be enough. And the worst part? She wanted this. The job was everything she had ever dreamed of.

A finger jabbed her arm, snapping her out of her spiraling thoughts. Mo leaned across the empty chair, watching her with an amused tilt of his head.

"Well?" he asked.

She swallowed hard, then picked up the pen and signed the paper.

"Excellent," Fran said, handing the contract to Disa, who filed it into the same metal box. "Of course, you'll need some time off for the wedding. And we'll need to make plans for Graham to join you here in Italy. Perhaps when the school year is finished?"

The question caught Aida off guard. Her heart thudded painfully. The room felt suddenly smaller, her chair more confining. The image of Graham and Erin resurfaced. Pushing down the surge of emotion, Aida responded with finality. "Actually, I'd like to return to Boston as soon as possible. And I plan on moving all my belongings. Graham will not be joining me."

Fran hesitated briefly before nodding, her face placid as though this were a minor detail. "Very well. We'll transfer your bags back to the jet. The driver will be waiting downstairs. Have a good sleep on the plane, and you'll be there first thing in the morning. Trista will contact you to determine what you need for the move, but you can plan for the movers to arrive in the morning."

"Leave now?" The idea of it sounded so absurd.

"Yes. That's no problem." Fran almost sounded sympathetic, as though she understood Aida's predicament.

At the thought of confronting Graham in person, Aida's pulse quickened, her vision narrowing momentarily, the room blurring at the edges like a vignette photo. How on earth could they arrange movers so quickly? It was almost as though they had been prepared for this. None of what had happened to her in the last two hours made any sense.

She tried to focus on the rest of Fran's words but found her attention beginning to wane. She'd just signed away five years of her life. The suddenness of it all made her head spin. She had pivoted from ending her engagement to plunging into an uncharted future in just a short span. It was hardly believable that a transatlantic flight awaited her, a literal journey toward a new undefined horizon. But what would her life look like in Boston now, stripped of the man she thought she'd share it with? Rome certainly seemed like the better option.

Yet, as she rose from her chair, a wave of vulnerability washed over her. What if she had made the wrong decision? Then she caught Disa's eye, and there was something in her piercing look and encouraging nod that gave Aida a newfound resilience. She had made her choice. She could do this. *One day at a time.*

"Before you go, Aida, let's discuss your publisher folding," Fran said.

Aida turned, unsure why this was up for discussion. "What about it?"

"Trista will be helping you arrange for a literary agent to represent you," Fran declared, as if it were the most natural next step.

"An agent?" Aida was shocked. "It's an academic book. I'm not sure an agent is ne—"

Fran didn't let her finish. "Have you considered writing fiction?"

Fran's question hung in the air, almost too casual, but with an edge that suggested this was more than a passing thought. Aida's chest tightened. "Fiction? I don't think that's quite my thing. I've always been focused on history and analysis, not creating stories."

Fran leaned back in her chair, gaze unwavering. "But you've been gathering stories your entire career, haven't you? Cataloging them, interpreting them, and making them resonate with readers. Fiction is just another way of doing that—of exploring truth, just through a different lens."

Aida's mind churned. She had once dabbled in fiction—a mystery novel set in the Tuscan countryside, drawing from the rich historical tapestry she knew so well. But she had shelved it years ago. The manuscript still sat in a file on her computer, untouched, a relic of a different time. "I appreciate the suggestion, but I'm not sure I'm suited for it. Writing fiction requires a whole different skill set."

Fran's lips curved into a knowing smile. "The best fiction often comes from those who understand the depths of what they're writing about. Your expertise in history gives you a foundation most fiction writers can only dream of. And let's not forget your recent work with MODA—it shows you're not afraid to step outside your comfort zone."

Aida's gaze flickered to the floor, uncertainty knitting her brow. "I wouldn't even know where to start," she murmured, her voice barely audible.

"That's what the agent is for," Fran replied smoothly. "They'll guide you, help you navigate this new path. And let's be honest, Aida, you're not in academia anymore. That world can be challenging to break back into when you're on the outside. This new path frees you from those constraints. Think of it as an opportunity, not a departure from your current work. You're not abandoning your past but building on it."

Aida bit her lip. The memory of her unfinished manuscript tugged at her thoughts. She had loved creating that world, even if she hadn't fully believed in her ability to bring it to life. "I don't know . . . I've spent so much time in academia. I'm comfortable there. I understand it."

Fran's expression softened. "Comfort can be the enemy of growth, Aida. Think about it: With fiction, you can explore the human experience in ways you never could with purely academic writing. You've already shown a knack for capturing the subtleties of emotion and experience. Why not channel that into storytelling?"

Aida had spent years piecing together the lives of historical figures, reconstructing their worlds. And she really had loved writing that novel. Perhaps Fran had a point. Maybe this was the natural next step.

Fran seemed to sense her wavering resolve. "Just meet with

the agent," she urged. "See what they have to say. You don't have to commit to anything now. But you might find it's not so different from what you've been doing all along."

Aida nodded, though her mind was still spinning. "All right, I'll meet with them," she agreed. She glanced at Fran, then back to the door, her grip tightening around the strap of her bag. She was standing at a precipice, the unknown stretching out before her. Yet there was a small almost imperceptible thrill in the idea of a new beginning. "I'll hear what they have to say."

Fran's smile broadened, a spark of satisfaction in her eyes. "Good. I have a feeling this will be a turning point for you. Sometimes, the best stories are the ones we don't plan."

As she left the room, Aida's thoughts raced. She had always trusted her instincts, and maybe, despite her hesitations, this was another moment to do just that. Things were shifting so drastically—with Graham and the plans they once shared fading into the background. Maybe this was her chance to redefine everything.

To not just write a new chapter, but an entirely different story.

MO OFFERED TO walk her back to the lobby. The thought didn't give Aida pleasure, but she wasn't comfortable protesting.

"Bravo," Mo said when they had closed the door to the main part of the suite behind them. "You even managed not to fall apart and cry."

A chill tickled the back of Aida's neck. What did Mo know about her and Graham? She put on a brave face. "Why would I have cried? For god's sake, I was talking about happiness."

"Yes, it was for the gods' sake," Mo said, "but that's beside the point." He pushed the button for the private elevator.

Aida had no idea what he meant but didn't think it was worth the trouble of asking. He would only offer more sarcasm.

As the doors slid open and they stepped inside, Mo looked her up and down with a peculiar intensity. "So, your book didn't sell."

Aida's lips pressed into a thin line. "The publisher folded. It's not exactly a reflection on the book itself. And sure, it faced rejections before, but that's how publishing works."

Mo's smirk was sharp, almost as if savoring a joke only he understood. "Right, the old 'blame it on the market' defense. Tried and true. Or maybe just tired."

Aida narrowed her eyes at him. "What are you suggesting?"

Mo chuckled. "Maybe it's time to try your hand at something people actually want to read."

Aida stared at him, taken aback. "What on earth do you know about publishing or what people want to read?"

"Not much, but I do know a thing or two about illusions. People don't really want happiness; they want the semblance of it. That's what sells, not just in publishing but in life."

Aida blinked, confused. "Are you saying I should've written a self-help book instead?"

"No, but perhaps Fran is right. Perhaps a fiction where happiness is the villain, and despair the hero. That'd be closer to reality, wouldn't it?"

Aida was about to retort but stopped herself when she saw the twitch at the corner of Mo's lips. She folded her arms. "You enjoy trying to rile me up."

Mo smirked. "It's a skill I've honed over years of tedious interactions. You, however, make it remarkably easy."

The doors opened and Aida strode out, glad she was no longer trapped in the little space with him. He didn't follow.

"*Buon viaggio*, Miss Happiness!" He gave Aida a salute and the doors closed in front of him.

She breathed a huge sigh of relief when the light on the elevator showed it moving upward.

April 2019

A S THE JET cut through the sky, Aida had quick calls with both Trista and Yumi before knocking back a sleeping pill. She couldn't—wouldn't—spend the night replaying the image of Graham kissing another woman. It felt like her head had barely grazed the pillow when she was awakened by the gentle tap of the flight attendant on the plane's bedroom door.

Rubbing her eyes, she moved to the window. Boston's skyline unfurled beneath her, a city waking up to greet her. She had considered having Yumi accompany her to confront Graham, but as she stepped off the plane and onto Boston soil, she texted her friend a change of plans. She was going solo. Four years with Graham weighed on her mind. Despite his betrayal, he deserved to face her in what was bound to be an awkward, uncomfortable moment.

She let herself in the front door. Music was playing, louder than she normally would have set it. Beneath it, she could make out voices drifting from the kitchen—Graham's, and a woman's.

Erin.

Fuck. Aida couldn't believe that after confronting him yesterday, Graham would so callously continue forward, as though calling the wedding off meant nothing. It wasn't even 8:00 a.m. Clearly, Erin had spent the night.

She stood in the entry for a moment, her eyes closed, willing her breath to calm. At least now she knew that she had made the right decision. This thought bolstered her and, steeling herself, she went to the kitchen.

When she reached the doorway, her heart immediately tightened at the sight before her: Erin—whom she had once believed was a dear friend—perched on the bar, the very embodiment of allure with sun-kissed skin and auburn hair flowing past her shoulders. The oversize denim shirt she wore, one of Graham's, was lazily buttoned, teasingly hinting at the curve of her breasts beneath. Seeing Graham, shirtless and in boxer shorts by the stove, spatula in hand with eggs sizzling, deepened the stabbing sensation in Aida's chest.

"Making me breakfast, I see," Aida said, her voice laced with a toxic sweetness that even she found chilling.

Graham looked up, eyes widening in alarm, spatula frozen midair. Erin shifted her gaze, meeting Aida's eyes in a fleeting moment before darting away. A quick flush colored her cheeks as she self-consciously tugged at the shirt.

"Aida . . . what are you doing here?" Graham stammered.

"Oh, I think I'm the one who should be asking *you* what you are doing here," she said, leaning against the wall, every ounce of her trying to exude control despite the tempest inside. "I'd love to know what this story is." She gestured vaguely at Erin.

Erin slid off the bar, clutching Graham's shirt around her. "I'm going to go—"

"Don't mind me," Aida interrupted her. "We're old pals, aren't we, Erin? No need for formalities. Remember all the pinkie swears we made to be friends forever? Of course you do. But really, I have to admit, while it might have made sense if you wanted to borrow some clothes, I'm not so sure our friendship will survive you borrowing my fiancé."

Erin paused, her eyes avoiding Aida's, her fingers twisting the shirt's fabric as if seeking something solid to hold on to. "Aida, this isn't how I wanted you to find out. This is . . . It's complicated."

Graham put the spatula down, his gaze falling to the floor. "Aida, I can explain—"

"Explain? Oh wait, I'm the storyteller. I can do the explaining. You're standing here, cooking breakfast for someone who is not me—for my oldest friend—who you just spent the night fucking, in the home we live in together. Do I have that right?"

The room fell silent, the eggs on the stove sizzling filling the void.

"See, the funny thing is," Aida continued, "I had really hoped, perhaps, maybe, you would have a good explanation for a one-time lapse. But thank you, Graham, for clarifying where I stand. No, not thank you. Fuck you both for that clarification. Now, please, feel free to continue. I'll be doing a bit of packing before the movers arrive. I shouldn't be in your way long."

Not waiting for a response, she left the kitchen and went to the bedroom, where the sheets were a tumbled mess and Erin's clothes were strewn all over the floor. She held back the flood of emotions threatening to break through and began to organize her jewelry and clothes to make it easier when the movers arrived.

Graham appeared at the door. He swept past her, picked up Erin's belongings, and left without saying anything. A few minutes later, Aida heard the front door open and shut, followed by Graham making his way up the stairs once more.

"Don't do this, Aida," Graham said from the doorway. He had donned the shirt Erin had been wearing.

She backed away. "Don't do what?"

"Don't leave me," he said.

She couldn't believe he was even attempting to keep her there. "Why on earth would I stay?"

"Because I love . . ."

She interrupted him with a rueful laugh. "Oh, that's rich." She picked up the rumpled sheet and flung it into the air across the bed. "Was this a declaration of your undying love?"

"You were the one that left me," he blurted out. "We're supposed to be getting married in a couple months and you jet off to Italy . . ."

Aida stared at him. "I went there to help *pay for the wedding!* You encouraged me! My god. I was trying to hold my own in this relationship, to make sure I could chip in after I lost my job. I sure as hell didn't consider sleeping with someone else."

"You were planning this all along, weren't you?" He tried to turn this around on her. "How did you manage to find movers in just one day?"

Aida was furious. "You don't get to make this my fault. As for the movers, since I'm no longer helping to pay for a wedding, I thought paying a higher last-minute price was a worthwhile use of the money." This wasn't true—MODA had made all the arrangements, but that was a strange explanation, and it didn't have the bite Aida wanted it to have.

Graham sat on the edge of the bed, put his head in his hands, and began to cry. She watched him break down and part of Aida ached to comfort him, but self-preservation held her back. The ringing doorbell was her escape, and she walked away, leaving the remnants of their relationship behind.

A moving truck was parked outside, a feat in busy Somerville. She had no idea how MODA had managed the truck's parking permit, but there they were, two young men standing on the step with boxes and packing tape in hand. She led them inside and set them to work in her office.

As the movers did their job, the air inside the house grew heavier. Each box they packed seemed to seal away another chapter of her life with Graham, and each item moved another memory. Aida directed them with a quiet efficiency, her focus unwavering. Most of the furniture was Graham's, but there was the occasional piece or two that she had brought with her when she moved in. But most of the art and all the books were hers. She helped mark the items that would go with her to Rome and those that would go into storage. Mercifully, Graham hid himself away in his office while they worked.

When the movers were nearly finished, she texted Yumi and then went to say her last goodbye to Graham.

The door to the study was cracked open. Through the gap, Aida could see he was staring out the window toward the newly budding garden. She pushed the door open but didn't go inside.

"I'm leaving in a few minutes," she said to his back. "I sent you a Venmo to help with the mortgage and utilities for this month." They hadn't yet combined their bank accounts, and for that, Aida counted her lucky stars. He certainly didn't deserve the money, but unlike him, she wasn't about to brush off her obligations.

His response was hardly audible. "I'm sorry, Aida."

"Me too," she said, pushing past the threat of tears and back toward resolve by thinking of Erin sitting on the kitchen counter that morning.

He turned toward her and his eyes, once filled with warmth and humor, held a depth of sadness that was palpable. The slight graying at his temples, which she had once found so distinguished, now made him appear weary.

"Do you remember that night at Hojoko?" he asked, his voice cracking slightly.

"I do." Of course she did. There was a guy at the bar who wouldn't stop bothering her, and Graham gallantly swept in, pretending to be her boyfriend. But she wasn't going to give in to nostalgia now.

He smiled, albeit sadly. "I had been watching you the entire evening, trying to gather the courage to talk to you. That guy just gave me the perfect excuse."

They shared a brief silent moment, lost in the memory of that night, a night that turned into two nights, then four nights, and then she was moving in with him, a promise of something she thought would last forever.

"I wish we could have held on to that feeling," Aida said.

"Can I hug you goodbye?"

That broke Aida, and all the tears that she had held back came flowing forth. Graham went to her and folded her into his arms. She buried her face in his shoulder, the tears mingling with the slight perfume that lingered, a perfume that wasn't hers.

After a time, he lifted her chin up. "I will always love you. And I will always regret not being able to do this again." He kissed her, and she let him.

"Goodbye, Graham," she said when the kiss broke. She pulled away and went to the door, refusing to give in to the urge to look back—to run back. She hated that she loved him so much. But nothing could ever be the same.

YUMI WAS WAITING OUTSIDE, her silvery blue Volkswagen Beetle double-parked not far from where the movers were locking up the truck. She gave Aida a quick hug, ignoring the honk of the taxi waiting for her to move.

"How are you doing?" she asked after they were on the road. "You look a wreck."

Aida flipped down the mirror to inspect her visage, then flipped it back up after she saw how right her friend was. "I'm exhausted, and god, this is all so hard."

"I still can't believe you're here, and you've already moved out." She pointed at the dashboard clock. "It's barely been twenty-four hours! They just put you on a plane? And found movers for you?"

"I apparently work for an extraordinarily efficient company," she said. But she tapped Yumi's arm and waved her phone at her friend. Yumi nodded that she understood. They had exchanged enough illicit texts and stolen phone calls to thwart MODA's secretive side. "I don't think it's all hit me yet." She sighed. "Ugh, and all the wedding plans."

"I'll help, don't worry. For what it's worth, I think you're doing the right thing."

A little bit of the tension within her gave way. "Oh, thank god. I had hoped you would say that."

"And you're taking the job, right?"

Aida nodded.

"Good. I mean, I'm going to miss you to pieces, but you have so much opportunity there, and aside from me, you have a lot of sadness here. Most people would be glad for such a break to start over."

"Yeah, I guess that's a good thing," Aida agreed, although she wasn't sure anything at the moment was good.

WHEN THEY REACHED Yumi's little condo in Boston's Back Bay, the first thing Aida did was take her MODA phone out of her pocket and set it on the counter. "Let's hit up the Esplanade. I need to take a walk."

Yumi immediately took Aida's hint. She set her own phone on the counter next to Aida's and grabbed her keys and a jacket off a hook in the nearby hallway. "Lead the way."

As they walked to the Dartmouth Street footbridge that spanned busy Storrow Drive, Aida told her friend what had happened when she'd confronted Graham. But it wasn't until they reached the bridge that she finally felt comfortable enough to freely talk about MODA. On the bridge, they could easily see anyone coming from either direction, and the noise of the traffic below would mask most of their conversation from anyone approaching.

"While I appreciate them helping me return to Boston and with the movers, it's so weird. All of it," she confided. "It doesn't make any sense."

"I always feel like my best friend is some sort of superspy with all the secrecy," Yumi said.

"And that's the worst part about it. I'm just a weird version of an historian," she conceded. "Mostly, I am trying to understand what role happiness has played in everything I'm studying. I don't understand why they are so hardcore about keeping it under wraps. It's strange, but not anything that will hurt anyone or even interest most people, for that matter."

"Have you had any warnings lately?"

"No, I've been a lot more careful. It's not worth the hassle of Trista's scrutiny."

During the first few weeks with MODA, Trista had regularly warned her about talking too freely with Yumi or Felix. When Trista once saw Aida using her personal phone to talk to Yumi on the Via Giulia outside the palazzo, she left a copy of the NDA on Aida's desk. Aida had asked her about it, and Trista only shrugged and suggested that sometimes it's good to have reminders on MODA policy. After that, Aida was more careful about using her personal devices where Trista might see her, despite the fact that the assistant had been clear on that first day about her ability to use them.

"I'm going to put some extra secure encryption on your laptop and phone while you're here. Just in case," Yumi said.

"Honestly, this secret skulking around to talk with my friends is the only thing I dislike about the job. Well, maybe not the *only* thing, but certainly the worst of it. I could never have dreamed of having a job where I see so many wonderful things every day." She rattled off some of the places they were planning on sending her next: the Sacro Bosco, a Mannerist garden full of monstrous statues; the Baci chocolate factory in Perugia; and the underground Domus Aurea, once the home of Emperor Nero.

"It sounds incredible. But is it really all roses? It seems way too good to be true." Yumi leaned against the rail. She bent over, hanging her head down toward the racing traffic.

"I guess it does sound that way," she admitted. She thought back to all the conversations with Graham. About a month into her time in Rome, she had felt so guilty about the beauty around her that she had started glossing over her work during their conversations. It made everything he was doing in Boston feel pale in comparison. Maybe all this was her fault. Maybe she drove Erin into his . . .

No. She refused to follow that line of thought and shifted her attention back to MODA. "It's rosy, but not all roses. There are a few thorns. The whole NDA thing hanging over my head sucks. Trista is a downer and I still know as much about her as I did the day I arrived. But I've gotten used to her and I don't let her get to me. And then there's Mo. He drives me up a wall."

"Maybe he's into you," Yumi teased, lifting her head to give her friend a little grin.

"God, I hope not." But the thought had crossed Aida's mind. Mo seemed to delight in making fun of her. He showed up randomly at places where she was working, and sometimes at the palazzo, where he took considerable pleasure in making Pippa mad and Trista sad. But with Aida, Mo's edge was slightly tempered, and while still biting and sarcastic, bordered on playful. He clearly enjoyed their back-and-forth, and the fact that Aida too often succumbed to his jabs. However, most of the staff could hardly stand him. Dante, who Aida thought was ever unflappable, patently refused to be in the same room when he was there. "He's manageable in small doses, but I think I'd be driven to murder if I had to spend a full twenty-four hours with him," Aida told Yumi.

"I wish I knew what he looked like. Or that you could draw like a sketch artist." Yumi laughed. "How was London?"

Aida groaned. "Awkward. I have no idea if I gave them the right answers or not."

After exhausting the more specific details about Aida's work for MODA, the two continued over the bridge to the Esplanade, a grassy park that lined the banks of the Charles River.

"Oh, I forgot to tell you," Yumi said as they headed down one of the paths along the river. "They tore down the Hatch Shell."

Aida stopped in her tracks. "What?" The Hatch Shell was an iconic wooden concert venue that had hosted countless events over its nearly eighty-year lifespan. Millions of people across the nation glued themselves to the television to watch the Boston Pops play there every Fourth of July in celebration of the country's independence. Just the year before, it had finished undergoing a renovation. What Yumi was saying to her literally made no sense. There was no reason to tear down the structure. None.

"Don't you remember? It was in the news for most of last year that a shady activist group filed a lawsuit claiming that the crowds on the lawn, the boats on the river, the fireworks—everything about the Fourth of July celebration—was an environmental disaster. They won, maybe right after you left for Rome. The ruling didn't force the city to tear down the shell, just to stop holding concerts. But then, in a rather suspicious way last month, it caught fire. Half of it burned, and the structural integrity was shot. Since they couldn't use it for performances anymore, and restoration would have cost a fortune, the city just . . . got rid of it. Damn, I'm sorry, Aida. I can't believe we didn't talk about this. Or that you didn't see the news."

"I put my *Globe* subscription on hold," she explained. She didn't want to admit to Yumi that she couldn't remember hearing anything about the activist group or their lawsuit—or how much that bothered her. How could she have forgotten something so important? "Did they catch the person?" She picked up the pace, wanting to see for herself. She didn't want to believe what Yumi was telling her.

"That's the even weirder thing. You know they have security cameras everywhere since the bombing at the Marathon. They didn't record anything. They had intended to keep the shell as a monument, even if they couldn't have concerts there. It's so beautiful and historic. But out of nowhere, it burst into flames. The fire department says they can't determine the cause. It was a clear night—no lightning. And they didn't find any evidence of explosives. But it's rather convenient timing."

When they reached the space where Aida remembered the vast grass expanse and little shacks for food vendors, there was, instead, an ugly chain-link fence circling the area where the Hatch Shell once stood. The whole area had been dug up, and there wasn't a trace left of the once beautiful Art Deco half dome and the bronze lettering on the steps with names of great composers. It was a Sunday, and no one was working. Two bulldozers sat on the edge of the dirt oval, silent big yellow monoliths. The shacks were gone.

"So that's it?" Aida was so upset she could barely get the words out. "They're just . . . leaving it like this?"

"No. Apparently, the surviving wife of the man who originally owned the land had a clause in her will—back in the twenties—stating that if the property ever stopped being used for performances, it had to be turned into a park, a playground, or a memorial. Since the lawsuit banned big gatherings, they decided on a memorial in her name."

"To a dead woman no one remembers? Not a park? Or a playground?"

"Nope. The activists ruined that. I think they've now turned their sights on the entire Esplanade, claiming that even bike paths and joggers disrupt the natural habitat along the riverbanks."

Aida gaped at her friend. "But that's just absurd. How can biking or jogging be bad for the environment?"

Yumi gave a snort. "Apparently, the argument is that the foot and bike traffic near the water's edge contributes to erosion, disturbs nesting birds, and affects the river's health. They want to limit human impact altogether."

Aida stared at the empty space where the Hatch Shell had once stood, memories flooding in like a tide she couldn't hold back. She remembered sitting on a picnic blanket with Erin and her parents, playing cards and sipping cold Cokes from the concession stand while the Pops warmed up in the background. Her father had always loved watching the symphony, and her mother had cherished the rare moments when the four of them were together. Erin had been like family then, Aida's closest friend.

Now it wasn't just the Hatch Shell that was gone; it was the last trace of those happy times. Her parents were both gone too. And Erin—who had not only betrayed their friendship but shattered Aida's life by sleeping with Graham—was gone in a different way. Aida's throat tightened, and before she realized it, tears were streaming down her face. It wasn't just the physical loss of the Hatch Shell; it was the loss of the life she once had, the people she once loved. "How can it be gone?"

"Ohh, Aidddy." Yumi put an arm around her and hugged her tight. "I forgot that you used to come here all the time. It really is terrible."

A black weight of grief filled Aida's heart. How could she have so much loss in just a day?

Yumi let her cry on her shoulder for a little bit, then wiped Aida's eyes with her thumbs. "Come on. You must be so tired. Let's get a little food and some coffee in you. You need to stay up and push past the jet lag."

Aida let Yumi lead her back into the city, across another foot-bridge and then down the street until they were in the Public Garden. On a whim, Aida suggested a ride on one of the swan boats, a gimmicky tourist attraction but something that had always given her a little childish joy. Yumi crushed that idea quickly when she told Aida that a child had fallen off and struck her head on the boat the week before. The child was still in the hospital. Out of an abundance of caution, the boats were closed indefinitely.

They found their way to a sushi restaurant on Newbury Street to eat. Aida was quiet during the meal. Between leaving Graham and the destruction of the Hatch Shell, she was terribly unnerved. None of it added up for her. The city's changes also gave her a weird feeling of déjà vu—not that she'd seen any of these specific things happen before, but rather that she'd had the same feeling, that something had been taken from her, wrested from her memory.

"Aida, did you hear me?" Yumi waved a chopstick at her.

"Sorry, what were you saying?"

Yumi gave her a sympathetic look. "You have so many reasons to be distracted. It's okay. I was waiting till you visited to tell you that I'm going to come hang with you in Rome."

Aida lit up. "Oh my god, that would be incredible!" Aida's excitement banished all thought of the Esplanade and the Public Garden. "When?"

"I have projects that will tie me up for most of the year, but once those are done I'll have nearly three weeks of vacation saved up that I have to take before the end of the year. I was thinking of coming to see you in Rome after Thanksgiving. I just need to figure out where I'll stay. No offense, but I don't think I want to stay with you. I'd be too creeped out about being watched."

Aida was so pleased she almost started crying. "I'll hook you up with Felix. He may know of a good place. Oh, I'm so thrilled!" Then it hit her that Yumi would be returning home right before Christmas. And Aida would have nowhere to go for the holidays.

II

11

June 2019

A FTER RETURNING TO ROME, Aida threw herself into her
work with a desperate fervor, trying to escape the emptiness that had settled within her. Two months had passed since
she left London, since she cut ties with Graham and called off the
wedding. She hadn't spoken to Erin. The betrayal still festered,
but beneath the anger was something heavier—grief for the
friend she had once trusted, the girl who had been part of her
life for as long as she could remember.

Rome was alive with the energy of tourists flocking to the
city as the season ramped up, but the bustling crowds and vibrant streets only served to highlight how isolated she felt. At
least her days were consumed by the demands of MODA, and
she welcomed the distraction, using her work to numb the lingering pain. Each site she recorded, each artifact she cataloged,
was a small victory toward keeping the ache at bay.

But even the rigor of her work couldn't fully silence the
thoughts that threatened to overwhelm her. So, following Fran's
suggestion, Aida had turned to a different kind of escape. Mo's
words about writing something that people would want to read
continued to ring in her ears, prompting her to dig up the manuscript she had nearly forgotten, a mystery titled *The Shadows
of Tuscany* that she had abandoned years ago, doubting her talent for fiction.

It became her refuge. Aida threw herself into editing *The*

Shadows of Tuscany with a single-minded intensity. Each chapter she revised allowed her to escape the relentless replay of her last moments with Graham, the bitter taste of betrayal, and the void of their abandoned future together. She wrote at a breathtaking pace when she wasn't working for MODA, and before she knew it, the edits were complete. She passed the finished manuscript to Mara, the new agent that MODA had arranged for her, feeling a strange mix of relief and trepidation.

But Aida didn't let herself linger in the uncertainty of what would happen next. She immediately began working on a new project, *The Botanist's Muse*, inspired by her earlier conversation with Felix about Goethe's *Italian Journey*. This novel, set in eighteenth-century Italy, would weave together art and science through the eyes of a young woman caught between the ambitions of a famous German writer and a charismatic Italian painter. Diving into this fresh narrative, Aida found a different kind of solace, a way to channel her academic interests into something imaginative and compelling.

As she crafted scenes and developed her characters, she was no longer just working to forget her past. She was beginning to imagine a future where she could create something beautiful from the wreckage. It was a means to reclaim a part of herself, to find meaning beyond the pain. With every page she wrote, Aida felt the faint stirrings of hope—the possibility that maybe, just maybe, she could write her own new beginning. It made her feel alive. No, it made her *happy*.

ONE SUNNY JUNE MORNING, Aida sat at the breakfast table in the garden loggia. "*Mamma mia*," she said aloud. She put down her coffee cup, alarmed at the news she read on the tablet before her.

"*È tutto ok?*" Chef Ilario set a plate of eggs and sausage on the table before her. He prided himself on being able to make a proper American breakfast, which had always amused Aida. She was more partial to a good chocolate-filled cornetto pastry but a couple times a week she indulged the chef.

"*Sì*. It's just that they're closing the Goethe museum indefinitely. It lost its funding. They may have to sell off the collection."

"Is that tragic?"

"It is to me. It was the first place I recorded when I first came here to Italy. I have such love for Goethe and his *Italian Journey*," she said. Losing the museum was like losing a part of her connection to her research and the novel she was pouring herself into. "It's also vital to my research. I was hoping to revisit some of Goethe's original manuscripts and personal letters there, to weave more authenticity into the story I'm writing."

"MODA certainly has enough money to support it. What if you talked to them? If you recorded its history, it must be important to them too." Ilario poured her a glass of fresh-squeezed orange juice from a carafe on the marble counter next to them.

"I'll mention it to Trista. Or Mo, whenever he shows up again."

"That bloody bastard," Pippa said from her spot on the other side of the counter, where she was mixing something Aida couldn't see.

Aida grinned. Pippa's hatred for Mo wasn't anything she tried to hide, not even from him. He egged her on every chance he got. Aida and Ilario had to intervene on more than one occasion before Pippa completely lost her cool and threw a knife at him.

"You're right. He probably wouldn't be the right one to ask. I can always try Disa and Fran next time I'm in London."

"MODA won't do nuffin' for ya." Pippa stopped her mixing. "Johannes asked 'em more than once to chuck in a few quid for stuff 'e reckoned was important, and they always said nah."

Ilario cocked his head at her, his mouth twisted, eyebrow raised. He switched to English. "I don't recall this, Pippa."

"My memory is better than yours, ya ol' goat."

"No! You can't remember a single recipe. But I have them all here." He tapped the side of his head.

Pippa rolled her eyes. "'Cause yer makin' 'em up every bleedin' time ya cook."

Ilario winked at Aida. He lowered his voice. "She might be right about that."

AFTER BREAKFAST, AIDA went to find Trista, who was where she almost always was, bent over her desk in her office.

"Trista, did you see the news about the Goethe museum?"

She lifted her watery eyes from the computer in front of her. "Yes."

Aida was surprised by her assistant's response. "Doesn't it upset you?"

"No, being upset by something like that does no good."

"We spent so much time there though. It was the first place I researched for MODA. I'd hate to see it close. It's also crucial for my novel research. Losing access to those collections would be a huge blow."

Trista clicked her nails against the desk. "What are you asking me?"

Aida's frustration rose within her, a tight ball that sat at the back of her neck. "Do you think MODA might consider giving them funding? They must have charitable obligations. Or Lady Ozie might."

For a moment, Aida thought that Trista might laugh.

"No, they wouldn't consider it. After MODA records a location, they never go back."

Aida had stopped asking Trista why she was doing this work, because the aide never had an answer for her. But now she couldn't keep that curiosity in.

"I don't understand. Why wouldn't MODA care about the location afterward? They went to all the trouble to understand it in the first place."

"The project is over. There is no need to go back to it."

"That doesn't make sense. Why doesn't it matter anymore? The very reason we cataloged it is to record how it makes people happy. And now the happiness will be gone."

Trista returned to staring at her computer. "And your point is?" She didn't look up.

Aida knew she wasn't going to get anything else out of her assistant. Angry and disheartened, she left Trista to her work and retreated to her own office. She slipped through the glass double doors to the balcony that overlooked the garden, leaned on the marble railing, and stared down into the squares of cypress below.

Several parakeets flitted between the bushes, their green wings a blur, their song a balm to Aida's frustration. She had found herself coming to this spot more and more often lately, as she mused on the increasing uneasiness that had started to creep into her work at MODA. During the first three months of the job, when it was just a trial period, she could ignore the weird ways of the company. Now, where there was once just weirdness, there was a *wrongness*, an undercurrent that could sweep her under if she let it. She tried to pinpoint when the unrest had lodged. She suspected it was before she returned to Boston, but she couldn't fix her feelings about any specific place or incident. When she attempted to recall those moments, her memory was hazy and indistinct. And when she reflected on her duties for MODA, she could only find enjoyment in her work, an extremely lucrative paycheck in her pocket, and full support for her shift toward work in fiction. She especially loved writing novels. So why did she feel so weirdly discontent?

"I'm only thirty-four," she said to the parakeets. "I can't be losing my mind yet."

One of the birds flew up to the railing near her and alighted for the briefest second. It noted Aida, then swooped back down to be with its friends. Aida sighed and went back inside.

She'd barely settled into her chair when her phone buzzed. She almost sent the call to voicemail but paused when Mara's name flashed on the screen. Her new agent was another strange thing to come out of this bizarre MODA arrangement. It still baffled Aida that she had been assigned an agent before she even had a finished book to show for it, let alone the credentials to justify one. The whole process had been surreal, moving at a speed that didn't quite seem real. Mara had been enthusiastic from the beginning, oddly so, as if she already knew *The Shadows of Tuscany* was destined to sell. And sell fast.

It turned out she was right. "Aida, I've got fantastic news!" Mara's voice crackled with excitement. "HarperCollins is thrilled about *The Shadows of Tuscany!*"

Aida's breath caught in her throat. "What? Are you serious?"

"Yes, I'm very serious. They loved the concept—the suspense, the layered narrative, the way you've crafted the mystery against the beautiful backdrop of the Tuscan countryside. They think it's exactly what readers are looking for, especially with the growing appetite for atmospheric, character-driven mysteries. But here's the thing—they want to fast-track the publication to hit the holiday market. That means moving straight into copyediting and printing galleys almost immediately. They're sure it will be a big hit for Christmas, and they want to capitalize on that momentum."

Aida blinked, trying to process the information. "That's . . . incredibly fast." Her mind flashed back to her colleague Celia, a seasoned novelist who had once lamented how glacially slow the publishing world could be. *Months,* Celia had said, *often more than a year* between signing a contract and seeing it inch toward publication. But this was nothing like that. This was breakneck speed. And while part of her was thrilled, another part couldn't ignore how strange it all felt. How—and why—was this happening to her?

"It is, but they believe the book is solid enough to move directly to the next stage. This *is* highly unusual, but that's why it's such good news! They're convinced this will be a big book, and they're prepared to put significant resources behind it. I think you'll be quite pleased with the advance they're offering."

Mara named a sum over seven figures, and Aida was glad she was sitting down. "Wait, how can that be?" she asked, stunned.

From everything she'd read, new authors typically received far less—somewhere between $5,000 and $20,000 for a debut.

"It's a rare opportunity, Aida. Just say you're ready to go. The contract details will be coming over soon, and I'll walk you through everything. But for now, I just wanted you to know how excited they are—and how excited I am! This is huge, Aida. Really huge."

Aida was still reeling. "Thank you, Mara. I'm . . . I'm excited too. This is just . . . incredible."

After a few more minutes of enthusiastic chatter and a promise from Mara to email over all the details, Aida ended the call. She sat there for a moment, staring at her phone, the reality slowly sinking in. She had sold her book. Her book. To one of the Big Five publishers. And they wanted it out by the holidays as a lead title. She should be overjoyed; part of her was, but another part felt a familiar unease. Why was this happening so smoothly, so quickly? Why would MODA be so invested in her success as a fiction writer? It didn't quite add up, but then again, little about MODA ever did.

LATER THAT MORNING, Aida met up with Felix at the entrance to the Jesuit church of Sant'Ignazio di Loyola in Campo Marzio, not far from the Pantheon. She had been inside the Baroque church dozens of times before—its magnificent ceiling was one of her favorites in all of Italy.

"Morning, love, you look radiant," he told her after he gave her the customary kiss upon each cheek.

"Oh, that's just because I may have a book deal."

"No, you don't. Didn't you just finish it?" Then he realized she wasn't joking. "Wait, you do have a deal!" He stepped back, taking a moment to absorb the news, then stepped forward again, his hands clasping hers. "That's fantastic, Aida," he said, his admiration for her evident in his tone. "Wow, there are so many good things happening for you. And you only have me to thank for it."

That sent Aida into laughter, which was interrupted by a

spindly old priest in a black cassock who opened the door with a scowl. Felix presented his guide badge and the man ushered them in, locking the door behind them, muttering to himself.

"I'm sorry," Aida said to him in Italian. "I didn't hear what you said."

"I don't like it, this locking of the doors, keeping the people out."

"It's only for a day, and I'm sure the donation my employers gave the church will be worth it," she told him.

He fixed a rheumy eye on her. "There are people out there that need guidance more than we need money. I don't agree with the bishop on this, no, no, I do not."

Aida kept a smile plastered on her face. "I understand. Tomorrow, the doors will be open again, and my work will shift to observing and interviewing tourists. But I promise we will work hard to complete our work quickly today so you can open the doors again."

"If you need me, I will be in the offices in the hallway." He pointed toward a nondescript door and shuffled off.

"What a crusty old man," Felix said once the priest had gone. "I promise you, we won't need him." He laid his jacket on the back of the pew closest to the door. "Ready to get started?"

Aida nodded. She pulled her recorder from her bag and hit the record button. "Ready."

For the next two hours, Felix went over every last detail of the church, ranging from the magnificent forced perspective ceiling that depicted the life and work of Saint Ignatius to the fake dome—a masterful illusion that, when observed from the right spot in the church, gave the viewer the feeling that it was real, not painted on a flat surface. Most of the scene represented the Counter-Reformation and the Jesuits' desire to defend the Catholic faith. Aida had done considerable research before she visited so much of the information was not new, but Felix had a particular perspective on the life of painter Andrea Pozzo and on the Baroque times he lived in.

"I've been in the church in Vienna that Pozzo painted," Felix told her. "The dome is better executed, but it lacks the richness of the full ceiling above us."

Aida's neck was beginning to hurt from looking upward. She rubbed at it, but could not keep her eyes on the ground.

Felix was still going on about the ceiling. "The blur between the physical edifice and the painted world is what I find the most miraculous. It's as though we're having a spiritual vision. There's a sense of movement. Nothing in this painting is static. It's all wild energy. You can almost see the movement of the clouds, the force behind the avenging angel's javelin, the strength of the angel holding Christ's shield."

Aida simplified it for him. "This ceiling . . . to me it represents joy. Every time I see it, I'm filled with pure happiness."

They stared upward together in companionable silence until the priest interrupted them to explain that he was locking up the church while he took lunch and they would have to come back in an hour.

"The photographer will be here then, so that works out," Aida said to Felix as they followed the priest out of the church. "Besides, I am betting you won't mind if I treat you to lunch."

They found a little restaurant a block away, tucked between two ancient Roman columns that had been built into the building's infrastructure. Felix secured a table for them while Aida found her way to the restroom. When she returned, he was gaping at his phone, alarm etched across his features.

"What's wrong?" she asked.

"You know the Chapel of the Madonna di Vitaleta near Val d'Orcia?"

Aida reached for a thin breadstick from the cup in front of her and began to unwrap it. "Yes, remember, I recorded it not long after I came to Italy."

"It was destroyed this morning in an earthquake."

She dropped the breadstick. "What?"

"I can't believe it. It's literally one of the most iconic Italian images. The pictures are horrible. It's just rubble now." He handed her his phone.

"*Dio mio.*" As Aida scrolled through the photos, the same grief welled up within her as when she saw the empty space where the Hatch Shell had once stood.

"They'll rebuild it, I'm sure. But what a tragedy," he said.

They talked a bit more about the earthquake, and how no one was hurt, so that was a saving grace. Then Aida told Felix about the Goethe museum.

"How odd is it that twice in one day I find that places I've researched are gone."

"Coincidence, I'm sure," Felix assured her.

Their conversation turned to other news of the day: the impeachment of Donald Trump; endless Meghan and Harry Royal Family controversy; devastating bushfires in Australia; and the Arctic experiencing record-breaking high temperatures, pushing the thawing of permafrost, which was releasing carbon dioxide and methane at rates faster than the earth could compensate.

"This is depressing," Aida finally said, realizing that she didn't want to carry the weight of the world on her shoulders that afternoon. "It's a dogpile of awfulness. Let's talk about art instead."

But underneath the discussion about the Caravaggio in one of the nearby churches, Aida couldn't shake her sadness that places she had cataloged were changing and disappearing.

THAT EVENING AT DINNER, Aida asked Trista if she had heard about the tragedy of the little Tuscan church.

"I have." She deftly swirled her pasta with her fork.

Aida wanted to shake her. Despite Trista's often somber appearance, she seemed curiously detached from most emotions. Aida had grown used to these peculiarities, but sometimes, like at this moment, they just made her angry.

"It's really awful. It's one of the most iconic images of Italy."

"You mean it was." Trista sipped her wine.

Aida couldn't stop her jaw from dropping. "You don't care at all?"

Trista wiped at the corners of her mouth with a napkin. "It's not that I don't care. It's just that it doesn't affect me, and I can't do anything about it, so it does me no good to give it much thought."

"That sounds like you don't care."

Trista raised an eyebrow at her but said nothing.

Aida could no longer control her exasperation. "It's two terrible things that have happened to places we've cataloged. It baffles me that it doesn't bother you."

"It's a coincidence, Aida. Nothing more." Trista set her napkin down on the table and stood up. "You shouldn't let this get to you so much." She took her half-full wineglass with her when she left the room.

After she was gone, Pippa came over and refilled Aida's wine. "She's right about one thing, luv," the sous-chef said to her. "Don't go lettin' 'er get under yer skin."

Aida sighed and took a big gulp of her wine. "I just don't understand her at all. Two MODA projects gone in one day? How can it not affect her?"

"She ain't got no bleedin' 'eart, that one. But listen, I reckon yer onto somethin'. Always thought there's summat dodgy goin' on, like there's somethin' rotten in the state of Denmark." Pippa gave her a little wave good-night, then slipped off into the kitchen.

THAT NIGHT, AS Aida settled into bed, she tried to calm her mind by focusing on how much her life had transformed. MODA had opened doors she'd only ever dreamed of, giving her a generous salary, a beautiful home in the heart of Rome, a new book deal, and endless inspiration for future projects. Professionally, she had never been in a better place.

Still, a faint unease tugged at her, Pippa's mention of *Hamlet* flickering in her thoughts. But for now, Aida brushed it aside. If something truly was rotten in the state of Denmark, she wasn't sure she wanted to know.

12

June 2019

Aida asked Trista to schedule her arrival in London for the day before her quarterly MODA report so she could feel better prepared. It was a luxury in and of itself to spend time at the hotel, and that afternoon, Aida decided to partake in the hotel's famous afternoon tea. The staff seated her in a corner and promptly brought her a glass of champagne. Then followed the tea and an array of little artistically shaped sandwiches of cucumber and lobster with the crusts cut off. Aida had become accustomed to not taking photos, but she snuck a quick snap of the snacks in front of her. It was the kind of thing that would make Yumi squeal in delight.

Aida sat back and sipped her tea, thinking about her upcoming report. Her gaze wandered across the restaurant, unintentionally landing on a man who, judging by his features and attire, could only be Italian. He sat alone at a table across the restaurant, looking at her with open curiosity. He averted his eyes when hers caught his.

Italy seemed to have a disproportionate number of beautiful people, and this man fell neatly into that pretty stereotype. A two-day scruff of a beard, aquiline nose, and dark hair, longer on top, with a lock falling into his blue eyes. He was smartly dressed in a dark ocean-green corduroy double-breasted suit, with a white shirt underneath, open at his chest and cuffed at the sleeves.

Her mind wandered to Graham momentarily, a habit not yet

unlearned. They hadn't spoken since she had moved to Italy—just a few necessary emails to untangle the last of their shared obligations. Thankfully, he had spared her any pleas for reconciliation. Aida was grateful for that, and to be four thousand miles away. Yumi had been right about the clean break being good for her. It dawned on her, as she observed the Italian's fleeting glance, that she had no need to feel guilt over the flicker of interest in someone new.

He looked back up and this time it was Aida who averted her eyes.

When she had the courage to take another glance, he was no longer at the table, but standing a few feet away, talking to a waitress who pointed him off in some direction. Aida hoped he might have just visited the lavatory, and she was surprised to feel so disappointed when he didn't return.

BEFORE GIVING HER report the next day, Aida intended to raise the issue of the Goethe museum closing, but Mo's antics prevented her.

"You *are* happy working for MODA, aren't you?" he asked her the second she sat down across from them. This time, Disa was absent.

"Yes, I love my work," she said, hoping she wasn't coming across too defensive. She had come to learn that's what Mo did to everyone around him—took them down at the knees with sarcastic comments, forcing them into emotional traps like inferiority or anger. She refused to fall for it.

"Sometimes you don't seem so happy," he said, leaning back in his chair and folding his arms across his chest.

"I didn't realize you were observing me, or I would have dished out a few more smiles," she said placidly.

"I always have my eye on you." He gave her a cryptic half smile.

Aida only nodded, although inside, she was confused by his statement. Was he flirting? Warning her?

"Mo, you're being counterproductive to the goals of this session," Fran said, her voice stern. "I'm meeting with Ozie later today and perhaps it would be a good idea for you to accompany me."

Mo scowled. "I only asked our spunky little historian if she was happy working for us. It's a reasonable question."

"We don't have time for questions that don't accomplish our objectives. If you don't want to stop derailing the process, you can leave." Anger tinged Fran's words.

"Fine, fine, fine. Carry on then." He waved a hand dismissively.

"Please, Miss Reale, tell us about your visit to Paestum."

Aida seized the moment. "Actually, before I begin my report on Paestum, I wanted to raise something important. The Goethe museum is closing due to lack of funding. It's a significant loss. I was wondering if MODA might consider providing some support to keep it open, given how integral it is to the cultural history we're cataloging."

Mo rolled his eyes, but Fran responded first. "We appreciate your concern, Aida, but we move on once MODA has recorded a location. There are countless other places that need our attention and resources."

Aida felt a sting of disappointment. "But isn't the whole point of our work to preserve the joy these places bring? If they close, all that happiness we recorded just . . . disappears."

Fran looked unfazed. "The happiness was recorded—that's what matters. Our task isn't to maintain it indefinitely. We document, we move on."

Aida pressed her lips together, trying to keep her frustration in check. She glanced at Mo, who was watching her with a bemused expression, clearly enjoying the show. She decided to drop it—her passion for her work wasn't for Mo's amusement.

"Please, Miss Reale, tell us about your visit to Paestum," Fran prompted again.

Mo didn't say anything else during the meeting. He sat there and stared, an amiable smile tugging at the corners of his lips. At the end of the session, he stood and, like he had during the last meeting she had attended in London, offered to escort Aida out.

"Brava, little historian." He pushed the button to the elevator. "Another happy meeting on the books."

She considered calling him on the diminutive title but thought that would likely backfire. "Does working for MODA make *you* happy?" she countered. But as soon as the words were out of her mouth, she realized that was likely an even worse thing to say.

He raised an eyebrow and huffed. "Oh, that's a good one!" The door opened, and he ushered her in. "You dare ask me about *my* happiness?"

"I didn't know it was an off-limits topic." She stared at the numbers above the door, willing the elevator to hurry and reach the bottom floor.

"Fair enough. For one, despite your terrible taste in fashion, and your ongoing inability to find a good hairstylist, I do find particular happiness in *this*." He gestured with his hand back and forth between them.

"And what, pray tell, might *this* be?" Aida's heart rate accelerated.

"Oh, Aida . . ." His tone was a confusing mixture of condescension and charm.

The door broke the tension with an opening swoosh, and Aida hurried out, almost crashing into an older woman who was waiting for the elevator. She was smartly dressed and looked to be in her seventies. Her golden hair was streaked with white but held in an elegant upsweep. She greeted Mo, then stepped into the elevator. Mo winked at Aida. The doors closed and the two of them were gone.

Aida decided to make a rare midday trip to the bar, hoping a drink might calm her nerves and help her think. The hotel bar, named after the famous early-twentieth-century literary club, the Bloomsbury Group, was known for its ties to bohemian occultist ideals. Unlike most London bars, which only had tables and no bar seating, this one was more like the familiar haunts Aida loved back in the States. It was usually a popular spot, so busy that finding a seat at the bar was nearly impossible. But it was a quiet Monday at 2:00 p.m., and the place was unusually empty, save for a robust Asian man with a very pink face nursing a glass of scotch at one end of the bar and, seated right in the middle, the mysterious Italian, a golden-brown cocktail in a martini glass in front of him.

Aida took a deep breath and crossed the threshold, past the myriad velvet armchairs and shelves full of antique books. "Is this seat taken?" It was cheeky, considering there were five empty spots on either side of the man that were free.

He turned from his drink to her, and Aida was relieved when a smile lit upon his face.

"Please," he said, shifting a little to make climbing into the high chair easier.

"What are you drinking?" she asked after she was settled. She couldn't remember the last time she had ever been so bold— had she ever? With Graham, he had been the one who made all the moves.

"The Siren Call. It's very good." He slid a card toward her, a tarot card of sorts, with *CHARISMATIC* etched across the bottom. On it, a woman with a flaming crown held a fiery heart in one hand and was emptying a cup of blood into a river at her feet. A hyena stood nearby, laughing. Aida flipped the card over. It was seemingly part of an elaborate cocktail menu. The drink and its ingredients were listed on the back.

"'Drink this to increase charisma and attract favorable attention,'" she read aloud.

"It seems that it worked." The man smiled.

His English was perfect, but he had a definite Italian accent.

"Parli Italiano?"

His eyes widened. *"Sì!"*

"I thought so," Aida said, continuing in Italian. "Where are you from?" She signaled the bartender to bring her what the Italian was having.

"Bologna. But I live and work in France. I come here periodically for business."

"I'm from the US, but I live and work in Italy now, and I too come here periodically for business."

He grinned. "Luciano Leto."

"Aida Reale."

"Your parents are fans of Verdi?"

She laughed. "They were, very much so." Occasionally, people asked her about the famous opera, but with the name becoming more common, it happened much more infrequently. "How do you like France?" Aida wanted to know what he did for a living, but it was a very American thing to ask that off the bat, and she didn't want to appear rude.

"I love it. There is so much history, so much culture. I find myself very happy there. And you? What brought you to Rome?"

"A job. I'm a historian of sorts. But I'm also a novelist," she said, realizing with a heavy heart that she couldn't really tell this charming man what she did for a living.

"What kind of novels?" Luciano asked, intrigued.

"I write historical fiction set in Italy. It's a blend of my love for history and storytelling."

"That's fascinating," he said. Then he grinned. "There is also another coincidence. I'm a bit of a historian too. What is your specialty?"

"General Italian studies."

"Ah, the same is true for me, general French history."

Aida thought this answer was odd—and, like her own response, seemed to be an obfuscation. What were the chances that neither of them specialized in some specific historical era like most historians did? Aida decided to probe a little.

"What era of French history have you found to be the most fascinating?"

He took a sip of his drink. "All of them! But I have been

spending considerable time in the Baroque and Renaissance lately, with the châteaus of the Loire Valley. Have you been to the Château de Chambord?"

Aida shook her head. "No, but I hear it is magnificent."

"There is a staircase there they think da Vinci might have designed!" Luciano began to describe the château in earnest, drawing Aida in with his passion. As he spoke, Aida noticed that he often referenced other recent trips—the spa town of Aix-les-Bains, the vineyards of Château Margaux, the beautiful carousel in Montmartre at the foot of Sacré-Coeur. The things and places he spoke of were found throughout the country, of various eras, and seemed to have no common thread. *Unless . . .* She made sure the bartender was out of earshot, then said, "It sounds like a job where you're always encountering happiness."

Luciano was lifting his glass to his mouth but paused midair. "It's a funny thing you should say that."

"Is it?" Aida said, realizing that she had guessed right. She pulled her phone out of her pocket and showed him she was turning it off. She indicated with a nod that he should do the same.

He raised an eyebrow, but reached into his pocket, removed his phone, and pressed the button to its side.

Once it was off, she asked him in a low voice, "Might it be accurate to say that you work for someone who is *collecting* happiness?"

Luciano gave a soft snort, then took a big swig of the cocktail. He lowered his voice a bit. "I suppose that is accurate. Yes, it's true. I like that. A *Happiness Collector.* But you ask this as though you too might be one."

"I haven't described myself that way, but yes, that sounds right." She knew she was in dangerous territory even having this conversation with her employers only a few floors away. She pulled a pen out of her bag and took up the napkin before her. On it she wrote a single word in tiny letters: *MODA.*

Luciano laid a hand on her arm. Their eyes locked. He nodded his head. Then his hand went to the napkin. He placed his glass on it, tipping some liquid across the napkin. The ink blurred. Aida took the napkin and wadded it up.

Her arm tingled where his hand had touched her. "I need to take a trip to the ladies' room. Will you be here when I return?" She hoped he would understand she was making the trip to flush the napkin into the depths of the London sewer.

He looked at his watch. "If you're not gone long."

She reached a hand to his shoulder and squeezed—a message, she hoped, that he should stay. And maybe a message of something more. "I promise."

She took her phone from the bar and turned it back on. Then she made her way to the bathroom and ensconced herself in a stall. She dumped the napkin into the bowl and flushed it down, then took a piece of paper from the little notebook she always carried and hastily scribbled her name, a note that Luciano should download Signal if he didn't have it, and her number.

She returned to the bar, relieved to see he was still there, his glass empty before him. When he saw her, he got up and stood next to his chair. "I paid the bill," he told her. "I have to go—an important quarterly meeting." His tone and the look in his eyes suggested he was about to head up that same elevator from which she had just come down.

Reaching out to take his hands, she slipped the paper between them. She hoped he wouldn't notice her hands were shaking. "I am glad to have met you, Luciano."

He hesitated, then leaned forward and gave her a peck on each cheek. "And I you, Aida," he whispered in her ear.

She watched him go, her heart swelling, euphoria at the touch of his lips against her skin surging through her.

Aida climbed back up on the barstool, her mind a whirlwind. She downed her drink in one, seeking clarity in the burn of the alcohol, and ordered a gin and tonic. As the cool glass touched her lips, a shadow of Graham's memory momentarily darkened her thoughts. She was only a couple of months removed from the raw wound of leaving him; was she ready for what was stirring inside her now?

Happiness Collectors. She turned the title over in her mind, thinking about how apt it was.

She had thought she was the only one, working on behalf of a miserable, eccentric billionaire. Yet here was Luciano, a mirror to her own secretive existence. And the thought of that—of not being alone in this peculiar vocation—brought both comfort and a new kind of longing. To feel such emotion was a shock, yes, but also an intrigue that was hard to ignore.

How many people she saw at the hotel on the days she visited were there also giving reports to MODA? How many hearts were collecting happiness while nursing their own hidden sorrows?

And more importantly, what did it mean that she wasn't the only one?

LATER, AIDA LEFT her MODA phone in her room, then snuck out of the hotel using the stairwell to take a walk to a nearby park. Trista hadn't scolded her in the last few weeks, and she hoped, in this case, that they would assume she'd stayed in her room. She settled in on a bench to video call Yumi on her personal phone. Her friend squealed with delight when she mentioned she had met a handsome man at the bar.

"Okay, tell me everything. Is he single?"

Aida paused. It wasn't something she had considered, but a little anxiety crept in now that the question had been proposed. She'd assumed he was single. More importantly, she *wanted* him to be single. "I don't know."

"You don't know?"

"We didn't talk about that. But I found out something else even more important."

Yumi looked skeptical. "And what might that be?"

"We have the same job. We decided that we should be called Happiness Collectors."

"Wait, there are more people like you?"

Aida filled her friend in on the limited interaction she'd had with Luciano, including the whisper of her name and pecks on each cheek at the end. She also mentioned the woman she had seen going up the elevator with Mo. "She knew Mo. I wonder if she's also a Collector."

"Okay, so this is turning out to be bigger than some rich old lady whose eccentric hobby is having you catalog all this Italian stuff," Yumi said.

"I know. It makes no sense. Why would she need other people to do this? How many Collectors are there? And why bring us together in the same place at the same time? Wouldn't that be a risk?"

Yumi looked thoughtful. "They're probably relying on the NDAs you signed to keep it quiet. You know . . . I could see about hacking the hotel's database and getting the records of people who stay there on the days you have your interviews. If there is a lot of overlap with other people, we'll have a good idea of who the other Collectors are."

At that moment, an old man sat at the other end of the bench. He looked harmless, but she hastily stood and moved on.

"Gah," Aida said when she lifted the phone back up to see Yumi. "It gives me no small amount of anxiety every time you mention hacking something."

"I won't get caught, Aida. Don't worry."

"I do worry. It wouldn't be a little slap on the wrist. They'd lock you away. Don't do it. Maybe I'll learn more if Luciano gets back to me."

The conversation turned to Yumi and her recent string of bad dates. Aida tried to appear interested, but her mind was simultaneously racing with two things: the thought of Luciano's smile and the implications of a world with more Happiness Collectors than just her.

AIDA RETURNED TO Rome the next morning. She didn't hear from Luciano for another three days, at which point she had reluctantly given up the hope that he might find her on Signal.

Then, one morning when she was out for a walk to enjoy the early summer air before it became too stifling, she felt the buzz in her pocket. She almost dropped her phone, her excitement was so great, when she saw the text on her personal phone from an unknown number.

Aida, sono io, Luciano.

Ciao! she texted back.

Sei libera? Puoi parlare con me? È sicuro?

Aida's stomach fluttered. Yes, I'm free to talk. It's safe, she wrote back in Italian.

She flipped off her MODA phone, then climbed the stairs of the nearby closed church. It was the perfect vantage point to see if anyone was coming. Her phone screen came to life just as she leaned back against the centuries-old stone.

"I'm sorry we couldn't continue talking in London," he said. He was also outdoors, walking along what looked like the Seine. He stopped at a bench and sat. His hair was tousled with the wind, which gave him a wild look that made Aida's heart jump. "Mo is such an asshole when I'm late for my interviews. Tell me, how long have you been working for them?"

"Not long. Six months. I thought I was their only historian."

"Ahh, just getting started. I've been with them for nearly four years. I thought I was the only one for a long time too. But there's a man I keep running into in London, and over the years, I've come to the conclusion that we're always at the hotel at the same time because we do the same thing. But I haven't had the opportunity to speak with him."

"Have you ever met Lady Ozie?" Aida asked.

He shook his head. "No. I asked Disa once if I ever would and she told me I never wanted to. I've the impression she's a miserable sort."

"Mo told me the same thing. It sounded almost like he despised her. Do you know why we're collecting . . . happiness?"

Luciano scoffed. "I wish. When I began working for them, I was so desperate for money and a job that let me use my degree that I didn't question my incredibly good fortune. I had concerns but was determined not to let them think I was ungrateful with too many inquiries. But since I realized there might be more than one of us, I have to admit that there are too many strange things to ignore. Why all the secrecy? What we do isn't illegal. And we're collecting places that are already familiar to people."

Aida was giddy with the knowledge that someone else felt the same as she did about MODA. "I don't understand either. I hate not being able to talk about my work with people close to me. My friend set us up with Signal to talk, but I worry I might be found out at any time. I feel like a child; if they catch me, they will take my phone away—or worse, my job."

"My aide, Dolores, always has her eye on me. It's tiring."

"My aide too. I wonder how many Collectors there are," she said.

"I collect happiness all over France. You collect it in Italy. Maybe it's country-specific?"

It was an intriguing idea, but of course, they really had nothing more than ideas to go by. They spoke for a little while longer, comparing stories about Mo, their aides, and their experiences at their London interviews. Finally, they both reluctantly had to admit they should go before they were missed by their respective handlers. Neither of them had answers, just more questions. But as they ended the call, Aida found it had been a profound relief to talk to another who understood the MODA weirdness so exactly, and who had the same misgivings as she did.

Mixed in with that relief was the butterflies she had when she thought of Luciano. No one had stirred these feelings in her since Graham. The wisdom of that experience had tempered her expectations, but her heart didn't seem to know the difference.

13

September–October 2019

T HE DEEP AZURE of the ancient mosaics echoed the tone of the sky as Aida stepped into the cool shadows of the Mausoleum of Galla Placidia. It had been almost a season since London, since Luciano, but there in Ravenna, time seemed to stand still, suspended amid the glint of glass and stone that had watched over the resting place of an emperor's daughter for centuries. Just as she finished recording her thoughts on the awe-inspiring beauty surrounding her, the familiar vibration of the MODA phone disrupted the morning stillness. She signaled to the photographer to continue while she stepped outside to take the call. The smell of the nearby ocean wafted on the breeze.

"*Pronto.*"

Her agent was ecstatic. "Aida, I have good news for you! Your book has made the longlist for the National Book Award!"

Aida looked around her, convinced she must be in the sights of a hidden camera. There were only the nearby brick walls of the church complex. "Mara, is this a joke? You can't be serious. The National Book Award? That's ridiculous. It hasn't even been published yet."

Mara was adamant. "I assure you, this is no joke. It's possible to submit an advance copy, and we just skated in under the deadline. *The Shadows of Tuscany* is a finalist."

What Mara was saying made no sense. While she knew she

was a decent storyteller, there was no way her writing was National Book Award level.

"I think I'll have to believe this one when I see it."

"You better start believing it. I've been working with Trista to arrange for you to finish early there and head back to the palazzo to meet up with the press for interviews. A car should be there for you in half an hour."

"Wait, meet with the press?" She was still trying to take all this in. How could she possibly be a National Book Award finalist? Even in her wildest dreams, she hadn't seen that coming.

"You need to get back to the palazzo and freshen up. Foreign correspondents from *The Times* and *The Post* are on their way to us now."

The palazzo Mara was referring to was an oceanside mansion MODA had rented for her. Aida pictured the main living area, with its expansive views of the sea, an elegant backdrop for these interviews.

"Call me afterward," Mara said.

Aida watched her phone disconnect. Stunned, she went back into the little tomb to wrap things up with the photographer before heading up the path to the waiting car. On the way to the palazzo, she texted Yumi to tell her the news. Aida didn't expect a response right away; her friend was likely still not up for her day yet.

Trista was waiting for Aida at the palazzo and quickly ushered her into her room, where a makeup artist and hairstylist were ready to transform her. "Do I really need all this?" she asked her aide.

"This is a big moment. You want to look your best," Trista told her. "There will be many photos."

So Aida let herself be pampered. She was reminded of the scene in *The Wizard of Oz* when Dorothy was whisked to the beauty salon and all the attendants swirled around her. Was this what it was like for celebrities readying for movie scenes or red-carpet ceremonies? There was a perverse pleasure in all of it—that she could just lie back and let them make her beautiful.

After, Trista ushered Aida into the wardrobe. Several outfits were laid out for her, carefully selected to look great on camera. Aida's eyes were drawn to a pale citrus-colored suit with a darker pink chemise and matching pink shoes. When she finally was allowed to look into the mirror, she gasped. She was sure Yumi wouldn't even recognize her if they passed each other on the street. The stylist had worked magic with the length her hair had grown over the past months, sweeping it into an elegant updo that accentuated her features beautifully. Her makeup was far heavier than she liked, but it sculpted her face into a visage of sophistication she hadn't known she possessed.

"I feel like someone else stepped into my shoes," she said to Trista.

Trista adjusted her collar. "Maybe they did."

"What do you mean?"

Trista didn't answer her. Instead, she handed her a tablet.

"What's this?"

On it was a list of talking points for the interviews: themes from *The Shadows of Tuscany*, her inspirations, her writing process. As she skimmed the notes, she couldn't help but notice the careful omission of anything related to MODA. That wasn't a surprise—she'd known from the start that MODA was strictly off-limits in public conversations. But seeing it so neatly excluded still made her uneasy.

"You know the rules," Trista reminded her, as if reading her thoughts. "The focus is on the book. Talk about your writing, your characters, your inspirations. They're here to discuss your creative journey, not MODA."

"I know," Aida said quietly. "But I know this book . . . I'm not sure I need specific talking points."

"This is how these things work, Aida. It's about presenting yourself as the author, the storyteller. This is to help shape the conversation so there is no need to mention how MODA helped you get here."

Aida nodded, flipping through the talking points again. She had expected some guidance for the interviews, but this was more than that—a major narrative of her life was being shaped for her. She was being packaged, every detail of her public persona meticulously controlled. She wasn't sure this was how most authors did their interviews. It left her feeling like a puppet on invisible strings.

The interviews were a blur. No matter what question was thrown her way, Aida had to steer the conversation back to the approved topics, her responses already half written for her. Each time she spoke, the real Aida sank further into the background, replaced by this polished version of herself that MODA had crafted. When the last reporter left, Aida collapsed onto the salon's divan and closed her eyes, exhausted. The room was finally quiet, but her thoughts were a whirlwind. She had never been less in control of her own life.

A clap in her face startled her. "No rest for the wicked!"

She sat up with alarm and opened her eyes. Dressed in a tux as though he were going to an award ceremony, Mo settled into a chair across from her. He was far more handsome than Aida wanted to admit.

"What are you doing here?"

His lips curved into a subtle, knowing grin. "I came to congratulate you."

Aida raised an eyebrow. "You came to Ravenna for that?"

He cocked his head, regarding her for a moment. "So skeptical. Why is that a surprise?"

"It seems a bit out of the way, that's all. I mean, we're in the middle of nowhere."

Mo made a dismissive gesture. "Nahh. Anything for you, Aida." He slipped a hand into his jacket, retrieved a folded piece of paper, and handed it to her.

Aida unfolded it. It was a memo from MODA that they were boosting her salary by 10 percent.

"Close your mouth, little novelist. We wouldn't want you to swallow a fly."

Aida reread the memo. "This . . . is . . ."

"A lot. I agree. I tried to tell them that you aren't worth so much, but I was overridden."

"Wow," Aida managed, unsure what else to say.

"*Wow* is right. But I suppose you did manage to win the National Book Award. So, that's another ten thousand in your pocket too."

Aida stared at him. "The winners haven't been announced yet."

He stood. "Oh, of course you'll win. I declare it." He headed toward the door. "Don't spend all that in one place."

AN ACCOLADE-FILLED MONTH LATER, Aida met Felix at his apartment in the Roman Ghetto. The late spring light filtering through the buildings seemed especially luminous to Aida. Her heart swelled with the beauty and history that surrounded her. She was living in Rome! And her book was up for the freaking National Book Award! She tried to focus on these events, but it was hard to ignore the little nagging part of her that told her it was all too good to be true.

Aida's reverie completely dissipated when she reached Piazza Mattei, where a crew of men were repaving the little square with the black *sampietrini* cobbles that were prevalent over most of the historic districts in the city. The piazza was empty, just a strange flat spot in between the medieval buildings. It tugged at her . . . Something was missing from the center of the piazza. *A fountain*, she thought, although the details were hazy. Puzzled, she walked along the edges of the construction, past the *umarelli*—the old men that hovered at the perimeter watching the workers—toward Felix's building, a block past the piazza. When she arrived, she found Felix sitting on a rickety chair beside the door, scrolling through his phone.

"I can't get the image of a fountain out of my mind," she said to him.

"A fountain?" Felix asked, puzzled.

"Yes. And turtles. Turtles." She couldn't shake the thought that there were turtles connected with the fountain that was no longer in the piazza.

"And Bernini," he said, furrowing his brow.

Aida threw up her hands in excitement. "Yes! Bernini made the turtles. There was a fountain in the middle of Piazza Mattei with young boys reaching toward the top basin and the turtles on the edge."

Felix nodded. "I remember now . . . Bernini made the turtles about a hundred years after the fountain was added."

Aida dug into her bag for her MODA phone and pulled up her calendar. She scanned through the entries and looked for Piazza Mattei, but nothing came up. She pulled off her scarf and wrapped it around the MODA phone to muffle the sound, then put it in the bottom of her bag and pulled out a notebook, flipping it open.

"What on earth is that?" Felix asked, picking up the notebook. "Alien script?"

"I take it you've never seen shorthand?"

Felix boggled. "Shorthand? You know shorthand?"

Aida laughed and explained that her grandmother had taught shorthand in schools before it went out of vogue and had taught it to Aida when she was growing up. She used it often to take notes, particularly when she was doing interviews for her research.

"I keep a list of all the jobs I've been on."

She took the notebook back from her friend and looked over the page. Her confusion grew as she scanned the list. At least three dozen locations were written down, some of which she remembered, but far more she did not. She looked for Piazza Mattei, and sure enough, she had cataloged the fountain and the piazza shortly after she had moved permanently to Rome.

"I walk through that piazza every single day. Why is it so hard for me to remember that fountain?" Felix said after Aida had confirmed her suspicion. "Or for you to do so, for that matter. I mean, you practically live next door *and* you studied it."

"Why would they have removed it?" Aida asked. "Why can't I remember most of the places on my list?"

Neither of them had an answer.

The first location listed seemed especially baffling. "There was a Goethe museum in Rome?"

Felix raised an eyebrow at her. "There was? Are you sure about that? It seems odd there would be a museum here for a German writer."

The date next to the name was a few weeks after Aida had begun working for MODA. She wracked her brain, trying to remember what she had done when she first came to Rome. She could picture herself moving into the palazzo, meeting the staff, and all of Trista's weirdness, but now that she looked back, there was no recollection of her first assignment. She vaguely recalled making recordings on the tape recorder, and that she and Trista had trudged across town for a few jobs, but she couldn't recall much more. She'd never had memory issues before . . . What on earth was happening?

Aida took her phone back out and looked back through her calendar. All the days before the last six months were blank. Her stomach churning, she hastily powered down the phone and returned to the list in her portfolio.

Most of the locations and items were unfamiliar, but she could still recall some of them. And as the dates became more recent, the more Aida's memory seemed to fill in the gaps. "Dear god. I think I understand. The locations are disappearing." She found a pen in her bag and added an explanation at the top of the list about locations disappearing so the next time she looked at it she would remember. "But why are we forgetting about them?"

"I need a drink." Felix nudged her toward the door. "I ordered us sushi while I was waiting for you." He led her through his apartment to the interior courtyard of the building and his little patio. She followed, her mind clouded by their discovery.

Felix deposited a bottle of wine on the table before them.

"There must be some sort of explanation," Felix said as he poured the wine.

"Do you remember any of these?" Aida read the list to him, including the dates she'd visited the locations.

He listened intently, his lips pursing as he concentrated. "Some of them. The most recent. Some of the others *seem* like they should be familiar, but I can't really pull any information out of this poor broken head of mine. Like this one, the Palio di Siena horse race. I feel like I should know what that is. I've been to Siena many times—my cousin lives there. I used to go there every July when I was young. But I don't remember anything about a horse race."

The food arrived and they tucked in. In between mouthfuls of maki, they tried to remember other locations on Aida's list. Felix searched Google for some of the names and came up with either scant information or entries that were very old, highlighting the history of a location or item that no longer seemed to exist.

Aida had an idea. "Do you keep records of all the tours you give?"

Felix nodded. "Of course."

"Even the ones you do for MODA? The tours you took Johannes on?"

Felix lit up. "Yes! I do. Especially for MODA. I have to do a lot of research before each visit, and I keep fairly extensive records of all the details." He was already scrolling through his phone.

Aida sipped at her wine while he searched for the information. Finally, he looked up. "This is fucked up. There are a bunch of folders in my digital storage, but nothing in them." He scrolled through his phone a little more. "It's only the ones related to MODA. The folders are still there, but they're empty— like someone wiped the contents but left the shell behind." He frowned at the screen. "Some still have names but reading them feels . . . off. It's the same feeling as when I try to think about the Palio di Siena. I know I worked on these, but I couldn't tell you a single thing about them."

"Tell me the names, and I'll add them to my list. At least my records seem to be staying intact. I wonder why though. If your files are vanishing, why isn't my list?"

Together, they went through Felix's folder names. None of them rang a bell for Aida. As he read them aloud—Pantheon Fountain, Barcaccia, Trajan's Column—his expression tightened. He pressed his fingers to his temple, eyes narrowing as if trying to pull something from the depths of his mind.

"I feel like I should know these," he muttered. "Like I can almost see them, but—" He shook his head. "It's like grabbing at smoke."

THEY GOOGLED A FEW. Most came up empty. Trajan's Column had results, but it was long closed after a terrorist attack had toppled the ancient monument four years ago.

"All of them . . . gone."

"I don't like this," Felix said.

"What on earth could be happening?" Aida whispered. A chill ran down her spine.

"We've talked about this before, I think." His brow was furrowed in thought. "About things you've researched closing. Like the earthquake in Val d'Orcia that destroyed the church."

"Oh, yes, we did talk about that." Aida could easily recall the little *chiesa* and its Madonna over the altar, as well as the conversation she'd had with Mo there. "Why can I remember that but not these other things? None of this makes sense."

"Can you ask Trista? No, maybe that's a bad idea."

"I don't think she would be helpful. But wait, maybe I know someone who might be." She reached for her phone and found the Signal app. She dashed off a quick note to Luciano.

A few moments later, her phone buzzed with a call. Her heart skipped a beat when his face appeared on her screen. "*Ciao, Aida! Come stai?*"

Felix gave her a sly grin. Aida hadn't told him about Luciano, but she knew Felix would get the story out of her as soon as she ended the call.

She explained their findings to Luciano. "I don't know if this is just some anomaly. But so many locations I've cataloged have disappeared . . . or been destroyed like the *chiesa* in Val d'Orcia. Has that happened to any of the places you've researched?"

His jaw dropped, and he gazed off toward a spot near his feet, lost in thought. "Yes, yes . . ." he muttered, then turned his attention back to the screen. "France has its own share of earthquakes. I'm sure you've heard about the one that destroyed half of Carcassonne three months ago. Then, of course, there was the fire in Notre-Dame this spring. And the Luxor Obelisk at Place de la Concorde. I researched it before it was toppled and destroyed during the first days of the Liberté Révolte protests. But smaller locations . . . I'm not sure."

"Think back to your first assignment when you became a Collector," she said. "What was it?"

His brow knotted. "I, uh . . ." There was an uncomfortable pause as he stared back at the ground, trying to recall.

Aida let out the breath she had been holding. "You don't remember, do you?"

"I don't. This doesn't make sense. I have an excellent memory." He gritted his teeth.

"When we met, you told me about a few places you had visited. Aix-les-Bains, vineyards in Château Margaux, and the Sacré-Coeur carousel," Aida pointed out.

Luciano nodded. "*Sì, sì*, I did. But I researched those locations in just the last few months, so the memory is quite new. But if I try to remember where I went when I first began working for MODA, that's harder. *Merda!* This is very disturbing, Aida. I can't recall much of what I did in the early part of the job. How can that be? And how haven't I noticed it before?"

"Maybe this is why MODA doesn't want you to keep any records?" Felix mused.

"Who is that?" Luciano asked, his eyes widening with concern.

Aida shot Felix a look. She didn't know if Luciano would be fine with the idea that she had broken the MODA vow of silence about their work. Reluctantly, she turned the phone toward Felix, who waved. "I'm Felix!"

Aida turned the phone back toward her. "He's an old friend who does guided tours in Rome. He got me the job at MODA. And no, before you ask, he's not supposed to know any of this. But I trust him. He's the one that helped me realize some of the places I've researched have disappeared."

"We should be careful," Luciano said. His voice held a note of warning. "I think MODA might be capable of dangerous things."

Aida thought about Johannes and his sudden death. "I know. I think that too."

They chatted for a few more minutes before saying goodbye. "Aida, *stai attenta*." *Be careful*. The video winked out.

THAT EVENING AIDA went back through her notebook, digging deep into the shorthand about places she'd researched, including the Casa di Goethe. She read about her exchange with Mo, which she didn't remember at all. How could she not recall when she met him? He was truly unforgettable in every way. Reading the passage was like reading a novel that someone else had written, not words she herself had recorded.

Her heart skipped a beat when she read her notes about the conversation she had with Ilario and Pippa about the Goethe museum closing. She couldn't recall anything about that, but she did have a perfect memory of the details about Johannes suddenly dying, as well as what Pippa had said before Aida had retired for the night—*Always thought there's summat dodgy goin' on, like there's somethin' rotten in the state of Denmark*. Only the details about the museum itself were hazy.

Aida didn't know what was rotten, but she was fairly sure she had stumbled upon the stench left behind.

December 2019

U M, THIS IS UNEXPECTED," Yumi said, her eyes growing round with surprise as they crossed the threshold. The apartment she'd be calling home for the next three weeks was an arresting visual symphony of minimalism and color.

Aida took in the sight: the stark white space cut through by the clean lines of modern furniture, accented with audacious splashes of color—a desk highlighted by blue plexiglass, a rebellious panel of red glass fragmenting the transition to the kitchen, and a solitary yellow triangle setting off the wall around the flat-screen TV. It was an avant-garde heart beating within the chest of a sixteenth-century palazzo, just a stone's throw from Piazza Navona.

"My friend is an architect," Felix explained. He handed Yumi the keys. "The Italians . . . well, their style is rarely understated." He chuckled.

"I'm just a ten-minute walk from this place," Aida mentioned while they navigated through the hallway with Yumi's luggage. "The layout can be a bit of a maze at first, but you'll map it out in no time."

Yumi brandished her phone like a talisman against getting lost. "I have GPS for backup."

Aida exchanged a knowing glance with Felix, and their shared mirth bubbled into laughter.

"It can't be *that* bad," Yumi said.

Aida reassured her that the technology had greatly improved

in recent years. "But trust me, there's a charming rite of passage in getting lost here. Even the best GPS can't unveil all the secrets of Rome."

"Well, you'll be in London for a couple of days, so you won't even know if I do." She stuck her tongue out at Aida before suddenly sobering. "Guess who I saw at the airport."

The hint of distaste in Yumi's voice was a giveaway. "Graham," Aida said, a slight unease settling in her stomach.

"He was there with Erin. They were at the gate to the Bahamas. I wish they would have looked over at me. I would have flipped them off on your behalf."

Aida felt a twinge of discomfort, a remnant of what once would have been a sharp pang of jealousy or anger. She hadn't thought much about Graham lately. For the first few months after the breakup, she had slept terribly, unable to get him out of her mind. As the summer passed, she found that Rome, her writing, and her work gave her the distraction she needed for her heart to heal. And of course meeting Luciano. The news that Graham and Erin were still together didn't affect her as profoundly as it might have months ago.

"She can have him."

Felix snorted. "What a silly time to go to the Bahamas. Isn't it hurricane season?"

"Sadly, I think that might be nearly over," Yumi said.

Aida didn't want to spend more emotional energy on Graham than necessary. "Forget about him. I'm more excited about us finally being in the same city together."

"Sounds good to me," said Yumi. "So, tell me, what's the 404 like?"

Aida pulled out her MODA phone to double-check it was turned off. "All clear. But I shouldn't leave it off for long." Trista had tried to reach her a few days ago when Aida had turned it off to call Yumi and hadn't been happy when she didn't answer. Aida tried to pass it off as signal issues, but she wasn't sure if Trista believed her.

"I feel bad rushing off to London right after you arrive."

Yumi shrugged. "Don't worry. I'm here for a few weeks, re-member? I wish I could go with you though." She threw one of her bags onto the bed and unzipped it. "Okay, so after you told me about the disappearing places, I went ahead and looked into the list of people who've stayed at the hotel at the same time you were there."

Aida normally didn't want to know about Yumi's hacking forays, but this time she was grateful. "What did you find?"

"There are about fifteen people who are almost always there at the same time. They arrive quarterly and stay for a day or maybe a couple of days, but never for long."

"That's interesting," Felix said.

"Where are they from?" Aida asked.

"All over—mostly European and Asian countries. But when I dug deeper, I noticed that the hotel hosts different groups from other countries every month, always the same people arriving on a quarterly schedule."

"So maybe there are many Collectors? And we all have to give quarterly reports?" Aida asked, trying to grasp what this information meant.

"Maybe there is a Collector for every country," Felix pos-ited. "And there are one hundred and ninety-five countries, if my memory serves me right."

"That's a lot . . ." Aida sat on the edge of the bed, which sported a red duvet—the only pop of color in the otherwise white room.

"There are exceptions for larger countries. The US has three Collectors—one each for the East and West Coasts, and one for the middle. MODA seems to rotate their quarterly check-ins to avoid overlap," Yumi continued. "It looks like MODA sets aside a week every month for reporting, and each group reports on a different quarterly rotation."

"I don't get it," Felix said. "Wouldn't the Collectors start to recognize each other? It seems like MODA wouldn't want that.

I mean, they haven't indicated there are other people like you, have they?"

"No, they haven't. But we travel alone, and my bet is that most of us aren't spending much time in the hotel common areas. With strict rules about discussing the company, they probably assume we'd never put two and two together."

Yumi opened another bag and began hanging her clothes in the mirrored wardrobe. "I went through five years of this, and the same pattern holds. Some people come and go, but it's been remarkably consistent."

"Wait, you have names and contact information for all of these people, don't you?" Aida pushed the idea of Yumi's illegal methods of obtaining such data to the back of her mind.

Yumi turned away from the wardrobe, a wide grin spreading across her lips. "Why yes, yes I do."

"Are any US Collectors there at the same time as me?"

She shook her head. "No, the US Collectors are on different rotations. But I can't be sure where everyone's really from— MODA seems to assign people to work in countries other than their own."

"That makes sense." Aida stood to help her friend hang her clothes. "It means they won't be jaded when they're cataloging happiness. The Romans, for example, barely seem to notice they are living among such priceless treasures, whereas tourists walk around with their mouths open in awe." She thought about it for a moment. "It makes perfect sense. We can experience happiness differently in a new place, so the Collectors need to be foreign."

"Actually, *that* is the real mystery here," Felix said. He had sunk into a plush white chair near the door to the flower-lined balcony. "Why are they collecting happiness at all? And why do they need a couple hundred people to do it?"

"True, that's fucking weird, but let's start small. Aida, I have something for you." Yumi set the empty suitcase aside and started rifling through her bag until she found her phone. A moment later, an AirDrop notice popped up on Aida's device. She accepted, and the document opened.

"Those are the people who are usually in London at the same time you are," Yumi explained.

Aida stared at the document, surprised. Yumi had curated a detailed table—names, short biographies, employers, and even photos of each person. Yumi had gone deeper than just tracking hotel guests; she had compiled background information from public records and pieced together details from social media and professional networking profiles.

A couple of them were vaguely familiar, though Aida couldn't be sure if she had seen them in passing during her trips to London. Then, two faces stood out: the older woman who had gone up in the lift with Mo, and Luciano. Aida couldn't help but smile when she saw his photo.

"He *is* quite the snack," Yumi teased her. "Way better than your last love interest."

Aida gave her a sock in the arm. "He's not a love interest!"

Yumi's only response was to cackle at her.

Felix gave Yumi a conspiratorial look. "I agree, snack is apt." He grinned at Aida. "I'm sure you aren't sad at all to leave us for London."

"Oh, stop," Aida said. "I *am* sad to leave you!" She tucked her phone away in the bottom of her purse. "Well, a little sad." She chuckled. "Come on, let's grab lunch and a spritz, and Yumi can catch us up on life in Boston."

Aida remembered to flip her MODA phone back on when they had settled into the heated tent of the café. It wasn't even a minute later that it buzzed in her pocket. Her heart began to hammer when she saw Trista's name on the screen. She briefly debated not answering but decided that would only lead to more problems. "*Pronto.*"

"Where are you?" Trista sounded more irritated than concerned. "Why is your MODA phone not working again? It went right to voicemail."

"It did?" She paused for a second. "You know how hard it is to get a signal inside some of these buildings. It's so frustrating. Yumi and I have been ducking into shops and finally settled in at a coffee bar. When I went down to the basement for the bathroom, there was a line, so I might not have been accessible for a bit." This was perfectly plausible. Getting any signal through centuries-old layers of marble, brick, stucco, or cement was impossible in many places.

Trista paused, as if deciding whether to believe her. "Very well," she finally said. "Your flight to London has changed from tomorrow morning to this evening. The pilot called in sick, and her replacement can only take you this afternoon at 17:00."

Five o'clock. "All right. We're having a little midday *aperitivo*, then I'll be back to pack." Aida hung up and briefly shut off the phone to relay the conversation to her companions. "We're going to have to be more careful. I think she knows I've been turning it off."

"I'll see if there is anything I can do about that," Yumi said. "Turn it back on, and let's get that spritz."

She did, and they easily filled the conversation with trivialities in case her phone was listening, but underneath it all, Aida knew they were burning to get to the bottom of the MODA mystery.

IN LONDON, THE onset of the holiday season had subtly transformed the city, and its festive touch was evident as Aida arrived at the hotel. The lobby was tastefully decorated with discreet strands of twinkling lights and a modest, elegantly adorned Christmas tree in one corner, creating a cozy, welcoming atmosphere. As she navigated the softly humming common areas, Aida paid attention to the individuals she encountered, hoping to recognize someone from the list Yumi had given her. She sat in the lobby for a while and observed guests coming and going. The only familiar face was Luciano, who entered with a single carry-on suitcase. Their eyes met for a moment before he quickly masked his expression, diverting his gaze and moving swiftly toward the check-in desk.

Aida made her way to her room, and not long after, her phone buzzed—it was Luciano on Signal.

Ciao Aida. ☺

Aida's heart fluttered. I'm glad you're here. I have something important to share with you.

He responded immediately. Are you staying in town after your meeting or returning? If you are staying, would you like to have dinner with me tomorrow night?

She gave a little fist pump to the air, glad she hadn't planned to return to Rome right after her meeting with MODA the next day. I'd be delighted.

Meet me under the clock on the corner of High Holborn and Southhampton Row at 19:00. There's a Thai place about 15 minutes away, if that would interest you? Better if we aren't seen together at the hotel.

As soon as she hit Send on her affirmative response, her MODA phone buzzed, startling her and sending her blood pumping. They couldn't know she had been communicating with Luciano, could they? She willed her voice to be calm as she picked it up and said hello.

"I hope your report is ready." She was surprised to hear Mo's voice, as she'd never spoken with him on the phone before.

"Now? I thought we were meeting tomorrow afternoon?" Aida said, confused that they would want her report in the evening before she even had a bite to eat. She glanced in the mirror above the hotel dresser, wishing she had time to redo her makeup.

His response was terse. "You're here now, and I'm waiting."

The phone disconnected, leaving Aida to stare at the glowing interface.

She wanted to text Luciano back to warn him that his schedule might change too, but the timing of Mo's call at the end of their conversation worried her, so she decided against it. She rushed to pull herself together and made her way to the private elevator.

AN ATTENDANT LET her into the penthouse and walked her to the dining room. The table was there, but the chairs had been removed, except for two. Mo stood behind the one at the far end of the table and motioned for her to sit in the other. Fran and Disa were nowhere to be seen.

"This looks like an interrogation," she said, hoping her voice didn't betray the unease simmering beneath the surface.

"It is," he said with a sly smile.

"Well then, officer, let's get on with it." Aida took her seat, determined not to let him see her flustered.

Mo came around the table and perched on the edge so that he was inches away, peering down at her. His proximity was unnerving, but there was something soft in his gaze. He suddenly reached into a pocket. Aida drew back, unsure of his intentions. He chuckled at her discomfort.

"Just the recorder," he said, placing a small black rectangle on the table before her. "So my *partners* can catch up later." He said *partners* as though it were a funny joke.

"Where are Disa and Fran?" she asked, trying to shift the subject and escape the strange energy between them.

"They're visiting with an old chum. Someone has to report back on your work, so I volunteered to stay here with you, my funless friend."

She wished Mo wouldn't sit so alarmingly close to her. It was meant to intimidate, and she hated that it was effective.

"Let's begin." Mo's voice broke through her spiraling thoughts.

Aida drew in a breath, steadying herself.

"Explain happiness to me," he said, his blue eyes searching her face, lingering for just a moment too long.

"It's the supreme good. Being able to live a life that enables us to use and develop our reason . . ."

Mo cut her off with a wave of his hand. "You think I wouldn't know Aristotle?" He folded his arms against his chest and frowned at her.

"I was about to credit him, but I couldn't finish my sentence." Aida tried to keep calm and not let an edge creep into her voice. She knew Mo enjoyed riling her up. Or riling *anyone* around him up.

"Do I make you happy, Aida?" His blue eyes were hard ice, daring her to answer.

"Yes," she said.

A slow smile spread across his lips, the satisfaction unmistakable.

"If you consider amusement to be a component of happiness," she added, though she was more irritated than amused. But Mo liked it when she pushed back, and his smile broadened as she spoke.

"Ah." He leaned in, closer than before, and for a moment, Aida was certain he would kiss her. She tensed, not because she wanted it, but because part of her was curious. *Would she stop him?* To her relief, she never had to answer that question, as he pulled back suddenly and stood, beginning to pace the room.

"Did winning the National Book Award make you happy?"

Aida raised an eyebrow. "Is that a serious question?"

"Yes," he said, staring her down.

"Yes, of course it did. Why wouldn't I be happy about that?"

"How did winning make you happy?"

"It gave my writing public legitimacy, something I never had when working academically. It made me feel accomplished, successful."

It was his turn to raise an eyebrow. "And feeling accomplished makes you happy?"

Aida was so confused about this line of questioning. "Yes. Don't you feel happy when you accomplish something amazing?"

He laughed, a roaring belly laugh that made Aida bristle. He was laughing *at* her. "Oh, my dear, everything I do is amazing. Now then, explain the puppet show," he said, his tone more clipped, shifting the conversation in a way that left Aida feeling like she had missed something important.

She had spent the previous week cataloging the Teatrino di Pulcinella Gianicolo, a puppet show on the Janiculum Hill that had been running since 1959. She began to describe the children's reactions to the puppets before he interrupted her.

"What did you think when you first watched the puppet show?"

"I wished I could have watched it as a child, with the wonder that comes naturally to them."

"The puppets are violent. Why do children delight in violence?" Mo shook his head in mock disappointment.

"Puppet shows were originally satire for adults, and Pulcinella, like Punch from *Punch and Judy*, was often associated with characteristics of the devil. But in the eighteenth century he became a little more benevolent, representing the greater good, even if through violent means. People were used to seeing violence, and humor helped to balance such unsavory aspects of life."

"I didn't ask about the history. Answer my question. Why do children *delight* in violence?"

Aida tried not to show how flustered his questions made her. She had only tangentially explored the psychology of the puppet shows, preferring to stick to the history of the tiny theater. "They aren't responding to the violence—they're responding to the uniqueness of the mode of storytelling. There's excitement in watching a figure fight off injustice, even if it is only perceived injustice."

"They're watching a puppet beat the shit out of another puppet and they think it's hilarious." He was leaning against the far wall, his arms crossed, staring at Aida. "Did *you* think it was hilarious?"

"I did," she said, although she felt dirty as the words fell from her lips. In this context, it sounded terrible that she had found such behavior funny.

"Do you also delight in violence?"

"No, I don't."

"What a conundrum we have here," he said, chuckling and drumming his fingers on his upper arm. He stared at her, willing her to speak.

Aida held her ground and waited for his next question.

"It seems that violence can make even normal people happy. Would you agree?" Mo smiled again, but this time there was something softer behind it. "You ever think about the Colosseum? Thousands of *normal* people, rooting for real bloodshed. Makes you wonder how far we've really come."

Aida exhaled slowly, keeping her frustration in check. "There's a difference between enjoying a story and condoning real harm."

"Is there?" His smile faltered for a moment before returning. "People used to cheer for blood. And here you are, cheering on fake violence."

"You are distorting my words."

"But I'm not incorrect, am I?"

Aida couldn't deny that he was right. She thought of all the violent TV shows and movies, all the video games she had played, the books she had read. She had grown up watching the Road Runner repeatedly destroy Wile E. Coyote, laughing every time his head was blown off or he fell off a cliff.

"We delight in watching the destruction of bad things," she said, but she knew it sounded weak.

"What do you consider a bad thing?"

Mo's needling was starting to grate and her retort was sharper than she meant it to be. "I don't know what this has to do with the work I've done in the last three months."

Mo pressed on. "So now our conversation is a bad thing?"

"I didn't say that."

"Oh, but you did." Mo broke into loud laughter. Then he seemed to notice the recording device on the table. "But, my dear Aida, I will refrain from continuing this mode of inquiry lest my partners accuse me of scaring off our little novelist."

He gestured for her to stand and leave. Aida was surprised . . . She had not covered most of her work in the last quarter. She gathered up her bag and went to the door.

"You've done well today, Aida," he said as she put her hand on the door handle. "Very well."

Aida raised an eyebrow at the praise. He seemed sincere. But when she looked back, he wasn't interested in her and was instead fiddling with the recording device. Perplexed by everything that had just happened, she opened the door to go.

"Wait."

She turned and Mo was coming toward her, pulling an envelope out of his jacket pocket. He handed it to her, then gestured for her to go before turning back to the recorder.

Aida waited until she was in her hotel room to open the envelope and gasped when two stacks of €50 banknotes fell onto the bed. She stared at the money in shock. They had just boosted her salary when she was longlisted for the National Book Award, and now MODA was throwing more money at her. Why? Then she thought of all the times she'd struggled to convince bosses she was worth her salt, and smiled.

THE NEXT MORNING, Aida set off for the Victoria and Albert Museum. Despite many past trips to London, she'd never found enough time to explore its vast collections properly. Today, she was thrilled to have an entire day to wander its halls, finally fulfilling her long-held desire to see the famous Raphael Cartoons and tapestries.

As she walked through the building's grand entrance, the familiar sights and sounds of a bustling museum surrounded her. But she froze in shock at the signs informing visitors that the Raphael Court and the Renaissance Britain and Baroque Europe galleries were all closed due to a fire in the neighboring fashion gallery.

"There was a fire?" Aida asked the elderly woman behind the glass of the ticket booth. She cursed herself for not paying attention to the news.

"Aye, it's terrible what happened." Her Scottish accent was thick. "A few days ago, someone managed to break into the area behind the glass cases and lit up a bunch of 1950s dresses and some of the Alexander McQueens. It spread through the room, taking down half the collection before the flames were doused." She handed Aida her ticket. "Terrible, terrible. They have no idea who did it."

"Weren't there cameras?"

She nodded. "Worthless."

Aida was disappointed, but she decided to make the most of her visit and explore the rest of the museum. Yet even as she examined the Medieval treasures of the Simon Sainsbury Gallery, Aida couldn't shake the thought that it was related to all the other cultural disappearances MODA seemed to have a hand in. But why would they burn down the fashion gallery? Or destroy any of the other locations, for that matter. And how could they possibly erase memories? None of it made sense, and if it was all true, Aida didn't want to think about what that meant for her—for her job, or her future.

15

December 2019

HAT EVENING, A little before 7:00 p.m., Aida donned her hat and wrapped her scarf around the bottom half of her face, hoping to obscure her identity from cameras and passersby. After a brief text exchange, she and Luciano decided to leave their MODA phones behind in their rooms with the televisions on for noise, hoping to convince anyone listening at MODA that they'd both stayed in.

She kept her fingers crossed in her pocket as she navigated the hotel, hoping no one would notice her. It was an old habit from childhood that she fell back on when hoping for parking spots, restaurant reservations, and other fortuitous events. She had no indication that it worked, and she almost crossed the fingers of her other hand to hope it did.

Luciano stood beneath the grand weathered clock that adorned the corner of the building—once a bank, now abandoned, its windows boarded up and its former purpose long forgotten. The stone facade still carried an air of dignity, though time had dulled its grandeur. Luciano's long gray overcoat billowed slightly in the cool breeze, and a houndstooth scarf was wrapped loosely around his neck. A black leather messenger bag hung casually over one shoulder. He lit up when he saw her. "*Ciao*, Aida!"

When he kissed each cheek, Aida's heart thumped so loud she thought he must be able to hear it. She willed herself to be calm and to mute the giddiness that bubbled up inside her. God, she hadn't felt like this since the first days when she was dating Graham. *Fuck that guy,* she thought to herself, and gave Luciano a big grin.

"Come, let us walk, and you can tell me this news," Luciano said in Italian, gallantly holding out an elbow.

Delighted, she took his arm and together they crossed the street and headed toward Soho. As they entered the vibrant neighborhood, the festive ambience enveloped them. The streets were alive with a dazzling array of holiday lights, casting a soft ethereal glow on the bustling sidewalks. Strings of delicate twinkling bulbs hung above them, weaving a tapestry of light that danced across the facades of restaurants and shops. The December air was brisk, but she was warm inside, buoyed by Luciano's proximity.

"So we know that more than two of us are working for MODA collecting happiness, right?" she said, continuing the conversation in Italian.

"*Sì,* have you learned more?"

"What if I told you that there may be more than two hundred Collectors?"

"No!" he exclaimed. "Two hundred? But why?"

"That's the mystery." As they continued down High Holborn into Soho, Aida explained what Yumi had discovered.

Luciano guided her around the corner at Soho Street. "You said you had a list of people we can look out for?"

"Yes, stop for a moment, and let me send it to you." They paused in front of a construction site where a hole in the ground dominated what once must have been a public square, taking up the center block of the neighborhood.

"Wait," Luciano said. "This place . . . something doesn't seem right."

Aida looked up. She'd been in this part of town several times before when visiting an old college roommate who once lived in the neighborhood, so she tried to get her bearings as Luciano led her around the edge of the construction. On a corner down the street, one of the oldest buildings had a red banner around two sides with big yellow letters proclaiming House of Charity.

"I know that building," she said. Her friend had lived just a block past and down the street.

"So do I," Luciano said. He turned back to the dark hole in front of them. Running his hands through his hair as he stared into the darkness, he began walking the length of the fence.

Aida followed him as he wandered the perimeter, weaving around pedestrians and dog walkers until they came to a stack of wrought iron fencing leaning up against the chain-link barrier that surrounded the site. One of the pieces had a dented sign dangling from a paint-chipped black bar. Luciano stopped in front of it.

"I knew it!" He turned back to her and began digging into his bag, before extracting a Moleskine notebook and flipping through the pages. Sketch after sketch blurred by until he finally stopped and held the book so Aida could see. "This statue," he said, pointing at the sketch, "is of Charles II." The Baroque-era king wore a long curled wig and sported armor. One arm was on his hip and the other bent in front of him, empty of the great sword that his hand must have once held. "I drew it the last time I was here. It was summer, and a concert was playing." He pointed to a building on the perimeter of the park. "That's Paul McCartney's office over there."

Aida peered around him to see the words on the sign: Soho Square Gardens. She gasped.

"Wait, there was a brown-and-white gardener's hut in the center of the park, wasn't there?" she asked, remembering. "And a bench that . . ." She paused, unable to grasp the words that seemed to be on the tip of her tongue. "Why am I having so much trouble remembering?"

Luciano nodded. "It's not just you. It's me too. I think you might be right about the bench." He stared at the park momentarily, then suddenly gave a soft "oh" in exclamation. "Do you think this could be tied to what you were telling me? About places disappearing."

A throat cleared near them, and they turned to look. A woman stood a few feet away, her hand on the chain-link fence. She was breathtakingly beautiful, seemingly ageless and round of face, with ruby lips and coffee-brown hair coiled tightly in several elaborate braids against her head. Her clothes were elegant, with black riding boots over her jeans, a suede coat, black earmuffs, and a scarf resembling cashmere. She peered into the blackness of the construction site. "You're both right. There was a bench in that park. A memorial to Kirsty MacColl. Now it's gone. A tragedy, don't you think?" Her voice was measured and clear.

Aida wasn't sure if she meant the missing park or the singer's death in a motorboat accident in Cozumel. In high school, Aida had gone through a phase of loving The Pogues, and "Fairytale of New York" quickly became her favorite Christmas song. Mac-Coll's death had left her feeling a deep sadness. "Yes, a tragedy," she agreed.

"Interesting. You seem to know about the disappearances," the woman said, turning to them. It wasn't a question.

For a moment, Aida couldn't breathe. Was this woman from MODA? Luciano must have come to the same conclusion because he tensed next to her before hastily closing his sketchbook and returning it to his bag.

"What do you mean?" he asked, his tone brusque.

The woman exhaled, glancing around the square as if confirming something. "I've been following disturbances like this all over the city. I was drawn here because something about this place felt . . . off. Hollow." She looked back at them, her gaze sharp. "And then I saw you two. That made it even more interesting."

Aida exchanged a glance with Luciano. "Why?"

"This park is gone, much like so many other London attractions. The Twinings tea shop burned down a few months ago.

Madame Tussauds is long shuttered. Gunnersbury Park is being turned into a cemetery. No one is skating at Somerset House this Christmas." She shook her head. "Too much is wrong. The balance is tipping."

A light switch flipped on inside her with the mention of Madame Tussauds. "Dear god, the old folk's home . . . and that juvenile hall. That was where the wax museum was!" Of course. She'd gone there once with her parents when she was ten, and seeing the figures of Henry VIII, Queen Elizabeth I, and Marie Antoinette had fueled her interest in history. How could she have forgotten it? But even as she thought about the museum, the sudden bright memory the woman had given her became hazy.

The woman peered at her. "You're already starting to forget, aren't you?"

"I don't want to forget it . . ." Aida put her hand to her head. "What's happening to me?"

Luciano touched her shoulder. "Are you all right?"

Aida drew herself up, the memory sliding away. "I think so. What were we talking about?"

"Places disappearing," Luciano said. He pointed to the Soho Square sign.

"You only remember that because there's a reminder in front of you," the woman noted, looking at the dangling sign. "But something's ripping these memories from your minds. None of this is right." She put her hands on her hips and sized them up. "Yes. It seems it's a good thing I ran into the two of you today. You clearly know more than you're telling me. Come, I want to understand. My favorite Thai place is nearby, and I would like to hear your story." She started off down the street.

Aida exchanged a look with Luciano, who gave a slight nod. "It's probably the same place I was taking you. We might as well hear her out," he whispered. "But be careful." He held out his elbow once again.

She hadn't needed the warning. And as much as Aida was

intrigued by this stranger, she was also disappointed that she wouldn't be sharing the meal alone with Luciano.

THE HOSTESS RECOGNIZED the woman and immediately led them to a table in the back corner of the bustling restaurant. Once they were seated, the woman regarded them. "You don't know each other well, do you?"

Aida's mouth fell open, and she closed it again.

The woman chuckled. "Ahh, I'm intruding on your evening. You'll have to forgive me for that."

"Who are you?" Luciano asked.

"My name is rather challenging to pronounce. You can call me Sophie."

"Sophie who?" he pressed.

She smiled. "Just Sophie."

"You're with MODA, aren't you?" Aida blurted out.

Sophie's gaze flicked around the restaurant, her expression unreadable. Then, without a word, she raised her hands, palms up, and swept them outward in a slow deliberate arc as if shaping something unseen around the table. The air seemed to tighten, the murmur of nearby conversations dulling to a hush. "That's better. Your devices will no longer work, and no one nearby will overhear us now."

Luciano nudged Aida under the table with his knee. She pressed back, knowing her thoughts echoed his. This woman might not have all her faculties.

Sophie picked up the menu and glanced through it. "No, I'm not with MODA. I'm not with anyone. But I think it would be prudent if you explained to me what MODA is. Let's start there."

"We can't do that," Luciano said.

"I told you no one will overhear us," she said.

"We still can't tell you about MODA."

"Why not? Why ask if I am with MODA and then refuse to tell me about them? What binds your tongues?"

Aside from the archaic language, Aida marveled at how Sophie's expression didn't change. She was perfectly measured, her features neutral, not a speck of irritation or emotion to be seen. For a moment, Aida was reminded of Disa and her often unreadable expression.

"We've each signed an agreement swearing that we will not discuss the nature of our work," Aida explained.

The woman was unwavering. "I give you my aegis."

They stared at her. Aida tried to make sense of her strange proclamation. Finally, Luciano responded, "I don't think your *protection* trumps a legal contract."

Sophie nodded. "A legal agreement. Well, that's something." She waved a hand, and suddenly the waitress was there with a bottle of Chenin Blanc. After pouring the wine, she readied her notepad to take their orders.

"Chor muang, please, for the table. I'll have the green curry." Sophie gestured to Luciano. "He'll have the lamb shank." A glance at Aida. "And for her, the lobster tail pad Thai. Thank you."

Aida watched the waitress depart, dumbfounded. She likely would have ordered that—if she'd looked at the menu.

Sophie gave them a measured smile. "I suspect I've determined your likes well enough. Now then, since you won't tell me about MODA, let's discuss the disappearances. You've noticed them, and you've managed to not entirely forget. That makes you somewhat different from every other person I've met. These are places that slide from the memory, but you are aware of this slippage. Why?"

Aida took a large sip of her wine, hoping it would calm her nerves. Luciano said nothing.

"I see. You don't trust me. I suspect it has to do with whatever MODA is. There was fear in your voice when you mentioned it." Sophie stretched her hands across the table. "Fine. I am loath to do this, but time is short, and I need to know. Each of you put a palm on mine. I'll prove that your trust is not misplaced."

"What will that do?" Luciano asked, his voice on edge.

"Just give me your hand. All will become clear, I swear."

Aida gritted her teeth. She could have been having a nice evening alone with Luciano but instead she was here with this New Age weirdo. She reached out a hand, hoping to hasten along the evening so the woman would leave.

Sophie's hand was warm, her skin softer than Aida expected. She had braced for a firm grip, but Sophie didn't curl her fingers around hers—just let their palms press together. She jutted her chin at Luciano, who sighed and extended his hand.

The moment his skin met Sophie's, warmth surged through Aida—not just heat, but something deeper, something alive. It settled in her bones, humming with a quiet resonance, as if she had tapped into something vast and ancient. A presence older than memory itself. The world around her softened. Doubt unraveled. A quiet certainty took its place.

Sophie's hand seemed to glow beneath hers. Aida parted her lips to speak, but before she could form a word, the warmth unfurled into something else—a flood of understanding crashing over her like a breaking wave.

And then, just as suddenly, Sophie let go.

"You're . . ." Luciano breathed.

"A goddess," Aida finished. Her hand tingled. "But how can that be?"

"Now then," Sophie continued, "do you trust me?"

"Do we have a choice?" Aida asked, an automatic retort that she immediately regretted.

Sophie rolled her eyes. In an elegant gesture, she turned her palm toward the door. "Yes, of course, you have a choice. Get up, go, leave here. Then neither of us will be any further along in our understanding of why the fabric of the world is thinning."

"I trust you," Aida said. "Sophrosyne." She marveled at the deity sitting across from her. "You're the goddess of temperance and restraint."

"You know your myths, I see."

"I devoured the stories when I was young," Aida explained. "And studied Greek and Roman mythology as part of my literature degree."

Sophie gave her a small smile. "Few remember me. Few remember any of us save those whose voices were the loudest, those who are mostly no longer of the earth, who fled this world with Zeus in the Age of Stars."

"Age of Stars?" This was mythology Aida didn't know.

"There's a universe beyond ours that one of our most ancient gods, Uranus, created after the Olympians overthrew him. Tired of things on Earth, Zeus went after him, and many of us followed. Few are left here now. The world is changing. Our influence—and our power—has waned." She paused for the delivery of their food. "Let's eat while you tell me what you know about the disappearances in the world. And of this MODA."

Aida didn't feel much like eating. She was too overwhelmed by their situation. The beautiful purple flower dumplings on the table would have normally brought her great delight, but they paled in comparison to the situation at hand. Besides, who could eat in front of a god? Yet Sophie ate and seemed to revel in the flavors on the plate.

Aida pulled out her notebook with its shorthand scrawls and explained the situation the best she could.

"Which places do both of you remember?" Sophie asked.

Aida looked at the list and named a few, and Luciano chimed in on what he could recall.

Sophie nodded her head. "The places you remember were all destroyed dramatically or publicly. An earthquake, a terrorist attack, a fire." She reached out her hand and Aida relinquished her notebook. "Shorthand. How interesting." She perused the list. "Yes, that must be it. My guess is the places you don't remember, such as this here, the turtle fountain in Piazza Mattei, were quietly closed or dismantled without public fanfare. But the question is why?" She handed the notebook back to Aida.

"I think these events are connected to a deeper shift I'm sensing in the world. It began in the '80s."

"What shift?" Luciano asked.

Sophie sipped her wine. "Some things are subtle. For example, muted—and often boring—color palettes for furniture, cars, beauty, fashion. There's a rise in music with gritty, rude lyrics or dark moody undertones."

"And auto-tune," Aida joked.

To her surprise, Sophie agreed. "That's an excellent example. People no longer rely on talent or their own voices. Instead, they distort and mask it. But those are small things. Dark times are upon the world. It's a laundry list of awfulness that the media loves to cover, because humans have always fed themselves on a diet of fear. And there's a lot to fear in recent years: online trolls, the dark web, crushing economic debt, disinformation, the rise of incompetent and corrupt world leaders, and climate change to name a few. Those things give rise to the widening gap between the rich and the poor, gun massacres, the threat of nuclear war, Christian nationalism, blatant racism, authoritarianism, fascism, Nazism, antisemitism, and on, and on, and on. These are not random events.

"There has always been war, oppression, suffering. The world has never been without darkness. But before, there was balance. No matter how brutal the times, there was still beauty. People still found wonder in art, in nature, in each other. They fell in love, they celebrated, they dreamed. Joy and sorrow coexisted, each keeping the other in check. Now, something has changed. The happiness that once rose to meet the hardship is thinning. People feel it slipping through their fingers, but they don't know why. And in its absence, the weight of everything else grows heavier." She exhaled, her voice lower now. "The world is tilting further out of alignment, and I'm finding it harder and harder to restore equilibrium."

"*Madonna*," Luciano cursed. "Aida, maybe it has something to do with us collecting happiness?"

Sophie leaned in. Her voice was sharp, and her once placid brow lined with concern. "What do you mean? Collecting happiness?"

"We work for a company called MODA. And up until recently, we thought we were singular employees fulfilling the wishes of an eccentric billionaire. We shouldn't even be here together," Aida began. She looked at Luciano, and he gave her a nod to continue. "But it's more complicated than that."

Sophie's gaze darted between them. "What do you actually *collect?*"

Luciano stepped in. "It's not physical happiness. It's more . . . moments. Experiences. MODA sends us to different places, and we observe—people, events, interactions. The idea is to catalog what happiness looks like and feels like in all its forms. At least, that's what we've been told."

Aida nodded, adding, "The goal was never fully clear to us though. We gather details about what makes people feel joy— whether it's a child laughing at a puppet show, or a couple seeing a famous place for the first time. We report back on the nuances of these moments—what we observe and how happiness manifests in these different locations. But recently, we've started piecing together that we're not the only ones doing this."

Sophie raised one eyebrow. "There are others?"

"We think there may be more than two hundred Happiness Collectors, each assigned to a different country or region."

"We just observe and report back," Luciano added. "But as we've discovered the existence of other Collectors, it's raised more questions. What's MODA doing with all this data? What's the endgame?"

Sophie stared at her plate for a moment, then took another long sip of her wine. Finally, she spoke. "I believe that this MODA likely knows what happened to Effie."

"Effie?" Luciano asked.

"My sister Euphrosyne. She's gone missing."

Luciano stared at Sophie, not comprehending.

"Happiness," Aida breathed. "Euphrosyne is the goddess of happiness."

Luciano's eyes widened. "I don't understand. How can a goddess go missing?"

"That's precisely what I want to know," Sophie said. "She's been gone for decades, but we've only just realized it."

"What?" Aida and Luciano said in unison, disbelief etched on their faces.

Sophie sighed. "I know it sounds strange to you, but time doesn't work the same way for us. We're immortal—what seems like a lifetime to you is merely a moment for us. We often go years without seeing each other. Plus, it takes a long time for the effects of something like this to accumulate. We didn't notice her absence at first."

Aida stared at her, speechless.

"Trust me, I've searched to the ends of the heavens and earth for her. Places have been disappearing for a while, but it's only now, when the balance has been widely tipped, that they've come to my notice. I believe that the two are connected. And here you are confirming this suspicion. The work you describe . . . It's purposeful. You're taking stock of places that give people joy. And in doing so, I think you're removing them, which further brings everything out of balance."

"And then our memories of these places are being erased? From everyone? Across the earth? How is that possible?"

Sophie raised an eyebrow at her.

Aida's cheeks grew hot. "Gods, yes, that's right," she said.

"This doesn't make sense," Luciano said. "Why would gods need Happiness Collectors? Why would us writing down details about happiness make things disappear? And if that's the case, why isn't Aida's list also disappearing?"

"It's in shorthand." Aida glanced at the notebook on the table in front of her.

Sophie nodded. "It seems the gods haven't accounted for such ingenuity. Few write in shorthand these days. Your unique method may be why your list hasn't slipped away like every-thing else."

"Thanks, Grandma," Aida breathed.

"Now then, let's talk about why the gods need you. As you know, not all gods are benevolent. When Zeus departed during the Age of Stars, he set forth the Preservation of Order, a set of binding rules for those of us who chose not to go or whom he asked to remain.

"The first rule: Gods are not allowed to kill humans directly. The second is that we can influence or guide humans but cannot override their free will. We can nudge them in a particular direction, plant thoughts, or heighten their desires, but the final choice must always be theirs. Still, it's a small thing—you'd be surprised how easily humans are swayed by what they think they want. The third rule: Once a god has claimed influence over a human, no other god may interfere unless the first god agrees. If a mortal's fate is being shaped by one of us, the rest must keep their distance—unless we reach an agreement to intervene.

"But influence isn't the same as ownership," she continued. "A god can nudge a mortal toward a certain path, but until the mortal actively aligns with them—whether through belief, worship, or true devotion—the claim isn't absolute. MODA shaped your circumstances, yes. They placed obstacles, guided your choices, and made sure the only doors open to you led back to them. But you never gave yourself to them, not fully. You didn't sign that contract knowing who they really were. You followed survival, not faith. That gave me just enough room to act, to speak with you now.

"Those rules were put in place to avoid utter chaos. In the event the gods wanted to return, they would still have a world to return to. Zeus commanded me to remain behind and maintain the balance between good and evil within the world. This was not a difficult task, because with most of the gods departing, the power they had within this world went with them. Gods are only as strong as the worship other creatures afford us. And therein lies the problem." Sophie paused for a bite of her curry.

"And that is?" Aida asked, hoping she didn't sound too impatient.

"Those of us left behind have very little power. And gaining it isn't that easy when most of humanity has forgotten you exist."

"But if the gods can compel humans, can't you rebuild your power?"

"It's not as easy as you might think. You can only compel those who believe in you and are aligned with you. And often, that's subtle and takes place over a long period of time. What do you think of when you hear the word Nike?"

"The shoe," Aida said. "But if you said it in the correct Greek pronunciation, I would know you were talking about the goddess of victory."

"Do you know how many Nike shoes are sold every year?"

Aida shook her head. She'd never liked Nike, preferring sneakers from Superga.

"Roughly seven hundred and eighty million."

Aida's jaw dropped as she took in the unfathomable number.

"The shoe company was founded after the goddess was able to compel the two young founders, both athletes, to name the company after her. But to reach this point of sneaker domination, it took her nearly sixty years. It's a drop in the bucket of time for us but a long time for humans, who die, and more often than not, trends die with them. And it's an odd victory, don't you think? To be the goddess of the most shoes on the planet? But it's a victory, and that's what matters to her."

"But this doesn't explain why things are disappearing," Luciano said.

"I don't know what's happening there. But I have a feeling gods are involved. Tell me more about MODA. Who's running it?"

"It's headed by someone named Lady Ozie." It felt strange to say the name out loud; it sounded so silly. "We've never met her."

Sophie sighed. "I should have known. Another sister. Oizys."

Aida wasn't familiar with that goddess, but Luciano obviously was. "*Cazzo!*" he cursed. "She's also called Miseria."

"Misery?" Aida said, stunned.

"That's why you've never met her," Sophie said. "She sucks all the life out of the room when she enters it. She would cripple you with her nearness. You would have the weight of unfathomable depression upon your heart. She can't simply appear and force despair, so she's using a more insidious strategy. By removing joy—bit by bit—she creates a world where despair can flourish naturally. Without happiness to balance it out, everything tilts further into darkness, and her power grows with every moment of suffering."

She set down her glass, her expression grim. "As misery and chaos spread, it weakens those of us tied to positive forces. Gods like me, who represent peace, temperance, and joy, are drained of our strength. The more the imbalance grows, the less we can do to stop it."

Aida's chest tightened. "So . . . we're helping her? By collecting happiness, we're helping destroy it?"

"Unwittingly, yes," Sophie said softly. "That's how she's stayed hidden for so long. She used you to document happiness, so she could target and erase it. You didn't know, but now that you do, you can help me restore the balance. Happiness is one of the most powerful forces in the human experience. It brings resilience, hope, and connection—all things that protect humanity from despair. By erasing joy, Oizys is stripping away humanity's last defense against her influence. Once joy is gone, misery can take root more easily. If she succeeds, the balance will be shattered, and gods like me will fade. Oizys doesn't just want to cripple humanity—she wants to reshape the world in her image, create a place where only misery thrives."

Aida gripped the table's edge to ground herself, her alarm rising and her heart threatening to leap out of her chest. Her ears and scalp began to tingle. The last time she'd had a panic attack was at her grandmother's funeral, standing by the graveside in the cold, the metal casket gleaming in the sunlight. She'd needed to sit on one of the folding chairs the cemetery had set out for the elderly. Yumi had held her and rubbed her back until she could be calm. Oh! How she wished Yumi were with her now.

Sophie could sense her discomfort. "Aida, please," she said, holding out her hand again.

Aida swallowed and reached out her shaking hand. This time, Sophie curled her fingers around Aida's and she laid her other hand on top, her skin warm and comforting.

"Don't worry. Now I will give you my aegis."

Immediately, Aida's panic fled, and a sense of comfort and safety filled her. "Oh, oh, thank you," she breathed, grateful for the reprieve from the attack on her senses. "I'm . . ."

"No." The goddess stopped her. "Don't ever apologize for your feelings." She let go of Aida's hand and reached for Luciano's. "I give you my aegis."

Aida felt Luciano relax next to her.

"Now, keep in mind you won't be invincible. Gods gain power over humans when the humans believe in them, but my protection renders their direct influence upon you void. Yet careless decisions can still render you vulnerable to other humans under the influence of the gods, so be careful. But you don't strike me as average humans. Use good judgment and you'll be fine."

"Could Mo be a god?" Aida wondered aloud.

"Mo?" Sophie paused, then sadly shook her head. "He didn't even bother with a clever name. I'm impressed at his restraint."

"Who is he?" Luciano asked.

"Momus, my brother. God of, what would you say . . . Snark. Guile. Sarcasm. Cutting wit."

Aida gave a rueful chuckle, remembering the first meeting she had at MODA when Mo told her to get her snark on. "So much makes sense now. What about Fran and Disa?" She described the two women to Sophie.

"Fraus, who is better known as Apate. And Discordia. My sisters."

"Fraus . . . fraud," Luciano explained to Aida. "And discord."

"I'm afraid so. My more nefarious siblings seem to have teamed up. Hence the name MODA. Not all gods care about balance. Some thrive in darkness and gain strength from chaos, deceit, and suffering. This imbalance is an opportunity for them. The more suffering there is, the more powerful they become. It's their chance to rise again, to reclaim the influence they've lost. They don't care that the world is slipping into despair, because they're thriving on it. My guess is that they know exactly what happened to Effie." Sophie took another sip of her wine. "You'll have to help me find out what and why."

"Wait, what? No, I'm done with this. I can't go back to work for them knowing who they are. And you are a goddess! If they are your siblings, you should be able to handle this on your own." Luciano began fumbling for his coat. "Come on, Aida."

Sophie's voice remained calm and measured. "Luciano, this is one of those careless decisions I was referring to that might render my protection void."

He paused. "What do you mean?"

"If they suspect you know anything, do you think they will let you live? There are many ways for them to influence the coming of your death that will override my protection. You can skate below the surface, but as soon as you blatantly show them you are aware of who they are, they'll arrange for your destruction."

Luciano threw up his hands. "Why can't you do anything? After all, this is *your* family trying to destroy all joy in the world."

Aida put a hand on Luciano's arm. He looked at her, took a deep breath, and seemed to relax. She turned her attention to Sophie. "Help us understand."

"Of course. There are two reasons. First, I can't interfere as it would disrupt the very balance I exist to protect. My influence must remain neutral—if I act too directly, I shift the scales in ways I can't control. Worse, my siblings could use my interference as justification to do the same, and they have no interest in balance. If I overstep, I don't weaken them—I strengthen them. Like my siblings, I'm bound by the Preservation of Order. That's why I need you. Since you know of MODA and the missing happiness, you will help me."

Her tone left no question that this was a command. Aida reached for Luciano's hand under the table and squeezed it. He squeezed back and, to her relief, did not let go.

"I don't think I can talk to them again without it being obvious that I know something, much less work to help you fix this," Aida said. Despite Sophie's assurance that the gods couldn't hurt her directly, she couldn't push aside the idea of Discordia sending lightning bolts from her fingers to burn her to a crisp. She was confident the woman despised her.

"That's what my protection is for," Sophie said. "I granted you calm in the presence of gods."

"I don't feel very calm right now." Luciano's words were bitter.

"You don't need protection from me. And I prefer to see you as you are. But in the face of scrutiny by one of my sisters or brothers, you'll find yourself cool as a cucumber. This is important because you'll need to sleuth out where they hide all that happiness. Now think, have they told you what they do with your research?"

"There's a database of sorts." Aida wracked her brain to remember everything that Trista had said about it. "We submit our digital information into a database online. And we meet with them in person every quarter to report on our research. Come to think of it though, a lot of that report is on how the work makes *me* happy."

"That's it then. We need to find out what that database is and where they store it. It's not a real computer. It might have some digital interface, but I assure you, it's something else."

"And how are we supposed to do that? We can't just ask

them. My assistant is a locked box regarding information about MODA." Aida tried to imagine a conversation with Trista about the database. "I think questioning it would set off every red flag she has."

"Mine too," Luciano agreed.

"They must have offices or rooms you can search," Sophie suggested. "Start there." She waved a hand, and suddenly the waitress was there. Reaching into her coat pocket, Sophie pulled out a slim wallet. She extracted several bills and handed them to the woman, who took them with a smile. Sophie stood and put her coat on. "I'll see you soon."

"Wait!" Aida couldn't believe the goddess would just leave them there like that. "How do we find you?"

"You shouldn't need to. Now that you have my aegis, I can easily find you. But if you really have to, I suppose you recall how to pray?" She gave them both a sage nod and departed.

"Pray?" Aida said, looking at Luciano.

He frowned. "I don't remember the last time I prayed." He gathered up his coat and stood. "*Andiamo.* I know a pub where we can get a drink."

Aida followed, her heart pounding at both the idea of complying with a goddess's wishes and going with Luciano off into the night.

16

December 2019

T HEY DUCKED INTO a pub a few blocks from the restaurant, off a side street toward the hotel. Luciano led Aida to a cozy table in a corner, and they ordered beer. Neither of them had said much on the way, but after the waiter deposited their drinks on the table and left, they could hardly contain themselves.

"I don't know how we're going to do any of this," Aida said. She pulled the little red plastic monkey off the side of her glass and set it aside. "The mere thought of presenting to MODA again just brings me terror."

Luciano laid a hand on hers. "Me too. But isn't that what she said her protection is for? To give us calm in the face of the gods?"

Aida's cheeks grew warm with his touch. "Do you really believe that? Why couldn't she have given us a magic shield to keep them from killing us?"

"Well, if she's right, and the gods can't directly kill us, then shouldn't a calm spell protect us? We just can't let on that we know who they are."

"I'm not a great liar," she said, thinking of Mo. Their usual banter, the sharp exchanges that used to feel so effortless, now hung heavy. She hadn't ever fully trusted him—not really—but now, with the truth staring her down, matching wits with him carried a new weight. It would be harder to stay sharp, harder to fire back with the same ease when every word from him might cut deeper than before.

"We've both had our meetings for this quarter. If we're lucky, we won't see any of the gods till we return in three months," he reassured her. "Maybe we'll figure it all out by then."

The weight of those words slammed into her, and a surge of nausea twisted in her stomach. "But, then what? What happens to us? To our jobs? I love this job. I'll never have anything else like it."

"I know." He let go of her hand, which only heightened Aida's sadness. "My family didn't have much money when I was growing up. My father died in a car crash when I was a toddler, and my mother had stage-four breast cancer when I was just out of school. I spent several years taking care of her until she passed. The MODA job gave me stability. For the first time in my career, I've had a salary that means I don't have to worry about paying for anything—car repairs, travel, or a nice dinner out with someone I like."

Aida blushed.

He continued. "I too love this work. But I've always assumed it wouldn't last, so I've been saving and investing in preparation for that day. I never want to worry about how I might pay my rent again."

Aida nodded, understanding that feeling.

"I don't know how I'm going to convince Dolores, my assistant, to tell me anything," Luciano said.

"Me too. Trista barely has kind words for me on a good day."

Luciano drained his glass. "I wonder if we can enlist help."

Aida had been thinking about how she might find a way to safely ask Ilario and Pippa for advice, and she certainly wasn't going to keep this a secret from Yumi or Felix. "Sophie didn't say we can't. But let's be careful. If we have her protection, but others don't, we could . . ."

"Be putting them in danger," Luciano finished. He looked into her eyes.

She melted. "We wouldn't want that."

"We should get back." He broke the gaze to reach for his scarf.

Aida took a breath to calm her racing heart before tipping back the rest of her beer.

AS SOON AS they were out of the pub, Luciano took Aida's hand, which lit the butterflies in her stomach alight. They walked down the street, past the nightclubs and cute restaurants, back to Soho Gardens. As they were passing the dark construction pit in the center of the park, Luciano stopped in the dimly lit doorway of a nearby custom house that had been transformed into a WeWork center. He pulled Aida close.

"I have been wanting to do this all night." Luciano leaned in. His cologne was faint but familiar. He pressed his lips to her forehead, then to the bridge of her nose, the tip of her nose, and then he was kissing her, soft at first, testing. Aida clasped him to her, one hand slipping into his hair, pulling him closer. Their kiss was deep, and it sent shocks of pleasure throughout her.

A whistle and the whoops of some rowdy teenagers broke them apart. "Someone's getting a shag tonight."

"Get a room to bump yer uglies!"

Luciano waved them off with a grin and took Aida by the hand again. Laughing, they headed away from the park toward the holiday lights of Oxford Street.

"Much as I would like to bump your ugly," he chuckled, "I don't think it's a good idea to be seen together at the hotel."

Aida knew he was right. "I must admit my disappointment." She squeezed his hand.

"I think I might need to take a vacation soon. Go back to Italy. See people like you."

"I'd like that." Although she hated the idea of waiting. "I have some ancient Greek gods to contend with, and I'd rather not do it alone."

Luciano pulled her into an alley and kissed her again. "You

won't," he said after he broke the kiss. "Even when we're apart, we'll figure this out together."

Aida didn't have a moment to respond before he led her back onto the street, where he immediately flagged a slow-passing cab. He gave the driver directions, handing him a crisp bill, then opened the door of the cab for her.

She sighed. "I wish I could walk with you."

He gave her a broad smile. "This is safer. And I want you safe."

She leaned up to kiss him once more, breaking off only when the cab driver cleared his throat loudly.

AIDA HARDLY SLEPT that night, her mind turning over and over the meeting with Sophrosyne. The conversation seemed unreal, but the feeling when Sophrosyne touched her hand was undeniable. It wasn't just warmth or reassurance; there was something ancient, something alive pulsing through her skin. Aida had always been skeptical about higher powers, preferring reason and logic. Yet, how could she question the truth now, after feeling something far older than human history flood through her, grounding her to the earth? How could she doubt the existence of gods when one had touched her soul?

The following day on the two-and-a-half-hour flight back to Rome, she picked at her breakfast and barely touched her champagne. The thrill of luxury, which once felt like a dream for a girl from her humble beginnings, was now overshadowed by a growing sense of unease. Each sip of champagne, each bite of gourmet food weighed heavily on her conscience. She looked around the lavish cabin, her eyes tracing the opulent details she had once marveled at. The guilt gnawed at her—the environmental cost of private jets, the excessive indulgences of the wealthy while others struggled for basic necessities, the careless extravagance that seemed so far removed from the real world.

She knew she should savor the experience. How many more of these flights would she have? All this would be gone if she moved forward with what Sophie was asking. Then she felt guilty for thinking such thoughts, holding such selfishness close to her. An internal battle raged within her—the love for this newfound luxury, a life she had never imagined, against the stark awareness of its impact and the superficiality that came with it. It wasn't just the fear of losing the comforts but a deeper conflict about what enjoying these comforts said about her as a person. She used to be someone who cared about the 99 percent. And she hated to admit that she wasn't ready to—and perhaps couldn't yet—give it all up. But the fact that her lifestyle came at an environmental and moral cost began to nag persistently at the back of her mind.

TRISTA MET AIDA at the palazzo door upon her arrival. "You didn't answer my calls or texts this morning. Why not?"

Aida pulled her phone out of the depths of her bag and saw all the missed notifications. She'd been tired from lack of sleep, and so distracted by her thoughts that she had spent most of the flight staring out the window or blankly gazing at the cooking show she had put on the plane's viewing screen, her bag left on another seat on the empty plane. She wished she could have said she'd put it in flight mode, but the private jet had its own satellite service and there was no need.

"I'm sorry. I didn't look at my phone." There was no lie in this, but Aida knew that all the times she had lied about turning off the MODA phone so it wouldn't listen to her conversations with Yumi or Felix had finally caught up to her.

"This is happening too often." Trista frowned. "Why?"

Aida had not been prepared for this interrogation. "It's not intentional, Trista," she snapped. "I'm not trying to thwart you, if that's what you think."

Trista folded her arms across her chest. "A little defensive today, huh? Again, why?"

Aida wished that Sophie's supposed calm spell worked on her in situations that didn't involve the gods. Having Trista suspect her of anything was not wise. "I'm sorry. I didn't sleep well last night and didn't mean to take it out on you."

"Why didn't you sleep? That hotel is the pinnacle of luxury."

"Indigestion," Aida lied.

Trista unfolded her arms but her face didn't soften. "Very well. You're due at Palazzo Spada in an hour. I was texting and calling to remind you."

"Ugh." Aida had forgotten that she was capturing the details of the Galleria Spada museum and its Borromini's Perspective that week. Normally, she didn't work on the days she flew, but the museum was conducting some restorations later in the month that would have interrupted her research. She'd hoped to go right to Yumi and tell her everything about London, but that would have to wait.

"Fine. Let me unpack and I'll head there right away."

"This time, keep your phone handy."

"I promise." Aida sighed.

AIDA HAD BARELY started her walk toward Galleria Spada when Pippa called her name. "I'm off to Campo de' Fiori for artichokes. Can I tag along with ya?" she asked.

"I'd be delighted!" While Aida already adored Pippa, she was extra pleased to be able to walk with her that morning and pick her brain about MODA. Despite her promise to Trista, she slipped her hand into her pocket and turned her phone off, reasoning that her aide likely wouldn't need to reach her in the ten minutes it would take to walk to Campo de' Fiori, a stone's throw from the museum. "I have a question for you." Aida held up her phone and indicated it was off, and Pippa did the same.

"Sure."

"If you had to guess, how do *you* think Johannes died?"

Pippa gave a low chuckle. "Oi, ya feelin' a bit nervous?"

"Should I be?"

"Well, I don't exactly 'ave the answer to that, but I've said before, I don't think Johannes's death was as simple as what the coroner said. That bloke was a proper picture of 'ealth. He was a veggie, never touched a cig or even a spliff, and went joggin' by the Tevere every mornin'."

"But sometimes healthy people have genetic issues that no one knows about until it happens," Aida reasoned.

Pippa shrugged. "Could be, could be. But in the weeks before 'e died, I 'eard 'im and Trista fightin' more. And as a peace offerin', or at least that's what she said when she came to pick up the tray, she started bringin' 'im 'is afternoon tea."

Aida stopped in her tracks. "Wait, what are you suggesting?"

Pippa put a hand on Aida's shoulder. "I'm tellin' ya if Trista starts offerin' to make ya tea every day, ya might want to steer clear of 'er kindness."

Aida took a deep breath to stop the panic that threatened to overtake her. "What were they fighting about?"

"I don't remember much, 'cept that Johannes didn't like the way MODA was doin' things, and Trista was gettin' fed up with 'im questionin' 'er. One day 'e told me 'e was thinkin' of quittin', but we didn't finish the chat 'cause Dante arrived and needed my 'elp with somethin'. I didn't see Johannes for a few days, and then we got the news 'e died of a 'eart attack. We got a few weeks off, came back a couple days before you arrived. It was all very sad and strange. I liked the bloke."

"Was there any police investigation?"

Pippa threw back her head and laughed. "Oh, dear girl, do ya really think that MODA, with all that cash they've got, would ever get investigated? 'Specially 'ere in Italia, where it's easy to grease a palm?"

Aida knew she was right. Italy had long been listed as one of the most corrupt countries in Europe. While she had personally only met upstanding people, she knew the country's bureaucracy and authorities were rife with corruption. MODA often paid for access to the sites she cataloged, but this was a deeper aspect to the story.

Pippa's tone shifted, filled with concern. "So, what's goin' on? Why are ya worried?"

Aida hesitated, not sure if she should put Pippa in danger. She opened her mouth to speak and shut it again.

"Aida, you can trust me and Ilario. I don't think there's another soul in that 'ouse I'd say the same about, but we don't 'ave any great loyalty to MODA beyond our fat bank accounts."

Aida caved. She liked the idea of having an ally in the palazzo. "I have some worries about MODA that I can't explain just yet, but I want to find out if they are true."

"Come on, let's keep walkin'. Can't 'ave ya bein' late." Pippa started back down the street and Aida fell into step. "Tell me, 'ow ya gonna find out?"

"I want to search Trista's office, but I'm unsure how to get near it. She's always there, or she's with me." Aida was about to say she had sometimes heard people talking with Trista in her office late at night—it had happened several times during Aida's middle-of-the-night palazzo strolls when she couldn't sleep. She had always wondered who was with her and had come to assume these chats were video calls Trista was having with another part of the world. But if MODA were comprised of ancient gods, they must be able to show up at will whenever they wanted. The idea of snooping through Trista's office suddenly seemed even less intriguing, if that were possible.

"Ah, well, I can 'elp ya with that. Make it easy for ya to get in there."

"How can you do that?"

"She usually 'as a spot of decaf tea at night before she kips. I can make sure she'll really sleep."

Aida didn't want to know any more details.

Jumping out of the way of a passing Vespa, Pippa continued, "When do ya want to do it?"

Aida hesitated. What did she really think she'd find in Trista's office? And what would she do once she found it? She wasn't sure she wanted to be so quickly out of a job. Or in jail. And if she was looking for information about a database, she needed Yumi's help.

"Not just yet. I'll let you know soon." Campo de' Fiori loomed ahead at the end of the street, its white-capped market tents glowing in the morning sunshine.

"Right, then. You just give me the sign, and that night she'll be sleepin' like a baby." Pippa pulled her phone out of her pocket and flipped it back on. "Ahh, my artichokes." She gave Aida a little salute, then headed past several vendors with cheap tourist trinkets toward a stall laden with vegetables.

Aida turned on her phone and headed toward Palazzo Spada, just a few streets away. She paused to take photos of Giulio Mazzoni's stucco sculptures of Roman heroes and emperors, as well as the facade of the opposing building across the *piazzetta*, and a beautiful fountain adorned with a nymph with arms crossed over her breasts and a lion spewing water into a scalloped basin.

SHE SPENT THE next two hours in a sleepy haze, voice cataloging the collection of sixteenth- and seventeenth-century paintings. She felt blind to the beauty of the immense main hall with its statues and ceiling-to-floor arrangement of paintings. The rooms were filled with works by Guido Reni, Titian, Jan Brueghel the Elder, Guercino, Rubens, Dürer, Artemisia Gentileschi, Caravaggio, and others, but she would have to return to truly appreciate the beauty of the objects before her.

For the first time in her work at MODA, she was slogging through a job, rather than doing something she loved. Part of it was fatigue, but most of it was a heavy haze of worry about what she was supposed to do with the knowledge handed to her by the ancient Greek goddess Sophrosyne, who, up until yesterday, Aida thought was a myth.

But when she came to the most important feature of Palazzo Spada, the optical illusion added by Borromini to the courtyard over a hundred years after it was built in 1540, Aida perked up a bit. She stared down into the forced perspective gallery of columns toward the statue of Pompey the Great, trying to work out the trick of it. The statue looked far away—the length of two bowling lanes—and one sensed that it was a big piece of art. But she knew it wasn't, that instead, it was merely thirty feet away, and the statue was only slightly higher than her knee.

She was about to begin recording her impressions when an abrupt Zen came over her, an unusual calmness and connection with herself. She was no longer tired, and instead was alert yet placid. She could gaze upon this halcyon scene for hours and be perfectly content.

"Marvelous, isn't it?"

Aida turned toward the voice, intrigued at her lack of alarm at the sudden sound in the quiet courtyard. She'd heard no crunch of gravel signaling another soul crossing the expanse to reach her.

Disa stood a few feet away, adorned in a tailored jacket in ecru wool bouclé, stunning on its own but made even more so by the glossy black trompe l'oeil snake that formed the jacket's collar, its mouth latched onto its body a few inches from the end of its tail. Her black crop pants were simple by comparison. Her long black hair was smoothly twisted with a white ribbon and styled in an intricate updo, the strands artfully pinned in place.

Aida was aware that she should be alarmed at the sudden appearance of this woman, who she now knew was the goddess Discordia, but she wasn't. Sophie's spell really did work. Maybe too well. *A bit of surprise would be wise*, she thought to herself.

"Oh, Disa! You startled me," she said with an awkward chuckle that she hoped only lent to the deception. This time, she couldn't help but comment on the woman's wild outfit. "Is that jacket . . . Schiaparelli?" Aida had long admired the fashion house's work, famous for its outlandish designs.

"It is." Disa flashed her a rare smile. Only then did Aida realize the white ribbon in her hair wasn't a simple accessory but another snake, its tiny head clasped to the goddess's ear like an earring.

"It's stunning." Aida looked back at Borromini's Perspective, marveling at how she stood between two things that were not as they seemed. *And I am not what I seem*, she thought, grateful for the calm Sophie had given her. "I didn't expect to see you here."

"I'm in the city visiting my sister who's down on her luck. I had some free time, and I thought I would see how your work is going."

Aida didn't believe her. Perhaps the goddess suspected Aida knew more than she should. "I wondered why you weren't in London. I had no idea we'd exchanged locations." She emitted another forced laugh. "The work is going well. I'm always in awe of the genius of the Renaissance artists. And Borromini was one of the best. For someone whose life was full of darkness, he left us so much beauty," she said, referring to the artist's bipolar disorder, which eventually led to his suicide.

"His chaos was his best feature," Disa said, looking toward Pompey in the false distance. "It was the source of his genius."

Any doubts that Aida had about Disa's deism disappeared with that remark. Of course, Discordia would appreciate Borromini's eternal conflict. She was a being who thrived on the unpredictable and who reveled in bloodshed and strife. Aida's memory of the myths wasn't as strong as Luciano's, but she knew some of them, including the story of the golden apples.

The apples! The bowl on the table in the Boston hotel where she'd had the MODA interview—on top of the pile of apples had been a single golden one. The Apple of Discord. Calm from the aegis tamped down any emotion tied to that realization.

Disa left Aida's side and undid the rope that blocked visitors from walking down the colonnade. She strode toward the statue.

Aida watched, her mind swirling with the story of Discordia, the goddess who was not invited to the wedding of Peleus and Thetis. Furious, she went anyway and threw a golden apple inscribed "To the Fairest" among a crowd of attending goddesses. What ensued was a battle between Hera, Aphrodite, and

Athena over the apple that not only disrupted the wedding but also brought about the Trojan War.

Disa reached the statue, her elegant silhouette towering above the stone helmet of Pompey. She looked like a giant. "This is the best of his brilliance, captured in this illusion." Although she appeared very far away, she was close enough that she had no need to raise her voice.

Aida pulled her MODA phone from her pocket and lifted it to take a photo.

Disa's visage transformed into anger. "Don't. I didn't give you permission to capture my image."

Aida had half assumed she wouldn't be able to get away with taking a photo of the goddess, but it was the most natural reaction to such a scene. Any other person would have been delighted to have their photo taken in such a context.

"I'm so sorry," Aida said, hoping she sounded contrite. "I didn't take it, I promise."

Disa left the statue's side and walked toward Aida, her giant form growing smaller and smaller until she was at the gallery entrance and her height returned to normal.

"That reminds me," she said as she neared. "Trista tells me you've been having problems with your phone. Should we have it replaced?"

Aida marveled at how normal her heart was beating in the face of such direct confrontation about her phone. She should have known Trista would bring it to her superiors' attention. "No, I think it's more of a connectivity issue. The signal's been spotty when I'm moving around, and sometimes the reception cuts out completely in certain areas. Plus, I've noticed the sound randomly mutes when the connection is bad." She made an effort to look pained. "I apologize if I've caused any concern."

"Not concern. But being available is part of the agreement you signed."

"Yes, of course. I'll be more attentive."

Disa nodded. "Good. Although, I commend you for bringing some mayhem into Trista's life. That woman is such a bore." Without saying goodbye, she turned and walked back across the courtyard toward the entrance.

Aida could feel Sophie's calm sliding away, leaving her shaking and her heart beating so hard she needed to sit down on the nearby edge of a planter. She immediately texted Yumi to tell her that she would no longer be able to get away with turning off her MODA phone.

What will we do? I have so much to tell you.

It seemed an interminable wait for Yumi's return text.

Don't worry, I'll figure something out.

17

December 2019

L ATE IN THE AFTERNOON, Aida met Yumi at a café in busy
Campo de' Fiori, a place where she hoped the sound could
help mask some of their conversation. She had picked a café with
outdoor seating and heat lamps, with plush velvet couches facing toward the busy piazza, which had become a chaotic mix of
vendors tearing down their market stalls, little street-sweeping
trucks that cleaned up after them, and tourists wandering around
looking for a spot to get a drink. Aida also hoped that by sitting
next to each other on the couch they could whisper without her
phone picking up very much.

On her way over, Aida received a text from Yumi with instructions to check her email and download the app that she
had just sent her. Aida paused to install it, but when she opened
it, she couldn't understand what it was supposed to do. There
was just a blank screen with a big purple button in the center.
When she pushed it, the button turned a glowing, slightly pulsing pink, but it didn't seem to do anything else.

When Aida reached the café, Yumi had already secured a
couch in the back, off to the side, slightly apart from the other
couches and tables. She waved Aida over and gave her friend a
wordless hug when she arrived. They sat, and Aida handed Yumi
her unlocked phone. Yumi indicated with a few hand motions
to put both phones in her purse.

The waiter arrived and deposited two Aperol spritzes and a little bowl of potato chips.

"I took the liberty of ordering," Yumi said, keeping her voice a little lower than normal. "Okay, so that app is essentially voice camouflage. You won't want to use it all the time, but when we get together, it's a good idea. I have one on my phone too. And I sent it to Felix."

"How does it work?"

"Your voice can be easily listened to when you make a call, but when you aren't on a call and your phone is *listening* to you . . ." Yumi flashed air quotes with her hand. "It's actually doing a speech-to-text translation, which is more efficient, particularly on the battery. Then, whoever accesses it can check the transcript later. To listen to you 24/7 would be tedious."

Aida smirked at her.

Yumi laughed. "Sorry, but it's true! Now, transcripts aren't foolproof, but they can generally give the reader a sense of the conversation. The app you downloaded quietly broadcasts external sounds similar to your voice cadence to mess up that transcript. It will be clear that there are words being spoken, but they'll be pretty garbled. It's not that much different than if you were in a super busy place, so hopefully, it won't attract too much attention to you."

Aida was still nervous, but she trusted Yumi. She took a big gulp of her spritz and proceeded to tell her friend about London.

When she was finished, Yumi shook her head. "Unbelievable."

"I know."

"Not only everything you just told me about the nefarious machinations of what we once thought was a mythical pantheon, but also that you were with Luciano and you haven't bothered to share if you got it on with him yet."

Aida laughed at Yumi's elaborate speech and her friend's singular focus on her love life. "We kissed, all right? But that's all."

Yumi jabbed Aida in the ribs with her elbow. "That's a start."

Embarrassed, she changed the topic back. "We can talk about Luciano when I have more to tell you. But right now, we have more important things to worry about. Like how on earth I will figure out what this database really is."

"You mean how *I'll* figure it out," Yumi said, tipping back her spritz. "I'm the hacker, remember?"

Aida hesitated. "It's not just a regular database though. Sophie made it sound like it's something . . . different. Not purely digital."

Yumi raised an eyebrow but wasn't deterred. "If you're recording information into it, then technology is involved in some way. It might have a strange interface, but there's still going to be a system behind it, and I have a way with technology." She said this in a sultry, exaggerated voice that made them both laugh. "You have your work laptop with you, right?"

"I have my personal one too."

"Work first."

Aida pulled it out of her bag and dutifully logged in when Yumi asked her to.

"Wait, can you hack into it from that laptop?"

Yumi shrugged. "I'm not sure. In theory, it's possible. But I suspect you don't have access to the database itself."

Aida sipped at her spritz and scanned the crowd while Yumi fiddled with her laptop. Finally, her friend grunted in frustration.

"It's as I suspected. You can send commands to the database and input data, but it doesn't allow you to directly view or access the stored data. That's in case any of you Collectors get grand ideas. This device is mostly useless to us." She grabbed her phone and began to type into it, looking up periodically at the laptop screen.

"Mostly?"

She grinned. "I have all the network access I need now. It's interesting—aside from your one-way connection, the rest of your laptop is rather sloppily set up. That bodes well for us, and hopefully the rest of their systems are managed so haphazardly."

She handed the laptop back. "Okay, can you leave your personal laptop with me overnight?"

Aida swapped the MODA laptop with her personal one. "So, I still have to find my way into Trista's office?"

"Unfortunately. Meet me here tomorrow at the same time, and I'll bring you your laptop. You'll need it when you break in." She picked up her drink. "In the meantime, I propose a toast."

Aida squinted at her but raised her glass.

"To making our own *Mission: Impossible* movie!" She clinked the wineglass to Aida's.

Aida rolled her eyes. "Yumi, we don't want this to be impossible!"

"It won't be. Trust me."

THIRTY HOURS LATER, with her heart pounding and her messenger bag slung over her shoulder, Aida cracked open the door from her office to Trista's and slipped in, using only the dim light from her phone to guide her through the dark room. That morning at breakfast, she had told Pippa to go ahead and spike Trista's tea. After waiting an hour past the designated time, she made a brief reconnaissance walk through the palazzo, ready to feign sleeplessness if anyone stopped her. She walked by just as the light under Trista's bedroom door went out, signaling the coast was clear.

She settled into the desk chair, grateful for the lights from the garden that filtered into the room. She then set up her personal laptop, equipped with a network spoofing program Yumi had installed. This program was designed to mask her device as authorized on the network. Yumi had explained that, under normal conditions, an unexpected device might trigger alerts, but given the generally lax security measures they'd observed, she was hopeful the system administrators would overlook any minor discrepancies.

Aida logged on to the network, her fingers crossed that Yumi's setup would prevent her from standing out. She located Trista's computer on the network and set up a secure connection to Yumi for backup. Each second felt like an eternity as she waited, her anxiety mounting at the thought of Trista deciding to return and catching her in the act. But finally, she received a text from Yumi saying that her friend had figured out the password.

Aida held her breath as she attempted to log on to Trista's computer. When it failed the first time, she almost aborted the whole project, but then, she reasoned, she often put in her own computer password wrong, so she tried again. She closed her eyes, wishing for the password to work, and when she opened them, she was rewarded with the familiar MODA logo on a stark red background, along with an array of desktop icons.

Aida followed the rest of Yumi's instructions to establish a VPN connection between the two computers and allow remote access. A few keystrokes on the keyboard later, she was nervously watching a transfer of the data, the progress bar slowly inching forward.

When it reached the halfway point, there was a squeak of footsteps in the marble hallway. Aida tilted the covers of both laptops downward to minimize the light. She had a light scarf around her neck and hastily pulled it off to further dampen the light. The footsteps grew closer. Aida froze. She was afraid to even breathe. She didn't know what she would do if Trista suddenly opened the door.

If anyone opened the door.

At least it's not a god, she rationalized. Sophie's spell had not activated any sort of calm within her. The footsteps stopped somewhere outside the door, and for a moment, there was silence.

Aida took a thin breath and began counting, a method a past meditation teacher had once taught her to manage stress. On the count of eight, the sound of the footsteps started again, then faded away, and Aida let out a sigh of relief. It must have been the security guard.

Finally, the transfer completed. Aida opened Signal on her personal laptop and sent Yumi a message. Are you in?

There was a long anxious pause before Yumi responded. I'm in. Give me five or ten.

Hurry. Someone is wandering around out in the halls.

Her friend sent her a thumbs-up.

Aida stared at the screens, wondering what Yumi might possibly find. After a few long minutes, a message popped up on Signal. It wasn't Yumi. It was Luciano.

Tutto va bene?

They had briefly video-chatted that morning and even through the small screens it had been evident Luciano was more than a little nervous about her plan to break into Trista's laptop.

Everything's all right. Waiting for Yumi right now. Will update you on the successful mission later.

I admire your confidence. Be careful. xxxx

Aida's heart jumped at the kisses.

A crash down the hall made Aida physically jump. Her hand flew to the lid of her laptop, and as it went down, she saw Yumi's message on the open Signal screen. Finished.

She didn't have time to celebrate. She hurriedly closed out the programs on Trista's computer, grabbed her own laptop, and went back to her office. After dumping her laptop at her desk, she rushed out to see what the commotion was.

Far down the hall, a huge vase of flowers had been overturned from its pedestal, leaving a mess of water, pottery shards, and dahlia, snapdragon, sweet pea, and gardenia flowers everywhere.

Dante stood over the chaos, strangely dressed in a faded tracksuit and a set of AirPods in his ears. He waved his hands at two sleepy maids who had just arrived on the scene.

"What happened?" Aida asked as she drew near.

Dante looked at her, horrified. "I bumped into it. I was . . ." He trailed off, holding his phone awkwardly. Before he turned the screen off, Aida could see it was open to a TikTok video. Social media wasn't banned on the MODA phones, but Aida hated the idea of the company tracking everything she did and never used it while she was in the palazzo. Dante was clearly flustered to have her see him in such disarray. "I apologize if I bothered you, Miss Reale."

"No, no bother. I couldn't sleep. I was reading in my office," she said. It must have been Dante who had paused in the hallway, caught by some video.

"We'll have it cleaned up right away."

Aida nodded and made her way back to her office. She fell into her plush desk chair and sat there, staring at the closed laptop on her desk.

After her heart had stopped its frenetic dance, she opened the laptop and logged back on, grateful to finally have some sort of network access on a personal device within the palazzo, even if she hardly dared use it. She opened Signal and typed a message to Yumi. You got what you needed?

A few moments later, Yumi replied.

Not exactly, but I have enough information to dig further. Find me tomorrow.

AIDA COULD HARDLY SLEEP. She had sent one brief Signal to Luciano to let him know the task was complete, and afterward she lay in bed thinking about the break-in, the danger she was in, and that her whole life had suddenly been turned on its head. At some point, she drifted into dreams, and when her alarm sounded at 7:00 a.m., Aida's only thought was to turn it off and keep sleeping. A knock on the door later that morning startled her awake.

"Aida?"

Fuck. It was Trista. Aida sat up. *Does she know?*

She glanced at the bedside clock and saw it was nearly nine. "I'm coming!" She swung her feet off the bed and into her slippers. "I overslept."

Aida grabbed her robe and went to the door. When she opened it, Trista nearly fell in.

She straightened herself. "Well, out of all days to shirk your duty, I suppose this is a good one. I came to tell you the museum had a break-in last night, and you won't be able to return until after the investigation is wrapped up." Trista's brow was furrowed. She was wringing her hands, clearly irritated. It must be an actual break-in and not something MODA had planned. And even better, she didn't appear to know about Aida's intrusion in her office.

"What did they steal?"

"They aren't sure of everything yet, but so far, they've only verified two tiny marble busts on a table below the painting of Cardinal Bernardino Spada are missing. But weirder, the burglars knocked all the oranges off the trees in the courtyard, and they forked the lawn. Thousands of forks."

Aida couldn't keep her jaw from falling open. "Wait, they forked the lawn? Like a high schooler would? I thought that was a US thing."

"I'd never heard of it. But the entire lawn was full of plastic forks."

Aida kept herself from smiling at Trista's rare admission of ignorance. "Doesn't the museum have cameras everywhere?"

"The thieves cut the power, so they didn't work."

It was a lesser-known, privately owned museum, and Aida guessed they might have thought they would never need to worry about having a generator to keep the cameras from going down.

"Did they harm the Borromini?"

Trista shook her head. "But they put all the fallen oranges in neat lines on the arcade path leading to the statue of Pompey. An elaborate prank."

"What on earth?" Aida couldn't wrap her head around it.

"At any rate, they won't be allowing you back in for at least the next two weeks until they complete the investigation and do a thorough inventory. You have some time to yourself. Take a vacation."

"Oh," Aida said, stunned at this turn of events.

"Or go back to sleep if you want." She headed back down the hall, and when she turned the corner, Aida retreated back into her room to ring down to the kitchen to have them bring her some coffee.

It was Pippa who delivered it. "You done good, yeah?" she asked in a low voice as she deposited a tray of coffee and cornetti filled with Nutella on the table.

"I think so. I'm not the one making sense of things, but what you did helped me get the information I needed. I owe you one."

"Don't fret, it ain't nuffin'. I hope ya find what yer lookin' for. If ya need anythin', let Ilario and me know. These people ain't normal, and us lot doin' their dirty work need to look out for each other."

Aida had to smile at Pippa's offer of solidarity. If she knew ancient Greek gods were involved, the sous-chef might change her mind.

"I wish there were a shot of sambuca in that coffee," she joked.

Pippa nodded in approval. "Yer wish is my command, luv. I'll be back in a jiffy with yer liquid courage."

"I was joking, Pippa. But also, I thought it was liquid hope?"

"Today it's courage, innit? You seem like ya might need it."

Aida sighed. "I do, I do."

"Cor, then I'll be bringin' ya some. No, no, arguin'."

AFTER AIDA HAD dressed and downed the *caffè corretto* Pippa brought with a heavier dose of sambuca than she was used to, she headed out of the palazzo toward Piazza Navona, feeling a little fuzzy but glad for the warming liquor.

When she arrived at Yumi's rented flat, she was surprised to find Felix there.

He folded her into a hug. "Dear god, Aida, what have you gotten yourself into?"

Aida couldn't help but laugh. "Felix, you seem to forget that it was *you* who got me into this mess!"

"Ahh, yes, I suppose I did," he said sheepishly. "I am sorry about that. Never again will I try to help you find your dream job."

Yumi put a finger to her lips to shush them. "You can put your things in my bedroom." Yumi gestured at Aida's purse.

When Aida returned from depositing her MODA phone where it wouldn't register their conversation, Yumi waved them to sit on the couch and launched into an elaborate explanation of how she attempted to hack into the MODA database. It was all over Aida's head, and between her lack of sleep and the spiked coffee, Aida found it difficult to concentrate.

Felix finally snapped. "Stop! Can you simplify? You're putting Aida to sleep."

Aida startled at the sound of her name.

"Sorry. Let me make you a *caffè*." She headed to the open kitchen but didn't stop her explanation. "Long story short—I can see how the information gets to the database, but getting into it is, well, unusual. There seems to be some sort of key that is needed to unlock it."

"A key?" Aida asked over the sound of the espresso machine.

"Yes, but it's not like any other sort of passcode or access point I've ever seen."

"That doesn't sound promising," Felix said.

"It's not. I don't know what I can do at this point. I need to know more about the database."

Aida groaned. "And where are we going to find out that information? We don't even know where the database is."

"That's not true." Yumi came around the edge of the bar to bring Aida her espresso. "I *think* it's in London."

"But you aren't sure?"

"The IP address is attached to a firewall that obscures the precise location, but that address is in London and since MODA is based there, it's my logical conclusion. But standing in front of it doesn't get me the key."

"We also don't have any idea where it might be in London. It seems odd that it would be at the hotel," Aida pointed out. "I mean, they must only go there for meetings. I can't imagine they run the business out of there."

"Unlikely, unless MODA somehow owns the building."

Felix chuckled. "Well, if you say we're dealing with ancient gods, then why not?"

Her personal cell phone buzzed in her pocket. "It's Luciano."

"Go ahead, take it. We'll watch." Yumi exchanged an amused glance with Felix.

Aida rolled her eyes at them and took the call, smiling when she saw him brush away a lock of dark hair that had fallen into his eyes.

Yumi waved at her. "Tell him about the app!"

Aida turned the phone around to introduce Luciano to Yumi, who he hadn't yet met. She gave him the lowdown on the voice-canceling app, then Aida told him about the two break-ins: their attempt at the laptop, and the chaos at Palazzo Spada. "But the good news is that I've got two weeks off—which is two weeks without Trista always bothering me."

"They'll still track you," Felix pointed out.

"But it's less suspicious if I go places on vacation."

"I'm due for a vacation," Luciano said wistfully.

Felix raised his voice. "Come to Rome. That's where the party is."

Luciano shook his head. "I've been thinking, if they are tracking us, they'll see that we know each other, which is risky."

Aida's heart began to flutter at the idea of Luciano coming to Rome, but she knew he was right. In London, they were both supposed to be there. And now that she had explicit instructions to stop turning off her phone, that would make it even harder because MODA would track them to the same locations.

With a heavy heart, she changed the subject. "Have you had any luck with Dolores?"

Luciano shook his head. "I tried asking her more about MODA, but she seems suspicious of my motives. And I'm not sure I can trust anyone else in the château. I'm going to try a different tactic. Today, I'm working at the Luxembourg Gardens, focusing on the beehives and the beekeeping school."

"Oh dear god, not the bees!" Yumi exclaimed.

Luciano nodded. "I know. But I'm going to see if I can learn more from the school headmaster about how MODA works with him." He looked at his watch. "I need to get going. I'll let you know if I learn anything." He gave a wave, and then the call went black.

Felix began gathering his things. "I need to go too. Have a tour to give in twenty minutes. Stay out of trouble."

Yumi plopped down on the couch next to Aida when he was gone. "Are you sure about the whole ancient god thing?"

Aida sighed. "You don't believe me?"

"I do. You're Miss History, not Miss Fantasy. But you have to admit, it seems so far-fetched."

"I wish it weren't real." As the words left Aida's lips, the emotion of the last few days overcame her, and she began to cry. Yumi folded her friend into her arms.

"We'll figure it out. You aren't alone in this," she said, smoothing Aida's hair. "We've figured out a lot so far, haven't we?"

Aida nodded, then pulled away before she soaked too much of Yumi's blouse. She wiped her eyes with her hands. "We have. And you know what I'm good at?"

Yumi raised an eyebrow.

"Research. I want to know everything I can about this whole thing. About these MODA gods, now that we know who they are. Maybe we'll find a connection to a key."

"Now you're talking." Yumi jumped off the couch to grab her laptop. "And we should search for information on Euphrosyne too. The database is only one component of this whole thing according to Sophie."

Aida didn't want to mention that it was likely the captive didn't have the key to her own cage. But she couldn't just sit there—she had to do something, anything, to not focus on the fact that everything she had once loved about her work in Rome had completely and utterly changed.

December 2019

AIDA AND YUMI spent the rest of the day poring over Wikipedia, JSTOR, Academia.edu, and ancient Greek and Roman mythology journals, looking for every bit of information they could about Euphrosyne and MODA. They scoured countless images of the Three Graces, wondering if there was a hint of truth in them—could the goddesses have actually modeled for Botticelli? Or inspired him?

They only found one brief mention of Euphrosyne and Sophrosyne being sisters, and it was merely a passing note that they were both borne of the primordial gods Erebus—darkness—and Nyx—night. It turned out that Nyx was a rather prolific goddess, with over forty children, most minor gods, including doom, madness, prudence, and even the Fates and the Furies. And only one story mentioned that Sophrosyne was one of the good spirits let loose by Pandora when she opened the jar, which also let evil into the world.

Regarding MODA, there was also scant information about the various gods who seemed to make up the organization, save for a few mentions. Momus, who was Oizys's twin, was so annoying that Zeus had ejected him from Mount Olympus. In fact, the only being who Momus seemed to have little criticism of was Aphrodite, whose only fault, according to him, was that her sandals squeaked. Over the years, mankind had begun painting Momus as less of an ass and more of a lighthearted comedian, a harlequin. The French even began depicting him on their cards as the Fool, which gave Aida a chuckle. She wondered what Mo thought of such a portrayal.

"I'm starting to get a headache from staring at this screen," Yumi said. "And we've not found anything useful."

"We did discover that all the gods we know of at MODA were born of Nyx, which validates what Sophie said—that they are her siblings."

Yumi shrugged. "But how does that help us? We're still no closer to figuring out how to crack into that database. Maybe you should try to reach Sophie." She motioned toward Aida's personal cell phone on the table in front of them.

"She didn't give me her number."

Yumi's eyes widened. "Well, how are you supposed to contact her?"

Aida reached for Yumi's hands. "We pray."

Yumi started laughing, but she didn't let go. "Seriously? Okay, okay."

Aida squeezed her friend's hands, then closed her eyes and bowed her head. "Dear Sophrosyne . . ."

Yumi snorted. "You aren't writing a letter!"

"But prayers start with 'Dear God'!"

Yumi frowned, then rolled her eyes. "Forget I said anything, go forth and pray!"

"Stop the giggling, and I will!"

After a few starts and stops punctuated by bouts of uncontrollable laughter, they calmed enough for Aida to attempt an awkward prayer.

"Dear Sophrosyne, oh, goddess of balance and temperance, we ask that you come to us, so we may speak to you about the database."

Aida began to withdraw her hands, but Yumi stopped her. "Do we say *amen?*"

Aida shook her head. "That's Hebrew."

Yumi let go of her hands. "Now what?"

"I guess we wait."

Yumi flipped on the TV. "*Grande Fratello* is on. I'm obsessed."

"*Big Brother*? How can you watch that? You barely understand Italian!"

"Eh, the drama is all the same."

After an hour of watching the Italian Big Brother House guests do a whole lot of nothing, Aida began to believe Sophie wasn't going to respond, which she found equal parts disconcerting and annoying. Finally, she reached for the controller and flipped off the TV. "Let's get out of here. I need an *aperitivo*."

Ten minutes later, they were on the rooftop deck of a ritzy bar overlooking Piazza Navona, ordering big glasses of Aperol spritz. They had finished one drink and were about to order another when a blanket of calm enveloped Aida just as a woman approached their table and sat in the extra chair.

She was easily one of the most stunning people Aida had ever seen. Cloaked entirely in ivory, she had an ethereal aura. A delicate silk jacket hugged her lithe frame and a gossamer pleated scarf adorned her neck. Her platinum hair was styled in an exquisite updo, with wispy tendrils framing her alabaster face. Her eyes, like pools of liquid mercury, shimmered beneath gracefully arched brows, their allure heightened by her high cheekbones. Her nails gleamed with a lustrous pearl sheen. Everything about her was exceptional, and she seemed perfectly at home joining Aida and Yumi at their table.

"Hello," Yumi began to say, awe evident in her voice.

"Oh, aren't you lovely," the woman said, cutting her off with a smile. The gentle lilt of her speech carried a calming warmth. Every movement she made was with grace and poise.

"Who are you?" Aida asked, afraid of the answer.

"Aglaea, but you can call me Aggie."

Aida hadn't realized she was holding her breath, and she released it in a sigh of relief. "You're a Charis."

"Yes, that's right. Sophie asked me to meet you."

Yumi almost choked on her spritz. "You're the goddess of

beauty and splendor! One of the Charites! The Three Graces! I read about you today!"

Several people at nearby tables began to stare in their direction, and a few chuckled at Yumi's outburst.

Aggie waved a hand, and immediately they turned away. "Now, now, not so loud. We can't have everyone staring at us."

"How can they not? You're so . . ."

Aggie nodded. "Beautiful, yes, I know. But they see me differently than you are seeing me. To them, I appear as a rather mousy, boring-looking girl who barely managed to comb her hair today. It's easier that way."

"I can't believe I'm talking to a goddess," Yumi said, her voice much lower. "Until now, I didn't believe . . ."

Aida smacked her friend on the arm. "You didn't believe me?!"

"I did, mostly, but I was skeptical about the god part."

Aggie laughed. "Well, I'm here, and I assure you, we are quite real."

Yumi was still gaping. "I don't understand. Why don't you gods just appear to the masses? Who could help but worship you?"

Aggie gave her a kind smile. "It's never been like that. Our interactions are meant to influence human affairs indirectly, guiding or testing mortals rather than overtly altering destiny on a grand scale. Can you imagine? Sophie would go mad with the idea of so much imbalance."

They were interrupted by the scrape of a chair against the tiled floor and an angry shout. A woman threw her drink in her companion's face, then turned to rush off the rooftop, tears streaming.

"Ohh, the poor dear," Aggie said, watching the woman leave. She closed her eyes for a moment, concentrating. Then she turned her attention back to Aida and Yumi. "The tables next to the wet man are tittering about the scene. It seems the woman learned her fiancé has been cheating on her with two other women and confronted him. I fear you'll start to see more and more of that sort of thing as happiness dissipates. That's why I'm here. There is a shift in that precarious balance. We must find Effie. She is somewhere surrounded by sorrow, and her light has dimmed."

"Why did Sophie send you?" Aida asked.

Aggie grinned. "Because you were asking about technology."

Yumi knitted her brow. "You know about technology?"

Aggie patted Yumi's hand. "No, of course not. I can't be bothered with that. But I happen to be married to someone who does."

While Aida had been reading of the Charites earlier, she hadn't dug deep into the history of Euphrosyne's companions. "Forgive my ignorance, but who would that be?"

"Hephaestus, also known as Vulcan."

Of course, Aida thought to herself. The god of the forge, the maker of all the enchanted objects of the myths: Jupiter's thunderbolts, Mars's spear and shield, Achilles's armor, Apollo's bow and arrows, and Mercury's winged sandals, to name a few.

"This might be a silly question, but which names do you gods prefer? The Greek or Roman? I can never keep them straight," Yumi asked.

"Whichever you prefer," Aggie said. "We have many names and realities for humans. Apollo and the Hindu god Surya are the same. The Egyptian god Amun is the same as Jupiter, who is the same as Zeus and the same as Odin. Mithras is the same as Jesus. Ishtar is Athena, and Isis, and Mary. I could go on and on. We use many of the names interchangeably ourselves. Fear not, Yumi, you will not offend by using the wrong name."

"You think Vulcan can help us break into this database?" Aida asked, choosing the easier Roman name for the god.

"I know not, but if there is anyone who knows what the gods can do with machinery, it's him. I paid your bill already. If you are ready, we can go there now."

Aida looked at Yumi, who nodded vigorously. "Yes, let's do it."

"Wait," Aida said, stopping the two from standing. "My

phone tracks me. We think we are able to muddle what it hears, but I can't stop it from knowing where I'm at."

Aggie raised an eyebrow. "Then you'll have to turn it off."

Aida took a deep breath. "I'm not sure that's wise."

Aggie seemed to understand her discomfort. "Just for a little while. We can ask Heph about it."

Reluctantly, Aida found the MODA phone in her bag and turned it off. "All right, let's go."

She followed the goddess and Yumi out of the bar to the elevator. When the doors slid shut, Yumi asked, "Where is he? How will we get there?"

"Like this," Aggie said, taking Yumi's and Aida's hands.

There was the briefest flash of light, and then they were standing in the middle of the Roman Forum next to a fence in front of a sad-looking round brick structure that Aida recognized as the Umbilicus Urbis Romae, the Navel of the City of Rome, or the center of the city from which and to which all the distances of the Roman Empire were measured. Legend had it that the structure was built atop a gate to the Underworld. Aida had spent a lot of time in the Forum since she had come to Rome and knew the structures fairly well, and she was surprised to see the dark opening of a door on one side of the Umbilicus. She was quite certain she had never seen it before.

"I thought the Vulcanal is over there," she said, pointing to a roofed excavation behind the Umbilicus that, although hotly contested among Forum archaeologists, was considered to be the site of the god's ancient forge.

"Well, it is," Aggie agreed. "But under it. Come."

The gate opened before them, and she led them toward the Umbilicus. There were a number of tourists milling about the ruins, but none seemed to notice them. Aggie ducked into the dark space. Yumi didn't hesitate to follow, but Aida paused just long enough that her friend reached back and pulled her through—into a long hallway with a red runner. The atmosphere was surreal, as if the ancient world had collided with modern times. The walls were adorned with frescoes depicting various gods and mythical creatures, illuminated by sleek LED lights.

"How did . . ."

Aggie looked back and shrugged. "Gods, you know."

Aida and Yumi followed the goddess down the hall to a regal marble stairway that led to a landing and a large ornate door made of a strange alloy that seemed to shimmer with an otherworldly glow. Two silver lions rested at the door, and when one of them turned its head toward them, Yumi jumped backward with a shriek, almost falling to the ground.

"It's all right. They won't hurt you with me here," Aggie assured her. Then she placed her hand on the door, which opened with a low hum, revealing the inner sanctum of Vulcan's forge.

A booming voice greeted them. "My love! Give me a second to finish."

The moment Aida stepped inside, she found herself in a world where mythology had embraced the digital age. The room was vast and domed, with an immense anvil at its center, surrounded by all manner of futuristic machines and tools.

At the heart of this breathtaking scene stood Vulcan himself, his tall muscular form draped in a modern heat-resistant outfit. His hair was a dark fiery red that seemed to flicker with the energy of the flames he commanded, cascading down to his shoulders in unruly waves. A neatly trimmed beard framed his strong angular jawline. He was manipulating molten metal using a high-tech holographic interface, his eyes glowing with an intense fiery gaze.

The interface projected a 3D hologram of the workpiece, allowing Vulcan to visualize the desired end product and make adjustments with remarkable precision. Aida had been to a few forges as part of her historical research, but nothing like this. The forge itself was a marvel of modern engineering, seamlessly blending ancient elements with state-of-the-art technology. A central high-efficiency furnace provided the intense heat required for Vulcan's metalworking. Robotic arms with specialized tools waited at the ready. The walls were adorned with touch screens and panels that likely monitored and controlled every aspect of the forge's operation. Several golden humanoid figures worked at various tasks throughout the space. Despite the obvious heat of the forge, Aida was amazed at how cool the room felt. Surrounding the central anvil were multiple workstations, each equipped with a suite of tools and machinery for specific tasks, such as metal casting, welding, and engraving.

Aida and Yumi stood in awe, overwhelmed by the incredible sight before them. Aggie smiled and motioned them forward. "Heph, I brought some friends."

Vulcan looked up. When he saw Aida and Yumi, his face twisted into a scowl. "What is this? Aglaea . . ."

"It's important," Aggie said. "It's about Euphrosyne."

The burly god flicked off the hologram. As he walked toward them, Aida noticed something was off about his gait and understood that some of the myths about his one misshapen leg might be true. He was probably wearing some form of prosthetic.

"Why have you brought mortals to my abode, Aglaea?"

Aggie admonished him. "They can help us. Hear them out."

He folded his arms across his chest and stared down at them. "This better be good. I'd be happy to test out my new lasers on you." He waved a hand at the robotic arms, which Aida realized with shock were aimed right at them.

"Go ahead," Aggie said, nudging Aida.

Aida tried to explain the situation to the intimidating god, ending with the strange circumstances at Palazzo Spada. When she was finished, he let out a string of modern curses and turned back toward the forge. He stood there staring into the fire, which seemed to grow hotter and brighter with his anger.

"The oranges, and forking the lawn. That's my sister's idea of a good time," Aggie explained. "She is the goddess of discord, after all."

Vulcan snorted with derision. When he turned back to them,

his eyes glowed with a dark red heat. "They don't have the ability to create a machine capable of holding the world's happiness. I'm the only one who can do that."

"Then how did they . . ." Yumi began, but Vulcan cut her off with a wave of his hand.

"They must have found Zeus's storeroom."

Aggie gasped. "You mean . . ."

Vulcan nodded. "They have Pandora. And my other creations. Shit, they probably even have my golden dogs."

"I'm not sure we understand," Aida said, glad for the calm spell Sophie had given her. The lasers were still trained on them, and Vulcan's response to the news was terrifying. She could feel Yumi trembling next to her.

"Pandora is an automaton," Aggie explained. "She's a husk waiting for instruction. The first robot, you mortals might say. It is near impossible for humans or gods to see the difference between an automaton and a human. They behave just as humans do, react in all the same ways, and are even as fallible."

"I made hundreds of them, but she's the jewel in the diadem."

"And if she's like a robot, that means she could be programmed," Yumi said in a low voice, understanding tingeing her words.

"Exactly!" Vulcan boomed.

Aglaea sighed. "They're using her to store the world's happiness."

"Has she just been sitting in the storeroom for millennia?" Yumi asked, her voice halting at first but steadier the longer the gods let her speak. "And if so, how could the other gods bend her to their will? I thought she was curious, not malicious?"

"After she unleashed all the evils upon this world, her purpose was complete, and she was rendered immobile. Zeus hid her and the other automatons away." Aggie looked thoughtful. "My bet is that Oizys or Apate have been looking for his storehouse since he left, and finally found Pandora."

Vulcan sighed. "And that's bad."

"Why didn't the gods just keep all their items? Why were they locked away?" Aida asked.

"What we make on Earth is specific to Earth. The gods that went with Zeus during the Age of Stars wouldn't have been able to take them. They would be useless. But they can't be left lying around. So Zeus locked everything up for safekeeping until the day when the gods may decide to return," Aggie explained.

"As for Pandora, if they found her, all they would need to do is change the meander and give her a new purpose. She was already unlocked," Vulcan said. "But I'm sure they have since locked her up tight so other gods can't access her."

Aida didn't understand what he meant about a meander, but in her mind, he was glossing over the most important part. "What does that have to do with Effie going missing?"

"If they've imprisoned Effie somehow, she can't replenish the world with happiness as they remove it," Aggie explained, her voice low and tinged with anger.

"And if they have found the storeroom, they have the means to detain a god. They could do it with any number of items. The necklace I made for Harmonia. The throne I made for my bitch of a mother."

"We don't talk about that," Aggie told him, her voice sharp.

"We have to talk about it!" Vulcan boomed. "If they have the throne, you can bet that's how they've trapped Euphrosyne."

A shadow fell across Aggie's features. "It's how he forced Hera to give him Aphrodite as a wife," she explained to the young women.

"Ahh . . ." Aida breathed, remembering that the god had first been married to Aphrodite. "But that means they also have your net?"

Vulcan's features darkened and Aida wished she hadn't asked the question. "No, it was destroyed when I released them."

Yumi threw up her hands. "Net? Can someone explain all this to me?"

"Go ahead," Aggie said, turning on a heel and going toward a door opposite where they had entered the forge. "But I'm not going to listen to this."

"Don't try anything funny in here. All it takes is one squawk from Bubo there, and those lasers will be happy to take care of you." Vulcan looked toward the corner of the room where a little golden owl with ruby-and-silver eyes sat on the edge of a cabinet. It twisted its head toward them.

Aggie looked back. "Join us when you are done telling the wretched story."

Vulcan followed after his wife. When they had gone, Aida explained to Yumi how Vulcan had made the throne in revenge for being thrown out of Olympus by Hera when she saw that her child was deformed. Years later, Vulcan returned to Olympus as a skilled blacksmith, bringing a golden throne with him as a gift for his mother. She was so delighted with it that she sat on it immediately but was trapped by unbreakable chains that wound around her body. Vulcan agreed to release Hera in exchange for being allowed to marry Aphrodite, and Zeus agreed.

But Aphrodite had an affair with Ares, which Vulcan didn't take kindly to. So he created a net with fine golden chains that were so delicate they could not be seen. Then he pretended to leave for a trip. When Aphrodite lay on the bed with Ares, the chains sprang up and trapped them both. At that moment, Vulcan revealed himself and called the other gods to come and witness the humiliation of his unfaithful wife. Vulcan demanded his dowry back, then kicked her out of his bed and his life. It was said that Aphrodite, out of guilt, later encouraged the relationship between her ex and Aglaea.

"No wonder she didn't want to talk about it," Yumi said, shaking her head. She looked around the room. "Aida, what have you gotten us into?"

"Now you sound like Felix. And let me remind you that you helped convince me it was okay to take this job!"

Yumi hung her head, sheepish. "Fine, I did." She looked

toward the door where Vulcan and his wife had gone. "If you had told me at the beginning that I would end up helping you hack the database of the gods, I would have escorted you directly to McLean myself."

Aida raised an eyebrow at the reference to the psychiatric hospital in the Boston burbs, known for its famous patients Sylvia Plath, Anne Sexton, Ray Charles, David Foster Wallace, and others. "We might both need to visit when this is said and done. Come on."

The room they entered was vast, with high ceilings adorned with frescoes depicting scenes from ancient myths. Warm golden light emanated from sconces lining the walls. Intricately woven carpets graced the floor. Marble columns, masterfully carved with delicate patterns, framed the room, supporting the weight of the vaulted ceiling above. A well-stocked library lined one wall, containing both scrolls and tomes, complete with a cozy reading nook, plush cushions, and a warm flickering fireplace. A tablet, likely for reading, lay on a side table. Four golden women—automatons—stood stationed in each corner, immobile, but Aida was sure they were ready to move at a moment's notice. In the center of the room, there was a large circular seating area filled with comfortable oversize chairs and couches, upholstered in the finest fabrics. Aggie and Vulcan were seated there, locked in a low heated conversation.

Aida cleared her throat. Aggie looked up and waved them over.

"Now then," Vulcan said, looking at Yumi after she had sat down. "The gods seem to have accessed Pandora and probably all the other automatons. It will be up to you to find her, but first . . ."

"Wait, why us?" Aida broke in before Vulcan could finish. "If a god took your automaton, can't you just take it back?"

He grunted, but Aggie's hand on his arm softened his response. "I can't interfere with the machinations of other gods and how they are compelling humans. In this case, if we are right, the happiness of millions of humans is stored within Pandora. As I did not initiate it, I cannot meddle because it is an arrangement between another god and humans."

Next to Aida, Yumi sighed.

"But there are ways to figure it out. I built a fail-safe—an override, if you will—into the automaton in the event someone other than me took control of her. You'll need to find the key to override Pandora's instructions and subsequently control all the other automatons. What you need to find is the specific pattern of the meander."

"What's a meander?" Yumi asked.

Vulcan explained, his voice steady and clear. "A meander, or Greek key, is a decorative border constructed from a continuous line, shaped into a repeated motif. It's a design that dates back to ancient Greece and is often found in architectural friezes and pottery."

"Mazes often use a meander pattern. That's why it's called a meander . . . You wander within them," Aggie added.

Vulcan continued. "This particular pattern represents the eternal flow of life, the meandering path of existence. In the context of Pandora's key, the meander isn't just a mere design, but a code. It's crafted so that each turn and twist of the pattern aligns with specific mechanisms within the lock. You see, the key and the lock are uniquely intertwined, much like the lines of the meander—intricate, complex, and deeply interconnected." He looked at Yumi. "To find the key, you need to break the code by finding the pattern of the meander."

"How do I do that?" Yumi asked. "I think she's in London. The database IP tracks to a location there. And that's where Aida always goes for her work."

"Okay. Then you need to go there. If Pandora is in the city, the meander will imprint itself in some way upon the most important public locations, usually into the architecture. The meanders change based on how the city and its people change if Pandora is in one place for a long period of time—so the key may always be found. There are five meanders."

"But London is massive. There are countless museums and important buildings. How on earth will we know which ones are the right ones?"

Vulcan made a movement with his hand, then held out his palm to Yumi. A gold-encircled lens lay in its center. "Like I said, it will be the most important locations. If you use this, you'll be able to see the correct meanders and the specific part of the pattern you'll need."

Yumi took the lens and lifted it to her eye.

"You won't see anything unless it's the right meander," he told her. "Once you have identified all five, you must put them together into the correct pattern to fashion a key."

"An actual key?" Aida asked.

He shook his head. "No, not now. In the past, yes, I would have said that. But Pandora and the key adapt to the world around them. If she's being used as some form of database, then the key is likely digital—code that you would input directly into her.

"Each meander will be unique in design. The differences might be subtle, but they will be there. Each will have its own structure and its own number of turns and lines. The complexity of the lines, the length, the direction—these are not arbitrary. They each represent something, a different numerical or alphanumeric value." He glanced up at Yumi, ensuring she was following along. She nodded her understanding.

"When you find these meanders, you'll need to discern their unique features, and then overlay them, one on top of the other, in a specific order, based on the importance of the locations where you found the meander." He sat back and pointed at the lens in Yumi's hand. "That lens is a tool but also a guide. With it, you'll be able to see the meanders and their potential combinations. And when you look at the combined design through the lens, you'll see something new. Think of it like a QR code of sorts. The overlay creates a new unique pattern, which can be converted into a digital meander. This will be the key. Based on how my automatons have adapted—" he waved his hand around the room at the golden beings "—Pandora will have a way to scan this key from your mobile device."

"Wait, we can't do this remotely?" Yumi asked, horror evident in her voice.

"Unfortunately, no. You'll need to see the meanders in person."

"And she'll have to give you permission," Aggie added.

Vulcan nodded sagely. "That's right. She'll have to agree to it."

Aida gaped. "I don't understand—are you saying that Pandora was willing to house the world's happiness? That she took on the information willingly?"

"Yes. My guess is that Apate deceived her in some way and convinced her to take on such a task. But yes, that's exactly what happened. She agreed. I'm the only one that can command her at will. And of all my automatons, Pandora is the only one with free will to choose."

Aida didn't like where this was going. "Can't you just go to Oizys or Apate and ask them about taking the contents of Zeus's storeroom? Isn't that between the gods?"

"Yes, I could. And after we settle the matter of Pandora, there will be no limit to the wrath I will bestow upon them. But if I went to them now, they could do too many things with the contents of Pandora—and I would be powerless to stop them."

Aggie broke in. "They could move Pandora and better obscure her location. Or worse, convince her to destroy the happiness somehow, rendering it impossible to restore. And while they can't kill her, they could torture Effie, and break down her will, which would further worsen the situation for mortals. No, we can't risk interfering."

Aida frowned, her brow knitting as she glanced between

them. "But wait, if these gods are so nefarious, why store all this happiness in Pandora at all? Why not just destroy it to begin with?"

Vulcan exhaled, slow and thoughtful, his eyes darkening. "Destruction is simple. It's final. But these gods prefer the art of torment. Destruction doesn't offer control, and it doesn't draw out suffering."

"Does that mean it's not enough to erase joy?" Aida asked.

"Exactly," Vulcan replied. "By locking happiness inside Pandora, they gain leverage. It's not about the absence of joy—it's about holding it hostage, knowing that the world will feel its loss every day. In their eyes, that constant ache is far more exquisite than outright obliteration."

"This is all a game to them. It's about watching us suffer," Yumi murmured.

Vulcan gave a grim nod. "They don't just want to win; they want to savor every moment of the struggle. And that's why finding Pandora isn't just about restoring happiness. It's about breaking their hold on the world. These are gods who delight in the misery and manipulation of others. You have to find Pandora."

Aida stood. While Sophie's spell allowed her to be among the gods without fear, it didn't prevent her from feeling the vast emotions related to her own life and work. "Who are we to go up against *gods*?" She began to pace. "I didn't take this job so I could get killed! This is not what I signed up for."

"You don't have many options," Aggie said gently.

"What do you mean?" It was Yumi who asked the question.

Aggie gave Yumi a sympathetic look. "Well, *you* have better options. You could hop a plane and be long gone from here. But MODA will find a way to kill your friend if she attempts to resign."

"Then I'll just keep working for them. I'll do my job."

Yumi shook her head. "That wouldn't work for you for long. How could you keep doing that job, knowing you are literally stealing happiness from people?"

Aida hated that Yumi was right. How could she visit all the beautiful places in Italy, knowing she would never be able to visit again and that others would be deprived of the beauty and wonder she'd constantly experienced when she first began her work as a Collector?

And what would happen to the world as all the happiness disappeared? She thought of the terrible headlines that were already making their way through the papers and internet: yet another American mass shooting, this time at the Naval Air Station in Pensacola, Florida; the former Pakistani president being sentenced to death for treason; ongoing protests in Hong Kong; the way climate change was wreaking angry havoc on the earth; and in London, the impending Brexit. Things were never so turbulent when she was growing up, were they? Knowing what she did now about MODA, it made all too much sense. How much of a hand had she had in making those events happen?

Aida sighed. "Then I need your help." She explained the problem of the MODA phone tracking her and eavesdropping on her conversations, then handed the god her phone.

Vulcan took it without hesitation, waving a hand over the screen as a faint shimmer passed across it. "That should block their surveillance—calls, messages, even location tracking. They'll see only what you want them to see." He handed it back, then held out a hand expectantly. "Your personal phone too."

Aida hesitated for a fraction of a second before handing it over. Vulcan repeated the process, then did the same with Yumi's device.

"Now, whenever you need to obscure your communications, just tap the screen three times in quick succession and say the word *Hephaestus*. This will encrypt your phone calls and any ambient noise the phone picks up. Anyone listening in will hear only mundane chatter—discussions about the weather, idle routines—or neutral background noise like distant traffic or a quiet room. To deactivate, repeat the same action and say *Hephaestus* again. It's seamless and undetectable. It will also help you bypass any Wi-Fi restrictions they may have put on your device. Use it wisely and discreetly."

"But can I make it seem like I'm in a specific location when I'm not?"

Vulcan nodded. "Simply say *Hephaestus, location*, followed by the name of the place you want to appear to be. The spell will create a false location signal, making it seem as if you are physically present in the desired area. To deactivate this feature, simply say *Hephaestus, clear location*. Just remember that using this feature too often or in suspicious circumstances—especially with powerful ears nearby—could draw unwanted attention, so use it wisely." With the point of a finger, he adjusted the enchantment on their cell phones.

"Can you do the same for Felix's and Luciano's phones?"

The god nodded. He had Aida open their contact information on her phone, then touched a finger to each in turn. "When you connect with them again, they will have the same protection."

Another thought occurred to Aida.

"What about cameras? In hotels, or in my own room at the palazzo. Should I worry about that?"

Aggie laughed. "No, that's one thing the gods can't be distracted by—television, movies, videos, live cameras. Our 'Achilles' heel,' so to say. We find such moving fakery disorienting."

Vulcan grunted, displeasure evident in his eyes.

"Now, now, Heph, if this information will help them later, you'll fault me not."

"But couldn't they have mortals watching us?"

"Unlikely. The more mortals they have involved in their affairs, the more their plans are at risk. Humans are too unpredictable. They'll settle for listening to you, but even then, that's most likely only when they have reason to suspect you. And if they suspect you, they will probably just interrogate you instead."

"Wait, you said that the storeroom had hundreds of other automatons. What if they are using them to watch us?"

"Yes. I would assume they are using them to do that. And you would have no idea either."

The idea that anyone around her could be watching her at any given time sent a chill up Aida's spine. She had been lucky then, when she had talked about MODA in public, even with the precautions they had taken with the MODA phones.

"What about Effie? Don't we need to find her too?" Yumi asked.

Vulcan grunted. "Worry about Pandora. We'll look for Euphrosyne."

Aida sighed. "Well, it seems I need to make up a good excuse for why I want to go to London, of all places, for my vacation, particularly when I was just there."

Yumi raised her hand. "I'm your excuse. Let's go."

Aggie walked Aida and Yumi to the entrance of the forge, her expression both concerned and hopeful. As they prepared to leave, she looked into their eyes and offered a sincere smile. "*In bocca al lupo*," she said, invoking the Italian phrase that means "into the mouth of the wolf" and serves as a good-luck wish.

"*Crepi il lupo*." Aida gave the traditional response. *May the wolf die.*

They stepped through the doorway of the Umbilicus Urbis Romae, and back into the Roman Forum, leaving Aida hoping that she wouldn't turn out to be the wolf.

December 2019

AIDA KNOCKED ON the door that separated her office in the palazzo from her aide's. "Trista?"

"Enter." Trista's voice wafted through the closed door. When she saw Yumi standing behind Aida, the woman drew herself up and cleared her throat. "Miss Tanaka. I had heard you were in Rome."

Yumi reached out her hand. "It's good to meet you in person finally, Miss Acheron. Aida has told me how much she loves working with you."

Aida smiled, hoping she didn't appear on the verge of laughing at Yumi's bald-faced lie.

Trista seemed flustered at the idea, hesitating for just a fraction of a second before shaking Yumi's hand. That slight pause—was it surprise? Or calculation? Aida had never thought twice about Trista's measured responses before, but now, with what she'd learned about the gods' use of automatons, the thought slithered in uninvited. *What if Trista wasn't even human?*

"Well, that's nice to hear," Trista said. She sounded sincere.

Aida shoved the idea aside. She was letting paranoia get the better of her.

"The palazzo is beautiful," Yumi went on. "You must love living here."

Trista shrugged, but it seemed Yumi had cracked her hard veneer. "Tell me what I can do for the two of you," she said, her voice warmer.

"I've told Yumi a lot about London, and how much I love the city, and we thought it would be nice to spend some time there. I wanted to find out what mode of travel you recommend if I'm flying with a friend."

"The jet is fine," Trista said. "And I'll book you both rooms at the hotel right away." She turned to go toward her desk.

"Are you sure, Miss Acheron?" Yumi asked, stopping Trista in her tracks. "I have a friend with a B and B we can stay in." Aida doubted this was true, but Yumi was great at making a good impression, and appearing unassuming was one way to do so with Trista.

"Don't be ridiculous," Trista said. "Why on earth would you stay somewhere like that? I'll book you both now."

They opted for an evening flight, and just three hours later, they were being whisked north across the dark European countryside.

"I still can't believe this," Yumi said as she leaned back in the white leather seat. She sipped at her champagne. "This is how you travel all the time?"

"I'm lucky. And now, so are you." But Aida also knew this luck was running out. How many more of these luxurious flights would she be able to take?

"I have the most boring job, mostly sifting through code all day," Yumi said before launching into a complaint about one of her coworkers.

The small talk was just that . . . small talk meant to keep MODA from thinking anything else was going on between them besides a friendship that crossed years and distance. They reminisced about their younger days: meeting for the first time, nights out clubbing, Yumi's bad dates, her family, and life in Boston. Yumi even mentioned hating her job enough to consider moving into something non-software related, hoping to divert attention from her expertise in security.

A nervous energy that wasn't usually there vibrated between them, and Aida hoped it wasn't apparent to anyone who might be watching or listening. She eyed the flight concierge who sat behind a closed windowed door at the far end of the plane. The woman didn't seem to be paying attention, but Aida knew that wasn't likely true. She would report the trip details to MODA, as she had in the past.

Yumi finally decided she wanted a nap, leaving Aida alone with her thoughts. She watched her friend sleep, and then panic hit her, sharp, like a punch in the gut. They had never asked Aggie or Vulcan to give Yumi an aegis such as Sophie had given to her and Luciano. Every misgiving ran through her with the thought. She should never have dragged Yumi into this. She wouldn't have the same calmness if a god was in her presence. What if she inadvertently gave them all away? What if that lapse got her killed? Or got all of them killed?

The concierge opened the door and came to her. She spoke in a low voice so as not to wake Yumi. "Miss Reale, may I get you anything? Perhaps something to calm your nerves?"

Aida froze. Could the woman have known what she was thinking? "Calm my nerves? Why would you ask that?"

"My apologies, Miss Reale. You looked like something was terribly wrong and I thought I might try to help."

"Oh, nothing is wrong," Aida said, making a mental note to find a way to keep her features calm when gods weren't around. "I was just thinking I forgot to pack my favorite jacket."

"Do you want to describe it to me? I can have Trista ship it overnight for you."

"No, that's all right. It's a good excuse to go shopping," she said, forcing a smile.

She watched the woman return to her post, realizing that an aegis might not save them, after all. Mere mortals could be the end of any one of them.

THE NEXT MORNING, Yumi knocked on the door in the sitting room that connected their two rooms. "Up and at 'em," she called.

Aida wiped the sleep from her eyes and looked at the clock before heading to the door. "Seven a.m.?"

"We've a lot to do today, Miss Reale," she said, imitating every person who had talked to the two of them since they had arrived—the doormen, the bellhop, the front desk, the service staff that passed them in the hallway all knew them by name. "I've already called down for breakfast to be sent, and they'll be here in ten minutes, so throw some clothes on."

Breakfast was silent as Yumi and Aida texted each other on their personal phones to plan the day, not daring to talk about their plans aloud. Occasionally, Yumi would regale Aida with some TikTok video or other, purely for appearance's sake.

This is going to be impossible, Aida texted. There could be meanders all over the city.

Yumi, as always, was more optimistic. Vulcan said that there are five meanders, and they are located in some of the city's most important public places. I pulled a list of the top ten locations by number of visitors and antiquities to get us started.

What if they aren't at the spots on the list?

Yumi shrugged. That's for me to figure out. Worry not your pretty little head, Miss Reale.

Aida glared at her friend over their tea and croissants. Please tell me you're going to stop calling me that.

Certainly, Miss Reale. Your wish is my command. Yumi passed Aida her phone. On it was a GIF of a beautiful woman curtsying, with the words, Yes, Your Majesty.

Aida couldn't help but laugh.

THEY WERE LEAVING the hotel when a voice called out across the lobby, stopping Aida in her tracks. "Miss Reale!"

Aida turned and saw Mo coming toward her. The dread she first felt upon hearing her name dissipated with every step closer, leaving her with a deep sense of calm. She objectively knew that she should feel worried about Yumi's potential reaction, but no anxiety came to her.

"Hello, Mo," she said with a smile. "I wondered if I would see you."

"I didn't expect you here so soon after your last visit. And you brought Miss Tanaka with you." He reached out for her hand and kissed it. "I am honored to meet you."

Aida wondered at his odd, cordial demeanor. Was it just a show for her friend? "Yumi has never been to London," she said placidly. "We'll take in the sights for a few days."

"So, this is Mo!" Yumi exclaimed with a girlish giggle. "You were right, Aida. He *is* handsome."

Mo raised an eyebrow at Aida. "Handsome? I would never have guessed, Miss Reale."

Aida was shocked at Yumi's tactic for managing Mo, but she always had a knack for navigating awkward situations. "Admiration isn't the sole purview of men," she said.

He chuckled. "You are always full of surprises, aren't you, Miss Reale?"

"You live in London, right?" Yumi jumped in, putting on her best attempt at innocence. "Where should we go first today?"

He lifted his hand to his chin in a stereotypical gesture of thought. "The Crown Jewels in the Tower of London. I say start there."

"Perfect," Yumi said, going along with his suggestion. She pulled her phone out of her pocket. "Let's see if I can get tickets."

"Don't do that," Mo said, waving his hand at her phone. "Go talk to the concierge. He'll arrange it. You'll never get in on your own last minute." He indicated a young man at a nearby desk.

"Be right back," Yumi said, abandoning Aida to arrange for the tickets.

"Your friend is rather perky," he said to Aida once Yumi was out of earshot. "A bit too perky. How can you stand being around someone so annoying?"

"The same way I stand your criticism of my friends," she retorted.

"I suppose I deserved that." He seemed oddly contrite. "So, handsome? Of course, I am. How could you think anything otherwise?"

"There's no conceit in your family, is there?" Aida said, knowing she was being cheeky. "You've got it all."

He only gave her that damnable grin. Then he grew serious. "Are you really just sightseeing?"

Aida silently thanked Sophie for her aegis . . . Without it, she didn't think she would have been able to keep her cool at such a question.

"You don't think I came here to see you, do you?" she asked.

He stared at her for a moment, then shrugged. "Fine. Tower of London, British Library, Tate Modern, London Bridge, the Churchill War Rooms, and the Museum of London. Those are my suggestions."

Yumi reappeared at Aida's side. "The concierge pulled some strings so we could enter early. We'll be the first ones to see the Jewels today! Thank you for the suggestion, Mo."

"My pleasure, Miss Tanaka. Now then, I must be going. Ta-ta, little sightseers!" He headed away from them toward the elevator, his absence bringing her anxiety about the encounter back to the forefront.

Aida ushered Yumi out of the hotel and down the street. When they were a few blocks away, she pulled out her phone and did as Vulcan said, tapping it three times and saying, "Hephaestus." Her phone glowed brightly, then dimmed to normal. Yumi did the same.

"God, I hope that works," Aida said, pocketing her phone again. She gave Yumi the lowdown on the conversation she had with Mo. "Out of all the people I didn't want to see on this trip, he was at the top of the list." She swatted Yumi on the shoulder. "And what were you thinking, telling him I thought he was handsome?"

"I'm so sorry! It was the first thing I thought of to say. I was so flustered. I'm not used to this god thing. And he is beautiful. Although rather condescending and a bit of a misogynist. *My little sightseers?* Really?"

Aida didn't relate Mo's other condescending words to her friend. "So those places he mentioned—Tower of London, British Library, Tate Modern, the Churchill War Rooms, the Museum of London, and London Bridge—we'll have to go to them now. Were they on your list?"

Yumi sighed. "Of course not. All those places were ones I specifically crossed off because they're heavily documented online and it was easy enough to check the photos and satellite views. Nothing about them suggests there will be any meanders. Maybe we can try the location spell Vulcan gave us. Let him think we're at one of those locations when we're not?"

"I worry Mo will randomly show up to one of them—he has a penchant for doing that, trying to catch me off guard."

Yumi lifted her hand to hail a passing black cab. "Why would this adventure of ours be easy? Gah. Then we'll see a lot of London this week."

THE TOWER OF LONDON, while jam-packed with history and millions of dollars' worth of Crown Jewels, did not, as Yumi had predicted, yield a single meander. But they didn't dare hurry too much. Mo knew they were headed there, so Aida didn't use Vulcan's spell to mask their location and only used the audio block sparingly. She needed MODA to think they truly were on vacation. But she had to give Mo some silent thanks—they were the only ones viewing the Crown Jewels early. When they emerged from the castle into the light of the courtyard, a line of several hundred people snaked in front of them, waiting for their turn.

Yumi was keen to see the Tower's ravens, so they wandered in that direction. While Yumi took photos of the caged birds, Aida's phone buzzed. *Luciano.*

Leaving Yumi to her photos, she stepped away from the path and out of the way of passersby. After activating Hephaestus's privacy spell, she slid in her earbuds and answered the call, looking around to make sure she wasn't being watched. Her heart skipped a beat when his face appeared on her screen.

"It's good to see you. Were you able to find anything out from the beekeeper?" she asked in a low voice.

"A little," he said. "While Dolores was her main contact, she said all the contracts she signed were from a firm in London, which she found odd."

"If the firm is in London, that's another sign that our database is too." She didn't want to say Pandora's name aloud.

"The beekeeper also told me MODA paid an extravagant fee to close off the garden so I was free to conduct my research—a fee that the garden couldn't turn down."

Aida sighed. "I hope they don't kill the bees."

"Me too. I wish I could be there with you in London. But I couldn't fathom any way to go without raising suspicion. It figures, just as you leave Rome, I get word that one of my uncles passed away."

"Oh, I'm so sorry to hear that."

"Don't be. I barely knew him. But after my father died, I became his next of kin, and it turns out that means I'm the owner of his apartment near the Spanish Steps."

"Are you serious?" Aida could hardly contain her excitement at the thought. It seemed too good to be true. "I might see you in Roma?"

"If whatever you do in London doesn't leave you without a place in Rome to return to."

Aida's stomach plummeted at the thought.

"I'll be heading there after the holidays to see exactly what he left to me. We weren't close. He and my father had a falling out before I was born. I don't ever remember meeting him. I only knew he was some sort of city politician there."

Yumi waved at Aida, ready to depart.

Aida held up a finger, indicating she wanted one more minute. "I wish you could be here to help. And god knows, or should I say, the gods know what we'll do once we have all the meanders. If they are in London, after all."

"If you really need me—and don't care about suspicion—let me know, and I'll be on a plane right away."

Aida agreed and reluctantly ended the call with Luciano, her heart conflicted. If they found Pandora and released happiness back into the world, if that was even possible, what did it mean if she no longer had a home? Or a job? The thought left a dark spot inside her.

"How's your *bel ragazzo?*" Yumi asked as she neared.

"The handsome lad is just tickety-boo," Aida said, throwing on a smile and her best British accent.

"Come on! We have a treasure hunt to continue."

Yumi headed toward the exit, and Aida followed. The sightseeing adventure had been fun so far, but after they found all the meanders and had the key, then what?

THAT AFTERNOON, THEY had true confirmation that the database was in London. They found their first meander at the Victoria and Albert Museum. After their cab had dropped them at the exhibition entrance, they had wandered through much of the museum, eyeing every inch of the architecture, but it wasn't until they stumbled across the Grand Entrance on the opposite end of the building that they were rewarded.

"Look at this!" Aida exclaimed as they emerged from an upper corridor and the large circular space appeared below. She looked up, stunned by the Rotunda's beautiful glass-topped, dome-shaped ceiling. In the center of the dome hung a stunning blue-and-yellow-green glass Chihuly sculpture above a circular information desk.

"No, Aida, you need to look at *that.*" Yumi pointed to the black-and-white floor. Along its border was a simple meander, a repeating motif that added an additional layer of visual interest to the space, complementing the overall design aesthetic of the Grand Entrance. She held up the lens to her eye.

"Oh my god, it glows! Come on!" She pulled Aida toward the marble staircase that led down to the entrance.

When she began to kneel in the center of the front entrance, lens in hand, Aida stopped her. "Way to be conspicuous."

"Oh, sorry." Yumi stood and backed off to a corner, then lifted the lens to her eye. She handed the lens to Aida.

Aida peered through the glass. The meander was glowing a bright blue all the way around the edge of the room. She gasped.

"Now what do we do?" she asked, returning the lens to Yumi.

"I guess we take a bunch of photos. I'll have to figure out how this fits in with the other meanders later."

"When we find them all."

"Right," Yumi agreed, turning her phone camera toward the floor.

20

December 2019

AFTER FINDING THE first meander, Yumi convinced Aida to make one more stop at the British Library, to pacify Mo and make sure their GPS showed them following up on his suggestions. "Let's get it out of the way," Yumi said as she nudged a foot-weary Aida into a black cab. Ultimately, Aida had to admit she was glad they did. She had long wanted to view the Magna Carta. There were also the Beowulf manuscript, fragments of da Vinci's and Emily Brontë's notebooks, manuscripts from Virginia Woolf and Sylvia Plath, and even a Gutenberg Bible.

Finally, they ended their day at a gin bar in Soho near the hotel. Without the comfort of using Vulcan's enchantment, the conversation felt stilted. "What was your favorite thing you saw today?" Aida asked her friend as she fumbled to keep the conversation going.

Yumi thought for a moment, then launched into a list of things that had excited her during their first foray into London. Aida was about to ask her to narrow down her list when a blanket of calm enveloped her, muting the sounds of the restaurant around her and focusing her attention. There was a god nearby.

She didn't look around the room. She didn't kick Yumi under the table. Instead, she smiled and pointed out that Yumi needed to pick one favorite thing, not twenty.

"Yes, sir, Ms. Vacation Police." Yumi saluted her. Aida registered some relief that Yumi didn't notice anything strange about her or her response.

"The cast room at the V&A," she said, and ignoring Aida's instruction of only one thing, she began to list all the statues in the massive room that had caught her attention.

The calm grew heavier. Aida went through the motions, rolling her eyes at Yumi at one point, teasing her at another, and giving her facts about Michelangelo's sculpture of David when her friend began to talk about the museum's copy. Aida didn't dare seek out the source of the calm, and she burned inside to turn her head and see which one was spying on them. She didn't think it was Mo—he didn't seem like someone who could contain his commentary on their conversation—which meant it was Apate or Discordia. But why? Did they suspect something? Had she slipped up and forgotten to set Vulcan's charm on one of their conversations?

Eventually, Yumi realized that something wasn't right with Aida. "You're off your game, Aida. I feel like you are barely listening to me."

"I've been responding," she said.

"Yes, but you lack enthusiasm. I must have tired you out dragging you all over London today."

Aida nodded. At least that was true. "I am exhausted."

The calm now seemed like a lead weight. Wherever the god was, they were very close. "Very exhausted. Maybe we should turn in early tonight."

"Party pooper," Yumi said, but she didn't argue for one more drink, which she often did on nights when Aida was half-hearted about being out. She pulled her jacket off the back of the chair and put it on.

The heavy calm followed them on their walk all the way back to the hotel. Aida resisted turning to see who it might be for fear of catching their attention. The calmness gave her a sense of reason as well, and she knew that if they were to throw MODA off their trail, she needed to truly act as though they were just on vacation, unaware of any supernatural gods that might be fluttering around them.

When they crossed the threshold into the hotel, the calm feeling abruptly winked out, and the panic it had pushed downward came roaring back into her consciousness. Only then did she turn to see who might be behind her, but no one was there.

Back in the suite, they collapsed on the circular couch in the sitting room. Yumi flipped on the television and Aida immediately began texting her friend, waving at her to look at her phone. She explained what happened at dinner and on the walk to the hotel.

I wondered why you were being so strange.

We need a code word, so I can tell you, Aida texted.

Yumi stared off at a distance for a moment then typed, If you can touch me, tap me three times. Or ask me "do you remember the time when . . ." and make something up. I'll know.

THEY SAW NEITHER hide nor hair of any gods in the following days. To be safe, they peppered in the other places Mo mentioned, and while they were interesting, as expected, none yielded a meander, whereas Yumi's instinct to target locations with connections to antiquities proved useful. Finding a meander at the British Museum in the floor of the Elgin Marbles room was a given, seeing as how the ancient temple pieces had been plundered from the Parthenon in Greece. In Room 32 of the National Gallery, Aida spied an elaborate meander in the cornice. At the interior entrance to the National Portrait Gallery, another meander decorated the cornice around the room.

They were stymied about the fifth meander until they heard about the Sir John Soane's Museum and the nineteenth-century architect's collection of ancient Roman and Greek items. It was off-season and a weekday, so they had the museum mostly to themselves, which was good because the rooms were small and cramped. The museum was a meander in itself, a discombobulated maze of rooms full of statues and paintings. Everywhere they turned, there was something amazing to look at. And sure enough, they found a meander in the cornice encircling the domed skylight in the No. 13 Breakfast Room.

"Thank the gods," Yumi said as she lifted the lens toward the ceiling.

Aida nudged her friend. "Maybe don't invoke them while we are doing this," she whispered.

"Ahh, right," she said, pocketing the lens and pulling out her phone for photos.

After snapping pictures, they wandered through the museum a bit more, partly to play the guise of sightseers and partly because the house was so fascinating. But when they reached the Sepulchral Chamber and stood viewing the 3,300-year-old sarcophagus of Egyptian Pharaoh Seti I, Aida couldn't take it anymore. She motioned for Yumi to mask their phones.

"What do we do now?" she asked.

Yumi's normal level of exuberance was missing. "Fuck. I really don't know. Finding the meanders was an adventure. I'm confident I can figure out the key, but having a vague IP address isn't necessarily enough to track down Pandora. And then, what will we do when we get there? I mean, come on, Aida, we're meddling in something much bigger than us. We could die."

She said these last few words in a whisper. Aida was surprised to see tears gathering in her friend's eyes. Yumi was always positive, energetic, and ready to tackle anything that was headed her way. Aida had always admired her bright way of looking at the world. She didn't know what else to do but to enfold her friend in her arms.

Yumi cried into Aida's shoulder for a minute or so, then finally let go, wiping away her tears with her thumbs. She looked at the sarcophagus and cracked a grin. "I think we could use a change of atmosphere."

Aida put a hand on her friend's shoulder. "No kidding, Yumi. The atmosphere down here is so heavy, even the mummies are going to start shedding tears."

Yumi laughed. "Well, let's hope they don't demand tissues. I don't think the museum staff is ready for that!"

BACK ON THE streets of London, Yumi returned to her regular upbeat self. "I booked an Airbnb not far from here. I need to get cracking on figuring out this key." She patted her backpack. "Let's go."

"You really did book an Airbnb?" Aida was incredulous.

Yumi shrugged. "Yeah, this morning. I didn't want to try finding the key using the hotel network. If we're going to die, I don't want it to be because I did something so reckless to lead them to us."

After setting their phones to misdirect, Yumi led Aida down Oxford toward Soho. They wound through the busy streets until her GPS led them to a little art gallery. The owner had the key and led them upstairs to a cute one-bedroom flat. Yumi immediately set up shop at the dining room table.

"And here we go."

As she worked, Yumi gave Aida a blow-by-blow, overly technical explanation for how she would do the pattern recognition, which included using some sort of software and writing some code to overlay the patterns in various ways that she could view through the lens.

"This is going to take some time," she said, wrinkling her brow in frustration.

Aida watched her for a while, then eventually crashed out on the long leather couch for a nap. It seemed she'd barely fallen asleep when a whoop from Yumi awakened her.

"I found it! I found it!"

Aida rushed to her friend's side. Yumi handed her the lens. The glowing blue meander was, as Vulcan said it might be, a chaotic mess on the screen.

"That was pretty fast," Aida said, shocked that it was so easy.

"Well, I gave you the Scotty treatment." Yumi laughed.

Aida stared at her blankly.

"Like in *Star Trek*. Scotty always told Kirk fixing the ship was impossible or that it would take days to do what was needed. Then he'd fix it in a fraction of the predicted time."

Aida remembered all the afternoons when she was young, watching *Star Trek* with her father on their gold-colored couch. She rolled her eyes, annoyed at herself for not catching the reference.

"Okay, then, Scotty, now what?" She handed the lens back to Yumi.

"We have to find Pandora. Let me try the IP address again. If we're lucky, I can get past the firewall and it'll lead us straight to her this time."

Minutes passed, each one stretching longer than the last. Yumi's hopeful expression slowly turned to one of confusion, then concern. "This doesn't make sense," she muttered. "The IP address is bouncing all over the place. London, then Berlin, now it's showing up in Tokyo. It's like it's being deliberately obfuscated."

"Can't you narrow it down?" Aida asked, trying to hide the worry in her voice.

Yumi shook her head. "It's like chasing a ghost. Whenever I think I'm getting close, it jumps to a new location."

Aida leaned back against the couch, feeling the weight of their task. "So, we have a key with no lock."

Yumi sighed. "I'll try it again later. It could be temporary."

Aida stood. "Let's get back to the hotel. When we spoof our location, it always makes me nervous that someone from MODA will show up at the location and not find us."

AFTER ANOTHER DAY of trying to ping the IP address, there was still no clear location. Finally, Aida and Yumi linked hands and sent up a prayer to Sophie and Aggie for guidance. At first, there was no answer, but as they strolled along the Thames, Sophie fell in step with them.

She wore a black wool coat that brushed her ankles and a gray scarf wrapped snugly around her neck. The river breeze tugged at the loose ends, but the goddess herself seemed untouched by the chill.

Yumi tensed at the sudden appearance of a stranger, but Aida squeezed her arm in reassurance. "Yumi, this is Sophie."

Sophie nodded at Yumi, a brief acknowledgment, then turned her attention to the river. "Things are getting worse," she said, her voice as measured as always.

"What do you mean, worse?" Aida asked, alarmed.

"The balance of happiness and sadness is shifting in a dangerous way. And I can't quite figure it out."

"Can you explain?" Yumi pressed.

Sophie hesitated, her gaze drifting over the flowing river, reflecting an inner turmoil that seemed at odds with her usually serene demeanor. "The world is on the brink of some sort of profound change. There is a shadow looming over the collective spirit of humanity."

Aida and Yumi exchanged nervous glances.

Sophie gave them a sympathetic look. "It's not easy to explain. I can sense a massive cloud of fear and uncertainty beginning to descend upon humanity, enough to tip the balance of happiness and sorrow. It's small now, somewhere in the east, but will spread, slow at first, then catch like wildfire till it engulfs the whole world."

Yumi furrowed her brow. "But what could cause such a thing? Can it be stopped?"

"I don't know," Sophie admitted. "Whatever it is, it's powerful, something that will hit both the physical and emotional worlds. And it's going to deeply affect most of humanity."

"So, it's like Pandora's box all over again?" Yumi joked, but she wasn't smiling.

"I suppose you could think of it like that." Sophie nodded.

"Except Pandora held a jar, not a box. When it was opened, everything terrible that could plague humanity spilled out." She exhaled, watching the river churn below. "I think something similar might be happening now."

"Wait," Aida said, realization flooding into her. "The last thing left in Pandora's jar was hope."

Yumi's eyes widened. "That means we can't waste any time finding Pandora."

"Exactly," Sophie agreed. "But it's not just about Pandora. Finding her is crucial, yes, but hope alone won't be enough to turn the tide. We also need Euphrosyne. Without her light, her influence of joy, the world's ability to hold on to happiness weakens every day. Sorrow and despair compounded make it even harder for her happiness to reach those who need it. Even if Pandora unleashes hope, it won't last without Effie. She's the very essence of joy, and her presence keeps that hope alive."

"But if releasing happiness through Pandora works, wouldn't that be enough?" Yumi asked.

Sophie shook her head. "Not without Effie. Her light has been dimming for too long, and the world already feels the weight of her absence. Happiness is fragile and fleeting. Hope needs something to hold on to, something to nourish it. Effie is that force. If we don't find her, whatever happiness is left will fade as quickly as it's found."

Aida frowned. "But we're having enough problems locating Pandora. How will we find Effie?"

Sophie put a reassuring hand on Aida's shoulder. "I wish I knew. Aggie and I will keep looking. For now, return to Rome and enjoy the Christmas season. Revel in the world as you know it, for there will be challenging times ahead. In the meantime, Yumi, keep using your skills to find Pandora. And for both of you, don't despair. The clues may come in unexpected ways. I have often found that in the toughest times, the most significant breakthroughs happen. If I learn of anything useful, I will come to you."

Aida tried to push down the panic. She wished Sophie's calm spell worked in the goddess's presence. Then she remembered her friend. "Will you give Yumi your aegis?"

Sophie turned in her direction, her face unreadable.

"Please." There was a note of desperation in Yumi's voice.

The goddess took Yumi's hands in hers. "I give you my aegis. Use it wisely."

She let go of Yumi's hands and then left them, walking down the path.

Aida's phone buzzed. She looked down to see a message from Trista on her screen. It seemed they had no choice, after all. The jet would pick them up in three hours—the Galleria Spada was ready for her return and she would continue her research in the morning. She relayed the news to Yumi.

"This feels like defeat."

Aida agreed, but Sophie's words were fresh in her mind. "Pandora still holds hope. So we must too."

"I don't feel any different with this aegis thingy," Yumi said as they walked toward the hotel. "How will I know it works?"

"Oh, you'll know," Aida reassured her. "Trust me, you'll know."

RETURNING TO THE Galleria Spada was like a stab in the gut to Aida. As she went through all the motions of her job, she experienced none of the happiness that she was talking about. She wore a fake smile as she interviewed visitors to the museum, dutifully capturing their delight at seeing Borromini's forced perspective and their thoughts on the myriad of paintings by Titian, Dürer, Caravaggio, Guido Reni, Artemisia Gentileschi, and other masterpieces. She envied the museumgoers, their awe, surprise, and admiration.

Aida looked at the same paintings but could not tap into any of the joy. Instead, a dull ache had wedged itself in the space of her heart, dread for what was to come and a deepening sense of loneliness looming. Aida had to wonder how much of the happiness draining from the world was directly affecting her. On top of that was the immense responsibility of trying to save the world—and if she thought of it like that, she had to laugh at the ridiculousness of it all. Who was she to save the world?

Eventually, Yumi had to return to the States empty-handed. The holiday season rolled in, but for Aida, Rome's festive lights and decorations couldn't penetrate the fog of her growing melancholy. Christmas came with a muted celebration. Felix invited her to dinner with him and his visiting sister. They tried to keep the spirits high, sharing stories and laughter over *tortellini in brodo* and a modestly adorned table.

But Aida's heart wasn't in it. She felt like an actor in a play, going through the motions without being truly present. Worse, she couldn't shake the feeling that something was readying itself— just beyond her reach, just beyond the glow of the holiday lights, waiting to descend.

21

January–February 2020

THE NEW YEAR brought little change to Aida's disposition. She returned to work, this time at the Botanical Garden in Bergamo, northeast of Milan. The garden was quiet in January, closed to visitors and harboring a serene, almost melancholic atmosphere. Each day, as she cataloged the dormant plants, she couldn't shake a subtle sense of foreboding that seemed to linger in the air, like a delicate frost clinging to the bare branches. Still, when she talked to the locals about the garden, she was filled with their happy memories of walking amid the nearly 1,200 different plants, all carefully maintained within an area of only 2,400 square meters. The garden was on a hill, and Aida found she didn't mind the trek upward.

In its winter slumber, the garden held a silent beauty that was both haunting and comforting. In these moments, amid the sleeping flora, wandering through the hedge maze, Aida tried to feel hope. She was most hopeful about Luciano, who was coming to Rome at the beginning of March to manage the details regarding his uncle's apartment. Much to Aida's chagrin, a MODA project at the Belleville Market in Paris had prevented him from arriving earlier. At least Aida had his arrival to look forward to—if the world didn't completely turn inside out before then.

For now, one of the only bright spots for Aida was that the garden was a treasure trove of information for her new novel in progress, *The Botanist's Muse*. Losing herself in the story was a blessing.

Meanwhile, Yumi was relentless in her efforts to find Pandora. Day after day, she pored over her computer, the lines of code reflecting in her determined eyes. But the elusive IP address continued to dodge her every attempt. It's like chasing shadows, she said in one of their texts. Every time I think I've got a lead, it vanishes into thin air.

Aida understood her friend's struggle, the helplessness that mirrored her own. The weight of their mission, the uncertainty of their success, hung over them like a dense fog. They had no leads, and there was only silence from Sophie and her friends.

The third week of January, on the same day she returned to Rome, Aida received a text from Yumi to call her. When she finally had a moment to escape the palazzo in the guise of an evening walk and made the call, she was surprised to hear a noticeable tremor in her friend's usually steady voice.

"Aida, I . . . I got laid off," Yumi confessed, the words tumbling out in a rush. "They're downsizing. It's such bullshit. I know for a fact they had record profits in Q4. It makes no sense at all."

Aida's heart sank for her friend. "Yumi, I'm so sorry. That's awful news."

Yumi wiped at her eyes with one hand. "I'm sad about it . . . I liked what I was doing. But I can find another job. I'm not worried about that. It just sucks. The way they bow down to a few shareholders without any regard for how it will affect their employees or their customers." She let out a long sigh. "But there's a silver lining—they gave me a six-month severance. Plus, I plan on selling a ton of stock, which will easily tide me over for a while."

Aida was relieved. "That's wonderful. You'll easily be able to find something in that time frame. What a comfort."

"It is, but I've been thinking. I'm going to come back to Rome. I can stay without a visa for ninety days, and I want to use that time to help you. We need to figure out this Pandora situation, and I can't let you do that by yourself."

A knot loosened within Aida. "Are you sure?"

"Yes, I'm sure," Yumi affirmed. "It will eat me up to be here. At least if I fail at finding that IP address, I'll be with you in Rome."

"We can fail together," Aida joked. It was a bad joke, rooted in all too much probability, but at least Yumi cracked a smile.

"I've already reserved that dorky apartment again," she said. "I'll be there at the end of February."

When they ended the call, Aida's heart was lighter than it had been in months. The idea of both Yumi and Luciano in Rome at the same time gave her new optimism. She thought of Pandora, filled with happiness and hope. They couldn't let it all disappear. "We're going to find you, damn it," she said aloud, causing a passerby to give her a wide berth. Aida didn't care. It bolstered her. She would soon be in the company of friends.

THE FOLLOWING DAY, Trista gave Aida her next appointment. "The Colosseum?" Aida asked, aghast.

Trista looked at her, concerned. "What's wrong?"

Aida quickly whipped up her biggest smile. "This is wonderful! So far, I've been researching more obscure places, so this is exciting!"

But deep down, Aida was already thinking of the famous medieval prophecy of the monk known as the Venerable Bede: "Rome will exist as long as the Colosseum does; when the Colosseum falls, so will Rome; when Rome falls, so will the world." If everything she researched was bound to disappear, what did that mean for one of the most iconic monuments in all the world?

"You'll be there for three weeks. You'll start in the hypogeum, under where the gladiators fought, and will conclude your work on the Belvedere, the fifth level. Dress warm. It's cold on the underground level."

Trista was right, the hypogeum was freezing. Aida tightened the scarf around her neck as she moved through the labyrinth of narrow stone-walled corridors under the Colosseum where gladiators once prepared for battle. A faint chill hung in the air, adding weight to the low murmur of the crowds above. Unlike other locations she visited, MODA didn't arrange for her to be at the site without visitors. Instead, the staff blocked off areas so she could work, but the throngs of tourists were never far away.

The cold damp air clung to her as she switched on her recorder and began to walk slowly through the narrow corridors. "This was the pulse of the Colosseum," she murmured. "From here, warriors and beasts were lifted into the light of the arena above—into a world of blood and spectacle."

She paused near the faint outlines of ancient holding cells. Her breath clouded as she tried to imagine the atmosphere back then. "They were packed into these chambers," she continued. "Gladiators, prisoners, exotic animals, all destined for a fight that would bring them death—or fleeting glory. Above, the crowd was buzzing, thousands of voices rising in anticipation, waiting for the violence."

Aida leaned against the cold stone wall, her fingers grazing the rough surface. "This was happiness. The crowd's joy came from the bloodshed, from watching men and beasts tear into each other. For them, cruelty wasn't just tolerated, it was celebrated. It was entertainment, a source of delight."

She tried to picture the faces in the stands—their laughter, their cheers as a blade found its mark. *How could they find joy in this?* she wondered, a chill settling in her bones. "It's strange to think that happiness can be drawn from cruelty, but it often is. For the people who came here, the suffering of others brought them together, united them in their shared delight."

The air in the hypogeum felt heavier as she spoke. "Happiness built on blood," she said quietly into her recorder. What she really wondered was how joy like that could last. Could something so dark be the foundation of any kind of real happiness?

Yes, it could, she thought, *for gods like Momus, Oizys, Apate, and Discordia.*

She was reminded of her conversation with Mo, about the cruelty of the puppet show. Over and over as she walked through the ancient monument, she thought of his words: *It seems that violence can make even normal people happy.*

Aida shuddered, but not from the cold. Mo's voice echoed in her mind, the casual cruelty in his words as sharp as any gladiator's sword. *You ever think about the Colosseum? Thousands of normal people, rooting for real bloodshed.* She pictured the crowds again, this time with fresh clarity—ordinary Romans, their faces lit with anticipation, their cheers rising with every blow struck. Happiness, for them, wasn't just watching. It was *wanting* the violence, *demanding* it.

Her grip tightened on the recorder. "Happiness built on blood," she repeated, more to herself than for her notes. *But at what cost?* Even now, the monument remained a symbol of joy for so many—a tourist attraction, a marvel of history. But beneath that surface, it was always the same. A place where delight came from suffering.

She paused in one of the ancient holding chambers, her heart heavy. *When the Colosseum falls, so will Rome.* The prophecy buzzed in the back of her mind, insistent, inescapable.

She turned off the recorder and exhaled, watching her breath spiral toward the stone ceiling. For now, the Colosseum still stood, its legacy of cruelty and celebration woven into the fabric of the world. But as she stepped deeper into the maze of corridors, Aida couldn't help but feel that with every word she recorded, she was nudging it closer to the edge of oblivion.

The days Aida spent at the Colosseum dragged on. Each morning, as she made the long walk to the ancient arena, she would stop when it came fully into view, taking a moment to admire it—the way the sun lit up the two-thousand-year-old concrete, how the arches soared into the sky with a defiant grace.

She needed to drink it all in, to commit every detail to memory. How many more times would she get to see its grandeur?

She tried, often in vain, to push away the thought that nagged at her: the role she played in it all, the happiness she was collecting, documenting, and quietly storing away. More than once, she thought about quitting—leaving everything behind, boarding a plane, and returning to Boston to start anew. There was a certain comfort in imagining herself back there, admitting her failure, and shaking off the weight of this impossible task.

But two things always stopped her. First, she didn't think the gods would let her walk away. And second, she couldn't bear the thought of leaving it all unfinished—of knowing she had a hand in the destruction of so much happiness without ever trying to make things right.

THREE WEEKS LATER, Felix joined her to augment her understanding of the fifth level, the Belvedere, the highest accessible point of the Colosseum. The stairs were extraordinarily steep, and Aida had to admit to her friend that they freaked her out. "This is like mountain climbing," she complained.

"It's worth it though! Up here, you get the best view," Felix said, turning back to smile at her, his hands tucked into his jacket pockets. "You can see the entire layout of the Colosseum, the grand design, the bones of it all. It's something, isn't it?"

When they finally emerged onto the platform, Aida stopped, catching her breath. From the Belvedere, the Colosseum unfurled beneath them like an open palm. The entire structure was visible, from the crumbling stone arches to the outline of the arena below. The winter sun cast a golden hue over the ancient walls, making the worn stone glow.

Felix leaned against the railing, motioning for her to join him. "You're standing in a place few ever get to see," he said, his voice reverent. "This level isn't always open to the public. Back then, it was reserved for the plebeians—Rome's lower classes.

But even here, at the highest point, they still came to be part of the spectacle."

Aida pulled out her recorder but kept it lowered, more interested in listening to Felix. "The Colosseum could hold between fifty and eighty thousand people, depending on the event," he explained. "It wasn't just for gladiators either. They had animal hunts, public executions . . . you name it. They even flooded the arena once to stage an entire naval battle. Can you imagine the engineering that took?"

Aida shook her head, trying to fathom it all. "They really turned death into a show."

Felix continued. "It wasn't just a show. It was a political tool. The emperors knew that keeping the people entertained kept them loyal. Bread and circuses, right? They wouldn't question much as long as they were fed and had something to cheer for. It was an easy way to control them."

Aida leaned over the railing, staring down at the remnants of the arena. "I always imagined the Colosseum as a place for the elite, but it sounds like it was just as much for everyone else."

"That's the thing," Felix said, turning to her. "Everyone came here. Nobles, soldiers, merchants, and the poor. It was one of the only places where the whole of Roman society came together, united by the spectacle of it all. And they loved it—the thrill, the drama, the sheer extravaganza. For the people in those stands, it wasn't just about watching someone die. It was about feeling alive—about being part of something bigger than themselves. That's where the happiness came from."

Aida thought of the tourists below, wandering the ruins with their cameras, smiling for photos in front of a monument that had witnessed so much suffering.

Felix stood straight, the moment of reflection passing, and clapped his hands together. "So, enough with the heavy stuff. Want to hear something fun?" he said, his grin returning. "They say that even after all these centuries, on a quiet night, you can still hear the roars of the crowd. Ghosts of the past, cheering for another round."

Aida laughed despite herself, shaking her head. "You're just trying to spook me now."

"Maybe a little," Felix admitted with a playful smirk. "But hey, it's a nice thought. That even after all this time, the energy of this place hasn't faded."

Aida turned off her recorder, her voice quieter than before. "Not yet." She gazed down at the Colosseum below. "But how long before it does?"

Felix opened his mouth to reply, but Aida waved him off as a wave of calmness crept up her spine, unnatural and deliberate. A god was coming. Her heart skipped a beat. *Not here. Not now.* Felix had no aegis; if he let anything slip, they'd be in serious trouble.

Disa's voice rang out, smooth and nonchalant. "Hello, Aida."

Aida forced herself to turn slowly, willing her expression to stay neutral. *Act like nothing's wrong.* Beside her, Felix was already stiffening, doing his best to maintain a calm facade, but Aida could feel the tension radiating from him. She had to get through this without him losing it.

"Disa," Aida greeted with a forced smile. "I didn't expect to see you here."

Disa's outfit, as usual, was utterly inappropriate for the setting: a gaudy gold-and-blue puffer coat with gold high-top sneakers, fuzzy blue earmuffs, and silk track pants. She looked like she should be on a sleek Milan runway, an odd contrast against the ancient stones of the Colosseum. The casual arrogance in her movements and the way she surveyed the space reminded Aida that Disa was more than just another eccentric person. She was an unpredictable force, one capable of unleashing chaos at any moment.

Felix rose to the occasion, stepping forward to extend his hand. "Felix Goodman," he said, keeping his voice steady, though Aida saw the flicker of unease in his eyes. "Pleasure to meet you."

Disa's gaze drifted to Felix's outstretched hand, then slid past it as though it didn't exist. She smiled, but there was something dangerous lurking beneath her pleasant exterior. "Yes, I know who you are, Mr. Goodman." She turned her attention to Aida. "I thought I'd drop by to see how Aida's research is progressing."

"We were just wrapping up the fifth level," Aida said, keeping her tone light. "I didn't realize you'd be joining us. We would have waited for you to arrive before Felix gave me the tour."

"I don't need a tour. I'm merely checking in. Keeping an eye on things," she said, strolling toward the railing and peering over the Colosseum. "What you are doing is of prime importance. After all, you're documenting something that might not be here forever." She let the words hang in the air, her gaze still on the crumbling arena below.

Aida swallowed. What was she suggesting?

Felix forced a chuckle. "It's a remarkable place. Hard to imagine something like this ever disappearing."

Disa's eyes slid to Felix, her smile widening as though she found his comment amusing. "Oh, nothing lasts forever, Mr. Goodman. Not even something as grand as this." Her voice was calm, almost playful, but Aida knew nothing was playful about her.

Aida stepped in quickly, trying to steer the conversation. "It's incredible how the Colosseum has endured for centuries," she said, her voice a little too bright. "People still come from all over the world to experience it."

Disa let out a soft, almost mocking laugh. "Endured?" she repeated. "I'd say it's survived just long enough to witness the world around it crumble. People build things, Aida. But they also have a knack for tearing them down." She turned her gaze back to the ancient structure, her fingers trailing along the stone railing. "Civilizations fall. It's inevitable. They just need the right . . . push."

"The world's more stable than you think, Disa," Aida said, her voice steady with the help of the aegis. "Things don't just fall apart."

"Don't they?" Disa replied, her eyes bright with dark amusement. "All it takes is one small invisible thing. One change and everything you know comes undone." She turned her gaze fully on Aida, her expression unnervingly calm. "That's the beauty of it, really. You never see it coming."

Aida's breath caught in her throat. Disa wasn't speaking in hypotheticals. She was hinting at something dangerous, something Aida suspected she'd already set in motion. The realization hit her like a slow cold wave. Disa was planning something catastrophic. Not for the first time, Aida was grateful for her aegis, because without it she wasn't sure she could hold her emotions together.

Felix, beside her, gave a strained smile, his voice tight. "Well, let's hope nothing like that happens anytime soon."

Disa's gaze flicked to him, studying him for a beat too long. Then she smiled, as if she'd decided to let him off the hook. "Yes, let's hope."

Aida forced a laugh, despite the calm she felt. "What can I tell you about this project? I'm happy to give you a rundown of my last few weeks."

Disa tilted her head. "Oh, I can't stay. I have other matters to attend to. But I'm glad to see you are working in earnest on this project." She stepped back from the railing, her gaze lingering on Felix for a moment before she smiled at Aida. "I want you to finish early. Make sure you've uploaded all your research before you leave today. Then take a long vacation, why don't you?" With that, she turned and sauntered toward the stairs, her eccentric outfit glittering absurdly in the sunlight.

Aida began a stilted conversation with Felix about the ancient graffiti on the nearby wall, which they kept up until Disa was out of sight and the calm of the aegis gave way. She cloaked her MODA phone, then signaled to Felix that they were okay to talk, and he let out a breath he'd been holding, his shoulders sagging with relief. "Oh my fucking god."

Aida nodded, her heart still racing. "Yeah," she said softly. "That was a god."

"Why was she here?"

"She's the goddess of discord. Who knows. But it definitely wasn't for anything good."

"We're going to lose this place, aren't we?" he said, looking out over the ancient stones below.

Tears rose to Aida's eyes at the thought. "Yes."

Felix kicked the stone wall in front of him. "Fuck this."

There wasn't anything that Aida could say, for she felt the same.

SHE WAS FINISHED when the Colosseum closed, an hour before sundown. After saying goodbye to Felix, Aida decided to detour through the Roman Forum and stop by the Umbilicus Urbis hoping that Vulcan or Aggie might notice her lingering at the railing that separated the tourists from the brick structure. They didn't, despite the prayers she whispered: *Please, don't let them take the Colosseum.*

Reluctantly she left and decided to head up to the Campidoglio overlook next to the Palazzo Senatorio, Rome's city hall, one of the best views of the site. The fading sunlight cast a warm golden hue over the sprawling landscape. From her vantage point, the grandeur of the Roman Forum stretched out before her, its ancient stones glowing amber in the dying light. Beyond the Forum, the iconic silhouette of the Colosseum stood majestically against the horizon, shadows deepening between its weathered arches. She took a few photos, hoping they wouldn't be her last. Then she stood there, a dull ache inside her rising while she endeavored to memorize every part of the view, burning it as much as she could into memory.

A strange rumble shook Aida out of her reverie. At first, it was a sound like a jet plane coming closer, or the heavy murmur of a subway moving below. Then the ground began to shake violently beneath her, the ominous rumble growing until it became a deafening roar. She watched in horror as the Colosseum, that iconic symbol of Rome's enduring legacy, began to crumble.

"No, no, no, no, no!" she screamed. "No!"

The tallest part of the structure, the imposing outer wall that had stood for millennia, groaned. Stones that had weathered countless battles and earthquakes for thousands of years now cracked and split. Chunks of the ancient limestone tumbled from the upper arches, where she had stood less than an hour before, cascading like rain onto the tiers below. Dust and debris filled the air in a choking cloud, swirling through the last rays of the daylight sun.

Aida's hand clamped harder on the railing, her knuckles white, unable to tear her eyes from the ruin unfolding before her. This wasn't just stone falling. The world was breaking apart, history being stripped away by invisible hands.

The topmost arches, once the crown of Roman ingenuity, buckled as their keystones dislodged, collapsing into the void beneath. A thick crack snaked its way down the length of the wall, sending shudders through the massive structure. The distinct rumble of shifting earth, once distant, now became an unbearable crescendo as the outermost edge of the Colosseum crumbled away. The collapse was slow at first but then faster and faster as entire sections of the ancient monument caved in, sending rubble crashing to the ground with sickening finality. Although the Colosseum had closed, Aida was sure there must have been some workers who died in the wreckage. The thought stabbed into her heart.

The rumbling stopped, and the sound of sirens cut through the eerie quiet.

Aida's phone vibrated in her pocket. Shaking, she pulled it out. It was Felix. She hastily responded that she was okay.

Then she ran.

But there was too much distance to cover, and by the time she got close, emergency crews had already blocked off the street and weren't letting people get any closer.

Aida gripped the wooden barrier that had been erected, her fingers curling against the rough surface as the reality of the scene sank deeper into her chest. The crowd around her was a strange chorus of silence and sound—murmurs of disbelief, stifled sobs, the occasional gasp as people tried to make sense of the impossible. The air was thick not just with dust, but with something heavier: a collective grief that rippled outward from the rubble, much like the collapse itself.

A woman to her left whispered prayers under her breath, clutching a rosary as though it were the only thing keeping her tethered to the earth. Beside her, an older man stared at the ruin with hollow eyes, his lips trembling as he shook his head, over and over again.

The weight of their grief pressed into her, intertwining with her own. It was the pain of every Roman who had grown up in the shadow of this monument, every visitor drawn to it as if seeking something timeless. The Colosseum had been more than stone; it had been a constant reminder of resilience through the centuries. And now, it was a broken thing.

She glanced around at the faces in the crowd, all caught in the same disbelief. A group of teenagers, too young to fully grasp the depth of the loss, held each other in stunned silence, their eyes wide, still searching the horizon as if the Colosseum might reappear, as though this were some terrible mistake that could be undone.

Aida's own tears were quiet, slipping down her cheeks as she blinked back the dust, trying to focus. She couldn't remember the last time she'd cried in public. But here, surrounded by strangers whose hearts were breaking alongside hers, it didn't matter.

A man in a red scarf lifted his phone to record the wreckage, his hands shaking so badly that Aida was sure the image blurred. He wasn't alone—others raised their phones, trying to capture what remained, but it felt pointless. No picture could contain the depth of this loss, and no video could explain what had been taken from them.

Aida wiped her face with the back of her hand, the tears mingling with the grit of dust and ash. The sirens grew louder as more emergency vehicles arrived, but the crowd stayed rooted, unwilling to turn away from the fallen monument as if by watching they could somehow keep it with them a little longer.

"Aida!"

It was Felix, who had come back and somehow managed to find her. She collapsed into his arms, and they held each other tight, their tears mingling. She knew what no one else around them could understand.

She had made this happen.

III

22

February–March 2020

Two days later, authorities still hadn't confirmed the cause of the Colosseum's collapse. It wasn't a bomb—that much was clear—but uncertainty lingered over whether the giant sinkhole in the center of the wreckage had been caused by an earthquake or the ongoing metro construction below. Whispers of faulty engineering and geological instability swirled through the media. Some suspected corruption or negligence, but no one could quite explain how it had all gone so terribly wrong.

Eighty lives were lost—janitorial staff, security personnel, and a few unlucky tourists who had been caught in the surrounding area. Rome vowed to rebuild, but the cost would be astronomical, and no one knew where the funds would come from.

Aida spent her "vacation" that Disa had prescribed watching the television with a grim obsession. She couldn't shake the feeling that this was no accident. The gods, after all, didn't have to throw bombs or cast lightning bolts to cause destruction. They just needed to push the right pieces into place and let human error take care of the rest.

The only thing that kept her grounded was the imminent arrival of both Yumi and Luciano. She dreaded their questions, knowing she'd have none of the answers they'd want to hear.

On the day of Yumi's flight to Rome, Aida shuffled down to the kitchen for breakfast. Ilario and Pippa were uncharacteristically standing at the bar, looking at a newspaper.

"Is there more news?" Aida asked as she hauled herself up into the bar seat.

Ilario lifted his eyes from the paper. "*Buongiorno.* Different news. That virus, the one in China, it's growing," he said.

"You mean spreading?" Aida teased.

"Bloody right," Pippa said, pushing the paper away. "Spreadin'. The Chinese government's locked down that city, Wuhan, right? Shut it all down, lockin' people inside. No one's goin' anywhere. They're pullin' sick people out from their families, quarantinin' 'em. They reckon thousands might've died already."

"It's worse than that," Ilario said. "The virus is in Rome. People have been hospitalized. *È terrible.*"

Aida gasped as Disa's words came hurtling back to her. *All it takes is one small invisible thing. That's the beauty of it, really. You never see it coming.*

"Oh my god," she breathed as the gravity of the situation hit her. It wasn't the Colosseum that was the catastrophe. It was a virus, a small invisible thing.

"Aye, it's 'orrible," Pippa said. "But what can we do? We charge ahead. Now let me whip up that cappuccino for ya." She swept the paper off the counter and focused on the espresso machine.

Ilario brought a chocolate cornetto pastry and a bowl of cut-up fruit. "Signorina, *tutto* okay?"

Aida took a breath. "No. *Il Colosseo*, the news about the virus. What's happening?"

Ilario looked off toward the east and curled his hand into horns with his fingers. "*Tiè!*" he exclaimed, shaking his fist. *Take that!* "Now you."

Aida felt awkward making the sign to ward off evil, but she did it to appease the chef, even practicing the right way to say the word: *tee-ay.* If only a simple hand gesture could save the world.

THAT AFTERNOON, AIDA greeted Yumi at the airport, relieved to see a familiar face. "We've got this," Yumi assured her as they hugged, but Aida knew her friend was just putting on a brave face.

Yumi, fresh from the upheaval of her layoff, threw herself into the task of finding Pandora with a renewed vigor. The next few days were a blur of code, maps, and endless cups of coffee as she tirelessly scoured digital landscapes for any trace of the elusive IP address or any information she could find about MODA.

Reports of the virus's spread grew more alarming by the day. Flights from China were no longer allowed into the country, significantly reducing the number of tourists in the city. Italy had confirmed more cases, and the sense of anxiety in the city was palpable. The growing concern over the virus tempered the usual bustle of the city. At coffee bars and in shops, conversations were dominated by the latest updates and speculations, especially about the growing number of cases up north, in Lombardy. But when the government shuttered theaters, cinemas, and gyms across the country for at least a week, worry really began to set in.

It was amid this backdrop of uncertainty that Luciano arrived in Rome a week after Yumi. "*Bellissimo!*" he exclaimed that night when Yumi opened the door and ushered him into the apartment. "I like your style," he told her as he admired the colorful decor.

Aida had to laugh. Yumi had complained about the place since the first trip back in December—it was all style over substance. It looked great, but the plumbing was wonky, there was limited counter space, and the furniture was, for the most part, pretty uncomfortable. But it had a prime location, a particular charm, and Felix had somehow wrangled a discount from his friend for the new extended stay.

"So this is the mighty Luciano!" Felix said, coming forward to greet the Collector.

"I'm not sure how mighty I am." He laughed.

"How long are you here for?" Felix asked.

Luciano handed over his coat to Yumi. "Not quite two weeks. Till the fifteenth. Then they are sending me to a little town outside of Paris, Tonnerre, to catalog the happiness at some Renaissance-era châteaus."

"I'd agree with mighty," Aida said as Luciano folded her into his arms and kissed her cheeks. They held on to each other a beat too long, eliciting snickers from Yumi and Felix.

"Where does MODA think you are now?" Aida asked Luciano when they pulled apart. With Yumi in town, it was common for Aida to spend time at her apartment, so while she masked what the gods might hear, she didn't try to obfuscate her location.

"In for the night, watching TV in my uncle's apartment—well, I suppose it's my new apartment. Although I'm glad to be here with you instead of watching the news. Have you heard the latest?"

Felix grunted. "I have. Which is why I brought this." He lifted up a grocery bag that was sitting on a nearby chair. The group followed him into the kitchen, where he pulled out a bottle of gin, some limes, and tonic. Several pizza boxes sat on the counter waiting.

"What was the news?" Yumi asked as she started to cut up the pizzas and dole them out in pieces, American style.

"It's bad," Luciano warned. "They're closing all schools and universities in Italy until at least the middle of March."

"Damn it," Aida cursed. "This is Disa's doing, I know it. The prophecy about the Colosseum is coming true."

"Rome hasn't fallen yet," Yumi said.

Felix began shaking the drinks. He made an attempt to sound upbeat. "There have been lots of viruses and diseases in our lifetime, and it's always been okay. I mean, Ebola, mad cow. They'll figure it out."

"I fear you may be too optimistic. They can't contain it in China, and I don't think Italy is doing much better," Luciano said. "Do you ever recall this sort of quarantine?"

After her conversation with Pippa last week, Aida had immediately looked up everything she could about the virus and came across the videos of the Chinese quarantine. One still haunted her, of half a dozen men in white hazmat suits forcibly removing a family from their apartment to take into quarantine. Since then, she had been glued to Reddit news feeds on the growing crisis.

Felix set a gin and tonic in front of Aida, and she had to stop herself from downing it in one gulp. "Didn't you have an opera date canceled when they closed the theaters?" she asked him.

He winked at her. "We still had the date. We just skipped the theater."

"Of course. I should have guessed." Aida's laughter was cut short by her watch buzzing. She glanced at it to see a text from Trista.

"*Merda*," Luciano cursed at the same time. He was scrolling through his phone. "My aide says our quarterly MODA meeting has been canceled."

Aida dug her phone out of her pocket to see that Trista's message was the same. "But the meeting isn't until the end of the month. Have they ever canceled meetings before?"

"Not while I've worked for them."

"It's definitely not a good sign." Aida sighed. "I wish Sophie would give us more news."

"Have you tried reaching her?" Felix asked.

"Yes, every day. There's only silence. I don't know what they really expect us to do at this point. We can't find Pandora, and we're just measly humans. How can we do anything? Especially in the face of something like a virus?"

Felix lifted his glass. "We change the subject to something happier, that's what we do. Let's live in the present. Let me propose a toast. To friends!"

The lively banter continued as they shared slices of pizza. Aida tried to focus on the comforting aroma of warm dough and cheese, the bite of the gin, and the good company of her friends. But it wasn't easy to live in the present when such a deep unease about the future lingered.

As the evening wore on, Aida found herself glancing at

Luciano, the unspoken connection between them growing stronger with each passing moment. Eventually, the group decided to call it a night, and Luciano offered to walk Aida partway back to the palazzo.

The streets of Rome were eerily quiet as they strolled under the soft glow of the streetlights. Luciano immediately took her hand, and Aida wished it weren't so cold that they needed gloves.

"I like your friends," he told her. "*Felix mi fa morire dal ridere.*"

Aida laughed. "Yes, he makes me die of laughter all the time too. And he's absolutely brilliant. He knows more about history than anyone I've met. I'm not sure how he remembers everything."

"And Yumi, what a good friend she is to you."

It was an observation that warmed Aida's heart. "She is. We've known each other a long time."

"That's why she's so invested." Luciano squeezed her hand. "If I had just lost my job, I'd be panicking and spending every last second trying to find another one."

"She's always been able to land on her feet," Aida said. "She's very good at what she does. The fact that she hasn't found Pandora yet says more about their godlike capabilities than it does about her. But she loves a good puzzle. She won't quit till she's figured it out."

He paused then and pulled her close. "Neither will I." He leaned forward, his lips a warm contrast to the crisp air that touched her cheeks. Aida let herself be lost in the moment, savoring the tingle that rose within her when their tongues met, when his hands pulled her close. Around them, Rome stood still, its historic stones a silent witness.

Aida laughed when they finally pulled apart. "We really should stop doing this in dark alleys."

"At least we don't have teenagers heckling us this time," he said. "But you're right. We should have some sort of proper date."

That seemed highly improbable—the mere fact that they

were walking together in public was a danger in itself. Aida smiled, masking the stab of disappointment at the thought. How could they ever have any semblance of proper anything as long as MODA employed them? She leaned forward and kissed him again, with more urgency, channeling her worries into the passion between them. Who knew what would happen in their future? Aida would do everything she could to enjoy her now.

"*Dio mio*," Luciano whispered. "Maybe we should just skip the proper date."

"*Sì*, but not tonight," Aida said. "Later this week? But now I should go. If Trista is tracking me, she's probably wondering why I stopped a few blocks away for so long."

Luciano nodded and gave her a quick kiss on the nose. "*A presto.*" *See you soon.* He backed away, then, with a wave, turned back the way he came.

23

March 2020

FOUR DAYS LATER, the gravity of the situation had intensified. Aida, Yumi, Felix, and Luciano had reconvened at
Yumi's apartment when the news broke. Italy had been placed
under a nationwide ban of public gatherings, religious services,
and football matches. The streets of Rome were hauntingly deserted. Museums, cafés, and even hairdressers had been forced to
shut their doors, a tangible sign of the crisis gripping the country.

"I never imagined it would come to this," Yumi said, her voice
laced with disbelief. "The entire country on lockdown. Everything closed. The Pantheon, the Galleria Borghese. Hell, even
the Vatican is shut."

"How will we do our jobs?" Aida asked, looking at Luciano.
"Will we even have jobs?"

"I think so. Dolores sent me an email this morning with
more details for my next assignment. Surely, they know what's
going on. It seems they are still planning on having us do work
in some way."

Aida stiffened. "They still want you working? Now?"

Luciano nodded. "Apparently."

Aida found that suspicious. "Does Dolores seem . . . at all
concerned?"

Luciano frowned. "What do you mean?"

"I mean, the world is shutting down, people are terrified,

and yet she's acting like nothing's changed. Like she expects us to go on as usual."

"Well . . . I suppose." He hesitated. "She's always been practical."

"Or programmed," Aida murmured.

Felix gave her a sharp look. "You think she's one of them?"

Aida exhaled, debating whether to voice the thought that had been gnawing at her. "I don't know. But we know the gods have been using automatons as their eyes and ears. And Trista never takes a day off, never misses a detail. Now Dolores is carrying on like nothing's wrong, even while entire countries grind to a halt? It's strange."

Yumi straightened. "You'll need to be extra careful around them."

"Good thing we already are," Aida said. She thought back to all the times she had passed by Trista's door at night and it seemed as though she had been talking to someone. Suddenly, she was sure Trista had been conversing with some of the MODA gods.

For a moment, silence settled over the room, the weight of it pressing down on all of them.

"I've heard they are going to start restricting international travel altogether," Felix said. "You could be stuck here."

Aida's heart fluttered. She liked the idea of Luciano remaining in Rome. Their chances to see each other had been few.

Yumi bit her lip, contemplating. "I heard that too and considered whether I should try to get out of the country while I can. My parents are pressuring me to do it, but I've decided to stay. I can stay till May. I'm sure it will be better by then. There's still so much we need to do here."

"What about you?" Felix asked Luciano.

He looked at Aida. "I don't know. If we needed to come and go, MODA could pull any string they wanted. I'm not worried yet."

Aida smiled, happy with the thought.

Yumi uncorked a bottle of wine and began pouring. "I'm thinking you should go back, Luciano."

"What?" Aida couldn't believe what her friend was saying.

"Why would you suggest that?" Felix said, winking at Aida. "Clearly Aida doesn't agree with you."

Heat rose to Aida's face. She wasn't used to her affections being so generally discussed.

"I know, I know. But I think I figured out how to find Pandora. And you're the one to help me," Yumi said, looking at Luciano.

Aida wasn't at all happy about the suggestion of Luciano leaving but was relieved that Yumi had some sort of plan. "What's this idea?"

"I think we can use Luciano's next upload to MODA as a way in. If I can hack into it, it might lead us to Pandora. It needs to be you," she said, looking at him. "If I go through Aida, it will be far too obvious. They know I'm in cybersecurity. It could immediately link Aida to any hack."

Luciano looked at her, understanding dawning in his eyes. "That's brilliant, Yumi. I can't believe we didn't think of that earlier. It's risky, but it just might work."

Fear rose in Aida. "What if they detect it? They could come after Luciano."

He was more nonchalant. "I'll feign ignorance. That's what Sophie's aegis is good for. Remaining calm in the face of godlike danger. They won't know I have any idea."

"I don't like it," Aida said, shaking her head. "You're right, it's risky."

Yumi reached across the table and squeezed her friend's hand. "I've been trying to figure this out for months. I've exhausted all my other options."

Aida groaned. "All right, fine. How will it work?"

Yumi pulled a little box from her pocket and held it out to Luciano. "In this is a tiny USB drive that looks like a fob. Mostly unnoticeable. Before you start working, you'll plug it into your computer and run the program that pops up. Then do whatever you normally do to catalog the happiness. Of course, you'll want to do this when your aide—what's her name? Dolores? When she isn't staring over your shoulder."

"Do I need to let you know when I do it?" Luciano asked.

"No. Definitely not. You don't want to raise more suspicion. Don't worry, I'll know."

Luciano took the box from her and slid it into the front pocket of his jeans. "I'll arrange to go back tomorrow. It probably makes the most sense to leave early with everything going on with the virus. Maybe I'll get a couple days of work done there before France decides to lock down too."

Felix asked the question that Aida was sure everyone was wondering. "What happens when we find Pandora? Especially if we're on lockdown?"

Yumi raised a glass. "We drink. And tackle that problem when we get there."

Aida lifted her glass with everyone else. But it all seemed so hopeless, even if they did find Pandora.

After the toast, Luciano cleared his throat. "It's been good to spend time with you all. But Aida and I have an important date that needs to happen before I leave for France." He held out his hand to Aida. "Ready?"

She blushed at his forwardness.

"What are you waiting for?" Felix nudged her.

Aida stood and took his hand. She stuck out her tongue at Felix. "Nothing."

"Find me tomorrow," Yumi told her as they were leaving. Aida knew this was polite speech for *call and tell me everything.*

Aida promised, then briefly set her location to remain at Yumi's apartment before setting off with Luciano into the night.

AIDA LINKED HER arm in Luciano's as they traversed the dark Roman streets. Fewer tourists meant their path through the cobbled streets to the Spanish Steps was undisturbed.

"I wish I were staying," Luciano said. "But I think her idea might work. And we've been out of options for so long."

"I know. I just wouldn't want anything to happen to you."

"I'll be fine. My aide never spends time with me at my locations, so no one will see me use the drive," Luciano said.

"If Pandora's in London, how will we get to her?"

"This virus scare can't last forever. We'll be back in London before we know it."

As they approached the Spanish Steps, the grandeur of the location struck Aida anew. The steps, often swarming with tourists, were unusually quiet, casting the area in an almost serene light. Luciano led her around the corner to his uncle's apartment, tucked discreetly on a narrow street. When they finally entered, Aida was met with an unexpected sense of elegance and calmness. The space reflected a life steeped in art and solitude. Artifacts of a rich, carefully curated life lined the walls. As the door closed behind them, the noise of the city faded into a distant hum.

Luciano moved to help Aida out of her coat, but she caught his hand, pulling him toward her. The tension that had simmered between them during their walk was now impossible to resist and she pressed against him, her hands roving through his hair. The taste of him was familiar and intoxicating. His coat slid off with a soft thud as he gripped her waist, drawing her in as though he'd been waiting for this moment as long as she had.

Their lips barely broke apart as they moved through the apartment, discarding their clothes along the way, a mad rush of months of pent-up desire finally unraveling in the space between them. When they reached the bedroom, they collapsed in a blur of entangled limbs. Aida could feel herself dissolving, her body arching into his embrace, every sensation heightened. Her fingers dug into his back as she lost herself in the moment—every touch, every breath was like fuel to a fire that wouldn't stop burning. Aida became deliriously hollow, with Luciano filling her, her senses reaching upward, above them, soaring over the

Roman rooftops, straining against the sky, endless stars, pin-pricks of light pulsing, pumping in that voluminous dark, culminating in a collective hot sigh.

Afterward, they lay together in a haze, the quiet hum of the night filtering in through the open window. Aida felt as though she were floating, her body weightless and content. Luciano's fingers traced lazy patterns on her arm, but they didn't speak. They didn't need to.

Later, when he walked her back through the quiet streets, they still said very little, the spell of the night still thick between them. Aida didn't want it to break.

But it did when he pulled away from their final lingering kiss. "Be safe, Aida."

"You too." She watched him go, the lightness she'd felt replaced by a worry for what might come. When would she see him again? Would she?

Reluctantly, she headed down the street and let herself into the MODA palazzo.

THE FOLLOWING DAYS unfolded like pages from a dystopian novel, each bringing a new decree that tightened the grip of isolation around Rome. On March 11, the city's vibrant pulse was muted as a partial nationwide lockdown was declared. The usual hum of life in the streets, the chatter from coffee bars, the rush of the metro—all were silenced. Movement was restricted, borders between cities became lines not to be crossed, and places of learning and leisure closed their doors. Aida, Yumi, and Felix now found themselves isolated in their own pockets of the city.

Luciano, across the border in France, felt like a voice from another world.

They changed my assignment. Now they're sending me to
the Promenade Plantée, an old railway line they've converted
into an elevated park. Have you been to the High Line in
NYC? This place was the inspiration.

An emoji of some trees and flowers accompanied his Signal text.

I'm relieved you'll be outside, Aida told him. Maybe it will keep you from catching the virus.

Usually, the promenade is very busy, but I think people are already starting to stay home, he wrote. Macron closed schools and universities today. I think it will affect how many people I end up talking to for my interviews. I'm done here in three days and will upload everything then.

Aida replied with a fingers-crossed emoji. She hated the idea that he was mixing with people. You got out just in time. They announced a travel ban in and out of Italy with only a few exceptions, and those people have to quarantine themselves for two weeks! This is so awful.

Don't despair. We'll figure this out.

But the next day, they closed the park, and since Luciano had gathered so little data, there was no reason to do an upload. They were at the mercy of the pandemic. Luciano was furious that he had decided not to remain in Rome. I'm stuck here in this big château with only Dolores and a staff who has been mostly invisible to me. To which god should I pray to end this quickly?

The gods won't help you. We're supposed to be the ones that end it, remember? Aida responded.

Sono tutte stronzate. Why are we the ones to do this?

Aida sighed. I know. You're right. It is all bullshit. But what choice do we have?

There was a long pause. I can pretend I don't know about any of this. Go about my job like nothing has happened.

I can't, Aida said. Her heart pricked with despair at the thought of Luciano abandoning her to handle the gods alone. In my mind, the Colosseum falls over and over. Sophie said that the big things aren't as easily forgotten. I hate that. I wish it would disappear from my mind like other things have. I can't bear knowing that I had some hand in its downfall.

And now this virus, he said. How will we get through this?

Aida didn't have an answer for that question.

THE NEXT WEEK saw Rome transform into a ghost of its former self. Parks, once brimming with life, were abandoned, their gates closed as if to hold back the spring that refused to be ignored. The streets were lined with shuttered shops. And yet, amid the stillness, a storm raged—a storm of numbers that climbed each day, numbers that represented lives lost. Italy's daily death toll had reached a number too grim to comprehend, casting a shadow over the nation that no sun seemed strong enough to dispel. As Aida watched the city from her window, the world outside was both achingly familiar and irrevocably altered.

At first, Aida tried to convince Yumi to come and stay with her at the palazzo, but she refused, not wanting to be under MODA's watchful eyes. And when Aida suggested she should stay with Yumi for a while, her friend shot the idea down. "Absolutely not! If you're here, they'll have their eyes and ears watching everything I do."

Aida knew she was right, but she worried about Yumi there alone, locked away from other people. So, although her needs were easily met at the palazzo, Aida downloaded the self-declaration form from the official government website and meticulously filled it out a few times a week, marking the box for "necessities," as grocery shopping was one of the few permissible reasons to venture outside. Yumi did the same, and they met in the line at the grocery store, faces masked, six feet apart, and talked about nothing of import. Aida ached to hug her friend, or more specifically, for her friend to hug her. She hadn't realized how much she needed that type of human connection.

Felix couldn't join them—he had recently moved and now lived farther away, in a tiny studio near the Appian Way, and going to a grocery store in the city center could lead to a hefty fine. The *polizia* were very serious about the fines. If you weren't going to the grocery store or a specific critical job or to take care of elderly parents, it was expected that you were at home, locked up, not in physical contact with anyone but the people you lived with. Yumi had already received one warning for taking a long walk beyond the area around Piazza Navona. As an Asian woman, she stood out and was repeatedly asked to see her self-declaration form.

These people, they are so stupid. The virus doesn't give a rat's ass about our race, she would rail in their group Signal.

The frustration in Yumi's messages was palpable. Aida could only imagine how her friend felt facing the same unwarranted scrutiny every time she dared to step outside. It was a reminder that the virus had brought physical isolation and deepened unseen divides, casting shadows of suspicion where there should have been solidarity. Aida had a surge of protectiveness for her friend. The lockdown had become more than just a measure of safety; it had morphed into a mirror, reflecting the fragmented lines of a society under strain.

AIDA DECIDED TO take the downtime as an opportunity to work hard on her second novel. And when she wasn't writing, she gathered with the others still at the palazzo—Dante, Pippa, Ilario, and a housekeeper who Aida rarely saw as she preferred to keep to herself. Dante had somehow acquired a 25,000-piece jigsaw puzzle of the Sistine Chapel, which he spread across the massive table in the big dining hall. They spent days trying to piece it all together. Trista rebuffed Aida's numerous attempts to get her to join them.

"Why do you bother?" Pippa asked one afternoon. "She'd only drag us down, wouldn't she? And we ain't in need of any more of that, not with this bleedin' pandemic on."

"Maybe she would loosen up if she spent time with us."

That brought a chuckle from the ordinarily stoic Dante. "*Quando i maiali voleranno.*"

When pigs fly. Aida had to laugh. It was the first time she had ever heard Dante say anything negative.

"I just don't understand her at all," she responded.

"Let go of what you can't change," Ilario advised. "And that woman—" he nodded toward the empty door "—is not one you can change."

THE DAYS TURNED into weeks.

"I feel like we're frogs boiling in the water. We're at the point where they are turning up the heat more and more rapidly, and we're going to be cooked." Felix looked haggard. They were on their daily Zoom call, in which they were attempting to keep up pretenses and couldn't talk about anything related to MODA or what they all felt underneath it all—the deep despair that the world was spiraling out of control, and only they knew why. And there wasn't a damn thing any of them could do about it.

"Have you learned the anthem yet?" Aida asked Yumi.

"Not by heart. But my neighbors forgive me for having to look at my phone for the lyrics."

Every day at 5:30 p.m. all of Rome went out on their rooftops and balconies, or opened their windows, and sang the national anthem, "Il Canto degli Italiani." It was often followed by songs like "Volare" or "Bella Ciao." This moment of solidarity was uplifting in a way that Aida found difficult to describe. It was not a moment of happiness, but something different, something inspiring and comforting. It gave Aida a strange hope—that despite everything MODA was doing to destroy the spirit of the people, they couldn't take it all away. Deep inside, she began to think that maybe there was still time to fix the miserable mess that all the Happiness Collectors had gotten them into.

But as the weeks compounded, the oppression of lockdown began to take a toll on them all. Aida couldn't count all her crying jags into her pillow or with Yumi on Zoom. Yumi had planned on applying for a visa, but by the time it had arrived, she had already nailed down a new job working for an American software company that had an office in Italy and was happy to let her live anywhere within the country. She wanted to look for a more permanent apartment, but the pandemic made that impossible.

Felix eventually confided that he was starting to panic about money. While he had shifted to doing online Zoom tours using photos and video, the money wasn't the same, especially without tips being slid into his hand at the end of the day. Aida offered him help, but he turned it down. Without telling him, she sought out the landlord of his apartment and paid the year's rent in full. Then, she arranged for grocery deliveries of some of his favorite foods every week. When they Zoomed, he always told her to stop, but she knew him well enough to know he didn't mean it, that he was grateful for the reprieve on his wallet.

ONE AFTERNOON IN MAY, she wandered down to the grand salon to work on the third puzzle that Dante had laid out for them, this one of the Venetian Grand Canal. A heavy calm overtook her as she neared the door. She took a deep breath. The god likely knew she was there, so she didn't hesitate long. She entered the room, wondering who she would find there. It was Mo, alone, fiddling with the pieces.

"How did you get here?" she asked, although she already knew the answer. She wondered how that worked—could he arrive in a blink? Was there some puff of smoke like in the cartoons?

"MODA has its ways," he said without looking up. When she neared, he slid a huge chunk of sky into one of the puzzle's edges. It was a section that they had been working on for the better part of the week.

"What ways would those be?"

"Ways you don't get to worry your pretty little head about." At this, he did look up, and the stare he gave her was serious. If she hadn't been under Sophie's aegis, Aida thought she might have experienced true panic. There was danger in his eyes.

"Jeesh, I'm sorry for asking." Aida took a seat nearby and picked up one of the puzzle pieces, willing herself to act normal. "We can barely leave the palazzo without being stopped by the Carabinieri asking for a permission slip and you casually waltz in. It was a reasonable question."

"I'm not reasonable."

"Clearly." He didn't respond. She attempted to lock several different pieces together while they sat in silence. The quiet stretched out, punctuated only by the click of Aida's nails on the table as she searched for the right fit and Mo shuffling his feet as he placed his pieces. After it reached the uncomfortable stage, Aida resolved that she wouldn't be the one to break the silence.

Finally, after another ten minutes of noiseless puzzling, Mo stood and came around the table to where she sat. He pulled up a chair alarmingly close to her and sat down. "Here." He took the puzzle pieces she had been working with, deftly found the right companions, and slid them into place.

"What a useful skill to have," she said, marveling.

Mo put his hand on the back of her chair. "I have many useful skills."

"You're sitting awfully close. Are you trying to give me coronavirus?"

"I haven't been around anyone, and I've been masked," he said mildly. Aida didn't believe him about the mask, but she was sure he was immune to the virus.

"Then are you trying to seduce me?" she asked, grateful for the aegis miraculously keeping her heart calm.

"Hardly," he said.

She raised an eyebrow at him, then turned back to the puzzle, picking up a piece. "What other motive might you have for invading my space?"

Suddenly, his hands were upon her, twisting her toward him, his fingers gripping her shoulders. His face drew close to hers.

"Maybe I just want to scare the shit out of you," he growled.
If not for the aegis, and if she didn't know he couldn't harm
her, she honestly would have been scared shitless. No one had
ever held her in such a way.

"You don't scare me," she said. "And you are my *employer.*
What are you doing?"

He abruptly dropped his hands, and to her surprise, he actually looked sheepish. "True," he said, turning back to the
puzzle. He didn't move away.

Aida returned to the puzzle, trying to understand what was
happening. What did Mo know? If he knew they had found
Pandora's key, wouldn't he have done something more drastic—
fired her? Arranged for another mortal to harm her directly?
She thought back to the time she saw him alone in London.
His behavior then had been strange, and that was before she had
known about Pandora.

"I wanted to see what you would do," he finally said. "You
are unusual, Aida. Unexpected."

"I'm not sure if that's good or bad," she said, setting a puzzle
piece in place.

He chuckled. "Neither am I."

"Why are you here?" she asked.

"I like to periodically check in on Lady Ozie's interests."

"Will I ever meet her?" Aida had no desire to meet the goddess of misery, but it seemed like a reasonable question, to meet
the woman who was bankrolling her entire livelihood.

"Trust me, you don't want to be in her sights. Just keep doing what you are doing."

This time, it was Aida's turn to laugh, a rueful one. "A whole
lot of nothing? This pandemic doesn't give me much to do. And
I would really love to be able to find a bit of happiness right
now."

But not if it will entirely disappear.

"Are there places in Rome you want to visit? Maybe we can
make happiness happen for you." His face had softened, and he

was looking at her with what she thought might be some sort of actual affection. It struck her that he probably wasn't someone who had ever had a real friend in his life.

"There are so many," she said, suddenly at a loss. What places should she name? There was a consequence to her choice. If she chose the Pantheon, she was sure another earthquake would make it fall. If she chose one of the museums, the doors might close, or art might be stolen.

"What book are you working on now?"

"I just finished *The Botanist's Muse*, but my agent wants to wait till the pandemic cools a bit—or until we figure out what the new normal looks like—before she starts looking for a home for it. Now I'm starting on a novel about a Baroque-era steward that was orphaned as a child. He traveled all over Italy and grew to such prominence that the Pope gave him knighthood."

"Then you should go to Palazzo Barberini. I'll work with Trista to make it happen."

A shiver ran up Aida's spine. The steward she was writing about had spent some time working at Palazzo Barberini early in his career. Visiting it would help her research, but then it would disappear. What would happen to what she was writing if that was the case?

"That would be wonderful," she managed. "But I'm sure the museum is closed. I wouldn't want to put anyone at risk to open it just for me."

"There will be no risk, I assure you." He stood but did not step back from the table. He gazed down at the disarray of pieces before him. "You're quite the enigma, Aida. A woman with secrets."

Aida did not look up. She wasn't sure she could maintain her composure even with the aegis. Terror filled her at the idea that he might know she had figured MODA out. After a brief pause, she finally spoke. "Every woman has secrets. You should know that by now."

He huffed. "Touché. But you jest, and I do not."

"Ah. I see how this is. You can tease me, but I cannot tease you? Fine. What do you want to know?"

Mo paused, as though weighing his next words carefully. He leaned back slightly, hands stilling, and for a moment, Aida thought she saw something unfamiliar in his eyes—not the usual sharpness or sarcasm, but curiosity.

"What is it like, spending time with someone without an angle?" he asked.

Aida glanced up, surprised. "Are you saying you usually have an angle?"

His lips quirked into a smirk. "Let's just say I'm not used to idle company."

"And I'm idle company?"

He shrugged, leaning forward to rest his elbows on the table. "What other sort of company is there in the middle of a pandemic?"

Aida sighed. "I wish you weren't right."

Mo tapped a puzzle piece on the table, turning it in his fingers. "Do you find the company of other people enjoyable? When there's no . . . expectation. Just . . . talking?"

"Well, yes. Don't you?"

He chuckled, but it was soft, almost self-conscious. "Maybe. Or maybe I'm just . . . not very good at this."

"This?"

He met her eyes, and for a second, the air between them felt different—not charged with tension, but something closer to vulnerability. "This. Talking. Being . . . friendly."

Aida picked up another piece and turned it over in her hand.

"I get the sense that maybe you don't have many friends." Aida knew it was bold, but being bold had always been the best tactic with him.

"I have always found friends to be overrated. Few conversations ever take place where someone doesn't need something from the other person."

"That's true. But that's not always a bad thing. Conversations with my friends always have two underlying needs: curiosity and respect."

Mo tilted his head. "And what is it you're curious about?"

"In general? Life, people, how things work. But with you . . . ?" She glanced up, meeting his gaze. "I'm curious why you're here."

His brow furrowed, but he didn't look away. "I already told you. I'm checking in on Lady Ozie's interests."

"Yes, but why are you *really* here? This isn't exactly a *check-in* sort of visit." She searched the puzzle, looking for the right spot for the piece in her hand. "You're not the type to sit around for hours doing jigsaw puzzles with someone just because of a job."

"Maybe I'm the curious one. Or perhaps I'm trying to see what it's like to have a conversation where I don't need something from the other person."

She smiled. "Well, so far, you're doing okay. No major social blunders. Well, except the attempt to choke me."

He laughed, and it was a different laugh, at least for him—a genuine, happy sort of laugh. "I shouldn't have done that. It belied—" he faltered, as if not sure he should say the words "—the respect I might have for you." He turned toward the door but paused, glancing back at the puzzle pieces scattered on the table. "Palazzo Barberini. You said you wanted to go?"

Aida hesitated, her heart speeding up as she considered the outcome of the offer. But to say no would bring questions that she couldn't answer. "You really don't have to go through the trouble."

"Consider it a favor," he said with a small smile. "Friends do that, right?" He gave her a final look, one that was more curious than anything else, before sauntering toward the door.

When the calm from the aegis dissipated and the throbbing of her heart rose to take its place, she took a deep breath, trying to puzzle out what had just happened.

What did it mean to be friends with a god like Momus?

24

May 2020

AFTER MO HAD GONE, Aida went to her office and printed out a grocery permission slip, then donned her mask and grabbed her coat. She texted Yumi on the way. She was stopped once, not far from the palazzo, but after a check of her papers she was free to go, with the admonishment not to go anywhere but the store.

It was an admonishment Aida promptly ignored. Before she reached Yumi's building, she masked her location on her MODA phone for the first time in months. Yumi buzzed her in, and to her great relief, she didn't see anyone in the hallways who might have noticed this stranger who shouldn't be there.

She collapsed into Yumi's arms the second the door closed.

"Oh my god, a hug!" her friend exclaimed, holding her tight. "I didn't realize how much I've missed this. But you're brave, stopping here."

Aida shrugged. "I can afford the fine."

"Heh, we should have done this ages ago then." She sobered. "But what's going on? You look worried."

"I am. Something really weird just happened with Mo."

Yumi raised an eyebrow. "Let me get the wine. It sounds like we'll need it."

After clinking together their glasses of rosé, Aida explained Mo's out-of-character behavior.

Yumi leaned back on the couch, eyes wide with interest. "So, let me get this straight. Mo—your cryptic, cynical employer—decided to just sit next to you and, what . . . attempt a friendly conversation?"

Aida nodded, sighing. "Exactly. And I can't tell if it was genuine or some sort of ploy. He's never been that . . . well, not exactly kind, but almost . . . normal with me."

"Whoa. This might be an opportunity. If he's sympathetic to you, he may be more likely to turn against his siblings."

Aida bit her lip, considering Yumi's words. "Maybe. It didn't feel manipulative this time. But I'm wary. I have to believe that he *is* someone who always has a motive. Even if it's not apparent immediately. He said as much at the beginning of the conversation."

Yumi nodded. "Yeah, but maybe this is him learning to act without an agenda. Maybe gods can change?"

Aida looked down at her glass, swirling the wine thoughtfully. "It's just strange. Why now? Why me? He's had centuries to find a friend."

"Maybe you're the first person who's treated him like a human being. You dish it back to him. I mean, everyone else is afraid of him, or they're working with him for their own gain. You've stayed honest. That probably counts for more than you realize. You might just be the one to teach him what it's like to have a real friend. And hey, if it goes well, that's one less immortal on your case, right?"

Aida laughed despite herself. "I doubt it's that simple. But who knows?"

PALAZZO BARBERINI WAS a thirty-minute walk across the city center. Aida was stopped twice by Carabinieri, but when she showed them the permission slip that Trista had given her, they quickly apologized and let her go on her way. At the door to the museum, she was surprised to find Mo there, waiting with Felix. Despite his mask obscuring half his face, Aida could tell her friend was not happy.

"Nice of you to join us," Mo said. He knocked on the door and a few seconds later it swung wide to let them in. A slender woman with a mask and gloves instructed them not to touch anything and to leave their masks on. Immediately after she disappeared, Mo tore his off.

"Dreadful things. I know they save lives, but mine sure as hell doesn't need saving."

Felix muttered something about putting other people's lives in danger.

Mo guffawed. "Worry not, you beastly little man. I'm needed back in London, and I'll be taking my maskless self right back out that door."

"It was nice of you to meet us here," Aida said to break the tension. She had hoped his earlier friendliness might continue, but perhaps that didn't extend to other humans. "I wasn't expecting to see you."

Mo's eyes seemed to light up momentarily. "I wanted to make sure you could get in without any hassle. But apparently, Trista also thought it prudent to send your bumbling guide friend along."

Felix was about to say something, but Aida broke in before he could set Mo off. "Trista is good at her job. Felix is one of the best guides in the city. He's been crucial in helping me catalog everything to Lady Ozie's specifications." She turned to Felix and held out an elbow for him to bump. "Good to see you again."

"Thanks," he said, connecting his elbow to hers.

"This lockdown is becoming tiring. Something must be done about it," Mo said, almost more to himself than to Aida and Felix. He put his hand on the door. "London's calling and I must be away. I think London should be calling you again soon as well." He winked at Aida, then disappeared through the door. The blanket of calm that surrounded her abruptly ended.

Felix sagged in relief. "What a colossal asshole. Seriously, one of the biggest jerks I've ever met."

"For some reason, he seems to like me," Aida said. "What did he say to you?"

"He was standing at the door when I arrived. When I said I was there to meet you, he ripped into me, interrogating me. It was unnerving. It was clear he didn't want me to be there at all. I would have left, but I was worried about leaving you alone with that guy. Despite his damned good looks, everything out of his mouth was sarcastic and downright acerbic."

Aida had to chuckle. "Well, he is the god of sarcasm, after all."

"Wait, that was Mo?" Felix covered his masked mouth with his hand.

"It was."

Felix could hardly say anything for a moment. When he finally did, it was with a curse. "*Fuuuuuck.* I don't like this god thing. I'm so glad I didn't say all the things I wanted to."

"Lucky for you, he's unable to hurt mortals directly."

Felix snorted. "Directly. But perhaps he could compel the woman who opened the door to fetch her gun and put a bullet in my head?"

"In theory. But that would mean she already had a gun, and it's not so easy to get one in this country."

Felix looked at her, incredulous. "Aida! You know what I mean."

"I do, but I really think Mo is mostly all talk. His power is in his biting words."

Felix led Aida through the magnificent palace, which was now the Galleria Nazionale d'Arte Antica, including some of the oldest paintings in Rome. When they reached the Grand Salone, they stood in its center looking up at Pietro da Cortona's Baroque masterpiece, a fresco that Felix informed Aida was called the *Allegory of Divine Providence and Barberini Power.*

"It's one of the most important paintings of the seventeenth century," he told her. "That woman in the center, that's Divine Providence. Time and the Fates are below her, and she is commanding the personification of Rome above her to put the papal crown on the Barberini coat of arms."

"I should take notes, I suppose," Aida said, reaching into her bag for her notebook.

Felix stopped her. "No, just look at it with me. Please."

They admired the fresco in silence for some time. Staring up at Cortona's masterpiece, Felix seemed lost in his own world, his eyes tracing the intricate dance of figures across the fresco. The silence between them stretched, filled with the unspoken magnitude of the artwork above.

Finally, Felix turned his face away from the ceiling. Aida was glad for the reprieve and took a moment to stretch her neck.

"Thanks," he said.

"For what?"

"For indulging me. I needed the silence to think, and admiring art helps me gather my thoughts. I've always appreciated this fresco for its artistic merit, but today, I've realized this scene is more than a grand display of Barberini's power or a tribute to divine providence. It's about the human spirit, our enduring quest to find meaning, to assert ourselves against the chaos of existence. It's a reminder of how people have always grappled with forces larger than themselves. The gods, fate, now this pandemic . . . They're all part of a larger narrative of human experience."

"It's funny. Humans are always painting the gods, but the gods are nothing without us humans," Aida said, glancing back up at the divine figures above her.

Felix turned to Aida, his eyes reflecting a mixture of resolve and introspection. He motioned for Aida to mask her MODA phone. "That's exactly it. That's what we're facing now with MODA, and trying to find Pandora and Effie is another chapter in that narrative. Our actions, our choices . . . they matter, just like those of the people who put the painting on that ceiling. We're part of something bigger, and that's both terrifying and incredibly humbling. And the gods . . . they can't eliminate us completely because if they do, who will glorify them?"

"Maybe that's why Mo mentioned the pandemic was becoming tiresome," Aida mused. "I've been thinking about that. I wonder how much of this is him going along with his sisters, and not his own idea. If humans are locked away, it must be pretty boring for someone like him."

"Well, he did say that you may be returning to London soon. Maybe you're right, and he'll find some way to ease the lockdown."

"I hope so," she said as she took her notebook out to get to work.

As they wandered the empty museum, Aida thought about Mo's words. She would give nearly anything to have her pre-pandemic life back, or at least an end to the lockdown. But if Mo gave the world some reprieve from the pandemic, what did it mean for Aida in relation to the god? He was caustic and unpredictable. A friendship with him was bound to be volatile at the best of times.

BY JUNE, MANY of the restrictions began to ease, and museums and public places reopened with strict mask rules, temperature checks, and visitor limitations. Aida continued her work at Palazzo Barberini, interviewing masked museum visitors. But most importantly of all, Luciano returned to the Promenade to finish his observations and upload them to Pandora.

The next day, Aida messaged Yumi via Signal. Did it work? Any sign of her?

Still working on it, Yumi replied. MODA's encryption is dense, but I'm making progress. I'll let you know as soon as I have something.

Luciano's message arrived shortly after. Any word from Yumi?

Not yet, Aida texted back. She's still cracking through MODA's encryption. Fingers crossed.

Three days later, a new text from Yumi popped up in their group chat. I found her!

Grazie a Dio, cazzo! Luciano's vulgar response of relief made

Aida smile. Dolores walked in on me just as I finished my upload, and I pocketed the USB. I was so worried she might have noticed.

Aida was beyond relieved. Finally, a breakthrough. Let's hope they don't figure it out before we can get to her. Is she in London?

Yes, Yumi replied. Once Luciano's data cracked through MODA's layers of encryption, I was able to pinpoint her location. She's living in Hackney, near the big church by the morgue. She's going by the name of Helen Harrow. I didn't want to say anything until I was sure, but I've been tracking her digital footprint since the upload—IP pings, security footage, even local grocery transactions. It's all pretty routine. She works at a small grocery store, walks to a nearby park, and keeps to herself. No sign of anything strange.

Now we only need to get to London, Aida said.

Dolores told me they may have us return to quarterly meetings soon, so let's wait for that. Better to go when we're expected to than to make an extra trip that might get noticed.

Luciano was right. Just a couple of days later, Trista—whom Aida had barely seen for the last few months as she had shown little desire to mingle with the rest of the locked-down household—appeared at the door to her office.

"You're to return to London in the morning."

Aida tried to act surprised. "I didn't realize the lockdown had eased up so much?"

"Things are more lax in London," Trista said. "A car will be ready for you at eight."

"Very well. Thanks for letting me know." While she feigned boredom with the idea, she was a mixture of emotions inside— excited to see Luciano and terrified that MODA might know about them finding Pandora.

Her aide strode into the room and deposited an envelope on her desk. "Mo sent this for you." She turned on a heel and left.

Aida opened the envelope. Inside was a single puzzle piece of blue sky. They had been wondering about the missing piece, and Dante had torn the room apart trying to find it. Eventually, they decided the puzzle was faulty. But of course, Mo had taken it. She turned the piece over. On its back was a smiley face drawn in pen. She snapped a photo and sent it to Yumi.

Looks like you have a new bestie now, she texted, alongside a bunch of laughing emoji.

Aida replied with a smiley face rolling its eyes.

WHEN SHE CHECKED into the hotel in London, there was a note that after she had deposited her bags, she should make her way to the suite for her interview. Aida hoped she wouldn't be alone with Mo this time.

Fifteen minutes later, she stood before the elevator, watching the numbers move ever downward. With every number, calm wrapped itself like a cloak around Aida. A god was in the elevator. She sent a silent prayer to Sophie for her aegis. Beneath the heavy relaxation, she knew she was terrified.

The doors opened. Inside were Luciano and Disa. His eyes grew big at the sight of her. She quickly diverted her attention to the goddess, who was wearing an extreme, formfitting bodysuit made entirely of mismatched men's ties. Aida had watched all the 2020 spring haute couture shows online during the pandemic and recognized the look. Perhaps her reaction could be forgiven. She ignored Luciano as he exited the elevator. "Disa, your suit, is that . . ."

"Gaultier," Disa said. "His final show before he retired."

"I wish I were brave enough to wear something like that."

"Few are." As usual, her tone was brusque, as though she abhorred conversation. She didn't indicate that she had noticed Aida's moment of recognition.

Aida followed Disa through the massive suite until they reached the familiar conference room with the round table. She was relieved to see that Mo was, in fact, accompanied by Fran. She took the chair opposite them, and Disa sat to her left. None of them were masked.

"It's been a minute, hasn't it?" A sly smile crossed Mo's face. "Go ahead, you can take that off," he said, indicating her mask.

"I suppose it has been a minute," she said, glad for the calm that enveloped her. She removed the mask, only because she knew that if the gods intended to hurt her, it probably wasn't going to be with a virus. She wondered what had happened in Luciano's meeting. She reassured herself with the thought that they had let him leave after his appointment.

Fran folded her hands in front of her. "We'll go over the projects you were working on before the pandemic hit. And I understand the world has unlocked enough for you to do some work at Palazzo Barberini."

"I was lucky to do that, yes."

"Very lucky. A fortunate easing of the oppression that has weighed upon us all." She glanced at Mo, her brows knit in annoyance. "It's a miracle, to be sure."

"Now, don't sound so disappointed, Fran. You might be an introvert, but people like us—" he indicated himself and Aida with a wave of his hand "—crave human interaction."

Fran opened her mouth to respond, but Disa cut her off with a sharp clap. "We don't have time to dally. We have a full schedule today."

"My, my. Look at you, suddenly all order and organization." Mo shook his head at her in wonder.

"Enough," Fran said, like a mother scolding her children. "Miss Reale, please give us your account of Palazzo Spada."

Palazzo Spada. Aida had gone over her notes on the plane, but she was surprised at how much she remembered, considering that the job had taken place over six months before. She and Luciano had long talked about when the forgetting happened, and it seemed that it began within a few months after they did their MODA interviews. With the pandemic, this was the longest she had gone between her meetings. There was a profound sadness in knowing this interview would mark the beginning of the forgetting of the museum, the memories slipping from her consciousness as the final data—the interview and whatever thoughts the gods might have—was uploaded into Pandora.

Pandora. She and Luciano had agreed that they would let the events of the interviews determine if they should attempt to find her. Neither of them had known when their meetings would be held, so they couldn't really plan, but knowing that he'd also had his in the morning gave her hope that they could try to find the automaton that afternoon.

The interview went much as all her previous ones, save that Fran and Disa seemed far more annoyed than usual at Mo, who was fully fixated on Aida's every word. He was as snarky as ever, but there was something underlying it, something Aida interpreted as affection. It suddenly occurred to Aida that he must have had some sort of hand in reducing the number of COVID cases and the subsequent easing of restrictions, and they were unhappy about it. Had he done it for her? Maybe he really did consider her a friend.

Finally, the interview was over, with no indication that the gods knew about their discovery of Pandora. "I'll walk you out," Mo said, rising from the table.

"No, you won't." Fran's voice was dark and commanding. "You will remain here. Disa is correct. There is much to do, and your work for MODA takes precedence. Miss Reale, please go ahead and collect your bags. We've arranged for you to return to Rome right away. Thank you for your illuminating report."

Aida thanked them, replaced her mask, and let herself out of the suite. When the calm disappeared again, she frantically texted Luciano to let him know she had to return to Rome.

Why don't you go ahead and try to find her? she suggested.

I'm not doing this without you. And I think she might respond better to a woman. Let's figure out how to return to London.

An hour and a half later, Aida boarded the plane with both relief and disappointment. Relief that MODA was not aware of their discovery of Pandora, that Disa didn't notice her recognition of Luciano, and that she did not have to spend time with Mo.

But they still were no closer to bringing happiness back into the world.

25

June–September 2020

AS THE SUMMER UNFOLDED, a renewed sense of optimism was in the air. The streets of Rome, once eerily silent, began to thrum with life again. Coffee bars and museums cautiously opened their doors, welcoming locals and a trickle of tourists with new safety protocols in place. Masks, though a constant reminder of the pandemic, became part of the city's new normal.

Despite the cautious resurgence of life, the remains of the Colosseum stood as a stark reminder of the devastation that had swept the city. Once the symbol of Rome's resilience, the ancient structure's collapse had sent shock waves through the world. The area around it remained blocked off, fenced with towering barriers that kept the masses away. Rubble still filled the surrounding streets, and the nearby metro construction, meant to bring new ease to the city's transportation, had been abandoned. Now, the Colosseum's ruins loomed over the deserted streets like a wound that had yet to heal. Reconstruction efforts had been delayed indefinitely because of the pandemic, and no timeline for the area's recovery had been announced.

Aida's first assignment after returning from London was at a site immediately next to where Trajan's Column used to be, Palazzo Valentini, built in the sixteenth century and now serving as the seat of Rome's Provincial Administration. Beyond its stately facade, Palazzo Valentini hid a remarkable secret beneath its foundations: the ruins of ancient Roman houses. The site had been transformed into a multimedia museum, where cutting-edge technology, including light projections and sound effects, brought the ancient world to vivid life. As she strolled through the remains of Roman homes, peering into living spaces, baths, and kitchens that once teemed with activity, her usual wonder was infused with a new appreciation for the world beyond the pandemic.

But every time Aida approached the building, she felt a gnawing sense of unease. The collapsed Colosseum wasn't far—its ruins a constant, looming reminder of everything that had changed. The sight of it every day made her heart clench. What else could fall? The city itself seemed fragile, as if the ground beneath her might give way at any moment, swallowing what remained of the world.

During her time at the site, Aida kept expecting Mo to appear. But it wasn't until late in August when she was cataloging happiness at the Villa Farnesina on the edge of the Trastevere that Mo finally appeared.

The photographer had just finished his work in the Loggia of Cupid and Psyche and departed when Mo brushed past him into the sunlit room. "So, this is where you hide when the world starts breathing again," he remarked with an unusual, playful edge.

"I wasn't aware I was hiding," she said, welcoming the calm that had preceded the god's entrance.

She didn't want to look at him because then she would be expected to say more, so instead, she gazed up at Raphael's magnificent ceiling, which, ironically, featured scenes of the gods. On one side, there was the Council of the Gods, in which Jupiter decided to give the drink of immortality to Psyche so she could become a god and marry Cupid. On the other side was Cupid and Psyche's wedding feast.

"Look," she said, pointing up. "There are the Three Graces. Seeing the goddess Euphrosyne is a breath of fresh air after the weight of coronavirus upon us. Are you familiar with her?" It was a dangerous question, but when she first saw the fresco that morning, a seed of panic was planted within her. The pandemic had given them a taste of the world without happiness, and she had no desire to have what little joy she had left taken again.

"Happiness is always fleeting. Humans are greedy. They never get enough of it," he said, coming to stand beside her. He pulled off his mask.

"If the guards see you, they'll yell at you," she told him, disappointed that he didn't say anything useful about Effie.

"The guards won't bother us. I asked them for some time alone. You can take yours off too."

Aida hesitated but ultimately slipped her mask off and hooked it over her forearm. "So, you've come to check up on me?"

"Something like that." He turned his gaze to the fresco, lingering on the details. "Though I'm not here to scold or interrogate you this time."

"Oh?" She shifted her stance, surprised by his change in tone.

Mo gave a small nod. "I'm . . . trying something different."

"Different?" She turned to him, raising an eyebrow. "You?"

"Don't act so surprised." He sounded almost defensive but caught himself and continued more lightly. "We haven't spoken in a while. I wanted to know how you're doing."

"How I'm doing?" Aida echoed, suspicious of this line of questioning.

He didn't meet her gaze, instead watching the figures in the fresco, their eternal revelry. "I don't have to be your enemy, you know."

Aida studied him, feeling off-balance. "You've never exactly been my friend either."

Mo shrugged, his casual demeanor slipping just slightly. "Maybe I could be."

"I thought friendship wasn't your strong suit."

"It's not," he admitted, looking at her now with that same intensity she'd grown used to. "But that doesn't mean I can't learn."

Aida shifted, uncertain of how to respond. "Why would you want to?"

Mo let out a small breath, his lips twisting into a humorless smile. "Because I'm bored, and you're . . . different. You're not predictable."

"Well, thanks, I think," she said.

Mo leaned against the wall—a move that would have the guards yelling at him if he was seen. "You're not like the others I deal with. You don't try to manipulate, and you don't play games. You just . . . do your job. It's refreshing."

She was relieved that he seemingly had no idea about her scheming to stop the games he and his siblings were playing. "And you find that interesting?"

"I find that . . . worth investing time in." He said it so simply, as though it weren't strange to say.

Aida frowned, trying to piece together his motives. "So, you're trying out this whole friendship thing with me?"

He smirked, but there was less bite to it than usual. "Something like that."

For a moment, the only sound between them was the faint hum of the wind from outside. Aida wasn't sure whether to laugh or keep her guard up. Mo, the god of sarcasm and guile, genuinely trying to make a connection with her—it didn't quite seem real. Yet, here he was, talking like this was just a normal interaction.

"You know friendship requires a bit more than just showing up unannounced," she finally said, turning back toward her work. "It's not transactional."

Mo pursed his lips, considering her words. "I know that. Doesn't mean I can't offer something in return."

"Like what?" She glanced at him, half expecting him to revert to his usual cryptic self.

But instead, he seemed thoughtful, almost serious. "I could help you. Maybe not with your research—" he gestured vaguely to the notebook and equipment around her "—but with something else. If you ever need it."

She decided to test him. "I wish you could end this pandemic."

"It's eased up quite a bit, hasn't it?" he said. "Maybe I had a hand in that."

Aida gave a nervous laugh. She had been right. He had done something to change it.

"Well then, thank you very much." She said it in a jokey voice because, of course, she wasn't supposed to know he could actually have such an effect on things. "But it's not gone entirely." She nodded toward the mask on her arm. "Maybe you could keep working on that."

"Maybe." He smiled faintly, and it didn't seem like a calculated expression. He turned to leave, pausing at the doorway. "See you soon . . . *amica mia.*"

My friend. Aida watched him go, unsure what to make of it all. The calm she'd felt before was gone, replaced by something more unsettled—but not in a bad way. For once, Mo didn't seem to be playing a game with her. Maybe Yumi was right . . . maybe this friendship could be something that would make a difference.

UNFORTUNATELY, THE SUMMER'S coronavirus reprieve turned out to be fragile. As autumn approached, the initial relief and hope gave way to a creeping sense of unease. Case numbers, which had seemed to be under control, began to climb again. The news, once filled with stories of recovery and reopening, now bore grim forecasts and warnings from health officials. The virus, it seemed, was not done with humanity yet.

By the time the leaves began to change, the writing was on the wall. Governments, hesitant yet compelled by the undeniable surge in cases, began to talk of new restrictions, of tightened measures to curb the spread. Aida had been planning on her next trip to London to try to reach Pandora, but with the pandemic rearing its head again, despair crept in. Yet just as she began to believe there was no chance of reaching Pandora, Trista informed her that they wanted another interview with her before the subsequent lockdown occurred.

She's still there, Yumi said when Aida texted her the news. I checked again when Luciano uploaded yesterday.

Thank the gods. Now, if only we can reach her this time. There were so many factors riding against the possibility. They could send her home right away like they did last time. Mo's weird new friendship might be a drain on her time. And there was always the chance MODA might find out they knew about Pandora in the first place.

Yumi sent a prayer emoji and explained, I sent a prayer to Sophie. I don't know if she'll answer, or if she can help, but it doesn't hurt to ask.

Aida sighed. I pray to her almost every day. The goddess had been absent since before the pandemic.

I don't, Yumi texted. Maybe another voice in the mix will make a difference.

AIDA ARRIVED IN London in the early afternoon and, to her relief, was informed that her interview would be delayed until the following morning. She had just opened Signal to find Luciano when a message from him arrived.

I just had my interview, but I'm not leaving until tonight.
Andiamo. Meet you at Hackney Church?

She couldn't believe that they would finally attempt to find Pandora. She hoped beyond hope that Mo was tied up in interviews and wouldn't try to meet up with her. After a quick glance around to make sure she wouldn't be followed, she walked a few blocks away from the hotel, found a black cab stand, and set her location to her room. She had just climbed into the car while giving directions to the driver when someone stopped her car door from shutting.

It was Sophie. The goddess settled in next to Aida, unzipped her brown leather jacket, and waved a hand at the plexiglass between them and the driver.

"He won't hear us now. A little bird named Yumi prayed to me. You can take that mask off."

Aida pulled off her mask. She could hardly contain her relief at seeing Sophie. "I've been trying to reach you for months."

Sophie's expression softened. "I know. But my attention has been . . . divided." She sighed, and for the first time, Aida noticed the weariness in her eyes—an exhaustion that seemed ancient. "I've had no luck finding Effie, and the pandemic has torn open more cracks in the world than you can imagine. I've been working to hold back forces that seek to exploit the chaos. It's like trying to plug holes in a sinking ship, and I'm running out of hands."

Aida's heart sank, but Sophie's presence offered some comfort. "I just thought—I thought maybe you'd given up on us."

"Never," Sophie said firmly. "But gods are not all-powerful, Aida. Even we face limits. There are things I must tend to that you wouldn't understand, battles I have to fight to keep some semblance of balance in the world. But let's worry about what we can attempt to control. Yumi said you were going to meet Pandora?"

"We're going to try. Are you coming with us?"

She shook her head. "No, I explained already. I cannot directly interfere with her. You must do your best to convince her to release the happiness. Do you have the key?"

Aida pulled out her phone and showed Sophie the image. The meander shifted slightly with a bright blue pulse, as though anxious to connect to something.

"Good. I don't think you will have an easy time of it, to be honest. She's bound to know nothing about her situation. There could be guards in the neighborhood watching her, but they are likely to be mortal. My aegis will conceal your true nature. You'll appear as friendly and harmless or may not even be visible to them at all."

Aida had been worried about that but figured she and Luciano would take their chances and figure it out when they arrived. "What if she doesn't want anything to do with us?"

"Tell her you are friends of Hephaestus. That should get you in the door. Then, show her that Greek key. She'll recognize it. She may ultimately not help you, but she should at least listen to what you have to say."

That didn't exactly answer Aida's question, but she shifted attention to what worried her more. "Can you keep Mo from finding me? I set my phone location to my room, but what if he wants me to meet him somewhere in the hotel? Then he'll know I'm not there."

Sophie gave Aida a thoughtful look. "Why do you think he would be looking for you?"

"I think he sees me as a newfound friend."

At that, Sophie burst out laughing, an emotion Aida had not yet seen from the goddess of balance. "Now, that's not what I expected you to say," she said, sobering. "This is not a man with friends. Are you sure?"

Aida nodded. "I think in this he's genuine." She tried to explain the situation the best she could.

Sophie drummed her fingernails on the car's armrest, considering. "This is interesting." She gave a huff. "My dear brother must be softening a bit. Perhaps he's understanding the importance of balance, after all. Maybe we can use this to our advantage." She put a hand on Aida's arm. "But you're right. His interference when you're attempting to connect with Pandora would not be good. I'll tell you what. I can't keep him from finding you if he really wants to, but I can distract him. I may need him to come meet me urgently in Christchurch."

"New Zealand?"

"A woman who knows her geography. Brava." The car pulled up near the Anglican church in the heart of Hackney. "Don't worry about the fare," Sophie said as they exited the car. She gestured with her chin toward the corner where Luciano waited. He hadn't seen them yet. "There's your boy. Go on. I'll take care of Mo." She strode off in the other direction.

Aida replaced her mask and headed toward the corner. It took everything she had not to run to Luciano, but when he saw her, he came swiftly toward her and swept her up in his embrace.

"These masks are a bother," he said when he set her down again. "I wonder if Sophie's protection extends to the virus."

Aida could have kicked herself. "Damn it, I should have asked!" She relayed the details of the conversation in the taxi. Luciano looked around them as she talked.

"There they are," he said, tilting his head down the street. "The men on the bench there, staring at that apartment building. The one next to that old brick building with the red doors."

Aida recognized the red doors from Google Maps. They sported a green sign that read Public Mortuary. It didn't look like it was in use, and for that, she was glad.

"Sophie said they won't notice us. I guess we have to try."

"*Andiamo.*" Luciano held out his arm for Aida to take.

They crossed the small green in front of the church toward the morgue and the flats, purposefully avoiding eye contact with the men on the bench. When they reached the gated courtyard entrance, Aida hesitated. There were no names on the buzzer panel, just numbers. "How are we supposed to—"

Luciano smirked and pressed a random button. When someone answered, he quickly said, "We're looking for Helen Harrow."

"That'll be number six."

Luciano hit the number six button, and a long moment later, a crackly voice came across. "Hello?"

"Hi, Helen, we're friends of Hephaestus."

There was another long pause, and then the door clicked

open. Luciano grinned and held it wide for Aida. As the door closed behind them, she risked a look at the men on the bench. As Sophie said . . . they didn't seem to have noticed her and Luciano at all. They were chatting and laughing at something down the street.

Pandora met them at the door, three floors up. She appeared to be in her early thirties, with long wavy auburn hair that softly framed her face, bringing attention to the dark brown eyes above her mask. She wore a simple brown skirt and a cream-colored shirt that seemed decades out of style. "Who are you?"

Aida realized they hadn't discussed what they should tell Pandora about them. If they gave their real names, would she tell MODA?

"I'm Luciano, and this is Aida," Luciano said, rendering Aida's worry moot.

Behind the mask, Aida gave Pandora a weak, unseen smile. "We have something important to talk to you about." She held up the glowing blue image of the meander.

Pandora gasped. "Please, come in." She pulled off her mask. "You can remove yours," she said. "I don't know why, but because that—" she pointed at the meander "—is familiar. I feel like I should trust you, but only a little."

She led them into a small but tidy apartment devoid of much decoration. She indicated they should sit on the gray love seat near the window and went to the kitchen, whistling a happy tune. A few minutes later, she returned with a teapot and mugs.

"I don't know why you're here or where you got that picture, but something tells me it's important, so it must be. Please explain." Her accent was mostly British, but the rhythm of her speech was off—words spaced just a little too carefully, inflections borrowed from places far beyond England's borders.

Aida looked at Luciano and then back to the woman. "Oh, where to start? Do you know the story of Pandora?"

"Pandora's box?" she asked, an eyebrow lifting.

"I think it was a jar, but yes," Luciano said.

Her eyes widened. "Yes, it was a jar! A terra-cotta jar . . ." Her voice trailed off, her excitement muted, as if she were trying to reconcile this detail with the reality she knew.

"What else do you know of the story?" Aida asked.

Pandora knitted her brow and wrung her hands, trying to remember. "There was a Titan. And punishment. And foolishness."

"Yes, that's right," Luciano affirmed, nodding encouragingly. "There were two Titans, Prometheus and Epimetheus. They oversaw creating life on earth. Epimetheus created the animals and gave each a form of protection, but when he came to man, he was out of protection to give them. Prometheus decided to steal fire from the gods to give to humanity, which greatly angered Zeus, the king of the gods. As punishment, Zeus ordered Prometheus to be chained to a rock, and an eagle would pick out his liver every day, but every day it would grow back."

"How dreadful," Pandora exclaimed, her brow furrowing, the weight of the story clearly unsettling her.

"Very dreadful," Aida agreed. "But Zeus wasn't done. He asked Vulcan, I mean, Hephaestus, the god of craftsmanship, to create Pandora as the first woman on earth. Zeus gifted her with a jar filled with all the evils of the world—a jar she was explicitly told never to open. Then, he offered Pandora to Epimetheus. Prometheus had warned his brother not to accept gifts from the gods, but Epimetheus was so taken by Pandora's beauty that he immediately married her. It was a test of sorts, a gift meant to bring about man's downfall for accepting fire. However, it was also a gift that contained something else."

Pandora's expression was a mix of confusion and recognition. "Hope," she said, nodding.

"Yes," Luciano continued. "When all the evils were released into the world, hope remained inside the jar. It's what keeps humanity going, even in the darkest times."

Pandora sat back, processing the information. "But why are you telling me this? Why come to my house to tell me about a myth?"

"I think you might know why, even if you can't articulate it," Luciano said.

She only raised an eyebrow and waited for them to explain.

Aida glanced at Luciano. This was the delicate part. "Because," she said gently, "you are not Helen. You are Pandora. Epimetheus is long gone, but you've been brought back. Today, you no longer house all the evils in the world. There's also no jar. Instead, you are being used by some not-so-nice gods as the vessel that holds much of the world's happiness. And we believe you have the power to help us, to help everyone."

Pandora looked between Aida and Luciano, her eyes searching theirs for sincerity. The weight of their words seemed to settle on her shoulders, a burden she was suddenly compelled to bear. "This is ridiculous. How could I help you?"

Luciano tried to explain about MODA kidnapping Euphrosyne and the Collectors uploading happiness into Pandora. Aida pulled her phone out again and brought up the meander. "Hephaestus said you would recognize the key."

Pandora took Aida's phone and stared at the pulsing blue light. She seemed reluctant but finally said, "I do."

Aida and Luciano waited for her to do something, but she only stared at the phone. "Do you know how to use it?"

She nodded. "But I don't think you understand. I'm perfectly happy with my life. It might not be glamorous, but I don't want anything to change. If I use that key, *my* happiness will disappear."

Aida opened her mouth to respond but realized Pandora might be right.

"You don't know that," Luciano said.

Pandora stood. She handed back the phone to Aida, then took the teacups from the table and set them on the tray. "I can't help you. I must clean up now. It was nice to meet you both."

"Wait," Aida said, desperate. "The world needs you, Pandora. If you don't help, the pandemic will get worse. More places will disappear."

"But if I help you, I will have only misery. No, thank you. I'm quite content." She started for the door.

"Please, stop." Luciano went toward her and touched her on the arm.

Pandora recoiled. "You need to go."

Aida stood and went to them. "Pandora, what if we find Euphrosyne and bring her to you? Then it won't matter if you share the happiness with the world again. Effie will have more to give you."

Pandora thought for a moment, then smiled. "Yes, that would work. I'd agree to that."

"We'll find her," Luciano vowed.

Aida took Pandora's hands in hers. "Please promise me one thing."

Pandora nodded.

"Don't tell anyone we were here, please. It would put you and us in great danger."

"I understand." She pulled her hands from Aida's, then leaned forward and kissed her on the forehead.

"Go with love and hope," she said. "I still have hope, and now you have some too."

THE MEN WERE still lounging on the bench when the pair left the apartment and gave no sign that they saw Luciano or Aida. Aida sent Sophie a prayer of thanks, along with some extra information about Pandora's situation.

They returned to the corner, intending to call for separate cabs. "Before we go, I wanted to tell you that I'm going to Rome for the lockdown. I cleared it with Fran this morning."

Aida clapped her hands together. While she knew a lockdown would still keep them worlds apart, they would be in the same city, and knowing that helped even more hope bloom within her.

After a lingering goodbye kiss, Luciano and Aida took separate cabs to the hotel, staggering their return times. They texted Yumi and Felix via Signal the whole way back.

When I talked with Sophie, she said they had no leads on Effie, Aida said.

Maybe we should look at the Greek myths again. Or the Roman ones. There might be something we've missed, Felix suggested.

We've spent hours poring over them, Aida said. But if you want to try again . . .

We have to do something.

Aida agreed. She only wished she knew what.

AIDA BARELY SLEPT that night. Between Pandora's refusal to help them immediately and the worry that MODA would know they had gone to see her, her nerves were on edge. When morning arrived, she made herself look as presentable as possible despite the soft bags under her eyes, then headed to the MODA suite.

Mo was nowhere to be seen. When Aida inquired, Disa informed her that he was attending to personal matters in New Zealand. Aida merely nodded, but her heart was soaring with gratefulness for Sophie's interference.

When they were done, Fran told her that they expected a new lockdown within the next few days and that it might be a while before she was sent back out into the field to work.

"But do not fear. Your job and paycheck are safe," she reassured her.

Even if my sanity is not, Aida thought as she let herself out the door.

26

September–December 2020

A IDA RETURNED FROM London with a heavy heart, not just from the weight of their unfulfilled mission but also from the impending sense of isolation as the second lockdown began. The streets of Rome quieted once more, a somber silence punctuated only by the sound of sirens as more and more people were rushed to the hospital with the virus.

With the rise in cases, the Italian government announced a series of measures that would once again restrict movement and shutter businesses deemed nonessential. International travel was still banned, and flights were restricted, but the second lockdown was thankfully slightly less limiting on a local level.

People were allowed to go for walks, and there were provisions for *congiunti*, or cells of no more than six relatives. You were still required to be masked and remain at least two meters apart. But the terminology of *congiunti* caused a stir among the Italian people, who were frustrated by the idea that they could not include friends in their cells. The government quickly clarified that relatives meant spouses, live-in partners, civil union partners, anyone sharing a stable emotional bond, and blood relatives up to the sixth degree and kin up to the fourth degree.

I would consider what we have a stable emotional bond, Aida told Luciano with a wink emoji.

Anch'io, he said. *Me too.*

As far as MODA was concerned, this stable emotional bond

consisted of Felix, Yumi, and members of the palazzo household, but when they could, Luciano was regularly looped into their more private gatherings. There was a curfew in place, so most of their meetings took place during the day, outside, properly distanced, with Luciano spoofing his location to be his apartment. *I read a lot of books*, he said he told Dolores.

The rains of November didn't help the situation. The days grew shorter and the nights longer. A new puzzle appeared on the massive dining room table in the salon, this time one with 42,000 pieces. Dante informed them that it would go all the way to the table's edges. Ilario was elated until Pippa began crying. The idea of the world closing up again was beyond stifling.

But, on occasion, Aida would sleep over at Yumi's new apartment off the Via Margutta, a stylish street not far from the Spanish Steps, in an area traditionally known as the "foreigners' quarter." The best part about Yumi's apartment—at least in Aida's mind—was that she lived only a stone's throw from Luciano.

ONE NIGHT AT the end of November, Aida made a bold decision during one of their sleepovers. When the time was approaching midnight, she sent Luciano a text, then gave Yumi a hug and headed out.

"Be careful." She gave Aida a sock in the arm. "Don't do anything I wouldn't do."

"That gives me a lot of leeway." Aida grinned before letting herself out the door where Luciano was waiting so she wouldn't be walking alone in the dark.

"I hope this isn't a bad idea," she said as they hurried down the street, hoping to avoid detection by the *polizia* who were on the lookout for anyone ignoring curfew.

"Of course it's a bad idea," he told her. "Doesn't that make it more exciting?"

"I think you're exciting enough without the extra dose of danger."

"If there is any one thing I've learned in the last few months, it's that life is short," he told her as he opened the door to his apartment.

And then Luciano's mouth was on hers, his hands roaming across her cheeks, entwining in her hair. She was just as needy, her body heat rising, the tingle between her thighs building with every kiss. Aida pressed herself against him, running her fingers hungrily through his hair to bring his lips even harder onto hers, banishing any last thought she had about the gods. There was only *this*—the delirious feeling of Luciano, her longing and desperation for him to fill her.

They never made it to the bedroom. Instead, Luciano bent her over the low back of the living room's mid-century couch. When he thrust into her, Aida arched in pleasure. Then she was lost, her body merging with his in an intense, pounding beat. It took every last bit of restraint she had not to scream her pleasure.

Afterward, they found their way to the bedroom, where they dozed, woke, made love, dozed, woke, and made love again. For the first time in months, Aida didn't think about anything except how grateful she was for the beautiful man in whose arms she slept.

But then she was being jostled awake, the last vestiges of a happy dream abruptly slipping from her mind. "Aida, get up, get up. Get your clothes on now!"

Aida blinked, confused, then realized where she was. She scrambled from the bed and rushed to the living room, where her clothes were still all over the floor near the door. "What's going on?" she asked, dread filling her as she pulled on her panties and socks.

Luciano handed Aida her pants. "Yumi's been texting over and over, but I'm just now seeing it. She says your MODA phone has been buzzing for the last hour. She's getting really worried. We should have set an alarm. It's already ten."

"Fuck, fuck, fuck." Aida looked at her personal phone and saw all of Yumi's messages, missed because her ringer was off. She dressed faster than she ever had in her life. "How on earth did I forget my MODA phone? I must have left it on the counter after I texted you. Damn it.

"I love you," she said, giving Luciano a hasty kiss as he opened the door for her.

She was only a few steps away and ready to break into a sprint when she heard Luciano call after her.

"Aida, did you mean that?"

She turned around. "Mean what?"

He waved his hand at her. "Go, go, you can tell me again later. Go!"

Aida didn't hesitate. She made it the block and a half to Yumi's in record time and banged on the door, falling into her friend's arms when she opened it.

Yumi shoved Aida's phone into her hands. "It's Trista, and she's starting to sound pissed."

Panting from the run, Aida opened her messaging app to see at least fifteen messages from her aide. The last one was ominous.

CALL ME NOW.

After taking a second to calm herself, she dialed the phone with a shaky finger.

"Where have you been?"

Yumi had been right, Trista was pissed.

Aida tried to sound like she had just woken up. "I'm so sorry, Trista. We overslept and I had my phone in the bottom of my bag with the sound low. What's wrong?"

"I arranged for you to be at Castel Sant'Angelo this morning. I texted you but you haven't been responding. You were due there over an hour ago. They opencd the site just for you, and you aren't there."

This was beyond unusual. Trista hadn't given her any early indication she was supposed to be at Castel Sant'Angelo. She never did things last minute. Was this a test to make sure she had her phone on?

"This is not acceptable. I'll have to report your lack of responsiveness to Fran."

In moments like this, Aida thought of Trista as a version of Mussolini reincarnate. She wanted all trains to run on time, and she would not take no for an answer, or heads would roll. "Trista, you don't need to report this. It was an accident. I just overslept. I'll head there now."

"Don't dally, Aida." She hung up.

Yumi put a comforting hand on her shoulder. "That didn't sound good."

"It wasn't." She started stripping down on her way to the bathroom. "Can you call me a cab? I'll be out of the shower before they get here."

"You got it."

Seven minutes later, she hugged Yumi goodbye just as a heavy calm descended over her. Gritting her teeth, she opened the door to find both the cab waiting and a black car, the latter of which Fran was leaning against, her arms crossed, her face impassive. She was dressed head to toe in sapphire, her red hair a stunning contrast.

Aida dismissed the cab driver with a five-euro bill and went to the waiting car. Fran held the door open for her, then went around to the other side and climbed in.

"I didn't know you were in town," Aida said as she buckled her seat belt, a good excuse not to look at Fran until she had to.

"I thought I would be seeing you at the palazzo. But I understand you missed the alarm on your clock." Fran didn't sound angry or frustrated, but Aida wasn't sure that was any better.

"We were up late talking and watching bad TV and I failed to set one. I'm very sorry. It won't happen again." Aida hoped beyond hope that Fran believed her, but the very fact that the goddess had come in person did not bode well for her.

"You've been a good employee, Aida, and if it weren't for that, we'd be having a different conversation. But you need to work with your aide. Tell me, do you appreciate this job?"

"Yes . . . very . . . very much," she replied, her voice faltering as a deep sense of dread crept in. The thought of losing the job was terrifying enough, but the idea that they might literally silence her chilled her to the bone. Even the aegis couldn't steady her; the mere possibility of such an outcome made her stumble over her words. "It's the best job I've ever had." This, at least, wasn't a lie.

Fran nodded as though expecting the answer. "MODA believes in taking care of their employees. Not many employers would be so generous to support your work as an author. We've helped you find an agent and a publicist. And I dare say you wouldn't have won the National Book Award without that help."

"I owe a lot to you, I do," Aida agreed. "Please believe me, I don't take it for granted."

Fran looked out the window, clicking her red nails against the armrest. Aida desperately wanted to fill the silence, but she didn't dare. They drove in silence for a few minutes, until Castel Sant'Angelo could be seen in the distance.

"I believe you, Aida," Fran said. "But the next time Trista sends a report showing a disregard for the rules we set forth . . ." She paused, allowing the unspoken consequence to linger, though not as sharply. "Let's just say it will reflect poorly on your standing here."

Aida nodded her understanding, her throat tight. "It won't happen again."

Fran gave a small nod of approval. "Good. Then we'll move forward and put this behind us. You've done great work for us, and I have no doubt you'll continue to. Just . . . be sure to stay aligned with the expectations we've set."

The car slowed to a stop near the bridge leading to the castle that was once the tomb of the ancient Roman Emperor Hadrian. Fran gestured toward the door, her expression neutral but calm. "I'll see you in a few months in London," she said, her tone lighter now as if the momentary tension had passed.

Aida unbuckled her seat belt and stepped out of the car, her mind still racing but her breath a little steadier. As the black car pulled away, she stood there momentarily, gathering herself.

Whatever happened next, she knew one thing for sure: There was no margin for error.

IN THE DAYS that followed, Aida was on her best behavior, making sure every task was handled with precision, avoiding even the smallest misstep. She spent more time at the palazzo, limiting her visits to Yumi's and, with some regret, steering clear of Luciano altogether. It was a sacrifice, but she couldn't take the chance that their efforts might be discovered.

Aida managed to stay under the radar for a couple of weeks, focusing on work at Castel Sant'Angelo and keeping her head down. But just when she thought she had found some semblance of balance, a call came in on her phone one Saturday afternoon in early December while she was in the grand salon with Pippa, putting together the latest puzzle. She froze, her heart skipping a beat when she saw the name on the screen: Graham.

Why would he, of all people, be calling her?

When she reached the sanctuary of her office, Aida looked at her phone again. Graham had left a brief voicemail. "Please, Aida, call me. It's about Erin."

Her stomach dropped. Her first thought was that she wanted nothing to do with him or Erin, but the message was so strange and his tone was so bleak that against her better judgment, she pressed Call.

The line barely rang before Graham picked up. "Aida?" His voice cracked. "Thank you for calling back."

"What's going on?" she asked, a knot tightening in her chest. "What about Erin?"

There was a long pause, the kind that made her wish she hadn't called at all. "Aida, she . . . Erin caught the virus. She was really sick, and she didn't make it. She . . . she was your friend, and—I thought you would want to know."

For a moment, Aida couldn't speak. The air seemed to drain from the room. "What? When?"

"Two days ago," Graham answered quietly. "I didn't know how else to tell you. I thought you needed to know, given . . . everything."

Aida sat down, her knees weak. Memories of Erin flashed

through her mind. Their childhood—riding bikes, gossiping about boys, trading clothes. And then, her return into Aida's life as an adult—cocktails, laughter, and all the moments in the weeks before the betrayal.

"I can't believe this," she whispered, the words barely audible.

"I'm sorry, Aida. About everything. I know that she regretted . . ." He began to cough violently on the last word.

Aida felt a surge of anger and despair. "Are you sick too?"

"I . . . I got sick first. I didn't take the restrictions seriously. I thought it was all just being blown out of proportion."

Aida's anger flared, his betrayal now mingled with blame. For all her frustration with Erin, she hadn't wanted her to die.

"I should have been more careful. I'm so sorry, Aida. This is all my fault." Graham's voice broke, the guilt palpable even through the phone.

"I . . . I don't know what to say," Aida finally managed. "I can't process this right now."

"I understand," Graham replied softly. "I just . . . thought you should know."

Aida nodded, though she knew he couldn't see her. The line was silent for a moment before she found her voice again. "Take care, Graham."

"Of course," he replied. "Take care of yourself."

Aida ended the call and sat in stunned silence, the phone slipping from her hand onto the desk. Her mind swirled with disbelief, memories of Erin flashing in and out of focus. In a sudden burst of frustration, she grabbed the phone and hurled it across the room. It hit the bookcase with a dull thud, knocking several books to the floor.

Moments later, Pippa appeared in the doorway. "Aida, what happened?"

Aida didn't look up, her body trembling as the tears came. Then Pippa was by her side, arms wrapped around her, holding her tightly. Somewhere amid her anger and grief, she understood that Pippa had waved off Ilario and Dante, and maybe even Trista, who had surely also come to see what had happened. The sous-chef held her until she soothed.

Erin's death wasn't just the loss of a friend—it was the end of a chapter, a piece of her past she hadn't truly confronted. Erin had taken so much with her. The friendship and happy childhood memories. The relationship with Graham that Aida had thought was unshakable, destroyed by someone she had trusted.

For what? Aida thought bitterly, her chest tightening again. For a fling? A brief moment of selfishness?

She had loved Erin. Hated her. She wasn't sure which was more painful now.

THE FOLLOWING MORNING, she met up with Yumi at the Torre Argentina Cat Sanctuary, an open-air archaeological site in the city center, not far from the Roman Ghetto. It was a place Aida hoped she'd never have to catalog because she loved coming to spot the cats that lived among the ruins of the Largo di Torre Argentina, where Julius Caesar had been murdered two thousand years before. As Aida began to tell her friend about Erin, it wasn't long before she was sobbing, and Yumi broke the two-meter distance rule to fold Aida into her arms.

Yumi held her tight, letting Aida wet the wool collar of her coat. After several long minutes, Aida pulled away, wiping at her eyes. She began to fumble in her coat pocket for a new mask to replace the wet one on her face. Before either of them could speak, a sharp voice cut through the quiet of the archaeological site.

"*Signore! Distanza! Mantenete la distanza!*" A carabiniere was walking in their direction. He pointed sternly at them, his gloved hand gesturing to the two-meter rule. Aida and Yumi immediately took a step apart, guilt and tension written across their faces as they nodded in apology. The officer glared at them for a moment longer before moving on.

Yumi sighed, her breath still heavy with the weight of Aida's grief. "Well, at least we're still following some rules," she muttered under her breath.

Aida leaned against the railing, her gaze following a sleek calico cat as it stretched and padded away across the ruins. The reprieve gave her a moment to steady herself, but her mind was still reeling. "I can't stop thinking about what Fran said." Aida's voice was tight. "About consequences for our actions—almost like a warning."

Yumi knitted her brow, waiting for her to continue.

Aida's fingers gripped the railing as if to anchor herself. "Do you think . . ." She hesitated, swallowing hard. "Do you think MODA had anything to do with Erin's death?"

"I wouldn't put it past them. They destroyed the Colosseum, after all. How many people died in that event?"

"But lots of people have caught the virus . . . maybe . . ."

Yumi shook her head. "Um, Aida, the virus was their fault."

Aida sighed. "Yeah. Plus, it's just . . . the timing, everything. Erin suddenly came back into my life right before I moved here and then she hooked up with Graham . . ." She could hardly say his name aloud without the anger returning, fresh and burning.

Yumi's expression darkened, her mind clearly racing to the same conclusions. "Maybe they pushed you toward Rome. Maybe MODA orchestrated the whole thing—bringing Erin back, forcing your decision. And knowing your emotions were all twisted up about her and Graham, it was a fitting punishment to get rid of her."

A chill ran through Aida. The idea that she was a pawn in MODA's grand scheme made her feel trapped, like her every move had been orchestrated. It wasn't just Erin's death haunting her now—it was the thought that nothing in her life had truly been hers.

"We have to find Effie," she said for the hundredth time. "We have to."

"We will, Aida. We will."

Aida hoped so, because even with Sophie's aegis, she didn't know how she could stand in front of Fran again for another quarterly meeting.

27

December 2020–January 2021

A S CHRISTMAS APPROACHED, the usual excitement and preparations were noticeably subdued. The vibrant markets and festive decorations that typically adorned the streets were scarce, replaced instead by masked pedestrians hurriedly collecting necessities before returning to the safety of their homes.

Aida was deeply lonely: grieving for Erin; missing Luciano, who was only across the city center yet still so far away; and yearning for the company of Yumi and Felix, who she could no longer meet freely. As the year drew to a close, Aida clung to what little hope she had, her fingers often rubbing the spot where Pandora had kissed her forehead. The world was grappling with an unprecedented crisis, but amid it all were moments of kindness, resilience, and the unyielding human spirit. She clung to the promise of a new year, a fresh start, and the faint yet persistent hope that they would find Euphrosyne and fulfill Pandora's request, unlocking the happiness the world desperately needed.

On Capodanno—New Year's Eve—Dante brought up what he said were some of the best wines in the cellar. He set the case on the bar counter and pulled out a bottle. "This one is Trista's favorite," he said, waving it in the air.

"I heard my name," Trista said from the doorway.

Aida took the bottle from Dante and read the label. "Monfortino Barolo Riserva."

Trista nodded. "It's exceptional. I came down for a glass of wine, and if you are opening that, I'll have some."

"We'll pour you a glass, but since it's Capodanno, you have to drink it with us," Ilario said.

"Yes, please, Trista, celebrate with us," Aida chimed in, studying her aide's face.

Trista frowned, and for a moment, Aida thought she would decline, but to her surprise, her aide sat down at the bar.

Aida exchanged a glance with Dante. Trista loved a glass of wine, but she always took it back to her room alone. She had never shared a drink with them. Not once in all the time Aida had known her. It was unsettling.

More and more often, Aida had been wondering whether Trista was an automaton. She never seemed to tire, never missed a detail, and MODA's automatons were apparently indistinguishable from mortals. But Vulcan had said they were fallible. Nearly human. And humans broke down eventually.

Tonight, was that what was happening?

Ilario uncorked the wine and poured them each a glass. They toasted to the end of a terrible year and a hopeful start to the new. The first glass went down fast, and another was poured. Then another. Trista, who had always seemed untouchable, let her shoulders relax. The sharp efficient lines of her posture softened, just slightly. Aida kept an eye on her, curiosity gnawing at her ribs.

Aida, seizing the opportunity to finally glean any information she could about Effie's location, decided to introduce a game of silly questions. Each had to pose a whimsical question to another, who had to answer as truthfully as possible.

As the game progressed, Pippa asked about the strangest animal they had ever seen, Ilario had them make up a movie they would watch, and Dante questioned what their guilty secret might be. With each round, the wine flowed, the rich flavors of the thousand-euro Barolo warming them from inside. Aida made it a point to keep Trista's glass topped off, so she never knew exactly how much wine she consumed.

Aida had never seen Trista drink more than a glass or two before. Maybe she wasn't supposed to. But Vulcan had said his creations were nearly identical to humans. Which meant, if they could drink, they could also slip.

And tonight, Trista was slipping.

An hour or so into the game, it was again Aida's turn. She looked around, making eye contact with each person before settling her gaze on Trista.

"We're in the middle of a pandemic, right? If there was a place on earth where all happiness would be most likely to die, where do you think it might be?" she asked, trying to keep her voice light.

"Bloody hell! Way to dampen the mood, Aida," Pippa said, socking her in the arm.

"No, no, I can . . . answer that . . ." Trista, visibly more affected by the wine than the others, leaned forward, her eyes unfocused yet shining with a sudden clarity.

Aida's breath caught.

Trista's expression was unreadable. Had she even registered the question? Did she know what she was about to say?

"The Roman Catacombs," Trista slurred slightly. "That's where shadows swallow joy whole."

Aida's pulse kicked.

"*Ci sono molte catacombe*, Trista. Which one?" Ilario asked. Aida could have kissed him. Ilario was right. There were many dozens of catacombs in Rome, let alone the rest of the world, and only a few were open to the public. If she was too pushy, she might arouse Trista's suspicions, but coming from Ilario, she would likely be none the wiser.

"Callix, callexess, cal, cal . . ."

Aida's heart skipped a beat. Trista had to be referring to the Catacombs of Callixtus, an ancient burial ground in Rome.

Pippa suddenly stood. "To the roof!"

"Wha?" Trista looked up in alarm.

"It's almost New Year's, silly," Aida said to her, with an affection that she had never expected to feel for Trista. "Come on, I'll help you." She put her arm around her aide and helped her up.

Dante broke out the prosecco, and together with glasses in hand, they made their way to the roof and watched as Rome celebrated the first minutes of 2021 from private rooftops, alleys, and yards. Because of the health risks, the mayor had canceled the official fireworks displays and banned firecrackers and explosives with a hefty €500 fine to be imposed upon violators. But that wasn't going to stop the general populace. The flashes of colored light and the acrid smell of smoke brought tears to Aida's eyes.

"Look at all this," Dante said, raising his glass to the sky. "It takes a lot to kill happiness. It might even be impossible."

Aida looked back at Trista, who had passed out in one of the rooftop deck chairs.

She clinked her glass against his. "I hope you're right, Dante."

THE NEXT MORNING, Trista appeared at breakfast with slightly bloodshot eyes. "I need some water," she told Ilario. "And coffee."

"How are you feeling, Trista?" Aida asked. She hoped her aide didn't remember the question about the catacombs. She didn't dare ask and raise suspicion.

"What do you say in America? Like I was hit by a truck."

Pippa set a glass of water in front of her with a smirk.

"Do *not* say what you're thinking," Trista said.

Pippa only laughed and returned to her tasks.

Aida wondered if she had ever been drunk before. "Drink lots of water this morning. It will help."

Trista downed the water in one gulp. When she set the glass down, the old Trista was back, serious and devoid of much emotion. She sat up straight. "What happened last night? I woke up in bed this morning with all my clothes on."

"Dante and I helped you get to bed," Aida said. "You passed out on the roof during the fireworks."

"I see."

Ilario set an espresso before her. She took a sip and made a face.

"What's in this?"

"Fernet-Branca."

She put the cup down and pushed it away from her. "I didn't ask for a *caffè corretto*. The last thing I need is more alcohol."

Ilario pushed it back. "No, you must drink. It's best *per i postumi della sbornia*."

Trista looked at him blankly.

"For a hangover," Aida explained, unsurprised that her aide didn't know that bit of Italian.

After a moment, Trista picked up the cup again. When she put it down, she asked for another espresso and a carafe of water to be sent to her office. "We'll not speak of this again," she told Aida as she left.

Aida only nodded, all too glad to comply.

AFTER THE FIREWORKS, Aida had sent Felix, Yumi, and Luciano New Year wishes, but it was so chaotic that she had decided to hold off on telling them about the lead on Effie. In the afternoon, Aida returned to the roof to enjoy the briefly warm weather, a respite between heavy rainstorms. She sat on the couch to message her friends on Signal about the seemingly impossible—getting into the catacombs during a pandemic lockdown.

I'll research everything I can on Callixtus, Yumi said. We'll need all the information we can get.

The place is massive. We'll need maps, Luciano said.

Felix, do you know anyone who could get us in there? On the premise of research? Aida asked. Aside from being a guide, Felix lived just off the Appian Way near the catacombs.

Before he could answer, a heavy blanket of calm rolled over

Aida. She turned off her phone and slid it into her pocket right before Mo came around the corner of the veranda and sat beside her on the couch. Aida's stomach lurched.

"Happy New Year, little novelist."

"I am not terribly little," she retorted, her internal fear shifting to something more sarcastic in the spell of the aegis. "Seriously, how do you manage to evade the lockdown travel restrictions?"

He shrugged, a dark lock of hair falling into his eye. He pushed it aside. "I told you, MODA has the right connections."

Mo put an arm on the back of the couch. It reminded Aida of the old TV shows and movies where the boy attempted to be suave to get the girl to neck with him. She shifted on the couch so she could face him instead. "How did you know I was here? I didn't tell anyone I was coming up here."

He didn't miss a beat. "Dante said you often come to the roof."

Aida only raised an eyebrow. He was lying. She rarely came to the roof, but the fireworks the night before had given her the idea.

"I'm sorry about your friend," he said, his tone softening.

Aida was surprised. He sounded sympathetic.

"Thanks. It was very unexpected."

"There's not much I can do, but I can give you this." He leaned forward and enveloped her in a hug. "I'm so sorry this happened to you."

Shocked, Aida found tears coming to her eyes. His words weren't about Erin. Instead, he seemed to be apologizing for something else—perhaps the actions of his sisters. But it touched something deep within her, and her tears welled anew. She buried her face in his shoulder and cried. He held her and smoothed down her hair.

She pulled away. "I'm getting your jacket wet."

"It's just the rain," Mo said, tilting his head toward the gray sky.

Aida blinked. She hadn't even registered the rain at first, but now it was everywhere—running down Mo's jaw, dripping from his lashes, soaking through his jacket and into hers. She looked up. The clouds had been holding back, but now they gave in, releasing a downpour that flattened her hair against her scalp and ran in cold rivulets down her back.

She shivered but didn't move.

"I miss being in the world," she said. "Really in it—surrounded by people, by life. I miss all the things I took for granted: crowded cafés humming with conversation, the clink of wineglasses over a shared meal. I miss the smell of old books in the Biblioteca Angelica, the hush of a gallery, the jostle of the crowd at a concert."

While this was true, she also hoped she could shift Mo's sympathies.

"I don't," he said.

So much for shifting, Aida thought.

"People are mostly terrible, and terribly foolish," he continued. "Humankind is on a path of self-destruction. Let me count the ways—climate, politics, gun proliferation, religious disagreement, malware, identity theft, online bullying, thousands of robocalls . . ."

"I get it," she said, stopping him. "But with the lockdown, we still have those issues, plus heightened sadness, fear, death, disease, depression, unemployment, poverty, homelessness."

He was silent. Aida knew he couldn't refute that but seeing him grappling with his very nature was strange. If he couldn't lash out with a heavy dose of snark, he had only silence. It softened her feelings toward him, this god whom no one liked because, through the centuries, he couldn't just keep his mouth shut. And here she was, instilling silence within him. Had anyone else been able to do that?

"There are no easy answers," she offered. She let him keep an arm around her.

The rain poured over them, drenching them both, making

their clothes heavy and cold. Her sweater clung to her arms, her jeans stuck to her legs, and water ran down the back of her neck in icy trickles. But strangely, she didn't care.

She tipped her head back and let the rain hit her face, let it soak into her skin. The air smelled of wet stone, of damp earth and sky. The world felt so small these days, but this—this was something vast. Aida exhaled and stretched out a hand. She turned her palm up, letting the rain pool there before it spilled over.

When she looked at Mo, she found him watching her. He was just as soaked as she was, his dark curls plastered to his forehead, his jacket useless against the deluge.

When it finally broke, he removed his arm. His expression was troubled. "I have to go. Happy New Year, Aida."

When the blanket of calm dissipated, Aida remained on the couch, watching the sky crack from gray to blue, her thoughts a jumbled mess.

THE NEXT MORNING, Yumi and Aida took a walk to the Roman Forum. It was locked up tight as a result of the pandemic, so they went to the overlook at Piazza del Campidoglio, the hilltop square near Palazzo Senatorio, Rome's town hall. Their vantage point gave them a perfect view of the Umbilicus Urbis Romae and the other ruins.

"So unimpressive from here," Yumi noted. "It's just a pile of bricks amid all the rest of this greatness."

"All the better to be easily ignored, I suppose." Aida leaned on the wall and stared out across the empty Forum. "It's strange to look over this in broad daylight and not see a soul."

"It is. I suppose we should start praying."

"No need," said a voice from behind them.

They turned to find Sophie there, dressed head to toe in gray and black, her chestnut curls cascading down her back from beneath a wool hat. She held a finger to her mouth—a shush—then made the same gesture she had in the restaurant, her hands in front of her, palms out, thumbs and forefingers touching. She moved her hands to create the invisible sound shield.

"You're wondering how I knew you were here. It's my aegis," she said, registering the surprised looks on Aida's and Yumi's faces. "I'm connected to you and know where you are. When you came close to the Umbilicus, I assumed you may have news for us."

"We do. We think we may know where Effie is."

Sophie looked toward the Forum. After a pause, she held out her hands. Yumi took one, Aida took the other, and with a whoosh, they were standing in front of Vulcan's golden lions. One of them growled.

"Shush," Sophie said, ignoring the beast's warning and touching the door. It opened into the humming forge. Vulcan stood there, hands on hips, looking less than pleased.

"Sophrosyne. It's been a while." He looked at Aida and Yumi. "But not for you two. You know something useful?" His voice boomed.

"Y . . . yes," Aida began. Sophie's aegis didn't seem to work in her immediate presence. She remembered that the goddess had said they didn't need it around her, but now there was no calm to shield them from the wonder that was the god of the forge. Vulcan was like something out of a superhero movie. Larger than life, stunning in his appearance, and everything about him was otherworldly. It didn't matter that she had met him before—without the aegis, he was so imposing it practically took her breath away. His hair was almost fire, and he towered over them. She wondered how Yumi had managed to keep any composure at all when they first met him.

Aglaea emerged from a nearby doorway, and she was equally breathtaking. Her platinum tresses fell across her shoulders, and she wore a white dress on her lithe frame. She went to her husband and linked her arm in his.

Sophie seemed to notice the problem, as she snapped her fingers and abruptly the calm returned.

Aida realized she had been gaping in awe. She took a breath. "Thank you."

"Now then, tell us what you know," Aggie said, her voice gentle and encouraging.

Aida and Yumi explained everything, relating what had happened with Pandora and Trista's slipup about the Catacombs of St. Callixtus.

"Interesting," Vulcan said, raising a hand to stroke his beard. "Those catacombs hold popes now, but they are built on the remains of an ancient hypogeum."

"Why didn't I think of that before?" Sophie said, her eyes wide with understanding. "Many centuries ago, there was an altar to Oizys deep within the catacombs."

"There was an altar there?" Aggie looked skeptical.

"I wouldn't expect you'd have been aware of it. Our sister always kept to herself. Not to mention, your domains are far removed from the abode of misery and despair. And Oizys, ever secluded in her ways, always shrouds her sanctums in secrecy. A journey into the depths of sorrow to reach her shrine was the ultimate answer for those who sought solace in their pain. Think. How did they unburden themselves of their grief?"

Yumi gasped. "They killed themselves."

Vulcan crossed his arms. "An altar with so many years of sorrow and grief imbues the place with a power that likely reinforces the magic keeping Euphrosyne from the world. Trapping her in my chair wouldn't be enough; they'd still need to tamp down the happiness that naturally flows from her. The catacombs . . . they make sense."

"Our friend Felix says there is only one door to enter the catacombs," Yumi began. "I think I might be able to hack in and manage the cameras without too much problem."

"But we'll still have to pick the lock and find the room where she's kept, then—" Aida continued, but Vulcan cut her off.

"Free her. Yes, yes. And you'll likely have other godlike issues to contend with."

"Issues like what?" Aida asked, not sure she was going to like the answer.

He looked thoughtful. "The deeper you get, the more the weight of Oizys's power will discourage you. And if you set off any triggers to warn the gods, they'll surely throw whatever they can at you. Whether that's mortals doing their bidding, nightmarish apparitions, physical traps—"

"You mean Indiana Jones–style traps?" Yumi interrupted, then realized she had cut off a god and clapped her hand over her mouth.

Aggie raised an eyebrow but didn't engage with the comment. "I'm not sure what you mean, but my siblings don't need elaborate traps—they wouldn't even imagine a mortal could get close to the throne," she said coolly. "That kind of arrogance is their real defense."

Sophie agreed. "She's right. First, the mere weight of sorrow hanging over Oizys's sanctuary will be enough to keep all but the most dedicated mortals away—those who already know about the sanctuary. Average humans would be repelled by the misery without understanding it. One would need to be ready to give everything to Oizys to find her shrine. And aside from that, there's the natural age of the catacombs, which are certainly structurally dangerous in many parts. There's a reason that the lower levels have been closed off for decades."

Aida frowned. "But why us? You'd be helping another god—Effie. So why aren't you handling it yourselves?"

Vulcan let out a short humorless laugh. "You think it's that simple? Gods can't just go around stealing other gods' prisoners without consequences."

Aggie's expression was grave. "Yes, MODA took Effie. But under our laws, only the god who was wronged can retaliate. The rest of us can't interfere—not yet. That's why the balance hasn't shattered."

Sophie added, "The balance among us is delicate, but still intact, because so far MODA hasn't been challenged. If we move

first, we aren't just rescuing Effie—we're breaking the rules ourselves. And if we do that, every god left on earth has the right
to step in. That's when things spiral."

Vulcan leaned forward. "Think of it like a scale—MODA's
move tilted it, but not enough to send everything crashing down.
If we act now, we turn a violation into an open battle between
gods. But if you act first—if mortals free Effie—then the scales
shift. MODA is no longer holding her. At that point, her retali-
ation is justified. And then we have options."

Aida's stomach twisted. "So the balance is already breaking?"

Sophie exhaled. "It's holding. Barely. But once Effie is free,
we'll finally be able to work alongside her to seek justice. If we
jump in before then, we start a war. If you do it first, we can
control what happens next. That's why we need you. Mortals
aren't bound by our laws. You're our best chance at getting Effie back without setting everything on fire."

"How will we go up against these gods?" Despite the aegis,
Aida's despair pricked at her. "We're not superheroes. None of
us are particularly strong or athletic. This is madness."

Sophie laid a hand on Aida's shoulder. "Genuine power arises
not from your physical strength but in your thought, soul, and
intent."

Aida huffed. "Where there's a will, there's a way?"

She gave Aida a small smile. "Something like that."

Vulcan went to a wall near one of his workbenches and waved
his hand. A sleek drawer slipped open, and he retrieved something from inside. "You might not be warriors," he conceded, "but
you have qualities just as vital. Technological skills, intellect, resilience, historical knowledge, human resourcefulness—they are
your true arsenal. And with this—" he handed Aida a compact,
ornately engraved metal orb, about three inches in diameter,
pulsing with soft golden light "—you'll have a piece of divine
craftsmanship to aid you. This will shield you when you unlock Euphrosyne's bonds. Throw it on the floor in front of

you. It won't last forever, so your actions must be swift and sure. Once you free her, she'll make sure you can get out of the catacombs."

The device was warm to the touch, a comforting weight in Aida's hand. As she watched, the orb's engravings—a pattern of Greek keys—began to disappear. It slowly lost its light and became inert, a simple metal ball. She looked at the god, unsure, but he only nodded. Aida slipped the ball into her pocket.

"How do we unlock her from the chair?" Yumi asked.

"With this." Vulcan produced a small golden key from another drawer and handed it to Aida.

"Before we even get there, we have to find her. Felix tells us the place is bigger than Disneyland! He is trying to find us better maps. The ones they give out only extend to the areas where tourists are allowed on the first floor, so that's not helpful. Twelve miles of passages and four floors. And what about the misery?" Just the thought of going down there in the dark and wandering around, potentially lost, was enough to make Aida feel sick.

"Worry not." Sophie's voice was calming. "Your aegis will protect you from the worst of Oizys's gloom. But give me your hands." She reached out to Aida.

Aida let the goddess take her hands and a warmth surged through her.

"There. Now tell me. What is a smell that makes you happy, or nostalgic. Something you revel in that brings you joy?"

Aida was confused. It was the strangest question, but the answer immediately came to her. "When I was very young, I used to visit my grandparents in the middle of nowhere in Idaho. They lived on a cliff above the Snake River. There were Russian olive trees in their backyard. That smell . . . I haven't smelled it in years, but oh!"

Sophie let go of her hands. "Then my guess is that's how your nose will lead you to Effie."

Aida raised an eyebrow. "I'll smell her?"

Aggie laughed. "Effie smells divine! What a brilliant idea, sister."

"Everything about her brings joy to the people around her. I just helped you home in on it a little. But the aegis may not work the same way in the catacombs," the goddess warned. "It will dull the misery and keep you from falling into despair, but it may not alert you that a god is near in the same way it does above ground."

"Great." Aida let out a sigh of frustration. "You also said that the catacombs aren't structurally sound. What do we do if our path is blocked?"

Vulcan grunted. "Try and find another path."

Sophie nodded in agreement. "There's only so much help we can give you without directly interfering. To do more might only backfire and bring you harm."

"When will you go to the catacombs?" Aggie asked.

"I need to be sure about the security system. That will take me a couple of days. It sounds like we'll need to find a few things for our spelunkers," Yumi said.

"One more thing," Vulcan said. "You won't have much luck with your phones down there. The catacombs are ancient, layered with old magic and misery that interferes with technology. Even I can't cut through that."

Aida cursed under her breath. "Great. We're going in without a lifeline."

Silence hung between them for a moment, the gravity of what lay ahead sinking in. Yumi crossed her arms, her lips pressed into a tight line. The idea of wandering through the dark ancient tunnels with no way to call for help left a pit in Aida's stomach.

She tried to laugh it off. "Guess we've got to be our own backup this time."

"I'll take you home," Sophie said. "Get some rest. You'll need it."

Before Aida could ask another question, the goddess laid a hand on her shoulder, and in a blink, she found herself in Yumi's living room. Yumi collapsed on the couch behind her. The goddess was nowhere to be seen.

"I will never get used to that," Yumi said. "It gives me an upset stomach."

Aida fell onto the sofa beside her friend. "So, Felix can't go with us."

Yumi looked at her. "Why not?"

"He doesn't have an aegis, so he would have no protection from the misery. And I was thinking about that. I've long thought about asking Sophie to give him one, but I don't want him to be in danger because of us. He's only been peripherally involved. Now he definitely won't be. I don't want him down there."

Yumi huffed. "Well, guess you and lover-boy Luciano will have the most interesting date ever."

"I don't think this will be terribly romantic," Aida said, smacking her friend with a throw pillow.

"Felix lives right near there, at least. It's a good place for me to set up. I wish the cell or Wi-Fi coverage would travel with you."

Aida cursed. "We could be down there for hours. What if we get hurt? Gah. This is such a bad idea."

"I think the alternative might be worse."

Aida leaned her head back on the sofa and closed her eyes. She tried to think of all the places she'd been since she started the job with MODA. There were museums that seemed to tickle the edges of her mind, but then slipped away. Every morning, she looked at her shorthand list to try to remember, and she did, for a little bit as she read the secretarial scrawl, but then as soon as she put the list away, the memories were gone again. She had done that . . . She had helped remove those places from the world, and not just her mind, but the collective consciousness of the people.

"I hate that you're right," she finally said.

"We'll figure it out," Yumi said, her voice taking on the cheerleader tone that Aida had heard countless times over the years when she was feeling down. Yumi had always been a good counterbalance to Aida's natural cynicism.

"At least I won't be doing it alone." Aida's fingers hovered over the screen of her phone, her mind a whirlwind of apprehension and determination. As she typed out the message to Felix and Luciano, she couldn't help but feel a tinge of excitement beneath the dread. The possibility of finding Effie, of changing something in this messed-up world, gave her a sliver of hope.

28

January 2021

A WEEK LATER, THEY gathered at Felix's apartment. With no jobs lined up for the next week, Aida had told Trista she'd be staying with Yumi, and to her relief, her aide hadn't seemed to care. They arrived at dawn, then Luciano, Felix, and Aida made their way down the Appian Way, backpacks stuffed with emergency supplies slung over their shoulders. Felix had insisted on walking them to the catacomb entrance. After a few blocks, they reached a tall arched gate set into an ancient brick wall.

"We're close," Aida said, tapping her earpiece.

"Be careful." Yumi's voice crackled in her ear.

They waited until no cars were passing before Felix slid his key into the gate. It swung open with a creak. They entered, and Felix hastily shut the gate behind them.

"I can't believe that worked," he said as they began the trek down the cypress-lined path toward the main entrance to the catacombs.

At first, Felix didn't want to tell them how he got the keys to the catacombs, but finally, after some wine a few nights back, he had loosened up and confessed he stole them from a man he knew worked at the catacombs. He'd seduced him, plied him with booze, and slipped the keys into his bag at some point in the night.

Aida had been horrified. "Wait, you got him drunk to steal the keys?"

Felix had realized what she was implying. "No, no! It wasn't like that. We've been flirting for ages. He was very into it, and he was the one pouring the gin. I just encouraged extra booze to make sure he wasn't going to notice I was stealing his keys. I'm going to bring them back," he had sworn. "That is, if we don't get caught. I rather like the guy."

The catacomb grounds were quiet—too cold for the parrots to sing, with temperatures near freezing. Aida and Luciano had bundled up in anticipation that the catacombs would be especially cold, but Felix had thrown on a lighter coat, and he muttered the whole way about catching a cold. Finally, Aida smacked him on the arm.

"Stop! I'd give my right arm to trade you places right now."

Felix gave her a sheepish look, then wrapped an arm around her. "I'm sorry. You're right. I'll make it up to you with a big bottle of champagne when this is all said and done."

"How big?" Luciano asked.

"A jeroboam."

"That's only four bottles. I was thinking a Nebuchadnezzar," Aida said.

Felix laughed. "We'll need about twenty bottles after all this. Okay, you're on."

They were coming up on the little piazza where the main entrance to the catacombs was.

"We're almost there," Aida told Yumi.

"Okay, give me a second."

The second turned out to be several long minutes, but finally Yumi confirmed that she had the cameras off. "You have about thirty minutes to get into the corridors outside the camera range. I can erase the footage if you don't make it, but it would be less problematic if you could just hurry."

"Okay, here we go." Felix led them to the door. He unlocked it, then gave each of them a big hug. "A Nebuchadnezzar. I promise."

Aida and Luciano slipped inside the dark entry. With one last wave at Felix, she locked the door behind them.

"*Andiamo.* We've got a big bottle of wine that needs drinking and we're not going to get that standing around here," Luciano joked.

"I'm pretty sure Felix doesn't have a few thousand dollars to throw at an oversize bottle of wine," Aida said. "But if we get out of here, I'm going to splurge on one."

Aida pulled the caving headlamp out of her pack, an item Yumi had thankfully been able to purchase online. She slipped it over her head, adjusting her ponytail to keep it out of the way, then hit the switch, and the room lit up.

"Wait, turn that off."

Aida complied. "What's wrong?"

"I can't kiss you with that blinding me. And I want one really good kiss before we go down into those tunnels. Who knows if I'll get another one." Luciano pulled her into his arms. His lips were cold, but his tongue warm. He wrapped a hand around the back of her head, cradling her, and she relaxed into his embrace, pushing all thoughts of what was to come from her mind. For a moment, she wanted him to be all there was: his warmth, the woody smell of his cologne, the strength in his arms and hands. She wished the kiss would never end.

But it did. Neither spoke as they fitted their headlamps and fixed their gear to be more easily accessible.

Aida tested her earpiece at the top of the stairs leading down to the Crypt of the Popes. "We're heading down," she told Yumi.

"What's taking you so long? Jeesh! Hurry up, slowpokes."

Yumi's urgency pushed them to comply. They began the descent down the long steep staircase, the lights from their cave headlamps slicing through the darkness. When they reached the landing of the second level down, Aida tried Yumi again. "Can you hear me?"

"Barely."

Aida sighed. "I think we're going to lose you soon. Wish us luck."

"*In bocca al lupo*," she said, replying with the Italian words for good luck. *In the mouth of the wolf.*

"*Crepi il lupo*," Aida responded. *May the wolf die.*

"And only the wolf," she said to Luciano as she turned off the earpiece and stuffed it in her pack. "Let's go."

Rather than descending to the next flight toward the papal crypts, Aida and Luciano veered into one of the catacombs' deeper corridors, guided by the logic that Oizys's shrine would sequester itself far from the mundane curiosity of tourists.

Aida peered down the path and her heart sped up. The galleries were only a few feet wide, narrow enough that Aida couldn't put both arms out without touching the hard tufa stone. The walls on both sides were floor-to-ceiling burial niches that looked like empty shelves in a bookcase. The idea that all these shelves once held dead bodies was a shocking thing to consider. Her experience with cataloging happiness had never necessitated such a descent into the literal and metaphorical underworld, leaving her unprepared for just how terrifying the subterranean space would be. Stretching before them indefinitely was the catacombs' unyielding reality: the omnipresent chill of the stone, the oppressive cloak of darkness, and the stifling air, redolent with millennia of seclusion and decay. The corridors constricted around them, and though the floor-to-ceiling niches were vacant of their long-departed occupants, an intangible presence seemed to linger, giving a horror-movie feeling to it all.

"How many people were buried here?" Luciano asked.

"Half a million. Felix said that over the years most of the bones were taken as souvenirs by raiders, and then eventually, the Church moved the rest to various churches in the city. Some bones are still in the walled-up niches, probably much farther in."

"This is nothing like the catacombs of Paris. There are skulls everywhere there. I'm not sure which is creepier. This emptiness or all the gaping eye sockets staring out at you."

Aida shuddered. "I'll take the emptiness."

As they ventured deeper, the oppressive silence of the catacombs seemed to swallow even the sound of their own footsteps. The narrow beam of their headlamps barely penetrated the all-encompassing darkness, the air growing colder, heavier with each step.

To mark their path, Luciano drew arrows on the rough volcanic walls with a big stick of yellow chalk—the kind kids used on sidewalks. The corridor stretched on, seemingly endless, with side passages branching off like the fingers of a ghostly hand. Every few hundred feet, there was an entryway to a little chapel. Occasionally, they stopped to admire the ancient frescoes of saints and various biblical figures, but they never lingered long.

They mistakenly thought the map Felix found would be useful, but the catacombs laughed at such modern arrogance. Passages would abruptly end, forcing detours that felt like regressions. While they intended to walk to the farthest part of the catacombs, Aida knew it was a shot in the dark, quite literally. They had no idea where Effie could be, and there were miles of galleries to explore. Several galleries they had passed weren't on the map at all. She tried not to think about the reality of getting quite lost in this place of the dead.

After more than an hour of walking, Luciano suddenly stopped, his hand shooting out to halt Aida. Ahead, the ground gave way to a gaping chasm, the floor having collapsed into the darkness below. They shone their lights into the pit, but its depths yawned back at them, accompanied by the sound of dripping water.

"Damn it," Aida cursed, her breath forming clouds in the cold air. "We'll have to find another way." She checked the map, which indicated another possibility to reach their desired destination: A section of the catacombs they estimated to be in the area below the Baths of Caracalla or perhaps even as far away as the Circus Maximus.

"I think we can go this way," she said, tracing the route with her finger.

"*Merda.* That's much longer. Why did this have to happen in the only part of the catacombs that isn't laid out like a city street?"

"Yeah, I know. But it doesn't look like there's any other way." She sighed. "If only we had any clue if this was the best way to go. For all we know, we should be heading over here." She indicated a part of the map that was easily a couple of hours in the other direction.

"I think we're on the right path," Luciano said. "The other part of the catacombs is much more well traveled and mapped. And they would want to keep her as far from people as possible."

"*Andiamo* then," Aida said, folding up the map. She turned around, sending a prayer up to Sophie for courage.

Their detour took them through narrower, more claustrophobic passages, where the weight of the earth above seemed almost tangible, pressing down on them. The walls were lined with niches, thankfully all empty.

Eventually, they came to a rough-hewn staircase to a lower level. They descended into the depths, where the air was colder, and continued walking. And walking. The empty niches turned into niches that were still walled up, some with the marble covering them intact, some which had fallen to the ground in broken shards.

When Aida saw the first skeleton, she thought her heart might stop. They had been walking for so long through the empty cemetery that it was a shock to see the flash of a yellowed skull under the glare of her headlamp. As they continued, it became clear that all the niches still held bodies. She dug out the map.

"We're still in the mapped area." She pointed to the spot she thought they were at. "But I wonder if anyone has come this far since Giovanni Battista de Rossi made this map in 1849."

"You might be right. It's interesting that the Church left these bodies behind. I thought they had moved them all."

They continued, and the feeling that they were walking into the depths of a horror film amplified past ten. Aida could hear the uneven rhythm of her own breathing, a stark reminder of life amid so much death. The beams from their headlamps carved pockets of visibility in the pervasive darkness. In this subterranean gloom, shadows played tricks on the eyes, and it was easy to imagine bony fingers reaching out from the walls, yearning for the warmth they had not felt in millennia.

A chill that had nothing to do with the temperature ran up Aida's spine as they passed a niche where the marble slab lay cracked on the ground, its inscription indecipherable with age. The skeleton inside seemed almost to be straining against the space, the skull tilted at an unnatural angle, as if in its final moments, it had turned to witness some unspeakable event.

The air grew heavier as they delved deeper. Aida couldn't shake the feeling of being watched, of unseen eyes fixed on her from the darkness, witnessing her intrusion into this sanctum of perpetual repose.

"I think we're heading in the right direction," Luciano said. "I've never been depressed, not truly, but I'm beginning to understand that feeling—that weight upon the body."

"Miseria," Aida said, invoking Oizys's more common name. "Me too. It's terrible." It made her want to cry.

Suddenly, Aida smelled it—the familiar nostalgia of childhood. It was faint and fleeting but unmistakable: the scent of a Russian olive tree, pleasantly sweet and floral, like a slightly spiced jasmine flower. Aida paused, and this time, tears formed in the corners of her eyes.

"*Tutto bene?*"

Aida nodded, her headlamp bobbing. "I thought I could smell Effie. By the gods, you're right. We must be heading in the right direction."

Luciano pulled her into a hug, dampening her neck. He was just as terrified as she was. "*Finalmente*," he whispered.

The moment gave them new courage and they hastened their pace. The scent wasn't steady, but when Aida could smell it, she thought perhaps it was growing stronger. Yet the farther they walked, the denser the air grew, tinged with the palpable feeling of grief and depression. Even under Sophie's aegis, the shrine's mournful gravity pulled at her spirit, a reminder of the goddess's pervasive sorrow.

They pushed forward, bolstered by the idea that such sorrow meant they were moving closer and closer toward the shrine. The air grew even damper, and the smell of Effie began to mix with the scent of mold and decay. Rounding a corner, they found the source: A section of the tunnel ahead was flooded, water reflecting their lamplight in a still, dark pool that stretched into the shadows.

"We can't turn back now," Luciano said, rolling up his pant legs. "It can't be that deep."

Carefully, they edged around the perimeter of the tunnel, trying to avoid the deepest water, their hands grazing the cold walls for balance. Suddenly, Luciano's footing gave way, and he plunged into the water with a splash, his headlamp flickering out and succumbing to the darkness. Aida, illuminated by the dim glow of her lamp, let out a startled cry and pushed her way through the water toward him.

A skull floated up in the water next to Luciano and Aida screamed, the sound echoing dully off the tufa stone.

"*Calma, calma.* I'm okay," Luciano reassured, his voice wavering slightly as he pulled himself up, but the water was deceitfully deep, swallowing his legs up to the knees. "But my pack is soaked through," he lamented, retrieving the sodden mass. "And my lamp . . ." His voice trailed off as he fumbled in the inky water, finally retrieving the useless device. The grim realization that they were now enveloped in an even more oppressive darkness settled heavily upon them. "We'll need to get through this water to try to fix it. I don't want to open the packs and lose anything."

"You're sure you're all right?" she asked, concerned, barely able to conceal her burgeoning panic.

"*Sì*. The water at least broke some of the fall. *Andiamo*. We can do this."

Aida's heart was pounding so hard she was sure Luciano could hear it. Surrounded by the suffocating silence, punctuated only by the unnerving drip of water from Luciano's backpack and their labored breathing, a sense of foreboding engulfed her. The reality of their situation settled in—a misstep, a wrong turn, and they could be lost forever in this labyrinthine underworld.

Luciano sensed her hesitation and turned to face her with a look of concern. "Aida?" he asked, his voice steady but filled with worry.

She looked up at him, resolve warring within her. "I . . . I don't know if we can do this, Luciano," she admitted. "We can't even see the end of this water ahead." She waved her arm down the dark tunnel. "What if we can't find her? What if we get trapped? I can't—I don't want to die here, not in this darkness." Tears mingled with the cold water on her cheeks, the weight of their predicament crashing down on her.

Luciano put his hands on her shoulders. "I would hug you, but then I'd get you all wet." He leaned forward and gave her a soft kiss. "We knew this wouldn't be easy," he said gently. "We can't give up now, not when we're so close."

Aida nodded, trying to muster even the smallest amount of courage. She took a deep breath, closing her eyes for a moment, willing her heart to steady. In the previous months, she had often said little prayers to Sophie and Aggie for guidance, but this time, she spoke to Effie, a desperate request for help.

And then, miraculously, as if in answer to her silent plea, it came—the scent that stirred memories of sunlight and open skies, of running across green grass and into the arms of her Papa, who would ruffle her hair and laugh. The subtle, sweet fragrance of Russian olive trees, so intrinsically linked to her happiest memories, intensified, a burst of comfort in the darkness, then it dissipated.

Her eyes snapped open, a renewed sense of purpose washing over her. "Did you smell that?" she asked.

Luciano shook his head. "No, but if you did, that's a good sign. Let's get out of this water."

They trudged forward, their light greatly diminished by Luciano's darkened headlamp. Bones from the lowest niches had come loose and floated around them. Aida did the best she could to avoid their touch—to bother the dead in such a way seemed not just disrespectful but also unlucky to her. It didn't help her sorrow either. The farther they pushed through the water, the more the oppressive atmosphere of the catacombs seemed to concentrate, a presence that pushed against their minds with whispers of despair.

Ten minutes later, they reached a dry part of the tunnel and sat on the floor to dig through their packs. Aida wished she could tell Yumi how glad she was that she had insisted on packing everything inside the packs in plastic bags. Yumi had done so to help organize and save space, but they had helped save nearly everything inside Luciano's wet pack. They first wrapped the space blankets around them for warmth and broke open some of the hand warmers that Yumi had tucked into their packs. But Luciano's headlamp didn't work at all.

"Damn it," he muttered. He shook it, then flipped open the battery compartment. Aida leaned over so her light shone on the lamp. The batteries looked fine—but a thin sheen of water coated the inside.

"The seal must have been loose," he said, frustrated. "Water got in and shorted something."

Aida frowned. "Did you check it before we left?"

"I thought so." Luciano sighed. "Maybe I didn't close it right? Or it might've gotten knocked loose when I fell."

"We should have brought a backup," Aida lamented. She handed Luciano one of the extra flashlights in her pack. It was smaller to help conserve space and weight, and didn't have the impact of the headlamp.

"It's better than nothing though."

"I don't think we can stop for long, or we'll get too cold being so wet. I still think we could have brought a backpacker's space heater," Aida said. "Even if we didn't use it for very long."

"No, Felix was right to discourage us. There could be all sorts of gases down here we don't understand. And there's no ventilation."

Aida peered down the passage ahead of them. There wasn't a sliver of light. The idea of moving forward filled her with dread. "I can't smell the trees. Maybe we should go back."

"But you could smell it when I fell in the water, and we were heading in this direction. We must be going the right way," Luciano said. "Besides, do you want to go back through that? Come on, let's keep going." He scrambled to his feet and held out a hand to help her up.

After thirty minutes of trudging through the gloom, they reached another staircase heading down even deeper. Aida would have balked if not for the fact that the scent of the trees had returned and was growing stronger with every step.

But only a short way down the new gallery, they hit a wall, a literal wall, nicheless, blocking their path. It loomed before them, solid and seemingly impenetrable, an ancient boundary set in stone. The smell of her childhood was concentrated at the wall and Aida breathed deep, letting the scent fill her with courage. She ran her hands over the wall's cold unyielding surface, feeling the tiny imperfections and the chill of the rock seeping into her skin. She pressed her ear against the stone, half expecting to hear a heartbeat from the other side, anything that would give them a clue.

Luciano joined her, examining the wall with an intense gaze. "There has to be a way through," he murmured, more to himself than to Aida.

Aida pulled away, her mind racing. She recalled the stories of secret chambers and hidden doors that were common in places like this. She doubted all the movies she had watched and books she had read could be real, but she wasn't sure what else to do. "Luciano, help me look for any signs of a mechanism or anomaly, something that doesn't belong."

They split up, tracing the expanse of the wall with their fingers, tapping lightly, listening for the hollow sound that would suggest a passage. Minutes passed, and the only sounds in the silence were the soft thuds of their explorations and the distant water drip. The passage was narrow, and their backs bumped against each other, a comfort in the depressing darkness.

Aida's fingertips moved across the cold stone, tracing lines and patterns worn by age. The scent of the Russian olive tree was stronger now, as if urging them on. And then, in a spot low to the ground on the left side of the wall, a stone seemed ever so slightly recessed. It shifted a bit when she pressed it.

"Here," she said. She shifted so Luciano could try pushing it. "Nothing."

The olive tree smell intensified. An idea came to her. "Wait, what if there is another spot on the other side?" She leaned over to that side and felt around, and her heart lifted when she found the same sort of recession in the wall. "Yes!"

Together, they pushed. A faint grinding noise filled the gallery, barely audible at first but growing louder. The wall began to tremble, and dust fell from the ceiling above them.

Luciano's voice was a hushed undertone of excitement. "It's giving way."

And then, with a resonant clunk that vibrated through the stone floor, the wall began to move. It didn't swing open like a gate but descended smoothly into the ground, receding with a mechanical precision that was oddly modern in the ancient setting. Aida watched, breath held tight in her chest, as the slab sank and the perfume of trees rushed in. The wall's descent slowed, finally coming to a gentle halt with a solid, final thud.

They stood together, peering into the newly revealed passage.

"Incredible," Aida whispered. "It's like stepping into a time that should no longer exist."

The difference from one side of the door to the other was stunning. As far as they could see, the ceiling, walls, and floor were covered in shining black marble.

Aida and Luciano exchanged glances, a mix of excitement and apprehension in their eyes. They had found the way. Luciano reached out his hand. Aida took it, and together, they stepped into the passage. Somewhere down this path, Effie awaited them.

29

January 2021

THE HALLWAY STRETCHED before them, its length veiling the promise of an end. With every step, the oppressive weight of despair thickened. Ten minutes bled into twenty, the corridor mocking their progress with its interminable reach. Yet, paradoxically, an inexplicable calm wove through their anxiety, a serene assurance that Sophie's aegis was at work—they were drawing closer to divinity. The faint, pervasive scent of olive trees continued to mark their path.

Gradually, the monolithic smoothness of the marble walls fractured, giving way to a procession of Doric columns hewn from the same obsidian stone. Atop each column, a single lantern glowed with a dark blue light that grew more assertive with each measured step, eventually chasing away the need for their artificial beams.

"I'm terrified," Aida whispered as they stowed their headlamp and flashlight. "But at the same time, I'm . . ."

"Completely calm," Luciano concluded. His gaze was locked on the path unfurling before them. He gave her a weak smile. "It's a strange feeling, isn't it?"

"Will we ever get to the end of this hallway? My feet are killing me."

He helped her put her pack back on. Before she could resume her weary trek, Luciano cupped her cheek gently, pulling her into a kiss. It was a kiss filled with desperation, stirring a tumult of emotions within Aida, not the least of which was fear that the kiss might be her last.

"Aida, I might be falling in love with you," Luciano confessed as he pulled away. "So it would be better if you didn't die on me up there."

Aida's heart jumped—not just from his words, but from the enormity of what lay ahead. Love had no place in what they were about to do. And yet, here it was, unexpected and impossible to ignore. She searched Luciano's face, half expecting him to take it back, to brush it off as a fleeting thought born from fear and adrenaline. But his eyes held steady, the truth of it anchoring her when fear gnawed at the edges of her mind, urging her to turn away, to run—but she didn't. She concentrated on the steady weight of the aegis and forced a breath past the tightness in her chest. *He loved her.* That, and there was no room for despair. Not now.

"And by the way," he added, "you still haven't told me if you meant it. Back at the apartment—you said you loved me."

The memory struck her in the chest. She had said it in a rush, half panicked, but she had meant it. The oppressive sorrow of the catacombs threatened to swallow her, but the warmth of that memory, of Luciano's presence, cut through the darkness.

"I meant it," she whispered, her voice trembling. Love and fear collided in her chest. "I meant it then, and I mean it now. I love you."

Luciano's smile widened, though the darkness around them seemed to deepen. "Good. Because if we survive this, I want to hear you say it again."

She nodded, unable to articulate her whirlwind of feelings, and followed him as he beckoned her onward.

Time seemed to dilate as they navigated the seemingly infinite corridor, nearly an hour passing before the ambient light began to transform. No longer confined to the lanterns, it now bled from an expansive chamber ahead.

Despite the sadness that assailed them, Aida and Luciano

quickened their steps until they reached the opening to a massive chamber of shining black marble. They dropped their packs at the door and stepped into the vast opulent room. Aida's breath caught in her throat. The chamber was colossal, its grandeur dwarfing even the Sala del Maggior Consiglio in the Doge's Palace in Venice—the largest room in Europe at one hundred and seventy-four feet long and eighty-two feet wide. Yet it was not its size alone that was so shocking, but the macabre carpet of bones that blanketed the floor, a sea of human remains stretching across the marble expanse. There wasn't a single bare spot without a rib cage, a femur, a skull, or some other part of a former human. Piles of bones, some as towering as the room itself, jutted out like grotesque monuments, bathed in the ghostly luminescence of massive chandeliers fashioned from skeletal fragments.

At the chamber's heart lay two harrowing sights: a massive stone altar stained with the echoes of countless sacrifices to the goddess of misery. Draped across the slab, a skeleton lay askew, its arm dangling off the edge in silent testimony to its final despair. In front of it, an ancient ornate chair glowed amid the gloom—a stark anomaly in this somber space. It was Hera's golden chair, and in it sat a figure, small and still.

Aida tentatively stepped forward, her movement sending a cascade of bones clattering across the marble floor. Euphrosyne lifted her head, her ebony hair cascading over slender shoulders, framing a face of ethereal beauty. "There she is," Aida breathed.

Buoyed by the sight of her, Luciano pushed forward, the noise reverberating off the distant marble walls. Aida followed in his wake. Every step felt like torture. When they were within twenty feet of the chair, she faltered, the idea of pushing through the remnants of countless lost souls becoming all too much for her.

Trying desperately to disassociate, she attempted to imagine herself on a movie set, with bones that were mere props, until she remembered with horror that in the early days of cinema they used to buy real cadavers for films. The thought filled her with a deep aching sadness. Envisioning the despair that drove so many to this final resting place under Miseria's influence, she crumbled, her cries echoing in the vast, cavernous hall.

"Aida?" Luciano turned. "Come, we can't stop." He reached out, attempting to coax her to her feet, but in her frantic state, she stumbled over a femur, her fall sending a cascade of skeletal fragments tumbling around her. Panic surged through her veins, her heart a tempest of dread and desperation.

A mocking voice cut through the din of her despair. "What do we have here?"

Aida looked up. Momus stood a few feet away amid a pile of bones. "Mo!" she cried. Despair ripped through her; their mission seemed doomed beneath his mocking scrutiny.

"Aida!" Luciano tried again to pull her forward, but her legs were like lead, her movements jerky and slow. How could they have ever thought they could save Effie?

"Aida." Mo's voice was behind her now. She whirled and almost fell into him. He looked out of place in his stylish blue jacket, white shirt, and perfectly pressed trousers. A dark curl fell into one eye. "How did you find this place? And how do you know each other?"

Luciano yanked her forward. "Don't stop, Aida! He can't hurt you."

Suddenly Mo was in front of Luciano. He folded his arms and cocked his head as if in thought. "Now, who told you that?"

Momus lifted his arms into the air with a casual, almost bored gesture, and all the bones around them rose with them. Then, he demonstratively pushed his hands toward the ground, sending them crashing down. Aida and Luciano shielded themselves, trapped in the eye of a skeletal storm.

"Please, don't do this," Aida begged when the bones had settled.

"I have so many questions, Aida," Mo said, shaking his head like a disappointed father. "I thought we were friends."

"We are." She hated how desperate she sounded.

"Are we?" Mo flicked his hand toward Luciano. "It seems he might be a better friend to you than me." He scowled.

She tried to reason with him. "Mo, people have more than one friend."

He scoffed at her. "Do they now? I'm curious to know which friend helped you. There's no way you reached this sanctuary without someone's aegis."

Aida caught a glance of Euphrosyne behind Mo. The goddess closed her eyes and smiled. The air was suddenly even more deeply suffused with the fragrance that evoked memories of love and an acute sense of longing. It filled Aida with a resolve she didn't know she had.

"That doesn't matter. But you are right. If we had truly been friends, Mo, I would never have had a reason to come here. My happiness would have mattered to you. But look!" She spread her arms wide, indicating the thousands of bones around them. "Does this look like happiness? Do you think I want to be here? I loved my MODA job. I was so happy. And I was happy about our friendship," she said, lying about the last part. "But then I discovered you were busy taking it all away. Tell me, Mo, what did you think our understanding was?"

Aida couldn't read his expression, and he didn't respond. Instead, he stood there, arms crossed, contemplating her. She caught another glimpse of Effie. Her eyes, a piercing crystalline blue, a striking contrast with her dark skin, met Aida's with an intensity that propelled her forward.

Aida stepped around Mo, hoping Luciano would follow and Mo would take pity, allowing them to pass. She reached her hand into her pocket and closed it upon the mechanism Vulcan had given to her. She just needed to get close enough . . .

Luciano, quick to understand, moved ahead of her, guiding her through the scattered bones and clearing a path toward the chair. Aida pulled her hand out of her pocket and was just about to throw the ball against the black marble of the dais when suddenly hands were on her shoulders.

Skeletal hands.

Aida was ripped backward to the floor with a painful thud. Vulcan's precious sphere fell from her hand and rolled into the bones. She scrambled after it, not caring what force had pulled her away from Euphrosyne. Desperation lent her vigor as she pushed her hands through the osseous fragments. Their only chance was to find that device.

Instead, her hands hit a leather boot. She looked up to see Disa standing above her, garbed in one of her outlandish haute couture dresses—a wild ankle-length bloodred tulle piece, the torso wrapped in wide elastic bands, with the bodice and one arm half covered in feathers that rose to a point higher than the goddess's face. To Aida's horror, a dozen skeletons were standing behind her. With graceful poise, the goddess of discord reached down, and her fingers deftly extracted the metal ball from its ivory bed.

"Looking for this?" she said.

Despair flooded Aida. A new voice echoed through the chamber, a dolorous waver that could only belong to one being.

"Who are you?"

Each word was slow, soaked in sorrowful emotion.

Luciano was by Aida's side. He helped her stand.

"Lady Oizys," Luciano greeted the goddess of misery. His voice wavered.

Aida's gaze shifted from Discordia to the new arrival, her heart sinking as she beheld the embodiment of despair. Miseria stood draped in her mournful magnificence. Her form was slender, almost fragile, yet her presence filled the chamber with an overwhelming melancholy. Her skin, pale as the moon, seemed almost ethereal. Her hair flowed around her like a veil of shadows, shifting subtly as if stirred by an unseen breeze. Her attire was elegant, a gown that seemed woven from the very night itself, moving around her in fluid sorrowful waves. Miseria's eyes, a deep fathomless black, held within them the pain of every sorrow ever felt, their gaze penetrating and inescapable. Aida looked away. Sophie's aegis could hardly hold up. She wanted to lie down in the sea of bones and die.

"Hello there, sister. Good of you to arrive. Let me introduce you to Miss Reale and Mr. Leto, employees of MODA." Mo smirked at them. "I suppose you both know you're fired."

"Why are you doing this?" Aida asked. She couldn't stop the tears as she shouted at Mo. "Why do you want any of this?"

The god of guile stepped toward them, his lips twisted in a menacing scowl. Startled, Aida backed up, yanking on Luciano's sleeve. He was reeling in the depths of Miseria's despair and was difficult to move. She pulled at him, dragging him away from the advancing god until they hit the dais and fell backward on the step. When she fell, Aida's hand brushed against Euphrosyne's foot, and a jolt ripped through her, a bright light of delirious joy that seemed to light up all her senses. She reached out for Luciano's hand and took it, letting the happiness flow through him too.

"That will not help you." Miseria's voice was like a low roll of thunder. She gently moved one hand toward the bone-laden floor, and every last bone began to tremble. The sound was incredible, echoing off the chamber walls. They watched in horror as all the skeletons knitted themselves back together. Soon there was an army in front of them, thousands of dead trembling, waiting for a command.

Luciano raised his voice, defiant. "You can't kill us."

Miseria laughed. It was a terrible sound, full of dread that seemed to permeate the air. The undead legion at her command lifted its hands and took a step forward.

"We don't need to kill you." Mo chuckled. "There are chambers in these catacombs where no one will find you in a thousand years. Our friends here will be delighted to show you the way."

"There was never any understanding, was there?" Aida screamed at Mo. "Humanity is just a game to you."

Disa, her expression one of amused detachment, toyed with the sphere in her hand, her gaze flitting over the skeletal army with a hint of dark anticipation. "Let me assure you, this is no game. It's our time to thrive," she remarked, her voice laced with cold mirth. "Our essence thrives in chaos, in the unraveling of order."

"You made your choice, Aida." Mo winked at Luciano. "And your choice was a bad one." A sinister grin spread across his face. "Besides, your desperation is palpable, and it's delicious."

Miseria raised her hand, directing her macabre minions. Aida's heart raced with terror. Her eyes caught Disa's. "Please, please, I pray, don't do this." Aida's voice was barely a whisper, full of the dread of a fate worse than death.

The skeletal warriors advanced, their movements slow and deliberate, each step a chilling echo in the vast chamber. Luciano and Aida, rooted to the spot by a mix of terror and disbelief, watched the inexorable approach of the undead host. Even the transient joy that Euphrosyne's touch had instilled in them was quickly overshadowed by the palpable aura of death Miseria exuded. Bones clicked and clacked as the skeletons moved, a morbid symphony heralding their impending doom. The chamber seemed to contract around them, the walls echoing the dread pulsing through their veins.

The skeletons were mere feet away when Disa's expression shifted, a flicker of caprice crossing her divine features. "Let's see what chaos truly looks like," she mused, her gaze settling on the petrified pair before her. With a fluid, unpredictable motion, Disa hurled the sphere toward Aida and Luciano.

The little ball arced through the air. Aida instinctively reached up and grabbed it. Without hesitation, she threw it on the ground at Effie's feet. It exploded, a translucent bubble of gold forming all around them. The skeletons bounced off all sides, their hands rattling against the shield, the bones collapsing on the floor in defeat. With every fallen skeleton, another took its place.

"The key!" Luciano urged. "Here!" He pointed at a tiny keyhole low on one of the chair legs.

Aida fumbled for the key in her jacket pocket, not finding it at first, but finally she felt it, warm to her touch, in the deepest corner.

She crouched and slipped it into the keyhole just as the golden bubble gave way.

30

January 2021

AN OVERWHELMING SENSATION of pure, radiant joy pierced the gloom that had wrapped itself around them. It was akin to a sudden burst of warm sunlight breaking through the darkest of clouds, infusing Aida with a lightness that banished Miseria's oppressive weight from her soul. Her heart swelled with an all-consuming love. The feeling lingered for a moment before a happy scream pierced Aida's euphoria, pulling her back to reality.

Disoriented, Aida stumbled and fell against a . . . couch? Luciano was nearby, pulling himself up off the floor.

"Aida!" Yumi rushed toward her, pulling her into a fervent embrace. "I wasn't sure we'd ever see you again! You did it! You really did it!"

Aida hugged her friend back, holding her tight. She knew her tears were wetting Yumi's hair and shirt, but she didn't care. She was alive.

A gentle voice brought her back to the present. "We don't have much time." Aida looked up to see the goddess of happiness and joy smiling at her. Effie wore a perfectly tailored white suit with a subtle shine that caught the light. Her hair cascaded around her shoulders in a profusion of obsidian locks.

They were in Felix's living room, which seemed like a sanctuary compared to the horrors of the catacombs. Felix had collapsed into a nearby chair, his eyes wide and his mouth agape. Effie went to him and took his hand. "I give you my aegis." As soon as their hands touched, the tension drained from Felix's body, replaced by a serene calm. A slow smile spread across his face.

Aida let Luciano pull her up from the couch. He put a protective arm around her, and she leaned into him, relieved they were both in one piece.

"Now we go to Pandora," Effie said. "Come close. You all need to be there." She held out her hand, and each of them laid a hand on hers.

In the blink of an eye, the five of them stood in the middle of Pandora's kitchen. Muffled voices seeped in from the living room. Effie put a finger on her lips.

"Helen, listen carefully. The idea of Pandora being real is a dangerous myth. Whoever fed you that story was manipulating you, trying to take advantage of your good nature. They want your money, your identity. This is why you need to come with me."

Aida recognized Fran's voice. Luciano recognized it too, grabbing her hand and squeezing it.

"I don't know," Pandora said in a wary voice. "Maybe it's you who is trying to manipulate me."

Fran sighed. "That's not the case, Helen, and you know it. I've supported you every step of the way. I helped you build this life—this apartment, your job. I found you when you were lost, with no memory. If I hadn't helped, you might have been in a far worse situation. Please, let's not waste time. We need to leave now."

Pandora's voice was firm but calm. "While I appreciate your help, I'm choosing to stay here. I'm happy with my life."

Fran gave a harrumph. "Of course you are. You are the happiest woman on earth."

"I'm glad you agree," Pandora said brightly.

"But happiness is delicate, Helen. I'm trying to tell you—these people will take it from you. That's why they're here. They've found you and now they'll try to drain you dry."

A pause. Helen's voice was small. "Drain me?"

"Yes," Fran pressed. "Your job—the one you don't even realize you've been doing—is to maintain all this happiness. But if they get to you, if they use you the way they plan to, it will be gone. Like a water main break. You'll be left in darkness once more. Do you really want that?"

Pandora hesitated. "I—I don't want to go back to the darkness."

There was the creak of a chair as someone stood.

"I see how this is," Mo's voice said from a few feet behind Aida. "You fickle cow."

Aida thought her heart might stop. Sophie's aegis calmed her in the presence of all the gods, but it did not stop her internal horror at the idea of the rest of MODA showing up and forcing Pandora's hand.

"Who's there?" Pandora's voice spiked in alarm. "Someone's in my kitchen!"

"Momus, you bastard," Fran cursed under her breath.

A few seconds later, Pandora appeared in the doorway, her face tight with fear at the sight of so many people in her kitchen. The tension hung thick for a moment, but then Pandora's eyes landed on Luciano and Aida. Recognition flickered across her face.

"How . . . how did all of you get in here?"

Effie held out her hand to the automaton, but the goddess of deceit pulled Pandora back. Her voice sharpened, full of fear that sounded too practiced. "That's the scam artist," Fran cried. "They've come to deceive you—to take everything from you. You have to trust me!"

Pandora shook Fran's hands off her. "Don't touch me!"

Aida caught the flicker of real panic on Fran's face. She hadn't expected that. If Pandora's happiness made her powerful, then her choices mattered. If she refused Fran's influence, it could weaken her.

Fran held out her hands, trying to regain control. "Helen, you must believe me. They're going to take everything. You need to leave now."

Pandora stood taller. "My name isn't Helen."

"Oh, you silly woman," Mo said, striding toward her. "You should have gone with her while you could have because she's right. We're going to take it all away from you." He indicated Effie and the rest of them as though they were all part of some merry band.

"He's lying to you! He's not with us. He's with her." Luciano indicated Fran. "They've been using you to steal all the happiness from the world."

Felix nudged Aida. "Show her the meander."

Aida felt around in her pocket for her phone. "Oh dear god," she breathed. "It's in my pack."

"In your pack?" Felix asked.

Aida nodded, picturing her pack at the doorway to the skeleton-filled room of black marble. "In the catacombs." Tears came to her eyes.

They had lost, after all. After the catacombs, after everything . . .

Fran straightened, her panic shifting to a look of resolve when she saw that Aida didn't have the key. "Helen, think about it. How did they get into your kitchen? Not by any normal means. Run! Come on!"

Pandora's mouth fell open with this new revelation. She hesitated, then began to turn toward Fran.

"While we're all being dramatic," Yumi said, "Pandora, let me show you *this*." She held out her phone toward the automaton.

Pandora's expression changed. "You still have the key."

"And we brought Euphrosyne," Aida said, indicating the beautiful goddess beside her.

Pandora smiled at Aida and Luciano. "You fulfilled your promise." She squinted at Fran. "Who are you? I mean, who are you really?"

"She's Fraus, or Apate to many. The goddess of deceit," Aida said.

Fran scowled.

"I'll give you a promise!" Mo threw something at Yumi. She went down with a scream, the phone flying across the kitchen floor, stopping at Fran's feet.

Luciano surged forward in a sudden burst of motion, a blur of intent and desperation as he lunged for the phone. Aida's heart leaped with him, her hopes soaring on his momentum. His fingers stretched out, grazing the device in a brush of almost-there, almost-success. But Fran was quicker, her divine reflexes snatching the phone away at the last possible instant.

Aida ran to her friend, who had sat up, cradling an arm. A toaster lay on its side next to her, the cord sprawling across the linoleum. "I tried," Yumi said in a weak voice.

"Oh, brother, throwing toasters at mortals? Stop being so pathetic." Effie gave Mo a calm smile. "You're acting like a child who didn't get his way."

"You're the one who won't be getting their way." Fran held Yumi's phone up. "You won't be needing this." With a twist of her wrist, it disappeared.

Aida let out a cry.

But Pandora's eyes sparkled. "You're right. I don't need it. It was only important that I see it and choose to honor it."

The goddess Euphrosyne extended her hand. Breath caught in Aida's throat as Pandora moved forward. Their hands met, and a surge of soft and warm light erupted.

The light enveloped Aida, filling her with a swell of joy so profound and pure she could scarcely believe it was real. Memories flowed through her, a jumble of impressions across the years of her life: the first time her parents held her and looked into her eyes, their smiles bright and delirious with happiness; swimming at the lake with Erin; graduating from college with honors; her first kiss; the surprise birthday party Yumi threw her when she turned thirty; her parents celebrating her first writing award when she was thirteen; the triumph of learning to ride a bike; on the swings at the playground at the age of four, her parents photographing every laugh and squeal as she rose and fell. It seeped into her, chasing away the remnants of fear and uncertainty. Around her, even the gods seemed touched by it, their eternal facades cracking under the weight of genuine happiness.

Pandora stood at the center, the origin of this newfound joy, her being radiating the very essence of contentment that had been locked away for decades. It was as if a dam had been broken, and all the happiness that had been hoarded, compressed, and contained was now released in a flood of laughter, warmth, and a sense of well-being. Even the air seemed to shimmer with the lightness of a long-lost hope.

Aida beamed, joy filling every part of her, and she sensed it mirrored in her friends. The happiness was tangible, a chorus of silent music that filled the room, spilling over, unrestrained and beautiful.

It was a fleeting moment. A surge of light momentarily blinded them, and the world shifted, twisted, and reformed.

When Aida's vision cleared, they were no longer in Pandora's kitchen but in a wide grass field. Aida, Luciano, Yumi, and Felix stood side-to-side in the center of a semicircle made by the gods: Euphrosyne, Sophrosyne, Aglaea, Oizys, Apate, Momus, and Discordia. Above them an impossibly wide full moon filled the field with light.

"Where are . . ." Aida's words were cut short when the gods around her dropped to their knees.

The moon turned from white to blue and the stars in the sky became brilliant sparkles of light, like shining glitter in the heavens. Aida reached for Yumi's and Luciano's hands, a touch of solidarity in the midst of uncertainty.

The cosmos began to shift, forming a face that radiated tranquility and authority. Stars gathered to craft her eyes, galaxies spinning within them. Her skin was the void of space, a canvas of dark beauty, dotted with the light of distant suns. The nebulae served as her hair, flowing and curling in the celestial winds, framed by the silhouette of the universe.

The being's gaze met Aida's, and in that moment, a silent exchange passed between them, a transfer of understanding. This was Nyx, the embodiment of the night, the primordial mother of dreams and shadows—and of all the gods who stood behind her.

She said nothing that Aida could hear, but the gods around her all bowed simultaneously, then stood and lowered their heads in deference.

Oizys didn't glance at the mortals before winking out, but Fran turned to face Aida. Without a word, she reached out and brushed Aida's hand with her fingertips. The moment their skin touched, a flood of memories surged through Aida—images, sensations, emotions.

Aida had been right. MODA had used Erin to manipulate her, to break her down, to leave her vulnerable and ripe for recruitment. Every part of her unraveling life had been a carefully constructed ploy to push her into MODA's grasp. Aida staggered back, her breath catching as the cold realization washed over her.

Fran's lips curled into a leering smile—a knowing, silent acknowledgment of the pain she had caused. With one final disdainful glance, Fran vanished, leaving Aida reeling from the truth: her heartbreak, her lost engagement, Erin's death—it had all been part of MODA's plan from the beginning.

Discordia parted with a rare smile, a little salute, and a wink. Euphrosyne and Aglaea went to each mortal in turn and bestowed upon them a soft touch to the forehead, then disappeared before their eyes.

Then Momus was before Aida. He had a smirk on his face. "It was fun while it lasted," he said. He pressed a brief tender kiss to Aida's forehead, then vanished before she could react.

"Thank you, Mother," Sophrosyne said, addressing the fading image in the sky. She turned to Aida and her friends. "Come now, hold hands, and let me take you home."

They linked hands, and the world shifted again. It took Aida a minute to realize they were in Felix's apartment. It didn't look quite the same. Where there was once a wall of art, there were now bookshelves. The once bare balcony now held a few potted plants.

"Thank the gods," Felix said. "I have never been so happy to be home in my life." He didn't seem to notice anything different.

Sophie stood near the apartment door. "That worked out rather well, I think."

"What just happened?" Luciano sat down in a nearby chair. He looked dazed.

"You saved the world. No big deal." But there was the hint of a smile on Sophie's lips.

"So now what?" Aida asked.

"Happiness is making its way back into the world. It won't be the same as before—it can't be. Some things that disappeared might come back. People who have died won't come back to life. But a museum could reopen, or a fountain may flow once more. But other things cannot revert. For example, a planetarium turned into a nursing home still has usefulness to the world even if the levels of happiness therein are different. It cannot change back without altering some of the fundamental fabric of humanity. But I think you'll find there are new places for hope and happiness."

"No, what happened in the field . . ." Luciano squinted at her. "What was that?"

"*That* was Nyx. I called upon her to give you all a boon. One that only she could give."

"What sort of boon?" Yumi asked.

"She's our mother and one of the only gods who has the power to command my siblings not to touch the hide nor hair of the four of you or anyone else in your lives. They cannot seek retribution for what you have done in restoring balance."

Aida had tried not to overthink what would happen if they were able to free Effie and convince Pandora, but the idea that their lives might be perpetually in danger had always been in the back of her mind. She closed her eyes in relief. But then she thought of the memories that had rushed through her.

"Sophie, I think MODA chose me to be a Happiness Collector when I was very young."

"Why do you say that?" she asked.

"I was filled with happiness when Pandora let it out into the world. And two memories stand out for me—one when my parents were pushing me on the swings. I was laughing. And my father told me I must be the happiest child in the world. And there was another when I won a VFW writing award. My parents were in the audience, clapping, so proud."

"What does that have to do with my brother and sisters?"

"In the first memory, Fran sat on a bench watching us. In the second memory, Disa was sitting in the auditorium next to my mother. And then Erin." She told Sophie about Fran's revelation in the clearing. She began to cry, unable to wrap her mind around the idea; the gods had warped her life to convince her to become a Happiness Collector.

Luciano put his arms around her. "You're not alone, Aida. I have similar memories."

Sophie nodded. "I wish your words surprised me. But we gods have long toyed with the lives of humans. Most of the time, you are blissfully unaware. You will become so again."

Aida felt Luciano tense. She thought he might scream at the goddess, his anger overcoming him, as her tears had done to her. But instead, he asked a calm, practical question.

"What happens to us? We no longer have jobs or even a place to live. And there are hundreds of us in the same position."

Sophie put her hand on the doorknob, ready to leave. "While you may no longer have official roles, rest assured that more benevolent forces have generously secured your wealth. Your homes remain yours, but now, the power has shifted—you'll be the ones in control, employing the staff who once served MODA's interests. But all MODA employees will begin to forget how you ended up in such a situation. New stories will form. Nyx has proclaimed it."

"What about our assistants? They're all automatons, aren't they? And what happens to Pandora?" Aida asked.

"They are. Nyx has collected them all to her, and will keep them safe until Zeus returns."

Luciano put an arm around Aida. "And us? Will we forget each other?"

Sophie shook her head. "No. But you won't remember me."

She opened the door and was gone.

"I THOUGHT YOU were going to order lunch," Yumi admonished Felix. "I'm starving. It's like I ran a marathon."

"Me too," Felix said. He pulled out his phone and began thumbing through the food app. "Say, Aida, let's do dinner at your place tonight. Ilario makes the best freaking carbonara."

Aida tried to understand what was happening in front of her. Yumi's and Felix's words felt strange, like there was something else they should be saying instead. "I need some air."

"I'll go with you," Luciano said, following Aida to the balcony. He shut the door behind them.

"Do you remember coming over here tonight?" he asked her. His brow was knitted with concern.

Aida shook her head. "No, I don't. And the apartment seems strange to me. Like things are out of place. And Yumi looks different." She peered into the living room, where Felix was making Yumi a drink from his bar cart. "She doesn't have bangs . . . I thought she always had bangs."

"You're different too," Luciano observed, taking her hand and turning over her wrist. "You have a tattoo." He ran his fingers across the skin.

Aida gave him a little sock on the arm. "I've had that tattoo for a while. We got them all together, silly. A tiny black star. Protection from the goddess Nyx, remember?" She paused, the idea of it seeming strange. "Nyx, Nyx, from, from . . ." She trailed off, trying to recall.

"Right, that role-playing game . . . the day I met you three," Luciano said, turning his right wrist to show her his little black star. But he looked at it like he was seeing it for the first time.

Aida leaned on the railing, looking out over the grass courtyard below. A group of children were playing some game with
a ball, which involved them tackling each other to get control.
Their laughter bubbled up and echoed off the building.

"They seem so happy," she said.

Luciano looked over the rail, then turned his body toward
hers. "So, Aida, I was thinking . . ."

"Of?"

He gave her a sheepish grin. "I was thinking of what it would
be like to always be with you."

Aida's stomach fluttered. "What are you suggesting?"

"This may sound strange, but I feel like I almost lost you. I
don't ever want to feel that way again."

Aida understood exactly what he meant, but she didn't know
why. "You didn't answer my question," she said, teasing.

"Want to grow old with me, Aida?"

She beamed. "Oh, Luciano, yes! That would make me deliriously happy."

EPILOGUE

Mount Auburn Cemetery, Cambridge

August 2022

THERE SHE IS," Graham said, pointing to a marble headstone etched with Erin's name.

A rush of emotions flooded through Aida. It was hard to believe that she hadn't seen Erin or Graham for three years. This was not the reunion she had ever expected. Aida knelt and placed the bouquet of white tulips on the grave. Below her name was etched a quote from Langston Hughes, a poet Erin had always admired. *Life is for the living. Death is for the dead. Let life be like music. And death a note unsaid.*

"I'm glad I came," Aida said. "Thank you." She stood and gave her ex-fiancé a hug.

"I'm glad you came too," he said. "Have a good trip home." Graham shook Luciano's hand and returned to his car.

"He seems like a nice guy," Luciano said after he was gone.

"I think he is?" she said, trying to remember. "I'm having one of those weird memory issues again," she admitted. "I think he was a nice guy, but just the wrong guy for me."

"His loss, my win," he said.

Aida turned back to the grave. She didn't want to leave just yet. "I can't even remember why she moved back to Boston," she murmured to Luciano. "I can't remember . . . so many things."

Luciano put an arm around her. "It's okay to forget details," he said gently. "It doesn't change what she meant to you."

Aida nodded, though the forgetting weighed heavy on her. It

wasn't just the details about Erin—it was everything. The past few years had been hazy, a common experience, she knew, but it was still unsettling. The pandemic had disrupted more than just daily life; for millions, it had left a strange fog over memories, making it harder to grasp the little things that once were so clear.

"I know." Aida wiped her tears with a tissue she'd pulled from her purse. "I feel like something important happened that I should remember . . . It's on the edge of my thoughts, but I can't quite recall it. But I remember her laugh, the way she made me feel loved." She smiled through the tears. "That's what matters, right?"

"That's what matters," Luciano agreed, his hand resting on her shoulder.

They lingered a little longer, silent, watching the shadows shift as the afternoon sun filtered through the trees.

Eventually, Aida kissed her fingertips and placed them against her friend's name. "I love you, Erin," she whispered.

As they walked slowly back toward the car Yumi had loaned them, Aida slipped her arm through Luciano's.

"I'm looking forward to the concert tonight," Luciano told her. "You've told me so much about the Hatch Shell, and we couldn't have asked for more beautiful weather."

"Me too. I'm glad the city decided to rebuild after that bad fire. It's a perfect way to honor both my parents' and Erin's memory." They had spent so many magical nights at the Hatch Shell, watching symphonies and movies, and when she was little, her parents would take the girls to puppet shows.

They paused at the pond in front of the Mary Baker Eddy Monument to watch a pair of swans gliding across the water.

"Do you ever wonder," Luciano said, "what the world would be like without this?" He waved a hand at the pond. "This beauty, this happiness? It seems strange to say that in a cemetery, but I've found so much joy walking through this magnificent place."

Aida knew exactly what he meant. Not just that the cemetery was beautiful, although it was.

"Do you really wonder that?" she asked him. "What the world would be like without happiness?"

He was silent for a moment, then shook his head. "No, I think I already know. I think we both do." He turned to her and pulled her close. "I feel like we're always collecting happiness, storing it up, living it, breathing it."

She grinned. "We are, Luciano. We are."

★ ★ ★ ★ ★

ACKNOWLEDGMENTS

My infinite gratitude to:

My agent, Amaryah Orenstein, who holds the torch that leads my way.

My wonderful editor, Dina Davis, who maps the depths and shines light into the unseen. And to all the extraordinary people at MIRA Books who helped bring this wild story of mine to light, including:

My editorial, production, and managing editorial team—Margaret Marbury, Evan Yeong, Dana Francoeur, Victoria Hulzinga, Bonnie Lo, and Katie-Lynn Golakovich—thank you for your keen insights, sharp eyes, and tireless dedication to making this book the best it could be.

The MIRA marketing wizards—Ana Luxton, Lindsey Reeder, Randy Chan, Ashley MacDonald, Diane Lavoie, Rachel Haller, Pamela Osti, Puja Lad, Alex McCabe, Ambur Hostyn, Riffat Ali, and Brianna Wodabek—and the publicity team, including Heather Connor and Laura Gianino. You have my infinite thanks for helping this book find its readers.

Elita Sidiropoulou and Sara Wood for imagining the perfect cover for this book.

The subrights team, Reka Rubin, Christine Tsai, and Nora Rawn.

MIRA publisher Loriana Sacilotto and associate publisher Amy Jones for your leadership and belief in this story.

The audio team—Carly Katz and narrator Jennifer Jill Araya—thank you for bringing this story to life with such skill and care.

To Bailey Thomas, Melissa Brooks, and the entire sales team—your hard work and enthusiasm make all the difference in helping this book reach its audience.

And to everyone else who played a part in this book's journey, whether named here or working behind the scenes—thank you. Your efforts, big and small, have made this possible, and I am deeply grateful.

To my early readers, who graciously gave their time to help me make this book better: Melissa Brenton, Kris Waldherr, Katrin Schumann, and Alyssa Palombo.

To the Salt & Radish Writers, Jennifer Dupee, Anjali Mitter Duva, and Henriette Lazaridis, who have been with me since the beginning.

To the Wonder Writers, my tribe who keep me afloat when the sea is rocky. And to all my author friends and people in the book world—there are far too many people to name, but know that you make my heart sing.

To Thomas Robinson, who shared with me his experience during the pandemic in Rome, which helped me write key parts of this novel. He may or may not have been the inspiration for Felix . . .

To my friends, Greg McCormick, Leanna Widgren, Graziella Macchetta, Joyce Guarnieri, Jason Alvarez, Phil Ayres, Kirby Crum and Dan Daly, Stacy and Thames Kral, Gracelyn Monaco, and Patrizia and Beniamino Bellini.

To my family, Mom, Dad, Misty, and Chase.

And to Joe. *Ti amo*, Giuseppe.